YEWSPRING

First paperback edition February 2023

Book design by Alaina Kowitz
Cover image © The Trustees of the British Museum

ISBN 979-8-9876057-0-7 (paperback)
ISBN 979-8-9876057-1-4 (ebook)

www.cecilyvancleave.com

To Ted, this story's faithful reader

CHAPTER ONE

When dawn came to the Midlands in a tide of gold washing away the rainclouds of the night, it found Clara Eastwood already at her desk. A little stub of candle still burned beside her, and the grate in her room lay ashy and cold. Fiona would not be in to lay the fire for an hour yet, and so Clara had bundled herself in nightgown and dressing gown and shawl to fend off the autumn chill. The blaze of light in the sky's eastern rim caught her eye, and she looked up from her work to gaze out her window over the quiet fields and hedges below. The grays and blacks of night were changing into the russets and golds and olives of autumn leaves on the Eastwood estate's trees, each one that Clara could see from her window as familiar to her as the face of an ancestor looking out from the frame of a portrait. The day illuminated hillsides of vibrant green grass cropped down to stubble by Yewspring's herd of cattle, and set the hedges burning with tawny flames as it touched their branches. Clara watched the dawn kindle them all and marveled yet again at the countryside's movement from beauty to beauty. It seemed to her as natural and graceful as a stream running in its course, as a line of dancing couples peeling apart, then coming together again.

She had risen as early as she could stand to make use of her unoccupied hours before breakfast, for she was forced to arrange her schedule around the light. Her pocket money could not stretch far enough to buy all the candles she would need to illuminate her work by night. Now she rose from the desk for a moment, stretching and looking down at the sketch of white dead-nettle she was working on, wondering if she had captured the arc of their uppermost petals that curved over the rest of the flower. It gave the blossoms the look of little nuns in white wimples, arranged on the stem all in a row to say their prayers. Muffled voices from the garden below came through the pane of her window, interrupting her contemplation and causing her to turn to look out through the glass.

Down below, her father and Clara's distant cousin George were walking through the walled garden to the back gate, their hunting boots crunching faintly on the gravel walk. The dogs bounded around their feet, yipping. George stooped down briefly to pat the head of his new pointer, her chestnut ears gleaming in the morning light, all the while talking to Mr. Eastwood. George was taller than Clara's father, but bent his head down a little as he spoke to the older man and leaned forward to make the height difference less apparent. She noticed again that George's complexion had improved in the last months, the morning light making his face glow ivory and pink rather than the grayish tan in which the marsh fever had bathed his face.

As they passed the spot nearest to her window, George turned and looked up in her direction. When he found her face in the window, he lifted his hand and waved to her. She waved in return, smiling a bit. She was glad he was able to go out today, even if it was only until dinner—he had been kept indoors so often on this trip to Yewspring, forced to make do with the company of herself, her mother, and her sister Rose. She knew that in some ways he did not mind, Clara's company being part of the reason he came to Yewspring to visit for the autumn shooting year after year, but she knew too that he wished to be out in the crisp air on a sleek hunter. She knew he did not wish to spend so much of his year in Bath, hoping that rest and taking the water would restore his health, and she was glad for each half day he could go out and forget about such things for a while, feel that he was healthy and strong and invincible. *Let him have his joys*, she thought, *and in the meanwhile I've still got a bit more time to spend on mine.*

The men's voices faded as they disappeared out the back gate and started across the fields, and she turned back to the desk, blowing out the candle whose pale flame could not compete with the strong silvery light of day. Her eyes lingered on a tacked-up map of Orion's nebula, then ran over the carefully pinned butterflies she had collected that summer, lying in their case like scraps of luxurious velvets and silks. They made her think of warm afternoons with her net in the meadows, of peering up at the starry sky on clear nights while the nighttime noises of Yewspring in summer rustled and murmured around her. The contrast between these moments and the ones that likely lay in store for her in the day ahead made her sigh. Though she could walk five miles up hills and through river valleys and follow the merest suggestion of a path through brambles and thickets, the hours ahead, filled with carriages and crowded streets and an assembly that night, taxed Clara's strength just thinking about them. She and George would walk through the streets of Daventry arm-in-arm if he was feeling well and had not over-taxed himself by bounding up hillsides after partridges. If he had, always reluctant to fully admit his fatigue, even to himself, she would sit quietly with him in the parlor while he closed his eyes on the settee. At least she could bring her books.

Knowing that there was nothing to be done for it, Clara sighed and sat back down. After gazing for a moment at the sketch and deciding she had done all she could with it, she lay it aside and pulled out her Latin primer from where it was concealed in an inconspicuous drawer. Her parents disliked her attempts to learn the language, and she knew even Rose could only be generous enough to call her desire "odd". It was slow and laborious going without a tutor; she had once requested one, after she had returned from the Bingham Seminary, and her father had laughed so hard he had had to wipe his eyes with a handkerchief afterward. She had only obtained the primer because she had bribed her cousin Ned to tell his teacher that he had lost his. Still, she had a volume of *The Flora of France* written in Latin and was determined to improve her understanding enough to be able to read it. She had so few things in her own control that she had resolved not to squander the things she did, even if that meant conjugating verbs that every schoolboy of ten would have known. So engrossed was she in her work that she was startled by the door opening when Fiona came in to make the fire.

On the threshold of Yewspring, Clara paused for a moment and straightened her bonnet. As she lifted her arm, she could feel the heavy weight of her reticule pulling on it—she had tried to tuck a third book into it, but its seams had bulged and threatened to split, so she had settled for only two instead. She lifted her face to the warm midday sun, glad that the ladies were taking the *landau* instead of the closed carriage.

From where she sat waiting in the carriage, Lady Constance Eastwood said, "Come now, Clara, we must not keep the luncheon waiting. And our detour to pick up Violet has put us behind. In you get."

Clara climbed in, and Yewspring's manservant William shut the carriage door. "Off you go, Leet," said Lady Eastwood to the driver, for the *landau* was her own, brought from Beechview to pick up her granddaughters, who had the pleasure of being seen in it with Beechview's crest displayed proudly on the door. Clara knew her sister Rose and the Eastwoods' cousin Violet Tapley were conscious of and grateful for this pleasure, and consequently made themselves agreeable to their grandmother, providing her with all the neighborhood news they had acquired in the last two days. These items were offered to Lady Eastwood like fine jewels on velvet as the carriage left Yewspring's lane and entered the outskirts of Exton.

As the carriage passed through the village square of Exton, Violet said, "Oh, look at the Vincents' window!" She pointed to a shop display with an ivory column of a gown at its center. "That looks very much like the dress I saw in *The Lady's Monthly Museum*—the one from Paris. I didn't think we'd get it here for another year. How smart it looks!"

Rose swiveled in her seat, nearly rising to her feet in the carriage. "It does look much the same. I wonder if Mrs. Vincent could make one up for me before we go to town."

"Oh Rose, this is your season, I am sure of it!" said Violet, patting her cousin's hand. "You'll need more than *one* new gown!"

Clara could feel an intake of breath, almost simultaneous, from her sister and grandmother as they both glanced at her, and then pretended not to have. And though her cheeks burned and she turned to study the hedges passing by more intently than she needed to, Clara knew her relatives' scrutiny was only natural. Her marriage and her sister's were inextricably linked, bound together like oxen in a yoke.

Mr. Eastwood had long ago pledged to be fair to his daughters and to give them an equal share in his fortune when they were married. Unless Clara married George, that is. In that case—and the Eastwoods had encouraged the relationship between their daughter and their young cousin for this reason—it seemed perfectly reasonable for him to settle his full fortune on Rose. George, and Clara through her marriage to him, would inherit Beechview, Yewspring, and both tenant farms in addition to what George's own parents had settled upon him and what Clara's grandparents would settle upon her. Clara and George would be more than comfortable without Mr. Eastwood's full settlement.

Rose receiving such a dowry as her father would then be at liberty to bestow upon her would entice any gentleman whose needs required the maintenance of perhaps several houses, a townhouse, and the carriages and servants that such a station in life demanded. And so she waited, not yet twenty, out in society despite Clara's unmarried status. But it had not done her any good, for gentlemen generally found out about the uncertainty over Rose's dowry and gently eased themselves out of her acquaintance with the delicacy and subtlety of slipping out of a theater before the play is over. Rose bore it patiently, but Clara knew her sister had been disappointed at least three times, most seriously just a few months ago, and would not be content with having her hopes dashed for much longer.

From behind the rim of her bonnet, Clara heard her grandmother say, "We must apply to George for the answer to the question of Rose's wardrobe, Violet, since her dowry depends on his addresses to her sister. And since such questions would be positively unladylike, let us keep silent on the matter to him."

"Very well, but Clara needn't keep us in suspense," said Violet. "What does he say, Clara? Is this to be the visit?"

Clara turned back to the center of the *landau* and saw Rose and Violet's faces turned toward her expectantly from the other seat of the carriage. Rose met Clara's eyes and held them. Breaking her sister's gaze, Clara looked to her right and saw Lady Eastwood also looking to see what she would answer.

"It does not matter," said Rose quickly. "We all have confidence in George, Violet. Anyone can see that he prefers our Clara. I have no doubt about it, at any rate."

Clara sighed. "We hope one more winter in Bath will fully cure him of his ague. Then perhaps this coming summer we will be free to wed."

"I have always marveled at this wonderful patience that

your mother seems to exhibit," said Lady Eastwood tartly. "I am not being duplicitous in saying so, for I have spoken to her of it many a time. She has two daughters and no sons, the younger girl depending on the attachment of the older to fully circulate in society, and yet she has the forbearance to wait out George's health until it is more agreeable. Forgive my indelicacy, but I do not think a touch of marsh fever has rendered him so unable to the physical…rigors of marriage should you and he be wed. He looked well enough to me at supper last night and certainly dispatched his allotted serving of sausage without any trouble. I do like to see a young man with a hearty appetite after a day out shooting. He was a little pale, perhaps, but nothing some sea air won't fix. Now, has he asked to speak with your father before he leaves on Thursday?"

"No, but we all are aware of the agreement between our fathers and the wish of our families. George and I are as committed to marrying as anyone can be without a formal offer. He is rightly concerned about his own health, a cause I am willing to wait until we are sure of. And anyway, Rose dear, you are not yet twenty. Since I am practically the age of an old maid, let me reassure you that I think you will have many opportunities to find a match of your own in the next year or two. And if I am engaged by the time we go to town, you could still be presented in the spring and have every chance of meeting a suitable man."

"I certainly hope so," said Lady Eastwood, before Rose could respond. "I ask you only to remember that suitors, whether for yourself or your sister, do not happen along every day, and life is far from certain. I would have had you married to George these three years past, with an heir in the cradle. I know your mother does not wish to force you into matches against your wills nor be seen as overly eager to bestow you upon a man who is not yet ready. But I do wonder sometimes how much she can have steered your courtship when she is always away in town or Bath or Brighton."

"Yes, Mama likes to be out and about. I am only thankful she does not demand that I go with her and takes Rose instead. I know how much you love town," she said to her sister.

"Well, I think it would have been good for you to travel," said Lady Eastwood, nodding to a tenant who was leading a heifer down the lane. "See the world, expand your horizons. A few years at school and then home to the country to wait for your distant relation to propose? Some young ladies would not call that a very satisfying life. But as you wish."

But everything I love is here, thought Clara, admiring the animal's sleek hide and gentle eyes as the carriage rattled by. *The countryside, my books, my solitude, my leisure. Yewspring is here— where else should I be?* When George asked, she knew her answer. For her *yes* to him would keep her here, where she belonged.

CHAPTER TWO

At the assembly that evening, after a whole day of her cousins' chatter, with the music of the violins turning from sweet to overbearing in her ears, head aching from too much punch, Clara could not help fetching her reticule from the inn's cloakroom and going up to the family's reserved parlor, finding it empty but for her grandfather snoring in an armchair in the corner, and the inn's maid cleaning the room from dinner. Clara motioned to the girl to keep clearing away the dishes, and crept to the window seat, making use of the full moon's light that spilled over New Street and into the room. She opened her reticule, took out her book, and opened it with a sigh of relief. She had just settled happily into tales from a minstrel on the borders of Scotland and England, marveling yet again at Scott's lively and evocative lines, when her mother came in. Mrs. Eastwood had followed her daughter up the staircase, and now came to stand at the window seat, taking the book from Clara's hand.

"You can have this back when we're home, my dear. There are only a few more sets, and you must get back down to George. He's dancing his second with Caroline now, and people will talk if you are not at his side. He's quite the catch, you know—there are girls here in Daventry who would take him for the farm alone, much less Beechview and Yewspring. I saw one of those Earnshaw girls eyeing him, and she's just turned twenty."

Clara sighed. She had hoped that if she left for a while George would take a reprieve from dancing, tired as he must be from his long day. She felt sure that while they were in the same room he felt obligated to stand up with her, and wished to spare him from a collapse that must offend his sense of dignity.

"Where were you?" asked George loudly over the music when she reached the assembly room again. He had dark circles beneath eyes and his forehead shone with exertion. He had just sat on a sofa next to her father but had of course risen when she approached.

"I—felt dizzy and stepped outside," said Clara, knowing that saying she had abandoned him for Walter Scott's minstrel would never do. Who read at a ball? Who concealed books in their bag like a child smuggling sweets?

She could see the relief all over his face. "Uncle, Clara is tired," he said, turning to Mr. Eastwood. "Might we have the carriage now?"

And though it was what Clara wanted, to be out of the warm and crowded room, away from the voices ricocheting off the paneled walls like bullets, she could not help feeling that it had been a waste of an evening, to stand up just so the neighbors would know she was intended for George. And when she had provisioned for her own delight so well, too, with *The Lay of the Last Minstrel*! Such parading of her and George's relationship, designed to keep other women away from him as if they were poachers waiting to slip in and make off with a prime pheasant, disgusted her. And yet she could not tell him that, not when they were so fond of one another, when she would have been happiest if he had been among the circle of quiet chat around the hearth at Yewspring. How was he to understand that she truly cared for him but did not desire to be in ballrooms a moment longer than necessary? She would not have a need for such gentle deceit once they were married, of course. She hoped it would not be long.

Clara stood at the dining room table the next morning,

gathering the last herbs from the garden strewn across the table into bundles, their scents filling the little room while George sat and ate his breakfast. Their reluctant chaperone Rose, cross at being awoken so early after a late return from Daventry, was sitting and plunking at the pianoforte in the sitting room, the sound coming through the open double doorway.

George studied a map spread out on the table before him. On this, his last day at Yewspring, he was planning a ride for the day for himself and his cousins, a privilege Clara granted with a greater alacrity than she might have been wont to do if it had not given him so much pleasure. He had several times been delighted by the idea that he had discovered new riding routes about Exton during his visits; each time he did, she did not have the heart to tell him that she knew them all already.

"I always think of Charles whenever I see a map now," said George, taking a sip of his tea. "And I wonder which one he's looking at that day. I wonder if he's frightened when he sees where they're going. And I wonder if he ever looks back across the leagues to England on the map, wishing he were home again."

"Charles went willingly," said Clara, bending to pick up some stray sprigs of thyme from the carpet. "So perhaps he is not quite ready to come back."

"Yes, I suppose I am only imagining what I would feel in his place. His letters do sound quite exhilarated at times, what with the ports they visit and the camaraderie amongst the officers. And even when they go into action, he always sounds gleeful afterwards."

Clara shuddered a bit when she thought of all the somber ways that George's brother's military career might end. "I suppose he is happy, then, as happy as one can be in the midst of war."

"I suppose so. I know he is proud of serving the Crown, of defending his country."

"Yes, it would give one a sense of—purpose, I would think."

Quiet fell about the dining room. Rose must have woken up a bit, for she was playing Scarlatti at a brisk tempo in the next room.

"You know, it is so strange for me to think that you and Charles have never met," said George, his voice thoughtful beneath the tinkling cascade of notes. "The two people I am perhaps fondest of—" He broke off in embarrassment and quickly began attending to the task of cracking the egg in his dish.

Clara could not help smiling at this, unladylike though it might be to rejoice in another's affection for her, but moderated her tone to a neutral one as she replied, "Yes, he was always at school when I was in town, and away somewhere when I came to stay at Reedbridge. But I hope to make his acquaintance one day."

He looked up at her. "Yes, that would be agreeable for us all, I think."

Clara went into the kitchen for more twine, and came back to find him intent once again on the map. "What about going to Bretford?" he asked her.

"Oh, might we go somewhere up north instead? Rose and I went to Bretford this summer already. I wanted to look for marsh clubmoss before it was too late in the season."

She had come home with mud up to her shins, a sheaf of drawings, and a sister who was cross from being out in the sun.

"All right, north it is," he said, running his finger over the map. "I am glad you've been able to pass the time so pleasantly here. Always sketching or chasing something through some meadow or other. And your reading is quite formidable, I confess.

But I admire your habits. They speak to your good sense and reflect a repulsion for idleness which must be to your credit."

"Thank you," she said. "I plan to continue my pursuits as long as I can—until I must be wheeled about the meadows in a chair as an old woman, at least."

He stopped and looked at her, a little smile on his face. "Your pursuits are a testament to your energy and dedication, Clara. And I know you will apply those qualities to our, er, your family when the time comes."

He blushed and added quickly, "I look forward to seeing what you make of those highest of aims."

Clara, flustered, busied herself with gathering up the now-tied bundles. "Oh," she said faintly to the stems neatly assembled at her fingertips, "You flatter me, George." But was she flattered? Suddenly her marriage seemed a cliff beyond which she could not see, whose edge she had never thought to peer over because she had never had the need. She had never envisioned what her life with George would be like, she realized, only pictured herself walking through Yewspring's fields, its woods, its barns. She mustered a smile and escaped with the armfuls of herbs to the scullery to hang from the ceiling, and came back resolved to be cheerful.

"Well," she said, wiping her hands on her apron and reaching behind her to untie it, "where are we to go today? Need we plan around your shooting schedule? I am surprised Papa is not down yet if you two are to go out first."

"We'll go to Frolesworth," he said, leaning back in his chair. "It's a long jaunt, perhaps, but Cook could make us a hamper and we could lunch outdoors. 'Tis a fine day."

"Are you quite sure you have time for such an expedition? Do you not want to go out with them in the afternoon, at least?" She knew his strength must have been sapped during his long stints out-of-doors during the previous two days. And yet he had risen early on his last day without complaint, and planned an expedition that must surely test his endurance once again.

"Oh no," George said in response to her question after a pause, and something in his voice made her turn in the doorway from where she was taking her apron away to the kitchen. He looked at her almost shyly. "I'd rather spend the day with you. There will be other pheasants back home in Kent, but no Clara Eastwood."

She blushed and looked down at the crumpled apron in her hand, dingy and stained by blueberries. "I'd like that too," she said. "I am pleased you're so fond of Yewspring, you know."

He stood and faced her. "I'll be even fonder of it when I know that I have a worthy companion to share it with," he said, making her go from pink to crimson.

Her heart pounded, and she drew in a deep breath.

In a daze, she noted that Rose's playing from the other room had paused. She heard her sister turn a page, and then begin the first bars of a mazurka.

George took a step toward her. "As soon as I'm strong again, I'll be back," he said.

She tried not to be disappointed, and chided herself for even feeling the flicker of regret, looking at his pale face and tired eyes with purple hollows beneath them. *What good was life without the strength to enjoy it?* she tried to ask herself. What joy could there be in their marriage if George thought he might leave her a widow, perhaps heirless, perhaps dependent on Charles for funds? She quieted the voice inside her that said at least, as George's widow, she was secure of Yewspring. George wanted them to begin their married life with the hope of many years together, just like any other young couple. And because he wanted this, she tried to want it too.

"Shooting or no shooting, invited or not," George said, "I have a question for my uncle Eastwood as soon as I feel secure enough of my future to ask it." He was the one blushing now, at what was so near openness. The earnestness and intentness with which he regarded her made her hands tremble as she twisted the cloth between them.

But she could not help smiling, and looked back at him.

She saw the table next to him still laid with his plate of kippers, the coffee pot beside him, and thought about how often they'd have mornings like this in the years to come.

"I hope the answer to your question is to your liking," she said, "and that subsequent ones are as well. I suspect they will be."

They heard a floorboard creak as Mr. Eastwood came downstairs, grumbling about Rose's loud playing so early in the day, and George took yet another step toward her, speaking in a low voice.

"As soon as I'm over this blasted weakness, I'll impose upon my aunt Eastwood's hospitality again, no matter what the calendar says. Believe me, Clara, I will. We've been patient enough, I think."

Thrill ran through her like a hot drink, her doubts in the scullery fading away, and she smiled at him.

"I agree," she said, and a glance passed between them of understanding, of anticipation—of something she could not quite name, a feeling hovering between friendship and passion without quite being either.

And when George drove off the next morning, she knew that it was the last time he would take his leave of Yewspring merely as its future heir rather than her future husband.

CHAPTER THREE

"Look, Phoebe!" cried Violet to her cousin across Reed's dry-goods in the main square of Exton, "Here are the green ribbons Mrs. Franks was telling us about on Tuesday at Grandmama's!"

Phoebe Morton, who had been standing at Clara's side while they examined a new book of pressed flowers that Mr. Reed had just ordered in, rushed to the counter. The cousins—there were five of them in total, the others being Clara, Rose, and Phoebe's sister Caroline—were on their way back to the Eastwoods' after taking tea with their former governess Miss Holt.

They had detoured into the shop when Caroline had looked over at the window display and said, "Oh, look at that *stunning* pelisse! And just my color! Oh, if only my pin-money was a bit more—perhaps I can convince Papa."

Rose had taken her arm and marched them all into the store so her cousin could have a better look. Caroline stood now at the mannequin with Mrs. Reed, reverently stroking the maroon velvet. They spoke in hushed whispers, as if the pile of the fabric would spontaneously crumple should they raise their voices. Rose had stood looking at the millinery displays with the seriousness of a sergeant inspecting the troops. From outside came the rumbling and clattering of carts passing through the square, and Mrs. Fulbright's flock of geese noisily honking as they traipsed down to the pond with little Daniel Fulbright trailing behind them.

Now that Phoebe had deserted her for the siren of emerald

ribbon, which Clara felt a feeble enticement in comparison to the one in her own hands, she paged through the book of flowers, noting the ones she had seen in bloom last year on her walks and looking forward in her mind to the walks she would take when spring came again. With her back to the door, she was examining a particularly interesting foxglove and did not think anything of the sound of the shop door's bell ringing as it opened. After a moment, utter silence fell over the store, making her lift her head and turn around.

The other young ladies stood with their jaws agape, and Mrs. Reed looked stunned. A young, well-dressed man had just walked in, and seemed embarrassed by the reaction this simple action had caused. Mrs. Reed recollected herself, and stepping forward from the mannequin, said, "Welcome, my dear sir. May I assist you in finding anything?"

The young man seemed determined not to notice the scrutiny of many pairs of young female eyes, the force of which he could not help but feel, like a hare cannot help feeling the eyes of the hawk.

"I am in search of blotting paper," he said, "for my aunt. Perhaps you have made her acquaintance? Mrs. Thurston is her name."

Mrs. Thurston was a widow who lived in the village, down one of its side lanes near the green. She and Clara's family often attended the same social events, and saw each other in the square or in church. But a nephew of Mrs. Thurston's had never been mentioned to Clara's knowledge, and certainly not a young well-dressed one with very correct manners. Caroline was now absent-mindedly stroking the velvet of the pelisse as she stared at the gentleman dreamily.

Clara studied him a bit to see if he deserved this sudden adoration. He was certainly very elegant, dressed in a fine tail- and waistcoat with a snowy white cravat adorning them. He was fair and tall, with broad shoulders and a strong square chin. In his manners, he seemed determined to please and be civil to all around him, though of course propriety dictated that he not presume to speak to the young ladies until he had been introduced to them, an office Mrs. Reed was not qualified to perform. The strangers were destined to remain strangers still, at least for today. Beyond that, Clara could not say, and decided a mere transaction in a store would not be enough time to determine his character.

Mrs. Reed led the gentleman to the selection of papers, and Phoebe and Violet quickly clustered around Caroline at the window, whispering with one another loudly and occasionally glancing over their shoulders at the gentleman. Clara exchanged a glance across the store with Rose, and wordlessly her sister began gathering the others to leave. The whispering of the three girls was loud enough to cause the young gentleman to look over his shoulder as he stood at the counter.

Clara loudly asked, "Mrs. Reed, would you be so kind as to order me a copy of this book of pressings?" as Mrs. Reed was in the middle of asking after Mrs. Thurston's health.

Mrs. Reed looked startled at Clara's rudeness and said, "Of course, Miss Eastwood."

Clara breathed a sigh of relief as Rose took advantage of the momentary distraction to herd the other girls out of the shop. As soon as the door clanged shut behind them, her cousins and sister began clamoring all at once.

"Mrs. Thurston has never mentioned a nephew before!" exclaimed Rose, willing to join in the excitement of the other girls now that they were out of earshot of the store.

"Did you see his eyes?" sighed Caroline. "A *most* becoming and elegant gray!"

"His eyes? How on earth did you get a look at them when they were so single-mindedly fixed on me?" asked Phoebe—whose recollections of the gentleman did not agree with Clara's. "He must fancy me! There is no other explanation!"

Clara smiled to herself at their astonishment, and their pleasure in the prospect that such a man had come to the village. Being older than they in years, and less prone to flights of romantic fancy, she thought it quite likely the young gentleman was there to pay a long-overdue visit to his elderly aunt, while of course conveniently availing himself of countryside's shooting if he was a sportsman, and they would never see him again. After all, the *ton* had little to do with their part of the country, and the young ladies had been forced to go to London to meet any of them at all. She could not envision that such a smart young man would dawdle in a country village. No, she decided, once his familial duty was fulfilled and he had shot enough ducks to satisfy himself, he would be off for London or Bath in his barouche. These smart young gentlemen were all the same, never satisfied with what they found in the country unless they were killing something or being entertained with some race or card game. She had seen enough of them in London drawing rooms to know. Her sister and cousins would have to wait until Violet's brothers' friends were at liberty to come to Exton in order to bestow their next dose of hysteria—George being so clearly earmarked for herself had denied the others any chance of achieving that enviable state through his presence.

The young ladies had no more crossed the square and started up the lane toward Yewspring when they encountered Ned, Violet's brother closest in age, walking toward the village.

"Oh, hello," he said, "I have just left Mama at Yewspring. She wanted to walk over straight away once she heard the news and tell Aunt Hazel. I shall trot over to the square and see if I can get a look at his black horse. They say it is very fine."

The young ladies were fairly frantic with anticipation. Clearly Ned knew of this young gentleman's arrival, and they were desperate to be filled in on the details.

"What is his name? Is he really Mrs. Thurston's nephew? Where does he come from?" demanded Caroline.

Ned found himself in the unusual position of having more information than his sister and cousins and was determined to savor it. He did not often find a captive audience in his female relations.

"Well," he began, "I wish I could remember what Mama was chattering about while we walked down, but I'm afraid I was rather distracted by the race results I'd just gotten from Newmarket. You see, I'd put five pounds on Crown Royal..."

"*Hang* Newmarket!" exclaimed Violet, in a most unladylike fashion. "Ned, if you cannot tell us anything interesting, we shall go to Mama and Aunt Hazel straightaway!"

"All right, all right," he said. "His name is James Creston, and he is from London."

"London? Why have we never been introduced to him in town? Surely our connection to Mrs. Thurston would have brought it about," said Rose, the most prone of all the girls to dreaming of a house in Kensington and a box at the Theatre Royal. "We have met all of Exton's other relations in town, why not him?"

"Mama says Mrs. Thurston usually goes to her house in Bath and her family visits her there, but she is so much better this year that she decided stay in the country," Ned said. "You remember that she was here all last spring, which is not generally her practice."

"How long will he stay?" asked Violet.

"A month or so, I believe. We may see him at the Doyles' dinner next Thursday, and to cap it all off, he has a sister who is here as well."

This was news that could serve in the young ladies' favor. A sister, should she be near them in age, would be a more suitable person with whom to make the acquaintance of the siblings, and the aunt would be sure to introduce her to them. From there, it was a hop, skip, and a jump to one of the five ladies—four, Clara thought wryly, excluding herself from the pool of eligible women—marrying the brother, and all would be well. Unless, of course, a lack of fortune would cast a pall on a match.

Rose's mind as well as Clara's must have turned to this subject, for she asked, "And is he a man of means, Ned?"

"Mrs. Roberts, who you know is Mrs. Thurston's good friend, and who was the one to bring the news to Mama this morning, says he has three thousand a year," said Ned. "Nothing to sneeze at, to be sure. I wonder if he needs advice on the races. He must have a fair amount of pocket money."

"Oh, how very suitable!" sighed Violet, and the girls, having exhausted Ned's usefulness, rushed up the lane together toward Yewspring.

Clara trailed behind the others and stopped for a moment, craning her neck to try and see over the hedge to Mr. Dillingham's pasture. She had been reading about cattle breeds after exhausting the rest of the natural history books in her grandfather's library and knew that the Dillinghams had recently purchased a Highland cow and calf during the fall sale at Southam. For some time she had wished to see them for herself, intrigued by the prospect of seeing such a shaggy creature that seemed meant for the wind-swept lochs or far-off mountains. Perhaps they had been put out with the rest of the cattle that she could hear lowing on the other side of the hedge. Being only of average height and the hedge higher than most, Clara found it difficult to see over, and walked on a bit further to try and find a more favorable spot. Up ahead, she spied a large boulder near the hedge, likely abandoned from when the lane had been built. Glancing about her, she scrambled up onto it and leaned over the top of the hedge to gaze down into the pasture.

"Clara, for heaven's sake, get down, you goose!" cried Rose when she glanced behind her to see where Clara had gone. "You'll fall and hurt yourself!"

"I will be careful," said Clara, now able to see down into the pasture below. "And I'll just be a moment, Rose—I'll catch up with you shortly."

She could hear Violet turn and say something to her sister, giggling, and heard the phrase "—such broad shoulders!" Soon the chattering of her companions had faded to a faint murmur as they went up the lane ahead of her.

There were a few cattle pastured below her vantage point, but they were Guernseys, well-kept with their glossy swirls of copper and white but not the object of her search. Clara had just turned to clamber down from the boulder again when a lone, very shaggy cow came ambling up a slope and into sight. Its pure auburn coat stood out against the green of the pasture grass, and Clara smiled at its forelock of hair hanging down below its eyes. Behind it came a miniature version of itself, although the calf's forelock had not yet grown over its eyes, giving it a curious, alert expression. It gazed at Clara, who smiled at it, rejoicing as she often did when a fact from her reading revealed itself in the physical world to be very much true. She always felt it made the world a friendlier place when she could recognize the goings-on of its seasons, animals, and plants. The woods and fields yielded more her contentment than most drawing-rooms, and she understood their rhythms and language, she felt, more so than she knew how to flatter or charm or cajole those of her own species.

"Aren't you the beauties?" she called to the newcomers who had so obligingly made themselves available for her admiration. They were decidedly unmoved by her flattering remark and placidly lowered their heads to graze. She stood, perched at the top of the rock, listening to the bramblings calling insistently to each other in the trees surrounding the field, not yet ready to lend their presence to Yewspring's garden as they would when winter came in just a month or two. She went on watching the herd and savored the feeling of sunshine on her face, knowing that there would be days ahead when she remembered it with longing.

After a few moments, she heard a throat, decidedly masculine, clear behind her. Startled, she twisted behind her to see who was there, slipped on the rock, still wet with the rain that had fallen briefly that morning, lost her balance, and fell backwards into the hedge. She landed in the ditch between the hedge and the road.

"Good day," said an unfamiliar man standing above her. From her vantage point, admittedly not a dignified one, as it highlighted the view up his nostrils, she could see he wore a bemused expression. "May I assist you?" He offered a hand down to her.

Blushing, Clara reached up and took it, and he raised her to her feet. Smoothing her skirts and straightening her bonnet, trying not to appear as flustered as she felt (as if it were her daily routine to tumble down in front of gentlemen), she said, "Thank you."

Now that they were face to face, she saw that he was not

ill-looking and certainly had a very pleasant expression on his face but was not what one would call classically handsome. He had an inquisitive face, gray eyes that seemed prone to crinkling at the corners, a nose that was larger and perhaps more slightly hooked than was strictly fashionable, and strong dark brows that were currently drawn together quizzically.

"I apologize for being so forward," he said presently, shifting several books he carried from one arm to another. "And I am sorry if I startled you. I was just curious why you were so eager to see Mr. Dillingham's herd. My name is Henry Kensington. I am Lord Chesterson's new land agent." He did her a courtesy.

She curtsied, noticing as she did that there was a clump of wet grass clinging to her skirt. "I'm Clara Eastwood," she told him, trying to shake the clump off unobtrusively. "My family lives at Yewspring, just up the lane there. You see, I've been read-ing about cattle and heard that Mr. Dillingham had purchased a Highland cow and calf. So I—wished to see them." She supposed she had appeared doubly improper to him, first for climbing up onto the rock and secondly to be peering over a hedge into someone else's field. Ladies were not supposed to appear to be intrusive into the business of another, she knew. And yet she had witnessed enough conversations to know that this disinterest was a façade, a veneer. She had simply not ever learned to apply it to herself, or to direct her interest toward fortunes and romantic intrigue as others did. Her curiosity was a ship she could not turn into more feminine waters, no matter how much such a change in course might have made her life easier.

Mr. Kensington smiled. "Had you been reading Anderson's *On Cattle and Their Fine Products*?"

"Yes," she said. "And before that, his volume on swine, though I must wait a bit longer to check the pens for piglets."

"Ah, naturally," he said. "Both worthy works, though I am not sure how many young ladies would share your desire to peruse them. And, pray, Miss Eastwood—it is 'Miss'?"

"Yes," she said.

"—were you rewarded in your rather surreptitious search?"

"Yes, they are just there on the other side, and just as friendly-looking as I'd thought they would."

He looked up at the rock she had been standing on. "Would you think it very improper if I borrow your footstool for a moment?"

"No," she said, laughing a little, "in fact, I think it an excellent idea."

He smiled. "Your ingenuity has inspired me. Would you be so good as to hold these?" He held out the books to her.

She readily agreed, and peered at the spines while he climbed up. The volumes were Hutton's *Theory of the Earth*, Bradley's gardening and animal husbandry book, and, most tantalizingly, Lamarck's *Philosophie zoologique*, which had been published just the year before. She could not help rifling through the pages, thinking yet again with dismay that it would take her eons to get through it—if she ever had the opportunity to read it—with her poor French.

"What fine specimens!" Mr. Kensington said from atop the boulder. "I wonder if Mr. Dillingham will acquire more. Is he the first in the area to buy a Highland?" He climbed back down, without losing his footing as Clara had done.

"Yes," said Clara. "These are the only that I know of, at any rate."

He took the books from her with a bow of thanks. "You seem to be most observant—I think you would have seen any others, if there were any about."

She could not resist saying, "I should love to read Lamarck, if you find yourself at liberty to part with it for a while. Once you have read it, of course."

He smiled. "I would be happy to lend it to you. You might be waiting a while, however—my French is atrocious. When my sister comes I shall have to have her read it to me."

"You and I are alike in our ineptitude, then. But Lamarck is so fascinating that I am always determined to try and learn his language better. I cannot be properly shocked by his radical ideas if I cannot understand him fully."

He laughed. "Might I inquire as to your interest in livestock? I confess I rarely encounter ladies attempting to learn of barnyards."

What to tell him? She knew it was unusual—and most would say unseemly—to be interested in animal husbandry. She wanted to say *Because the parts of the world that delight me are all out-of-doors, and barnyards are what are here.* She wanted to say *Because my mind longs for Latin and for scientific names, so I may as well practice on sheep and geese.* She wanted to say, *I must learn* something *or go insane—and since no one will take me to Africa or Scotland or America I am determined to take pleasure in what lies just beyond my door.*

Instead, she said, "Because barnyards are close at hand—and I should like to understand what is close by. I find it makes my walks and conversations with our neighbors much more interesting. It is easier to make one at ease if you can converse with them about what they care about—at least, I believe so."

She expected a baffled look, but he just studied her thoughtfully.

"Indeed," he said after a pause. "And you seem to have found enthusiasm there yourself—which always makes it easier to converse about a topic."

"Yes, well," she looked down at the dirt of the lane beneath her feet, "some would say I am foolish to attempt this particular one. Perhaps they are right."

"I must disagree with you on that score," he said, and she looked back up at him.

He looked up the lane in the direction she had gestured when mentioning Yewspring. "May I escort you home, or—wherever you were going?" he asked.

Propriety dictated that he not ask that question. Propriety dictated she refuse, if he should breach etiquette enough to ask. Neither of them heeded propriety in this instance.

"You may," she said.

They walked on together, in silence for a moment. Clara tried to peer down at the grass stain on her skirt unobtrusively, glad it was on the side not facing Mr. Kensington.

"You could find no companion for your livestock investigation?" he asked presently.

"Oh," she said, "I was with my sister and my cousins, but they went on ahead—they are more lady-like than I and are not interested in such things."

"Well, I wonder if you might allow me to be of greater service than they in your investigative mission. Of course, I can offer you full access to his Lordship's barns, but I have also been meaning to visit the Dillinghams to ask to see the Highlands up close—I did not anticipate the brief and unorthodox opportunity of seeing them that you have thought of. Once you and I are properly introduced, of course, would you like to accompany me and we shall see if our initial impressions can be expanded upon?"

"Oh, very much! Thank you, sir."

As they walked, she learned that he had lately come from Somersetshire to take the position on the Haythorne estate. Clara remembered seeing an advertisement for the post in the *Coventry Herald*, which she had surreptitiously stolen from her uncle's study while he was napping and devoured while the other girls were cutting out patterns one day. Mr. Kensington had taken a small cottage ("very derelict at the moment", he said ruefully) on the estate and planned to bring his mother, sister, and nephew to live with him when it was repaired.

They had soon reached the gated arch in the hedge that signaled the drive to Yewspring. Clara stopped. "This is my house— or, my father's, I should say," she said. "Yewspring."

Mr. Kensington looked through the open gate to the gravel drive and neat but unremarkable facade of Yewspring, with its symmetrical double rows of windows and pillars adorning the doorstep, then turned to her and bowed. "Ah, yes, his Lordship was praising your father's management of both this estate and Beechview Manor."

"He is very kind."

"Yewspring is how many acres? I cannot recall what he said."

"Only a hundred," she said, "but it is really just a part of the Beechview Manor estate, which is about a thousand. My father manages both estates for my grandfather, along with the agent."

"Ah yes, Mr. Graham, I believe?"

"Yes," she said.

"No doubt I will have the pleasure of commending him and your father myself soon. Good day, Miss Eastwood," he said, bowing to her. "I hope to make your family's acquaintance, and that we meet again soon."

She echoed his sentiment, curtseyed, and turned away. The

hedge that surrounded the house and its front garden blocked him from her view. She was tempted to look behind her but did not until she reached the porch, from which she saw only the empty gate behind her.

Mr. Cove hailed her from the side garden and said, "The garlic's ready to be planted, Miss Clara, if you'd like to help me. Oh, but you're in your fine clothes! No matter, the bulbs'll keep."

"Don't be silly," said Clara, stripping off her gloves. "I'll meet you in a moment."

She entered the house and heard from the sitting-room doorway the excited voices of her sister and cousins from the sitting room. She lingered a moment in the hall, shedding her pelisse, gloves, and bonnet, thinking about the morning's events. Who could have guessed that they would be so remarkable? And now a lovely garden diversion to keep her out-of-doors a little longer!

She put on her work apron and went to the garden door, spending the next quarter hour helping Mr. Cove set out and cover the bulbs. Reluctantly, she went indoors when the task, too brief for her wishes, was complete.

As she came back into the hall, Rose came out of the sitting room, from which still came the deluge of seven feminine voices. "I came to see where you were. We were afraid you had run into gypsies on the road and they had kidnapped you. Oh, you've been gardening already? Well, you must come at once and settle the matter of whether Mr. Creston wore a blue coat or a gray one. We are all at odds with each other."

"It was green," Clara said. "But you'll never guess what just—"

But Rose was already rushing back down the hall. "It was green!" Clara could hear her calling as she went.

CHAPTER FOUR

Clara entered the sitting room behind her sister. She found Violet and Phoebe squashed together in the window seat arguing on whether they had seen a watch chain in Mr. Creston's waistcoat pocket and whether it had been brass or gold. Mrs. Eastwood sat by the fire on a settee with the tea-table at her elbow and began to pour the cups. Her sister-in-law Mrs. Tapley sat next to her.

"Hello, Aunt Georgiana," said Clara, coming up to her aunt and bending to kiss her cheek.

"Oh Clara, such a lucky find!" her aunt exclaimed as she returned the greeting. "I am so pleased that his coat is green instead of blue, for I think it a more becoming color, and one that sounds as though it will suit his own coloring better—which, of course, speaks to his modest good taste. And Ned tells me he has a charming little estate in Rutland, as well as the family's London house! To think, if you girls hadn't been taken with that pelisse, you might never have seen him! I have a mind to buy it for Caroline in gratitude for the encounter."

"Clara, Clara, you silly girl!" interrupted Mrs. Eastwood, looking at her daughter for the first time. "How in the world did you get dirt on your face just walking to Exton? And your hands—they're filthy! Good heavens, what if someone were to see you looking like a grubby little gardener's boy? Pray go and make yourself presentable. Has she gotten dirt on your gown, sister?"

"Oh no," said Mrs. Tapley, though Clara could see that there was indeed a smudge of earth on her aunt's Indian shawl.

"Of course she did," said Mrs. Eastwood with a mixture of resignation and anger, peering at the spot. "Clara, go upstairs at once and wash. I shouldn't have to tell you such things—how will you ever be married if you are to appear in such a state? What would George say?" She picked up the bell at her side and rang it to summon Mrs. Huttleston, the housekeeper.

"I'm so sorry, Aunt Georgiana," said Clara, feeling truly terrible at her thoughtlessness. Being in the garden always made her so happy she forgot about the dirt, and other people's objection to it. Moreover, her aunt's shawl was a particularly lovely paisley and she knew it was especially treasured on account of just having arrived from her son Thomas, away serving the Crown in the East Indies.

"It's nothing a bit of scrubbing won't mend, Clara dear, don't fret," said her aunt placidly, and in came Mrs. Huttleston to be instructed to bring a bowl of hot water and soap to get out the spot. Clara went away to wash, cheeks burning like a schoolgirl rather than a woman about to turn six-and-twenty. As she crossed the threshold of the sitting room, she heard her mother begin to her aunt, "Her father indulges her in these unseemly past-times—" She was glad she could not hear more.

She soon came back, feeling tidier in person but irritated nevertheless after her mother's scolding, accepted the cup offered to her, and sat on the other pianoforte stool across from Rose, seats being scarce in the little reception room. It had clearly not been designed in anticipation of harboring all the females of the Eastwood line.

From where she sat at a work-table, Caroline was staring blushingly into her lap, which meant that someone had mentioned a Mr. Reynolds in the course of the conversation. He was a friend of Ned's, a young barrister from Manchester who had spent time with the Tapleys during the shooting, and shown special attention to Caroline during the dances in the village.

"Ah yes," said Mrs. Tapley knowingly, looking at her niece. She prided herself on being a conduit for young men into her nieces' lives through the connections of her many sons. Apparently the topic of "Mr. R" was still at hand. "I shall have to ask him to come and stay again soon, Caroline dear. Perhaps once another certain young man makes an offer to our Clara—"

Now Clara was the one blushing as the eyes of the others in the room turned to her.

Violet said, "Oh yes, I heard George telling Ned that he wished to return to Exton next spring before we all go to town! What else could it be but to propose! Oh, it is so exciting—a wedding here in Exton!"

Clara could not help smiling with pleasure at this welcome sign that George had been as open with her family as he had with her.

"Oh!" cried Mrs. Eastwood, clapping her hands in spite of herself and clasping them before her with sparkling eyes, as if she were the one in expectation of a proposal. Clara had not told her mother about George's wish to return to Yewspring that spring. "Oh my heavens, Clara, you really *have* captured his affections, and at what a most opportune time, now that—well, never mind!"

Clara blushed deeper at this reference to Rose's lack of suitors until she herself was engaged. She knew her mother was hoping that Rose might catch Mr. Creston's eye.

"George takes such delight in talking with you!" exclaimed Violet. "I declare I scarcely can make out what it is he is saying when he holds forth at dinner, but you two are so well matched—I know you like a serious subject, Clara, and he certainly has no trouble providing one."

"Heaven knows there are precious few to be found here most of the time," said Caroline serenely, looking at her sister where Phoebe pouted over having lost The Watch Argument.

"On the contrary, I think marriage is a most serious subject," said Rose to her cousin with a smile, "one that cannot be talked of too much beforehand—for what would be the point of avoiding the topic and then bumbling into a bad match that leads to years of unhappiness and unpleasantness for all? We should think of the hearts and good nature of the gentlemen who are so kind as to pay us attention—those are at stake in the decisions as well as our own. Our schoolroom days are meant to prepare us for such decisions, and why should we throw the subject aside once we are old enough to act on our preparation?"

"Well said," her mother replied, casting her eyes to her other daughter meaningfully. Clara pretended not to see. "Would that all young ladies would attend to the matter with such care."

"And George and Clara have always been a wonderful model of what might exist between those who are to wed," Rose went on, looking at her sister. "I have admired their friendship and good-natured relationship and hoped for the same for myself when I am considering the attention of a gentleman. If I am fortunate enough to entertain such attentions, that is."

"Oh, pish-posh," said her aunt. "You are a desirable match, my dear. An accomplished musician, descended from a very respectable family, —the name of Eastwood is known and thought well of in all the best circles, I dare say—of a most amiable temperament, *and* shall have a dowry of at least five thousand when the time comes. And your travels with your dear mama have done you good—you are polished indeed after your time in Bath and London and Tunbridge Wells. I hope your mama will consent to allow Violet to accompany the two of you when you go off again, for it would benefit her greatly. Trust me, Rose dear, the suitors will be vying for your hand."

Clara knew her aunt spoke truly of her sister's merits—if rather optimistically about the plethora of gentlemen crowding round Rose, if recent years were to be any indicator—but could not help feeling that they reflected rather badly on herself. She rose from her seat, saying, "Would anyone like another cup?" and luckily found that the teapot needed refilling, giving her an opportunity to excuse herself to the kitchen for more hot water.

When she returned, Phoebe piped up from the window seat. "I do not see how it follows that Mr. Eastwood means to propose just because he said he wants to come and visit. What if all he wants is to discuss a business matter with Uncle Eastwood?" As the youngest cousin, she categorized all masculine undertakings under this vague term.

Violet said, "Mr. Eastwood must ask Uncle's permission before asking Clara herself, of course! And a gentleman wouldn't write about such a thing, he must come himself."

"Even though…?" Caroline asked, trailing off in embarrassment. Clara was well past the age that she needed her parent's consent to be wed.

Clara's mother turned to face her niece. "Your uncle holds the privilege of bestowing Clara's dowry only for a match of which he approves," she said firmly. "Otherwise he could alter his will and give everything to Rose."

"Which he would not, of course," said Rose hastily, looking at her sister. "Papa would never leave us destitute unless he truly and gravely objected to the match. And George is so highly suitable there could never be an objection to him."

Clara knew herself well enough to suspect that there was unlikely to be another match for her beside the one her sister alluded to. She had often been grateful that her expectations prevented her from needing to preen and jostle with the others for a gentleman's attentions, and did not think she could if she had to. She was not worried about trying to secure her father's approval for her fiancé.

"It is merely a formality, to ask the father's permission," said Mrs. Tapley to Phoebe, "but one that any gentleman would adhere to. When we hear that he has asked to come visit again, Clara, we will all rejoice with you."

"Enough of Mr. Eastwood, as agreeable as he might be!" Violet said. "When shall we meet Mr. Creston?"

As it happened, the young ladies did not have long to wait to officially make the acquaintance of the intriguing addition to their neighborhood. At Beechview that evening they all learned from their grandmother that he was certainly to be at the Doyles' dinner on the following Thursday, a mere week away.

"That is a quarter of his stay!" moaned Phoebe. "What if he makes some other young ladies' acquaintance in the meantime, and then we are at a disadvantage? The Younges are quite close with Mrs. Thurston, and they have three daughters! What if they should get there before us?" Her tone was that of one explorer racing another to reach some vast, untapped continent.

"Then you must decide how you will take advantage of the time you *are* allotted with him," said Lady Eastwood, "and make the most of it, dear."

After the fine day on which Clara met Mr. Kensington, the weather turned inhospitable to any outdoor excursion far from Yewspring. Clara was no stranger to walking in foul weather, finding shelter by walking in the woods rather than the open fields, but even she took fewer outings during these days, content to stay by the fire with her books. One morning, however, she decided to walk down to the granary and see how the threshing was getting on. She bundled herself into pelisse, gloves, and bonnet against the damp chill, even though her journey was no more than a quarter of a mile. She was glad that they had gotten the garlic in while the weather was fine, as she passed by the bare earth where the bulbs lay waiting for winter's long rest.

She wound her way through the garden, out its back gate, and through the edge of Yewspring's western pasture to the granary, a long low building lying beside a cart-path that cut through the long block of pastures and fields running parallel to the lane to Exton. She went in through its front foot-door rather than the wide double doors that would have been open in fine weather to allow the carts and wagons to drive in and be loaded with the sacks of grain. They were closed today, of course. It was a day for staying in, and only the promise of an extra day's wages would have compelled the workers to come and finish the flailing to get the grain to market. Her eyes began to adjust to the building's dimness, and she gradually saw figures moving to and fro on the threshing floor. A group of about ten walked amid drifts of chaff and wheat stalks with their flailing sticks, beating the heaps at their feet. Another ten gathered the stalks into large baskets, sifting out the chaff, which fell back to the floor, and poured the grain into the bags that lay open and waiting. Clara looked with pride at the symbol of two yew branches stamped onto the bags.

Annie Clemons had seen Clara come in, and now walked over to her, wiping her brow with a strong forearm as she did.

"Good afternoon, Miss Eastwood," the forewoman said.

"Good day, Mrs. Clemons," said Clara. "I see everything is proceeding speedily enough. It looks like they'll finish before the end of the day."

"Yes ma'am, I think so. This crew here knows their way around the threshing floor right enough, especially Yewspring's. I only wish there were a bit more for us to do, if it isn't too forward to say so. I'd have liked to see a few more fields put into corn this year—it'd have kept us threshing a bit longer and not so idle this winter."

"Well, the winter is a slow time, isn't it?" said Clara. "We all must stay occupied as best we are able, I suppose. But—perhaps it would be better to hold back some of Yewspring's grain harvest in future years? Then you could all count on some work doing the last bit of threshing and bagging in the winter. And Yewspring's grain would go for a higher price, I think, since the stores are more depleted at that time of year. It would give us a bit of an advantage, I think."

"Aye, that may be worth trying," said Mrs. Clemons, looking at the bent backs of the workers. "And the grain'll store well enough during the fall and winter, as long as it's out of the weather."

"I'll speak to my father about it."

"Thank you, Miss Eastwood. Your father's a decent landlord, and a good employer, but we're all grateful nonetheless for your influence with him."

Clara blushed. "I'm flattered you think my word with him is effective," she said, watching the workers go back and forth. "It's the least I can do, really. All of you are the ones whose work really keeps the estate going. Tell me, is there any chance we can get your sons back down to Exton? I remember they were so good with the animals, and we seem to be building up more of a cattle herd. We could put them to good use next spring."

The other woman's brow constricted. "I don't think so, Miss Eastwood. My Frank's off on a ship—he's a midshipman already, though I don't know where the last three years went! And Sam's got a job now in the Corn Office they've built up in Liverpool—a shipping clerk, he is! Who would have thought any boy of mine would be keeping the account books?"

"You must be proud," said Clara. "I wish we'd have been able to keep them, though. I don't like seeing so many of our villagers leave for Liverpool or London. I wish we were able to do more for them here."

"Mrs. Clemons!" called a woman from across the granary, "where did you say those sacks were?"

"I'll get them," said Mrs. Clemons in reply. Turning back to Clara, she said, "We're grateful for all the work we can get here, Miss Eastwood, that's for certain. And we'll take each day as it comes and be grateful to God for every penny we're able to earn."

"I shall endeavor to make sure you have work aplenty here, Mrs. Clemons. I'll speak to my father about seeding more corn next year."

"You're a kind woman, and if I might be so bold—you'd be a landholder we'd all be proud to serve, if God wills that you stay here." And with that, Mrs. Clemons stepped away to fetch the sacks.

Watching her go, Clara was suddenly envious of the workers before her. Their task was clear, the need they must meet was right before them, and they earned enough—she liked to think—to be comfortable. She thought of coins clinking into an imaginary apron pocket, thought of going to the store for sugar and flour. She thought of paying for them herself. Why should she not pretend that was her life? She stopped a woman passing by on the floor, saying, "Mrs. Graves, could I relieve you for a while?" After all, there was nothing for her back at the house but Rose asking their father incessantly for the carriage to see the Tapleys—a request he had refused repeatedly because one of the carriage horses was lame—and another hand of whist with the family.

Mrs. Graves looked at her askance. "I—don't think that's a good idea, begging your pardon, Miss Eastwood. I wouldn't want to be seen idling. And it's dreary work, this. Though I'm glad to have it, of course," she added quickly.

Clara flushed, and nodded to the woman before heading for the door. Of course she couldn't take a turn at the threshing—she knew nothing about it. And of course she couldn't take Mrs. Graves's place, if even for ten minutes. There would be talk. She couldn't risk displeasing George if he should hear of it, that his future wife wished to labor like a charwoman. And so she went out, relishing the feel of the cold wind and stinging flecks of rain on her burning cheeks.

Instead of going back to the house the way she had come, she turned as she came out of the granary door and went past the barn, hearing the occasional lowing of a cow within as the animals all waited out the wet weather. She picked her way through the barnyard, knowing that there would be sharp words uttered under Mrs. Huttleston's breath if any hint of the farm—be it odor, manure clinging to Clara's shoe, or bits of straw—followed her back to the house. She went down the little slope from the barn to the stream running through a cleft in the field, crossing the cattle bridge that stood over the dark water. She was in Yewspring's chief pasture now, and paralleled the stream below as she made her way up the slope to the pasture's nearest edge, delineated by a thick hedge of hawthorn, blackthorn, and dog roses. On the other side of the hedge loomed the dark shapes of the tall yews that lent the estate its name, the barrier of the hedge meant to keep the animals from browsing the poisonous yew seedlings, a barrier broken only by a sturdy gate that Clara now reached and opened. She wished to walk through the groves before returning to the house, for though others shuddered at the sight of yews— associating them with cemeteries and therefore with death, Clara

guessed—she had always felt that they were protective guard-
ians, sheltering her with shade in the summer and in the winter
providing her with barer ground beneath their thick corky trunks
than the open fields.

She had a favorite path that wound through the trees, and
followed it now, stopping every now and then to reach out and
touch a tree's wide girth—it seemed to her that each one held
stability and yet life, marrying grounded peace and ever-changing
growth. These were qualities she needed, and imagined that she
could feel them rushing into her fingertips as she touched the
bark. Her thoughts were back on the threshing floor, on the hope
she had heard spoken on Mrs. Clemons's tongue: *You'd be a landholder we'd all be proud to serve.* And yet this privilege was given to
George on the basis of his sex, to become the landholder when
Mr. Eastwood died. She felt that her loyalty to and pleasure in
the estate gave her a greater natural right to that title, and for the
umpteenth time she wished Yewspring and Beechview had not
been entailed to the male line. Although marrying George was
not a harsh price to pay to stay at Yewspring, she wondered what
it would have been like if he had been attracted to her for herself
alone, without the ever-present knowledge that their marriage
would satisfy her family's wish to keep Yewspring associated with
the original Eastwood line.

She walked a bit faster as she traversed the slope, watching the rain fall beyond the canopy of the yew branches, which
formed a roof over her head. Why should she be sundered from
all this if she did not marry George? Why, when every fiber of
her being felt that this was her birthright, one she had gladly
formed herself in response to, should it be given to someone else
who would simply hire out its care? Mr. Graham was a good
agent, yes, but a landowner without attachment to his estate was
like a patient being treated by a doctor who expected payment.
Clara felt that her own regard for Yewspring was more like a

mother lovingly nursing a sick child, or a daughter tending to her father in his last years. And yet she was prevented from fully giving it by her unmarried state. By George's poor health. By his own hesitance. Her fondness for him was interwoven with a strange and startling anger when she thought of all that she was prevented from doing in her current state. Why had he not proposed during this last visit? Could he really be so cautious as to allow inaction to rule his life, and hers? He knew how much she loved Yewspring and longed to work for its good. Surely at some point prudence would demand that they marry. She pushed away insidious thoughts that her cousin secretly found her undesirable and delayed to avoid joining himself to a woman he was loathe to commit to. His behavior when they met did not support such a claim, and yet each time he had left her single still.

She was at the top of the knoll where the yews grew, and saw below her the stream, which diverted itself into a pond at the foot of the little valley with the house at its apex on the other side, below her now too. In the summer, terraced lawns stretched down from the house to the pond and stream, the former now silent beneath a sheet of opaque ice. She turned homeward, the afternoon light already failing. Yewspring's ground floor windows glowed a faint gold as the candles were beginning to be lit, and smoke twisted from its chimneys. She came down the slope, crossed the stream again—this time over a daintily arched footbridge meant to allow pleasure walkers to reach the woodland beyond the lawns. She ascended the walk that led back to the house, went in through the double doors that led into the main passageway, and made her way past the various doors. Her father's study door was closed, but the sitting room door was open and she could hear Rose playing on the pianoforte while her mother accompanied her on the harp. This was a rare occurrence and one that must have been precipitated by the inactivity forced upon the household by the weather, Clara thought as she took off and hung up her pelisse and bonnet. She was just bending to take off her boots and exchange them for slippers when she heard her father come out of his study and down the hall.

"Ah, Clara, there you are," said Mr. Eastwood. Rose's playing in the other room ceased.

"Here I am," Clara said. "Did you want me?" She sat in the hall chair and began unlacing her boots.

"Yes, we were all wondering where you were," he said. "His Lordship's new agent called while you were out, even in this wet, especially to make my acquaintance. He said he had already met you out on the road somewhere a few days ago." He lowered his voice. "You mustn't let your mother know you've been meeting strange men alone. She wouldn't like that one bit."

"Mr. Kensington was here?" asked Clara, sorry that she had not been indoors to meet him again. "How unfortunate that I missed him. He seems like a knowledgeable agent. I think he could be a good collaborator for Mr. Graham. But what does he have to do with me?"

"He wanted to invite you and I to look at the Dillinghams' new Highlands with him. Apparently you discussed this idea when you met?"

Clara had almost forgotten about the allusion to looking at the cattle, and now smiled with real pleasure at the idea. "Oh, how lovely! What did you say? Was a date set?"

"No, but I tentatively accepted for the both of us. We shall write him when the weather clears a bit. He is at liberty any day we name, he says."

"Wonderful!" Clara slid into her house slippers and wrapped a shawl about her shoulders, preparing to fetch her books from her bedroom. She paused on the lowest step of the staircase and asked, "What did you think of him, Papa?"

"He seems an agreeable man, to be sure," said her father, looking over at her from the sitting room doorway. "If he stays in the neighborhood, perhaps we could tempt him away from Haythorne when the time comes to replace Mr. Graham—but don't tell his Lordship I said so!"

CHAPTER FIVE

The next day brought continued showers that prevented anyone from going out in their carriage, but Clara's sister and cousins were still wild to formally meet the Crestons. Each mother, in her turn, was begged to send the grooms out to scatter sand or gravel or whatever would make the muddy roads tolerably passable. When their mothers acquiesced to their fathers' judgment, as they generally did in most out-of-doors matters, the girls were universally disappointed, for dispensing enough material to improve the roads all the way to Exton was an expense their fathers were unwilling to bear. Even Clara's uncle the apothecary had ventured out only for the severest of cases, going on horseback instead of by carriage. But around tea-time Mrs. Thurston most thoughtfully sent an errand boy, who became progressively wetter and muddier as he made his rounds, to each of the three families' houses with notes reassuring the anxious mothers and daughters that the intriguing niece and nephew would be brought to them at the earliest opportunity afforded by the weather. And, as Mrs. Eastwood and Rose concluded, the unfavorable weather that kept them all apart must also keep the visitors firmly fixed in Exton, lessening the evil of the delay.

Clara too, was anxious for clear weather, but because it would allow her to visit the Dillinghams' barns rather than converse with the young London gentleman. Accordingly, when the rain ceased as darkness was beginning to fall and the next morning dawned with blue skies and sunshine glancing off the autumn canopies of trees, both Clara and Rose were gladdened.

"Surely he must come today, Mama!" exclaimed Rose during breakfast. She had anxiously risen for the third time during the meal to look out the window at the obligingly bright day.

"Yes, I am sure he will," said her mother soothingly, "but they cannot call before three, you know. Thank heaven we have the altar cloths to work on and pass the time before then. And perhaps we should go and select another gown in case they do come today—that muslin is getting rather drab."

Clara's father had already sent a note to Mr. Kensington asking if visiting the Dillinghams would be agreeable that day, and now Mrs. Huttleston came in with a reply that had just been brought from Haythorne Hall—Mr. Eastwood opened it and said to Clara, "Mr. Kensington is at liberty and proposes that we meet at eleven. Shall that suit?"

"Of course," Clara said. "Would you like to ride over, or take the carriage?"

"Oh, we'll ride. I think the drive is still too soft for the carriage. Would you like to go, Rose?"

Clara's sister had taken her seat again but fidgeted with the tablecloth now, calculating how long the errand would take. Clara reached over and patted Rose's hand. "You should stay here in case they come early. I wouldn't want you to feel unprepared."

Rose looked both relieved and sheepish at being so distressed, and so Clara set off that morning alone with her father, bundled into her riding habit and in high spirits at having such a delightful excursion during the sunny morning. As they went, they passed carriages and buggies coming out of nearly every gate, and carts of sportsmen with their dogs and guns, ready to resume their autumn sport. The neighborhood was eager to circulate again.

Clara had thought this opportunity would be a good one to discuss delaying some of the threshing with her father, but she found that the ride over to the Dillinghams' was not long enough to bring it up, for riding out with her father always made her think of many other rides she had taken about Yewspring's grounds with him. When Clara was very young, just old enough to be lifted up onto her own pony, he had taken her out with him on his rides to help keep her out of the way at the house. Clara remembered many long days when her mother had not emerged from her bedroom, with nurses and physicians bustling in and out, and was grateful he had given her something else with which to occupy herself. And of course, after Clara had come home from school she had found her mother often away with Rose and the nanny for weeks at a time, and so she had continued to walk and ride with her father. There had been no point in staying indoors alone, and out-of-doors solitude was no burden to her.

Whenever they rode out together now, she was content to talk idly of the day, the livestock, and the neighbors they saw as they went. As they reached the Dillinghams' barnyard, however, she determined to ask him about the threshing on their way home.

Mr. Kensington stood in the mud next to the barn with Mr. Dillingham, who oversaw his own estate rather than employing an agent, for it was only fifty acres, much of it pleasure ground attached to the house.

The four greeted each other cordially enough, Mr. Dillingham showing toward Clara a deference that she could only suppose was the result of her being the only lady of the party, since he had not ever shown her such attention before. Mr. Kensington, on the other hand, greeted herself and her father with a mix of both cordiality and ease that could not help but lessen her embarrassment. And as soon as they went into the barn, Clara immediately forgot the awkwardness of the pleasantries outside.

The familiar sounds of animals shifting in their stalls, the smells of dusty straw and hay and the warm musk of cattle-hair and wool, and even the dimness of the barn's interior made her feel at home.

Mr. Dillingham led them through the narrow maze of aisles between stalls until he reached a particular one, and turned to Clara. "Mr. Kensington said you were interested in this little lass and her mama the other day." He pointed to the russet calf with her legs curled up under her next to the mother cow, who worked her cud beneath her shaggy forelock.

"Oh, yes!"

Mr. Dillingham swung the stall door open. "You can go see them, if you like. They're gentler than lambs. And I kept them back when I turned the rest of the herd out this morning."

Clara went in and sank to her knees on the straw. The calf and mother regarded her warily but serenely. She forgot about the men standing in the aisleway behind her, and gazed back at the calf. She loved the earthiness of its orangey-red coat, unbroken by white, and its shagginess. She held out a hand to the calf, who sniffed it cautiously and then let her touch her head before leaping to her feet and skittering around her mother's body to stand and watch Clara from a safer distance. Clara laughed, and heard Mr. Kensington chuckle behind her.

She shifted herself to face the group behind her and asked Mr. Dillingham, "Will you purchase more, do you think?"

"Maybe, Miss Eastwood," said Mr. Dillingham. "I was waiting to see if I can breed this one to my shorthorn bull, which won't be until the spring. The man I bought her from said they're good breeders. If this pair does well, I wouldn't mind buying some more to breed another group next year."

"Which is where Haythorne might be able to help, if I

can convince his Lordship to acquire some Highlands as well," said Mr. Kensington. "I'll tell him my impressions based on your animals, Mr. Dillingham, and perhaps we'll start a little flock of our own that can be bred with yours. And of course, you'll have access to our animals for breeding if you wish."

"That's a kind offer, Mr. Kensington, I thank you," said Mr. Dillingham.

"Mr. Dillingham has a fine flock of sheep as well, and a breeding ram that we all covet," said Mr. Eastwood. "How is his foot? Devilishly bad luck, getting that wire wrapped around it."

"We can go and see, if you like," said Mr. Dillingham.

Clara's father and Mr. Dillingham headed off down the aisle, while Mr. Kensington hung back to wait for Clara. She rose and came out of the stall, latching the door behind her. They followed the other two down the length of the barn, going past the solid rumps of cattle with their heads buried in the feeding troughs and the Dillinghams' plow-horses, which regarded them with placid intelligence, waiting for the day when they would be harnessed and called upon to perform their duty.

"Have you continued on your rounds through the neighborhood?" Clara asked Mr. Kensington as they went. "Are you becoming familiar with the different farms, and with Haythorne?"

"Yes, though I have been indoors more than I would like with this weather, of course. I did venture out one day and rode all the way to Newbold."

"Did you go by way of the Haythorne woodlands, or over the downs?"

"I felt it best to go through the woodlands, since I thought the downs would be too wet," said Mr. Kensington. "But I suspect that in drier weather the downs must be the more scenic ride."

"Yes, I quite prefer that way," said Clara. "You will have to go again in clearer weather. Did you sightsee in Newbold at all?"

"I just stopped at St. Botolph's for a moment, to go down to the river. While I was there I saw a colony of river otters playing on the bank opposite. They are the most charming little creatures! I confess I wanted to scoop one up and bring it home in my saddlebag."

"Oh, how delightful!" Clara loved otters and rarely got to see them.

"Yes, I was quite fortunate. When next you are in the neighborhood you must stop and see if you can spot them. Just go through the woods below the church to the river, where there is a little peninsula that juts out on the west bank. It looked as if there might be dens further downstream, but I did not have time to investigate further."

"I will," said Clara, already plotting the excursion for when George returned in the spring. He could stay up at the church and look at the building, if he wished, and she could go down to the water.

"Splendid," said Mr. Kensington. They were nearly to the other two of the party, who stood outside the lambing stalls. "And—how have you spent your days since last we met, Miss Eastwood? Do you have pursuits enough indoors to occupy yourself?"

She stopped and thought for a moment. "The days when I am confined indoors are difficult, I confess. I've been doing some sketching in the mornings and evenings. Reading, of course. And—" she stopped. Could she confess her pursuit of Latin, which in reality had consumed much of her evenings?

She decided not. After all, she barely knew Mr. Kensington, and though he had confessed himself inadequate in his knowledge of French, she still felt that her desire to learn such an intellectual language—her mother's word had been *useless*—was somewhat unseemly, somewhat unfit for the station of a lady. And it would be better if he did not find her so, better for her and George's acquaintance with him.

"…I am learning a new set of pieces on the pianoforte," she finished belatedly. Not wishing to draw attention to this awkward reaction, she asked as they continued down the aisle, "And how do you find Lamarck?"

He smiled. "You ask as if the three of us were friends, as if he lived in this neighborhood just a mile or two away! If only he were that immediate, for his mind is fascinating, truly fascinating. I am reading about his theory of use and disuse—do you know it?"

"No." She could not help stopping and turning toward him. "What is it?"

"You must read it yourself, really you must—for I think your mind would pick up its nuances better on the page than from my crude remembrances. But it is essentially the idea that animals acquire and dispose of traits through use and disuse rather than design, and that they pass those assemblies of traits on to their children."

"And a particular environment might encourage the use of one while discouraging the use of another?" Her mind was racing. She leaned against a stall door and drummed her fingers on its wood, looking up at the ceiling beams above in the dimness. "For example, a frog species that lives both on land and water must survive both conditions while one that lives entirely in the water may dispense with a thicker skin, since it does not need it?"

"Yes, exactly! You grasp it entirely. But I shall still endeavor to finish the book quickly so that you might have my copy to read. I am anxious to discuss the ideas with you, if you would be so kind as to permit me the pleasure doing so."

"Certainly," she said, and they continued their walk down the barn aisle toward the other two. After the ram's leg was deemed to be healing nicely by all, Mr. Dillingham begged to be excused from the group because of other commitments. He offered to let them linger in his absence, but the other three made their farewells and rode out of the gate together. Mr. Kensington had invited Mr. Eastwood and Clara to accompany him to Haythorne's barns where he would be surveying the threshing, but Mr. Eastwood declined, saying, "Another time, Kensington, we would be glad to accept your offer. But Clara must hurry home now for a long-awaited social call. You know how ladies are about these things, I dare say."

Mr. Kensington said only, "Indeed," and bid them good day with a polite tip of his hat to her, leaving Clara without the opportunity to explain that for her the social call was not in fact one of happy anticipation. She tried to convey a sense of cordiality to him, at least, in her farewell, thanking him for arranging the viewing as he had promised. She assured him, as well, that he would be welcome any time he should care to call at Yewspring.

True to Mrs. Thurston's word, her carriage appeared at Yewspring at three-thirty, as the afternoon light was just beginning to make its fall into dusk, and the Eastwoods soon heard their visitors taking off their coats in the hall before being ushered in to the sitting room. Clara had been pulled away from trying to decipher Homer in Latin, and her mind was still spinning with verbs and pronouns as Mrs. Thurston and the Crestons came in.

Mrs. Thurston was a fluttering, talkative elderly woman who gave off a vague impression of genteel sickliness and always dressed in black silk. Her speech was often punctuated with soft little coughs, and she carried a handkerchief in her fist with which she liked to make extravagant gestures. Clara thought this mannerism made her look like a sergeant trying to signal his troops on a far-off hill. And today Mrs. Thurston was especially fluttering and agitated with pride that she had come to introduce a very eligible bachelor nephew to the young ladies of the neighborhood. She had never been quite sure of her status in the county, being gone away to Bath so often and without any children of her own to offer as social currency, and so she positively beamed upon the group once she had been seated.

Mr. Creston, for his part, made no sign of recognition if he remembered the encounter with the young ladies at the store when he had been ogled at as if he were a zoo animal, but merely bowed and said, "How do you do?" upon being introduced to Miss Eastwood and Miss Rose Eastwood. He wore a black morning-coat and looked just as elegant as he had the first time they had seen him.

Miss Creston was a plump, very animated young woman of twenty who took after her aunt in appearance and in gentle good-naturedness, though hers was more energetic. She laughed merrily as Mrs. Thurston introduced her. "Oh Auntie, Tabitha is so terribly long! Do call me Tabby, won't you?" she asked the ladies, taking the hand of each as she went around the room. Mr. Eastwood she honored with a deep curtsy that even his Majesty the King must not have taken offense to.

"Heavens, what a lovely room, Mrs. Eastwood!" Tabitha exclaimed when they had all sat. Clara knew there was no better way to win her mother's affections.

Mrs. Eastwood thanked her guest for the compliment. She did indeed pride herself on the decoration and well-appointment of her home, and the sitting room got lovely light at this time of day even at this time of year. She was glad Rose was sitting near the window where the last illumination of day was strongest and wearing a becoming shade of blue, and that Mr. Creston sat just opposite her, where he might admire her unobtrusively. Ever since she had heard of Mr. Creston's coming to the village, she had determined that one of her daughters should catch his eye before one of her sisters' daughters—and since Clara was so soon to be engaged, she felt sure it should be Rose. She was very fond of her nieces and wished them every happiness in life, but a woman without sons, she felt, ought to have a superior claim when it came to potential suitors for her daughters. Indeed, she had pinned her hopes onto Rose even before hearing of George Eastwood's plans for an unusually-timed visit, for as to this elegant London gentleman taking a fancy to her odd Clara, well—she studied her eldest daughter and took in the nondescript threadbare dress, the untidy hair, and distracted expression despite the sitting room banter swirling around her. Clara was positively squinting across the room at Mrs. Thurston—was it possible she already needed spectacles? Such an accessory would be the final blow to Clara's prospects if George had not been so very agreeable to the match. Mrs. Eastwood had decided long ago not to pin her hopes on a very fashionable match for Clara and was grateful for the friendliness between the two cousins.

Mrs. Eastwood turned her attention to Mr. Creston. She inquired about his stay thus far, his plans in the time remaining in his trip, and his impressions of the countryside. He answered satisfactorily to each inquiry, praising the weather, the roads, the scenery, and the village society he had encountered.

"I always find that the country is so restful after London's hustle and bustle," he said.

"However, I suspect you shall be quite glad to get back to that hustle and bustle when you leave next month," said his aunt with a knowing titter. "Winter can be so very trying out here in the country, what with the weather keeping one at home without the diversions one can count on in the city!"

"I do like London," her nephew said, "but if it is agreeable to you, I hope to be much more with you than I have been in the past, Aunt."

Clara saw Rose and Mrs. Eastwood exchange a smiling glance at this. Tabitha (Clara could not yet bring herself to think of the other young woman as "Tabby") eagerly echoed her brother's sentiment. "I cannot think why we have stayed away so long! Perhaps because you always came and stayed with us, Aunt. Indeed, Mama never brought us here at all when we were young, and I am most vexed with her about it. I shall tell her so in my next letter. How I should have loved to take these walks and romps through the fields as a girl!"

"My daughters and their cousins, would be happy, I am sure, to walk with you any morning you choose, once all the paths have dried a bit, Miss Creston. They know the countryside about Exton quite well, especially Clara," said Mrs. Eastwood. She looked at her daughter expectantly.

Clara, upon hearing her name, started out of her study of the new arrivals and said, "Yes indeed. Have you been down to the mill pond yet, through Mr. Phillips' pastures? It is a lovely walk this time of year."

Miss Creston replied that she had not, and that she would be delighted to have the company of the Misses Eastwood, Tapley, and Morton.

"And perhaps you would like to take your exercise with the

young ladies as well some day, James?" his aunt asked, turning to him.

Mr. Creston's good manners dictated that he reply to this suggestion in the affirmative, although six young ladies seemed to be much more than any one gentleman could reckon with. Wednesday morning, the day before the Doyles' dinner party, was to be the day for the walk if the weather held. Once it had been fixed upon, the three visitors rose to leave, intending to stop next at the Mortons'.

"Well!" exclaimed Mrs. Eastwood when Mrs. Thurston's carriage had pulled out of their drive, "*what* a young man, girls! And his sister is so agreeable—a very good friend for you, while she is here."

"Oh Mama," sighed Rose, "he is quite elegant, is he not?"

"Very," agreed Mrs. Eastwood. "His morning-coat cost ten pounds if it cost a shilling. And *such* nice manners!"

"He must meet very elegant ladies in London," said Rose. "How can any of us hope to ever catch his fancy?"

"Country charm and innocence can go a long way, dear," said her mother. "But your aunts and I have been discussing when to depart to London this spring. We think the sooner the better—in a few weeks, perhaps, if all the houses can be got ready in time. And if you should see Mr. Creston while you are there, well...I only hope that George has time to come to us here before we leave, for I would hate for him to waste his journey if we shall see him in London. Oh, what a fine thing to have two suitors—potential suitors, that is, we musn't be *too* presumptuous—to think of!"

Clara was horrified at the talk of London as she sat there with her Homer, listening to this exchange. She had no doubt she would be shipped off to town should the chance arise, though she was no longer in need of the attentions of a London suitor. She thought of crowded ballrooms every night, cobblestone streets filled with carriages, horses, dogs, and people, and iron gates closing the houses in. To someone whose walks provided her an ease she could not find indoors, it was a miserable existence.

Mrs. Eastwood turned to Clara. "Perhaps you had better stay home from the walk after all. We cannot have him hear that his presumed fiancée was walking about the countryside with another man, family party or no."

"Mama, the entire outing with the Crestons is based on Clara's walk!" said Rose with amused exasperation. "Is she never to speak with another gentleman for the entire length of her engagement, which has not even occurred yet? At any rate, he will understand that her honor cannot be called into question with six other ladies there!"

"Well, you can never be too sure," said their mother, "and we must tread carefully until the ink of the dowry agreement is signed." But she said no more about it.

After the Crestons left, Clara's day was too disrupted for her to resume her studies. Violet and Ned called after four, and since the Eastwoods' carriage was brought out to take them home again, they all crammed in with the two cousins to dine *impromptu* at the Tapleys' and did not return home until late that evening. So it was not until the next morning after breakfast that Clara went gratefully back to her Homer, spreading the sheets of her notes out on the work table, cross-writing on them to make the paper go further. She had vaguely heard her mother and sister go out to the Mortons, and was in the middle of untangling a particularly fascinating passage when Mrs. Huttleston bustled in from the dining room, cleaning pail clanking.

"Oh Lord, Miss Clara, you startled me! I thought you'd gone with the others," said the housekeeper, going to the windows and opening them up despite the chill. "Where is that Fiona? She needs to put the tea leaves down on these carpets—they haven't been done in a month if it's been a day. Fiona! Fiona!"

Realizing that she was in the housekeeper's way, but that Mrs. Huttleston would never say so directly, Clara sighed and gathered her papers and book to go up to her room. As she left the sitting room and climbed the stairs, Fiona came down them toward her.

"Oh, you've not gone with the others?" Fiona said distractedly, going past her, "I've not quite finished your room yet, Miss Clara. We're all behind today because Cook's brother is so poorly and we had to do the breakfast."

Clara thought that explained the tepid porridge and overcooked bacon they had been served, but said, "No matter, Fiona, I'll go to the schoolroom. No need to fret about my room, just finish it when you can."

And so she kept climbing the stairs, past the middle floor where the bedrooms were, and on to the third floor that contained the nursery, schoolroom, and she and Rose's childhood bedrooms. It was not an area of the house she often visited, for the memories associated with it were not all happy ones. Though she knew there had been times of games and play with Nanny and Miss Regis, their first governess, she could remember all too well the mornings, before Rose was out of the cradle, when Nanny would tell her to tiptoe down to the schoolroom, for her mother was abed again and she must be quiet. Her uncle Morton would come every week for a few months, coming in Yewspring's door with spring rain clinging to his dark oilcloth cloak or white flakes of snow on his shoulders that would melt into drops and fall onto the slate tiles of the hall, leaving miniature puddles in his wake.

Those days meant that if her father had not taken her outdoors with him, she would not see her parents until just before bed, when she would go downstairs in her nightgown, hair plaited, holding Nanny's hand. Her father would ask her what she had learned that day, whether she had said her prayers, and beckon her over to bestow a timid kiss on his cheek. "Sleep well, dear," he would say with a rather absentminded pat on the head, looking all the while at his pale and quiet wife across the room.

Clara would then go to her mother, who would be wrapped in a shawl with feet propped on an ottoman but in full dinner dress with her cap tied firmly onto her head, and Mrs. Eastwood would take her hand, give it a little squeeze, and say, "Good girl, Clara. Thank you for helping Mother by being so quiet today."

"Do you feel very unwell, Mama?" Clara had asked once, and her mother had said firmly, "It's just a bit of illness. Even Mamas get ill sometimes. It will pass."

And then Mrs. Eastwood's gown swelled below the waistline, Clara had a little brother named Robert after their father, and just as suddenly as it had seemed to happen to her, at four years old, she didn't have a brother anymore after a frantic night when the servants scurried past her door and she heard her uncle Morton hurrying up the stairs. Then her father was holding her while a little coffin was lowered into the muddy November ground and her mother wept.

She was relieved when her mother's belly rounded again, hoping it would keep her father in the house and her mother at home, since babies seemed to please them. Rose was born on a cold December day, and Clara had thought the troubles would be over, that her parents' joy in their healthy baby daughter would be multiplied a handful of times more.

But then Uncle Morton's hurried, short-lived visits began again until they stopped, for the brothers or sisters who made Clara's mother feel so unwell after Rose never needed a cradle, never joined their older sisters in the nursery, never babbled or crawled or smiled.

After a few years, when Rose could toddle downstairs with her, Nanny would tell the two to pray every night that God would grant them a little brother, and they did so dutifully, Rose's childish lisp turning the phrase into "wittle bwother". But the little brother never came, and when Clara was old enough to move from the nursery floor downstairs, she found that her parents had taken up sleeping in separate bedrooms, when her mother was home at Yewspring at all.

Now, she entered the schoolroom, which had not yet been converted to the servants' sitting room that she knew one day it would be. It was clean but cold, since the fire was no longer laid there, and rather than go back down to her room for a shawl she lifted the cloth cover from a work table to wrap around herself. As she settled herself in a chair, she noted the ink stain in the rug beneath her feet, one that no scrubbing could remove. She remembered, too, the day it had gotten there—Rose had just progressed from writing on a slate to writing with pen and ink, and upset the ink-pot as she moved her papers to the side. Ebony rivulets ran across the table surface and off onto the floor. Miss Regis had leapt to her feet, exclaiming, "Naughty girl!" and gone to fetch a bucket and rags to mop up the mess.

Rose began to cry, and Clara had gone and embraced her, saying, "It's all right, Rosie, it was just an accident. It wasn't naughty of you at all. And anyway, look at the ugly pattern you've covered up with the ink—quite an improvement, I think."

Rose had looked down at the carpet and smiled through her

sniffles, and soon they were giggling despite themselves, chang-ing their expressions to solemn concentration when Miss Regis returned.

"I've a mind to slap you for being so clumsy!" the governess snapped at Rose, kneeling before the chair to clean up the ink.

Clara had looked up from her book and said, "I'll go straight to Papa if you do—he won't tolerate anyone laying a hand on us." She did not precisely know if this was true, but the thought of Miss Regis striking her sister filled her with an anger and fear that gave her sudden courage to speak authoritatively.

Miss Regis had scowled and said nothing, viciously scrub-bing at the stain. She had left Yewspring soon afterward, and the Eastwood, Morton, and Tapley households employed one governess for all five girls, a gentle middle-aged spinster from the village named Miss Holt. The quiet schoolroom was soon filled with French recitations, embroidery hoops, and several easels for painting. The music master came each week to teach the young ladies, and the sounds of the pianoforte could be heard drifting up the stairs from the sitting room as the girls took it in turn to practice for their lessons. Rose blossomed and thrived with the lively company of her cousins in their lessons each day, while Clara longed more and more for a quiet room filled with books, and a knowledgeable tutor to instruct and guide her study. One who would not be satisfied with a cursory knowledge of the constellation's names or by her reciting the titles of Shakespeare's plays, but one who would understand and enable her to accom-plish what she herself desired to achieve, even if she did not always understand it herself.

Clara knew her younger self would have envied the oppor-tunity to study uninterrupted for several hours, a luxury she could now afford. Even so, she could not deny that though her studies had been inadequate they had at least provided her with the semblance of companionship. The other girls had embraced Clara's role as the best mathematician among them, though their interest was confined to the household budget exercises put to them by Miss Holt, who told them with a wistful countenance that they must learn to be good domestic stewards when they married. Clara had spent many an hour with the slates and tables of figures before her, instructing Rose or a cousin on the markets and on household economy. Now, in the quiet, the sight of the books laid on the table before her filled her with both dread of the uselessness to which her ends seemed destined and anticipation of what else they might hold. She almost longed for the chatter of the long-ago mornings. She almost longed for her old routine of a long walk or ride about Yewspring with her father, followed by her own studies for the evening. But then she remembered that they were all engaged to play cards with the Mortons that evening, and set to work, determined to make good use of the solitude.

She was startled, several hours later, by Rose opening the door and coming in, saying, "Good gracious, Clara, you're quite the sight wrapped in that table cover!" Indeed, Clara had burrowed herself into the ample fabric, even going so far as to cover her head, leaving only her hands and face exposed. She had been hunched over the table and realized she must look like nothing less than a giant caterpillar wrapped in its cocoon, and laughed a little, unwrapping herself.

"You're back then?" she said to her sister. "What time is it?"

"Nearly three," said Rose. "I came to find you so we can practice our duet before we start dressing for the Mortons—I am anxious that it should go well on Thursday at the Doyles'. Josie Younge has had that new music teacher from Paris giving her lessons, and I am sure that she sounds quite elegant now! It would not do to—" Her voice trailed off delicately.

"—appear to disadvantage alongside," Clara said, finishing her sister's sentence. She knew too, that there was a gentleman whose name began with C for whom her sister especially wished to appear in a favorable light. "All right, I'm coming down." She stood and began gathering her things.

"Brrrr," her sister said with a shiver, going to the window, "however did we manage up here with this chill?"

"We had a fire laid," said Clara, "but I remember always wearing a shawl even so. It is terribly drafty."

"What tedious hours we spent here," said Rose. "It is much better to improve oneself as an adult than be forced to do so as a child, I think. I remember enjoying nothing but music and French. How glad I am that those days are done!"

"And I," said Clara as they left together, although she remembered the silent hours she had just spent, never certain whether there was any fruit to be harvested in the orchard that she kept returning to. At least when her cousins and Rose were here, she had felt as though she was helping someone else. She had felt as though she had companions in the girlhood sea of education and study, a sea her sister and cousins seemed to have left for the womanly waters of marriage and domestic concerns. She felt stranded and forlorn, and as she left the room determined to try and shake off the feeling by giving her sister her full attention in their practice together.

CHAPTER SIX

Two days after their first official meeting, the cousins of the Eastwood, Tapley, and Morton households accompanied the Crestons over the hills and vales of Exton's countryside. Mrs. Morton had at first thought it prudent to keep her younger daughter Phoebe at home, as she was only sixteen and not yet out. "I am not sure that she should be seen out walking with gentlemen in such a manner," she mused. However, Phoebe was joined in her earnest protests by her sister Caroline and cousin Rose, who all pointed out that such conventions should be relaxed by virtue of the large mixed party and the walk's location at home in the country, and Clara's aunt relented. The walk, however, was not destined for great success by most people's estimation. The recent rains had left deep mud in most of the paths, and the outing was much shorter than Clara would have wished because of the other ladies' aversion to walking through such terrain and a bracing northeast wind that had sprung up and whistled its way around them.

An indoor card game at the Eastwoods' was soon suggested instead, much to Clara's distaste, but she was grateful for some activity in an otherwise sedate day and even joined in the reigning merriment as she and the others bluffed and chanced their way through the hands.

"You are a terrible actress, Clara!" laughed Rose as Clara collected her share of tokens from the table. "No one will bid against you with that little smile always on your face—we all know you had a face card in your hand, you goose!"

By all accounts, the young people seemed to be getting on famously, momentum that was continued the next evening when the three houses were abuzz with the sound of four eager young women, their mothers, and their maids attending to their preparations for the Doyles' dinner party. Never had such a clatter of feet up and down stairs, the chatter of gowns being considered and fretted over, and the clang of curling tongs being heated been so aroused for a mere dinner party! Of course, no one considered this a mere dinner party, whatever the calendar may say. Mr. Creston's attentions must be captured by the young ladies of the family and not allowed to stray toward the Misses Younge or the eldest Doyle daughter, who had just turned eighteen.

Clara was coming down the stairs, ready well before Rose and listening with half an ear to the din above her as her mother and sister debated the best way for Rose's curls to lie, and through the open front door caught a snippet of conversation between William and her father, standing out on the stoop.

"—that Kensington has some outlandish ideas," her father was saying.

"Well sir, that's what'll come of being new to the county, I dare say," said William. "He's not yet learned how we do things here. I expect his Lordship will have him straightened out soon enough."

Clara paused on the steps, hoping to hear more and avoid them hearing her, lest they stop.

"But really," her father said, "A hazelnut orchard at Westlane Farm? There isn't a hazelnut west of Clackton, and if there was the potential he says there is, why has no one else attempted it? But I did think him very sensible when we met at the Dillinghams'. I suppose we must wait and see how his experiments turn out. *I* certainly would not try such peculiar things on Yewspring's ground."

The third step betrayed Clara with a sharp creak under her weight and the men turned to look up at her.

"There you are," said her father. "All ready before your sister? I might have guessed. Do you think there is any chance at all that we'll arrive less than an hour late?"

"None at all," she said lightly, and continued her descent down the staircase.

Clara endured the dinner party as best she could. Apart a rather interesting discussion of India springing from the news of a letter from Thomas to her aunt Tapley, and the quick sketch of an unusual lily from one of the dinner bouquets she had managed while pretending to use the water closet, it had contained just what she expected—a few pleasantries exchanged with the matrons who spared her a few moments in between gossip sessions, tedious turns at the whist table, and the young ladies each taking it in their turn to perform for the assembled group. Tabitha Creston was heard to particularly compliment Rose on her part in the Eastwood sisters' duet, and her brother, standing beside her, echoed her sentiments. Rose could not hide a blush of pleasure, and thanked the Crestons with an eagerness that Clara understood meant true gratitude, for Rose enjoyed none of her pursuits more than music, and particularly wished to be an accomplished musician.

As the evening was drawing to a close and the party made ready to leave, Clara went upstairs to fetch the family's wraps. Above her she heard Mrs. Doyle say to Mrs. Younge in a low, conspiring tone, "—Mrs. Eastwood said their nephew hopes to return in the spring."

Clara paused, hoping to hear more.

"Ah," said Mrs. Younge knowingly. "Perhaps to address

himself to his cousin?"

"Why else would he come back before the shooting in the autumn?"

"True, that is very odd. Well, between you and I, I have always doubted that such a sensible young man should really wish to attach himself to such a—well, unusual young woman as Miss Eastwood has turned out to be. My Edward said she was out in the Dillinghams' barn the other day with the new estate agent and Mr. Dillingham. Really, it is so unsuitable! Does she care nothing for her reputation? She is always hanging about the fields or out in the woods or holed up in her room with some nonsensical book. What a queer creature! I would be shocked if one of my girls were seen out in the barnyard, and the only woman in the party as well!"

"Perhaps she asked to do the farm chores!" laughed Mrs. Doyle.

"Oh, stop," said Mrs. Younge with a giggle. The two women went on ahead into the bedroom to collect Mrs. Younge's belongings.

Now Clara blushed as well as Rose, although her self-consciousness was born of much more unpleasant feelings than her sister's. She did not think particularly highly of either of the two matrons, but she did not want to be so ridiculed by the neighborhood. Nor did she feel as though she had done anything to deserve their mockery. She could not help the fact that she found drawing-room conversations so tedious, and like her face in card games she knew she could not hide it. Did they think she enjoyed finding such settings so inadequate for her mind and her soul? Did they not know that she would have changed herself if she could? If only she did not feel so alone in attending to things of substance, things that mattered, while the world around her seemed intent on dwelling on frivolity and uselessness, on disregarding the birds that frequented the trees of their own garden and the yields of their own crops. Instead, they talked of gowns and guns. She waited still on the stairs, giving the women some time ahead of her so they would not know that she overheard them, and made way for Miss Younge coming down.

"Good night, Miss Eastwood," said Miss Younge in a friendly tone of voice that betrayed nothing about whether the daughter shared the sentiment of the mother.

Clara murmured a good night, and began climbing the stairs again to retrieve the coats so that she might be home again at Yewspring that much sooner.

Despite the sting of the words she had overheard, the mention of George's return brought him to mind, and after returning home Clara lain awake until late into the night, watching the stars outside her window. She considered yet again how she would feel when her cousin made her an offer. In the past, her vision of their married life was one of friendly, warm comraderies. George had already alluded to the idea that she could have full authority over the kitchen gardens, the ornamental beds, the storehouse, the henhouse, guinea fowl yard, and the dairy, while he would rely on the estates' agent for the livestock, the barns, the fields, and the sale of any farm products.

"More a man's realm, that," George had said with easy authority on their last ride together as they passed Yewspring , "and while my Uncle Eastwood may enjoy the role of gentleman farmer, I fear I've no taste for it. But I'll happily shoot and ride and become a magistrate and make friends at the pub. I think we'll get on well here, Clara, I really do."

Now she thought of such a life, with a husband's allowance of such country duties in his wife—and his ability to restrict her from others. Would George share the opinion of every other married woman she had thus far encountered, that her vision must turn inward upon their wedding, to confine itself to the bounds of a house's walls or a garden's boundary? Would he wish to spend much of his year in London? How had they never discussed these matters? She determined to attach a post-script to her father's next letter to George and ask him what he thought. And she determined, too, to think about what her answer would be if he demanded a cession of her studies, her poorly administered self-education in the ways of the natural world.

She thought, too, of what it would be like if George did not object but also did not join her in her responsibilities to Yewspring. What would it mean for them to occupy such wholly different spheres? Could that division engender affection, understanding, and unity? Could she really accept the thought of decades of politely pleasant interactions with her husband? No closer to an answer than when she had begun, and unsure why the future she had always anticipated with pleasure now seemed to unsettle her, she arose after falling into a light doze in the gray light of early morning.

A week after the Doyles' party, Clara rose one morning, dressed and descended before the rest of the family, who were sleeping off their wine, their laughter, or their disappointments from another dinner engagement, this time at the Mortons'. After a very pleasing and marked attention shown to Rose at the beginning of the evening, Mr. Creston had withdrawn himself to the circle of the Younges and hardly stirred again, speaking primarily with Mr. Younge and several other groups of gentlemen. Mrs. Eastwood had commented on her notice of a look passing between Mr. Creston and his aunt as he was speaking with Rose, after which he had withdrawn himself. Strategizing how to understand and overcome this setback had kept Mrs. Eastwood up until late, and so Clara descended to a quiet house. She went to the work table in the sitting room to take advantage of the abundant morning light, deciding to try and salvage the crumpled lily sketch from the Doyles' party and put it down in color.

No sooner had she completed its outline than Mrs. Huttleston knocked and came into the room, saying, "There's a gentleman at the door, Miss Eastwood, and no one awake but yourself. Shall I let him in? Lord, there's no fire drawn yet! I could send in Fiona to lay it while you see what it is he wants, and I rouse Mr. Eastwood. That way there's nothing improper, if you'd like."

"A gentleman? Did he say his name? Do you recognize him?"

"It's that agent man, Miss Eastwood. Kensington, I believe, is his name."

"Oh heavens," said Clara. "You may show him in, and don't bother Fiona about the fire. It is so very early, I daresay he'll understand."

She had hardly a moment to compose herself before he was in the sitting room. He started when he saw her sitting there, but covered his surprise with a deep, courteous bow. He was dressed more formally than when she had seen him last, in a morning-coat and carrying a hat. Mrs. Huttleston pointedly left the door open as she left, and Clara knew Fiona would hover right outside the door in the hallway with a cleaning rag, should she need to intervene if Mr. Kensington assaulted Clara's honor or virtue. Clara had no such qualms—her agitation was all pleasant surprise at seeing Mr. Kensington again, and in such quarters conducive to a longer meeting.

"Good morning, Mr. Kensington," she said, rising from her seat and curtseying to him politely.

"Miss Eastwood," he said with a smile, "good day. I do apologize for the earliness of the hour. I had hoped to speak with your father, but I hear he is still abed."

"If you would care to wait, I am sure he will be down shortly," she said. "We dined at my uncle's last night, and so they are all sleeping in. Have you made the acquaintance of my uncle Morton?"

"I have not. Your father is the only one of your relations I have met, but I understand Morton is the apothecary here."

"Yes."

"Well then, I hope to know him socially but not need his professional services extensively."

"I am sure you will be introduced to him soon. I've wondered if you would be at several of the dinners we've attended recently—are you simply too busy with your work to accept invitations, or are there families you have yet to meet in the county?"

"The former, at the moment. And at present I must leave Exton for some time—two weeks or so, so my prospects of having the pleasure to dine with your family are slim for a while, I regret to say. I had hoped Mr. Eastwood would forgive my impudence in visiting without an invitation because I come to inquire after the very fine bull yearling I saw grazing in your field yesterday and see if he would consider selling it. His Lordship is looking to expand his breeding stock."

"I cannot speak for my father, but I believe he would consider an offer," she said. "You see, we have so few paddocks that we would have to sell him soon or take him to my uncle's. We cannot keep him away from the cows here."

"Yes, that can be difficult in smaller fields," Mr. Kensington said. He walked over to the window near her table, looking out over the back garden to the field in question. He surveyed it for a moment, rubbing his chin thoughtfully. "You have a paddock of perhaps three acres there?"

"Yes." She felt herself flushing as if he had paid her a compliment that she did not know how to respond to.

"I wonder if a more portable fencing would do the trick?" he mused.

"Portable fencing, sir?"

"Yes, something more lightweight and temporary that can be moved to create paddocks of whatever size and shape is needed. You could keep your bull on the northern half of the pasture and the cows in the south, then adjust the size of the southern pasture as you get feeder calves to sell."

She stood and went to look out the window with him. "We have never had enough room to raise calves in any number," she said, "but perhaps that sort of system would work. The dividing fence could go along that little ridge there," she pointed, "and the troughs could go in the center, so that each paddock would not need its own food and water."

His gaze turned from the field to her face. "Indeed," he said. She stood a moment in silence, looking back, then remembered herself and stepped back over to her table.

"I do apologize, Mr. Kensington," she said, "for forgetting my manners as your hostess. May I offer you some tea while you wait for my father?"

He accepted and sat down at the table while she went to the door and, as she had expected, found Mrs. Huttleston hovering nearby, who went hurrying off to the kitchen to fetch the tea. Clara knew the servants would be abuzz with the news of a gentleman caller at so improper an hour, and Fiona had already passed by the open passageway door three times on some imaginary errand to monitor the situation as best she was able.

Clara went back to the sitting room and found Mr. Kensington looking at her sketch of the lily, lying out where she had been working on it. He looked up as she sat across from him.

"Did you draw this?" he asked.

"Yes," she said. "I had just a few minutes to sketch that one, but I hope to expand on it." She uncovered the larger sketch from where she had placed it and handed it to him. He looked at it for a long moment in the manner he had studied the pasture, turned back to her.

"I feel I should confess that I came here today not merely to inquire after the calf," he said finally. "I enjoyed our meetings earlier this month and was hoping to speak with you again."

Stunned, she didn't have a chance to reply before her father walked in.

"Good morning, Mr. Kensington," said Mr. Eastwood, still straightening his cravat. "I trust my daughter has entertained you well enough in my absence. Ah, Mrs. Huttleston, will you—oh, tea is already here." He shot Clara an approving glance.

They sat, and Clara poured the tea.

"I beg your pardon, sir, for intruding at such an early hour," said Mr. Kensington once the cups had been distributed. "I come to inquire about the young bull in your paddock and see if you would consider selling him to Sir Chesterton. Mr. Dillingham mentioned that you have sold calves to his Lordship in the past. I must leave Exton this afternoon for a time, but if you are willing, we can establish a price and I will send a man over to collect him. He might as well eat his Lordship's hay rather than your own this winter, before he runs your supply quite down."

As the two men dove deeply into a conversation about the fair market price of the calf, Clara studied Mr. Kensington. He seemed determined both to get the minimum amount for the calf on behalf of his employer, and to not cheat Mr. Eastwood in the process. Her mind spun both with the sight of him and with his declaration. He had wished to meet her again? How could it be, when every man she had ever known had hardly been able to disguise the fact that they found her odd or endeavor to conquer it with a stilted, begrudging conversation? Even if such conversations were undertaken, she could not help feeling that the other party was concealing—with the faintest of veils—a profound regret that she had not worn a more flattering gown. And how could this stranger who had just two encounters with her come to such an outlandish conclusion?

She was not attending to the conversation at all, and was startled out of her thoughts by her father's impatient, "Clara?"

She turned to him. "Yes?"

"I asked you to fetch Mr. Kensington a pen for the bill of sale."

When she handed it to Mr. Kensington, their hands brushed against each other's.

"Thank you," he said with a smile, and turned to the paper. His writing was cramped but precise and possessing strong masculine jagged letters.

Mr. Kensington had just passed the bill to Mr. Eastwood to sign when the sound of a horse and rider on the gravel drive came through the window-pane. Clara shared a puzzled glance with her father, for who else could be visiting at such an early hour when politeness dictated that visitors should not come before noon? She rose and went wordlessly out to the hall, opening the front door to find a breathless messenger leaping down from his horse, arm outstretched to give her a letter.

"For Mr. Eastwood, miss," he said.

"Are you to wait for a reply?" she asked the man, who had already swung back onto his horse, still breathing heavily.

"No, miss," he said, "I don't believe a reply will do any good.

Good morning to you." And he was off, at a slower pace now that his errand had been completed.

Her head now spinning doubly from Mr. Kensington's compliment and from the unexpected, seemingly urgent message that had come, she returned to the sitting room, where Mr. Kensington and her father had completed the bill of sale. Mr. Kensington seemed to be saying that he would be away from Exton for a time. "—requested that I go to Manchester and get the seed myself. We are going to try a new variety this year that will hopefully do better in the wettest fields."

She had forgotten that he said he would be leaving, and was dimly aware that she was disappointed.

"Ah," her father said. "You must let us know how it does. For myself, I have very little wet ground and thus will plant Chevallier as usual—but you know, the Browns have very soggy fields and may be glad to hear of a new option."

Mr. Eastwood turned expectantly to his daughter, who had come to his chair and held out the letter to him. Despite Clara's apprehension at what it might contain, she could not resist the chance to learn a bit more of what had been said.

"Not only the Browns, Father," said Clara. "The whole western edge of the valley dries out dreadfully late, and I am sure there are several farmers who would like to know about another possibility that would fare better than Chevallier. They cannot even plant until May some years."

She glanced at Mr. Kensington, saw that he had risen in respect when she came back into the room, and then lowered her eyes to the floor when she saw him looking at her with a mixture of interest and incredulity that caught her off guard.

"I suppose so," Mr. Eastwood said in response to Clara, and

took the letter from his daughter. He opened it in an absent-minded way, eyes beginning to run over the page.

"Yes indeed, Miss Eastwood," said Mr. Kensington to Clara. She went back to her seat and looked over at him, still watching her father out of the corner of her eye.

"I believe there are six or seven farmers near the Browns—the Franks, perhaps?" Mr. Kensington asked her.

"Yes," she said. "Then there are the Younges, the Edwards, and the Halls."

"I shall remember to speak with them once we grow it this season. Thank you for mentioning their names. It is most helpful to have some local knowledge, as you do."

Clara looked back to her father to see his reaction to the letter in his hand. He was looking pained, and now burst out, "Good God!"

"What is it, Papa?" She went to his side and stooped down, trying to read the words on the page, but her father had cast the paper aside and dropped his head into his hands.

"Good heavens, Papa, what is it?" asked Clara, more urgently.

Mr. Kensington, too, rushed to his side. "Are you quite well, sir? Shall I fetch a doctor?"

"No," said Mr. Eastwood faintly from behind his hands. "I beg your pardon, Mr. Kensington, I have just received the most terrible news from Kent. But I am quite well myself, only distressed. Clara, Clara, George is dead!"

CHAPTER SEVEN

No news could have thrown the households of Yewspring and Beechview Manor into greater confusion or distress. The force and weight of the blow were magnified by its swiftness, for George had not succumbed to one of the weaknesses the marsh fever had sown in him nor suffered a reoccurrence of that fever itself. Instead, he had died in a manner that any other young Englishman might have, even if he had enjoyed fullness of health: he had been riding a horse he had been considering purchasing—*the groom tried to warn him, my poor boy, that it was prone to shying and trying to throw its rider, but he believed he was capable of controlling it*, wrote his mother Harriet—and been thrown when the horse shied at a flock of birds that came out of a tree. Striking the ground had caused a blow to his head, and he had died almost instantly.

Now the Eastwood families were thrown into dismay over their future as well as regret for George's own sake about his untimely passing. Inheritance of the estates, Rose and Clara's dowries, Clara's future—all were thrown into question now. Every expectation had been disrupted the moment Mr. Eastwood had broken the seal on his cousin Harriet's letter. All former plans must now be dismantled, and new ones put in their vacant places. It was no easy task.

The day after the news came, Mr. Eastwood sat in his study for almost a full day, turning over the ramifications of this unlooked-for change and debating with himself about what was to be done about the girls' dowries. Mrs. Eastwood came in with some tea and a cold luncheon tray for him, set them on the papers and account books he had laid across the desk, and then sat in the visitors' chair. Husband and wife regarded each other with a dazed weariness across the desk.

"We've had word from your mother about the mourning period," she said. "A full six weeks, in recognition of George's position as the estates' heir and his closeness to the family."

Mr. Eastwood sighed and closed his eyes for a moment, pinching the bridge of his nose between his fingers. "It is the correct thing to do, I imagine. Do you and the girls have the clothes you need?"

"We'll manage with what we have. No need to incur more expenses now—we've put enough into Rose's wardrobe for the season as it is. And Clara will need all new things as well, for she can't sit about in the country now. We must all get to town as soon as possible when we are out of mourning, for heaven knows Clara won't find another match here. And perhaps the ground we've laid with Mr. Creston—"

"—will remove the need for much casting about for a suitor for Rose," her husband finished, his delicacy necessarily less developed than his wife's. "Unless one of our nieces catches his eye, or he has a prospect in London. Without a substantial dowry I fear the prospect of both girls will be diminished. I know they will have something from my parents, but I have just been doing the calculations, and my dear sisters have so very prolific that even a large sum must be split so many ways. But at any rate, nothing substantial can be done for Rose until Clara's engagement is fixed. What is to be done with her?"

"I wish she were not so determined to remain at Yewspring, for I think it will make things difficult for her," said Mrs. Eastwood. "I must confess I think it unlikely that Charles Eastwood should share his brother's feelings about her. He has never even been to Warwickshire—there can be nothing of George's fondness for us and for Exton in him."

"Quite so. And especially given his time overseas," said her husband. "I suppose they'll send for him and bring him home, commission or no. All that military experience, wasted." He sighed longingly, for he was fascinated with warfare and the accounts of men who had fought for the Crown. If it were not very unpatriotic of him, he might have wished for the conflict with the French to continue on indefinitely.

"Oh, Charles will be home as soon as they can find a ship to bring him back on. Harriet won't want to lose another son after this."

"But what good will his homecoming do us if he does not also take a liking to Clara? There was already a disparity in years between her and George, and it will be magnified more so with Charles. I too predict that a marriage between them unlikely. But she will be devastated if she's forced to leave here."

"Yes," said Mrs. Eastwood with a sigh. "I wish she would look about her freely and perhaps find someone else that she liked."

"Someone she liked?" mused Mr. Eastwood. "And who would that be? A parson perhaps? She won't go for a rattle, you know, nor a rattle for her. A widower?"

"I doubt it. Except for Rose, she didn't much like children growing up, nursemaids or no."

"Too young to wish for children at present, too old to engage a young carefree heart. What a conundrum. One that I feel sure you're capable of meeting, my dear."

"I hope so. If only the estates weren't in trust—she could inherit it from you in her own right."

"Yes, but we might as well complain about the sky being blue. It will do just as much good."

"As it is, I fear she will try and engage Charles's affections, a scheme I feel sure would be doomed and cause her much embarrassment. And so I must insist, Robert, that you turn her over to me. She's barely fit for London as it is, much less to form another attachment."

"What do you mean, *turn her over* to you?" asked her husband. "Everyone knows a maiden is under the guidance of her mother, not her father."

"Most maidens, yes. This one has been allowed to put her nose into useless books and grub about in the fields too long. A decision," she said hastily, for Mr. Eastwood had opened his mouth to protest, "that was for the best when she was to marry George. We both felt that she would be a suitable mistress for Yewspring. But now—she is unlikely to stay here, and her little farm sketches and dawdling out-of-doors won't help her catch anyone's eye. And so I must get her smartened up and try to convince her to try for someone else. I can't have you pulling her away to inspect the barns or transplant the cabbage or whatever else goes on out there. It always was an indulgence, and now we cannot afford it."

"All right, Hazel. I think it's for the best, too—for Rose, for her, for all of us. But oh George, poor fellow, you have spoiled all our plans!"

As for Clara, she had shut herself in her room after Mr. Kensington left the day before, and her mother ordered trays to be brought up to her. The social life of the household must now come to an abrupt halt for the next six weeks, but even if she had been able to go out, Clara would not have felt equal to it. Grief and anxiety pinned her down in her bed like a butterfly pinned to paper, and she was unable to exert herself even enough to return Rose's well-meaning attentions with more than terse replies and stifled sobs. She wished only to be alone, and so her sister eventually went away.

Days passed, Clara's solitude broken only by the servants bringing in her tray and the timid taps on her door of her father and sister, who came in to check on her once or twice a day. Her mother, on the other hand, gave only a perfunctory rap before coming in to ensure that her daughter had not enacted some foolish scheme to reunite herself with George—she had heard stories of young girls throwing themselves out of windows or refusing all their meals in order to join some beau in the afterlife, schemes she found irritating and nonsensical. She grieved her nephew with them all, but this was not her first brush with unplanned tragedies, nor with the trials of loss or want. She was determined that Clara must live, and must rally when the time was right. She was evidently satisfied by Clara's condition, which was listless and silent rather than hysterical and frantic, and went away again as well.

But Clara loved the world too well to attempt to follow George out of it. Her anguish over George's death was as much composed of the fact that she would now be separated from Yewspring forever—for what course of event could keep her there now? Its heir was no longer the familiar face that she had seen for so long across card tables and drawing rooms. It was a name on a piece of paper, *my dear Charles* as addressed by her aunt in the letter. "Dear Charles" would be back in the country within half a year, and she dreaded meeting him, knowing that he would become the owner of the land she loved so well without ever having set foot on it before. Perhaps he would rent her a cottage somewhere on the grounds? She could be governess to his children, dear old cousin Clara with her charts and pencils and maps and telescope, destined to ask her cousin for new spectacles and material for a new gown. She shuddered when she thought about it, but where else could she go? There was nowhere else. Nowhere else was hers.

Days passed and nights followed them, light and darkness following each other like partners in a dance she was not quite attending to, one whirling after the other out of the corner of her eye. Her twenty-sixth birthday came and went, Clara refusing the cook's offer of making a cake to mark the occasion and listlessly opening a present from her sister while Rose sat at the side of the bed. Clara began to sob when she saw that it was a miniature of George, a scheme plotted by him and her sister in secret that autumn. "I thought you still might like to have it," said Rose, her eyes filling with tears at her sister's sorrow. Clara only handed it back to her so it could be put away again for a while longer.

Clara's thoughts were chaotic, ideas of departure and return and guilt over not thinking more of George and the sharp painful remembrance that she would never see him again to apologize for it. They all lay together like linen stuffed into a washing basket, sour smells drifting up, stains needing tending. Her only sources of relief were sleep and rising from her bed to stare out the window, where at least she could grant herself the privilege of looking at the landscape she knew so well. All else was a trial to her. She tried listlessly to read and found that she could not concentrate. She picked up drawings she had worked on only to put them down again, not even picking up her brush. The trays were set back outside her door with nearly as much food on them as they had before.

And then, a fortnight after the news had come, Rose came in one morning. "Clara, look at that beautiful sunshine! It's chilly, but let's bundle up and go for a walk, shall we? That always raises your spirits."

At any other moment, Clara would have eagerly accepted

her sister's suggestion. But at any other moment, she would not have confined herself to her room, would not have slept until the village clock struck eleven. The thought of walking and talking, of seeing the world go on as it always had—a continuation she found most unfeeling given her anguish—repelled her, and she replied, "No Rose, I haven't the energy. Have Mama walk out with you." And she turned back toward the wall.

She heard Rose say softly, "All right," and her sister left the room.

However, after another hour of alternating between lying in bed and standing at the window looking out over the garden and the fields beyond, she realized her sorrow now lived alongside a churning restlessness. It was painful, but it made her feel more like herself. She took her outdoor clothes and dressed for the first time in almost a week, since church the Sunday before, and was out Yewspring's back door before her father even knew she was downstairs.

She went back to the yews, certain that no one would find her there, and after leaving the sight of the house behind her she picked up her skirts and ran up the slope, wishing to feel an ache in her legs and a stitch in her chest. Wishing to feel anything at all. She made the top and looked out over the country that lay beneath her, Yewspring perched on its terrace just below the bottom of its little valley, smoke rising from its chimneys.

Longing and regret filled her now as she looked out over what she had thought would be hers to cherish and work for. Anyone else might have said that nothing had changed from the last fortnight to this one, save that the air was colder now and her breath turned to white clouds in front of her. But Clara knew this was a falsehood, because to her, everything had changed. Grateful at least for the tightness in her chest that helped anchor her to herself, she sat for a while underneath a tree with her back against its trunk, looking out over the view. Then she got up and descended the way she had come, determined at least to write a journal entry about how she might appeal to Charles for a position at the estate, and to eat supper with her family that night.

As she was coming back through the hallway to take off her wraps, Clara met her sister and mother coming through the front door from their own walk.

"Oh, so you've been out and about then," said Mrs. Eastwood, taking off her bonnet. "That should help shake the cobwebs out of your head, dear."

But Rose had stopped and was staring at her sister with an expression Clara had seen only a few times before. It was the same one she had worn when Clara had claimed a pony that Rose had wanted, one of profound anger and pain.

"You said you didn't want to walk!" cried Rose, all but stamping her foot in agitation. "If you didn't wish for my company, you need only have said so! I so dislike being lied to, Clara, especially when I was only trying to help you feel better. You needn't treat me like a child, but—oh, I only wished to talk with you!" Tears filled Rose's eyes, and before Clara could say more than "Rose—", her sister fled upstairs without taking off her pelisse and bonnet. Clara heard a bedroom door slam up above where she and her mother stood, startled at the outburst.

Clara went and knocked at her sister's door on her way back to her own chamber, determined now to keep to her room for a while yet. Venturing out into the world seemed premature.

Rose said, "Come in," and so Clara went and sat by Rose's bed, where her sister lay with a few tears shining on her cheeks, staring up at the hangings of her bed.

"I'm sorry," said Clara. "I didn't mean to leave you out of my walk. You were already gone when I started feeling better."

"I know," said Rose, sitting up and reaching for a handkerchief to swab at her face. "I've just been lonely, and I wished for your company."

Clara was unused to being sought after in this way, her cousins usually seeming to her better companions for her cheerful sister. "I'm sorry you're lonely," she said. She was so used to the state herself, and had overcome it with her own pursuits and reflections, that another person being unused to it surprised her.

"I'm sorry for being selfish," said Rose, sniffing and blowing her nose.

"Selfish? How so? You have been very kind to me."

"It is selfish of me to think of my own feelings while you grieve. You, who have suffered the greatest loss of us all! My loss is nothing to yours. But—"

"What loss?" Clara was genuinely confused. Was this about the dowry?

"Oh, it is silly to even call it so, but I did wish to meet with the Crestons again, and by the time we are out of mourning they will be gone back to Rutland for Christmas."

Clara sat back in her chair. The world of drawing-room visits and Crestons, of polite conversation over tea and card games seemed far away now. But to Rose, the loss of it had altered everything. George's death could not consume her as it had Clara. "You are fond of the Crestons' company?"

Rose looked at her sister. "Yes, I confess that I am. And I was eager to continue our acquaintance."

"I see. But surely you expect to meet with them in town this season? Surely this is merely a delay in becoming better acquainted, not an end?"

"Yes, but town is so difficult with all the other young ladies, and who knows if they will wish to renew our acquaintance? It is so uncertain who they might meet in London. The situation of being here in the country with them, without society pressing in—well, it was ideal. I regret that I cannot take full advantage of it, that is all."

Clara suspected this scrutiny of whom might meet whom extended to Mr. Creston only, not his sister, who seemed happy to meet any respectable person who was brought across her path without regard for her quantity of acquaintances. Clara was amused, as well, that Rose did not consider her cousins "other young ladies" who might interfere when it came to Mr. Creston. She knew they all loved each other too well to begrudge potential matches.

"Well, I am sorry for your sake, then," Clara said, and rose to go. "I will try and rally my spirits, at least, so you might not find the days so dull."

But when she got back to her bedroom, Clara found that the season's first snow had begun to fall outside her window, and felt a despair descend upon her like a stone. First her own hopes had been dashed to pieces, and now Rose's seemed likely to as well. Winter had begun, her grief still tossed her about like a leaf on the surface of a river. When would things ever be cheerful again?

Although she desired nothing but the quietest Christmas imaginable, Clara was coaxed out of her room by Rose for the festivities at Yewspring. Mourning had ended a week earlier, but Clara still kept to the house—the countryside was too snowy, anyway, for her to go out and walk, and she had no spirit for making calls. She endured the coming and going of her family over the ten days of celebrations with as much good grace as she could muster, though she knew she was still a sorry companion for them all, wishing for nothing more than to sit alone in a corner and not be asked to pretend to be merry.

On Christmas morning, she unwrapped Fordyce's *Sermons to Young Women* from her parents—she wished ruefully that she might reject the volumes because no one would consider her, at twenty-six, a young woman any longer. More pleasing was the news that two books she had ordered for herself had arrived and were waiting for her under the tree. She paged through them with real delight: *An Introduction to Botany* and the latest work by Rev. Dibdin called *Bibliomania* (the title of which had been enough to convince Clara that it was worthy of her pocket money). When the present-opening was done and everyone went upstairs to dress for dinner at Beechview, Clara took the Fordyce volumes reluctantly, feeling as though she had reached out and taken a poisonous plant. She carried them up to her room and purposely buried them under the piles of papers and drawings on her desk—she flushed with displeasure that her mother had had to buy new volumes after giving away the household's old copies, for years ago Mrs. Eastwood had thought her daughters finished enough to find husbands and given the old ones away to a charity fair.

Clara looked at her room's little clock, decided she still had ample time to dress, and took the botany book to her window seat where the light was best to begin reading. She was quickly entranced with the style of the instruction, for though she knew most of the material being covered, it was arrayed in a manner that was engaging and aimed for students to follow. After a quarter of an hour, it occurred to her that she did not know the writer, that information having been absent from the catalog description of the book. She turned to the front page, and felt herself gasp a little in excitement.

The author was a *Priscilla* Wakefield!

A woman had written this book? She glanced through the illustrations again, and then went to the desk to look through her own sketches. Though she had been taught but little, the two sets looked close enough in quality and detail that a thought spread through her like a warm drink: *could I do this too?*

She rose and stood at the window for a moment, biting her lip in thought with a shawl clutched about her—winter's damp chill crept in through the windowpane, and the little fire in the grate could not quite dispel it.

What if she should fail to engage a man's affections? What would become of her then? At the very least, it would create obstacles for Rose, for while gentlemen had been known to delight in the simplicity and gentleness exhibited by her sister, they were also known to have an eye toward their pocketbooks when they chose their wives. Clara thought of her sister's pain at the misunderstanding over her solitary walk the other day, and imagined it magnified twentyfold if Clara refused to marry. Yewspring had always been enough riches for the eldest Miss Eastwood, a promise she had been so certain in that she had never asked to see a document making it so. Now she realized that that document had been her and George's marriage certificate, and it was gone forever.

Would it not be prudent to think of how she might earn her own bread if circumstances demanded it? She could take her portion of the dowry, which her father might be induced to give her on her own terms, and give it back to Rose if she knew she would be able to earn enough for a roof over her head, for medicine, for clothes. All she asked was not to have to trail after her married relations in the decades to come, wiping their children's noses and teaching them to do their sums in return for whatever food and shelter they cared to give her.

Comfort and security—and Yewspring—she might have had with George, but death had taken these from her like it had taken his future. She went to the little stack of books by her bed and picked up Smith's *Botany of New Holland*, paging to its own title page.

"Sowerby," she murmured to herself, finding the illustrator's name on the page. It was not an unfamiliar one. In fact, she had seen his mineralogy work for years, a subject she nonetheless knew very little about.

She went to her desk, shivering either from cold or excitement, and picked up her pen.

December 25

Dear Mr. Sowerby,

I write in the hope of obtaining employment in botanical illustration and hope you might direct me to anyone who may be in need of such services. I have read several of your own works and am impressed by the quality of your illustration as well as the breadth of your knowledge of natural history. I am looking forward to your upcoming mineralogy work, for I know so little of the subject and am sure to be enlightened by your guide.

I have enclosed a small sample of my illustrations, taken from field samples in the Midlands, so that you might have some idea as to my abilities. I am very eager for improvement in my work and would be very grateful for any of your thoughts on how I might do so.

I hope to hear from you, though I realize you must have many obligations on your time.

Sincerely yours,

Clara Eastwood

She posted the letter before she could lose her courage, feeling like she was writing to a secret beau.

"Who is that to?" asked her mother when Clara brought the letter down for Fiona to take to the village.

"Aunt Harriet," Clara lied, knowing the missive's intention would horrify her mother. Fiona could not read, and therefore

Clara's deceit went undetected as she handed the girl the packet and the Eastwoods all went out the door to Beechview.

CHAPTER EIGHT

January descended on Exton with snow and cold winds that kept everyone at home except for church on Sundays. Clara longed to be outdoors but found that her weeks of inactivity in November and December meant that she tired quickly when struggling through the deep drifts. She was forced to keep to the paths that Cove cleared between the house and farm buildings, taking refuge in the dairy and the storehouse where she took it upon herself to organize all the preserves and tonics. But she felt underfoot as the maids came in and out, searching for what they needed for the day's dinner and uncomplainingly moving her stacks of jars aside while they did. And so she came indoors to try and occupy herself with drawing, reading, and time at the pianoforte, longing for spring, which she felt must be a balm for her restlessness, her sorrow that followed her from room to room. Mrs. Eastwood convinced them all to play several of the card games she had learned in her travels that year, and when that diversion was done, sighed that winter was so very tiresome in the country when one could not get to one's neighbors, and spent her evenings writing letters to her friends elsewhere.

But Clara and Mrs. Eastwood's discontents were nothing to Rose's. Mr. Tapley was in Parliament and always went down to town first so he could be there for the opening, and his household were all ready to go with him, exciting much envy amongst the family members who longed for the novelties of town. Mr. Eastwood, however, would not go until March, no matter how much his youngest daughter might plead. And in this time of shattered plans for the future, he wished for his wife to remain in Exton as well, to feel that his family was unified under one roof. Mrs. Eastwood agreed to it despite her preference for town, viewing this desire as a sign of her husband's esteem for her. And so Rose was destined to stay for another eight weeks at least, to read with longing in the London papers of the plays and concerts she was missing.

Violet, however, was especially close to Rose and determined not to sample the delights of London until the other could as well. She asked to stay at Yewspring and travel down when the Eastwoods came later in the spring.

"I shan't enjoy it without you," Clara heard Violet say to Rose when her cousin came to ask her aunt Eastwood if she might be welcome at Yewspring while they all remained in the country. The two girls were below her in the hall as she came down the stairs. "And perhaps these last few weeks of winter might be a bit more cheerful for you if I am here—they certainly will be for me. The end is almost here, and we shall all be in town again quick as a wink."

Clara's cheeks stung with the allusion to her sister's unhappiness, and she wished again that she herself had more sociable manners that were eager to please her sister, and a mind that could stand to traverse the territory of gowns and village news and the latest magazines. But when Violet settled herself at Yewspring with her maid, three trunks, four hatboxes, her sewing workbox, and an armful of sheet music, Clara could not help feeling relieved that her sister had an agreeable companion without taxing her own spirits to try and become one.

The Eastwoods and Violet attended church the next Sunday with glad spirits after another week of being confined to Yewspring. And a reward awaited them for their faithful attendance, for Mr. and Miss Creston attended their aunt into her pew. Clara was surprised to see them back in the county so soon after leaving it, and turned to see her sister turn pink beneath her bonnet. As she did, she caught the eye of Mr. Kensington, sitting with the Haythorne party in their customary pew. He nodded to her courteously, and she returned the greeting. She had not spoken with him since that dreadful day, and felt his solicitude for herself and her father at such a moment of shock. He had asked if there was anything he could do for them, and finding that there was nothing he could supply in terms of assistance, left the house after expressing his sympathies. He had detained Mrs. Huttleston for a moment at the door as he went, and the housekeeper had come back into the room with brandy for Clara and her father. She was sure Mr. Kensington had requested it for them on his way out, and remembered the small kindness with gratitude.

Knowing that her companions would engage the Crestons in conversation after the service and that she would no doubt hear all about their return, Clara went to the Haythorne pew rather than being detained with the rest. Mr. Kensington came out of it, swinging the little door shut behind him, and she said, "Good day Mr. Kensington."

"Miss Eastwood." He took off his hat and bowed to her, making way in the aisle for the choirmaster to pass by. "How do you do?"

"I am—" She knew not how to complete the sentence. She was weary and yet restless, she mourned George still and yet it had begun to feel natural that he was not there. Her heart was a mix of grief and dissatisfaction that both unsettled her and felt as though they had always been there.

"I am as well as can be expected, I believe," she said.

He looked at her. "You feel your family's loss keenly, of course. It must affect you profoundly in particular—" He stopped. "Grief is a long and winding road, I am afraid."

"Yes, I believe so. But—I came to say thank you for your sympathy and your kindness when you last came to Yewspring. I was not—sensible of it before, I think, and so my thanks are sadly overdue."

He offered her his arm as they began to walk toward the door of the church, with the backs of many of their fellow churchgoers still ahead of them to be greeted by Dr. Flemington upon their exit. "Do not mention it. I am only sorry I could not do more for you all. Your father must have felt this loss as well as yourself. I could see the affection that must have existed between him and his nephew."

"Yes, we were all fond of George," she said.

"Is there anything I can do for you now?" he asked, "or something from Haythorne that would make this time easier to bear? The hothouse oranges will be ready any day now—perhaps your mother would consent to let me send some over? It is a strange gift to offer those who mourn, I know, but I cannot think of anything that will completely answer for a broken heart."

"Oh," she said, stopping suddenly and looking up at him. Was her heart broken? Is that what these feelings were? "I—thank you for the thought. But I think what I most long for is news that does not come from my own family. How come the repairs on your cottage?"

And he told her all about it, while the church gradually emptied and Mr. Eastwood had to return to collect Clara for the carriage, the other ladies being ready to depart. Mr. Kensington bid Clara farewell, saying, "I expect that your spirits are too delicate yet for company—but whenever they are recovered somewhat, remember that my offer of a tour of Haythorne still stands. A note from you will settle the matter." She had thanked him, not knowing when she would want to have to rally her energy for such a venture.

On the way home, Clara learned that the Crestons had come back expressly because they had enjoyed Exton's society and wished to spend the last month or so of winter with their aunt. Their father also being in Parliament, the household at Rutland had begun breaking up after Christmas, and so brother and sister had decided to return to the newfound friends they had made in Warwickshire. "Town will always be there," Mr. Creston had said, according to Rose.

The oranges from Haythorne arrived at Yewspring two days later, and Clara could not help smiling when she saw them on the table.

Clara had long ago realized that her life afforded more opportunities for pleasure if she did not call others' attention to her joy, for it only resulted in one of two unsatisfactory outcomes. The first is that she found herself having to explain why she took pleasure in an occurrence or suffer from another's lack of understanding of it, as she did when she was fourteen and told Violet that the first woodlark had arrived in Exton four days earlier than the previous year, to be met with a blank stare—to be fair, her cousin was only six at the time.

The alternative to a blank stare tended to be having that pleasure taken away, as when she was sixteen and told her mother she had been spending her pocket money on coach fares to the next village in order to try and glimpse the rare roe deer that she had heard her uncles talking about. Shooting season was at hand and she wished to see it before it became the victim of a trophy hunter. She had subsequently had her pocket money rescinded and managed by Mrs. Eastwood, who had wished to cultivate more lady-like pastimes in her daughter.

And so when Clara found herself equal to the dinner parties that had erupted across the neighborhood, partially in honor of the Crestons and partially as a consequence of everyone else longing for company during the cold snowy month of February, she almost did not notice her willingness to be agreeable. When she went to the barn and found the year's first litter of kittens tucked into the hayloft, little auburn and gray slips of fur with impossibly tiny ears and bright eyes that stumbled toward her waiting lap, she almost did not hear the sound of hope in their squeaks and mews. She almost missed the arrival of these feelings, but not quite. They sat, quiet but waiting expectantly nonetheless, like books on a shelf she had just now noticed tucked behind the volumes she had already read. She was not sure whether she should look at them too closely.

The Doyles were so obliging as to throw another party for the Crestons, having a large enough house to hold forty, and Mr. Kensington was in attendance. He found Clara shortly after the Eastwoods arrived, Rose already tucked into a corner on a settee with Violet, Miss Creston, and her brother, who was obligingly moving back and forth from the dining room to fetch wine for all three ladies. Mrs. Eastwood had formed a cluster with her sisters-in-law and Mrs. Doyle, and so Clara stood with her father, her gown the only white in a ring of black evening jackets, hoping that he would find her. She could not help smiling and flushing a little at how quickly he sought her out.

They spoke for a few moments, he expressing how glad he was to see her in company again and she confessing that it still felt a bit like a betrayal of George to be cheerful. He smiled and said, "Most understandable, but you know—I think he would want you to be happy as soon as you could manage it."

He was presently receiving a tug on the elbow from a Haythorne errand boy, who reported that one of the ewes was having trouble with her lamb.

"I asked to be made aware of any problems," he said, turning back to Clara, "the shepherds have enough to do as it is. I fear I must make my apologies to Mrs. Doyle and go assist if I can. Poor thing, it's her first lamb, too."

He started to make his bow to her, then straightened and looked her in the eye. "Oh," he said facetiously, "would you at all be interested in coming along?"

She smiled, as he must have known she would, and said, "I'd love to, but I must find a chaperone. Let me see if my father—"

And she was off into the ring of black she had lately quit. Mr. Eastwood consented both to leave the party for a while and to have the Yewspring carriage brought around for all three of them, and before she could believe her luck Clara and her father were following Mr. Kensington into the Haythorne barns. They found the shepherds gathered around a stall, quiet yet hurried movement coming from inside it where some of them tried to push on the ewe's heaving belly.

"Can't get it to budge, Mr. Kensington," said one of them, a boy who looked no older than eighteen. His forehead shone with sweat in the light of the lantern, his mouth a worried line pulled tight.

"May I see?" asked Mr. Kensington, shedding his jacket and rolling up his shirtsleeves as he went in to the stall. He went and looked behind the ewe's tail.

"We've tried pulling the lamb, sir," said the shepherd, who seemed to be the head. "But it's still not coming."

Clara and her father received the polite nods of the shepherds who still stood out in the aisle, but they were all of them silent, knowing that extra noise would only distress the ewe and make it harder for Mr. Kensington and the shepherd to hear one another. Mr. Kensington reached down and pulled at something beneath the ewe's tail that she could not see, and the ewe gave out a squall that sounded like agony to Clara.

"All right," Mr. Kensington said in a soothing tone, "we won't try that anymore."

Clara had winced at the sound of the ewe's pain, and was tempted to clap her hands over her ears. But something she had read came back to her now. She took a step closer to the stall.

"Mr. Kensington, you said this is her first lamb?"

"Yes," he said, looking up at her, his shirtsleeves glowing white in the flame behind the lantern glass.

"And you think this is just a tight birth?"

"Yes, the head and front hooves are presented, but the lamb won't budge."

Steeling herself, Clara reached forward and unlatched the stall. "Clara—" said her father behind her. "Don't presume—"

But Clara had already gone to Mr. Kensington's side and peered down at the tip of a nose and two tiny hooves that were visible underneath the ewe's tail. The sheep grunted and moved on the straw, one leg kicking.

"Move her onto her back," said Clara, looking at Mr. Kensington. "It might make more room for the lamb. And someone can pull when we get her moved."

"My thoughts exactly," Mr. Kensington said, "You must have read Anderson's volume on sheep as well as swine and cattle—I might have known. John, come in here, please," said Mr. Kensington. None of their voices were above a murmur, but the urgency was in every tone displayed.

"I'll cover her eyes," said Clara, taking off her shawl, "to help keep her calm."

A shepherd from beside Mr. Eastwood unlatched the stall door and came in. "Daniel, keep checking the lamb while John and I turn her, and get ready to pull again when we get her settled. There, girl, it's all right."

John had moved so that Clara could only see his back in the light of the lantern, and she went and laid the cloth over the ewe's eyes.

"Ready?" asked Mr. Kensington, and they all assented. With one motion, John and Mr. Kensington turned the sheep onto her back while Clara helped move the ewe's neck and head. Clara caught a glimpse of Daniel tugging on something wet and shining, then looked down again at the ewe, who had begun to struggle again, flailing her head against Clara's shawl.

"Oh no," said Mr. Kensington, "keep her down, keep her down. She's bleeding."

The other shepherds rushed in, and Clara's place at the ewe's head was taken. There was a bustle, a frenzy, the ewe bleating in pain, the metallic smell of blood on straw, and the wet lamb, dark eyes just beginning to open against the white of its coat handed to Clara over the stall door. If it was distressed about its problematic entrance into the world, it made no sign. Clara supposed it did not know any differently. It just thought this was the way the world was, a cold place where men shouted and death and life brushed shoulders with each other as one entered the little lambing stall and the other was handed over the door.

The ewe was still, finally, her hindquarters stained rusty red, her eyes looking up at the far-off rafters.

"It's all right, boys," said Mr. Kensington, his hands and waistcoat covered in blood. "We did all we could. I don't think she suffered long—the labor was the evil here, not our treatment of it. I'll have the butcher up tomorrow."

He rose and came out, and Mr. Eastwood held the lantern high, looking a little green. "Well, Kensington, I can't say I'd have liked to join you in there, but it was a good show. Lord Chesterson will be pleased at your diligence."

Clara could feel the lamb's heart beating against her hand as she cradled it. She had dried it with her shawl, hoping that its mother's scent lingered there still.

"Let's get this little lad to another mother. We mustn't lose him too," said Mr. Kensington, taking the lantern from Mr. Eastwood, then looking at the lamb and at her in the ring of yellow light, the darkness so close around them it seemed to be velvet, wrapping them and keeping the world at bay. She met his eyes, could not help doing so, and met his gaze. The shepherds and Mr. Eastwood had already started off back down the aisle toward another stall, but she and Mr. Kensington stood there still.

"Thank you for your assistance," he said softly.

She could feel tears gathering in her eyes, for her assistance had felt more like harm. "But—she died. How can you thank me?"

"Because you knew she might, I think," he said, "and you came in anyway."

"I hate it when things are in pain," she said, looking down at the wool of the lamb's back.

"So do I," he said, "but all pain is mended, one way or another. That was a release from her pain. She suffers no longer, and as a result of our efforts—" he gestured to the lamb, "there is new life where there might not have been. Don't stop trying, Miss Eastwood, I beg you. Now, little fellow, let's find you a new home."

Twenty minutes later, Mr. Eastwood and Clara were back in the carriage and Mr. Kensington walking back to Haythorne. He had handed her into the carriage and thanked her again with a bow.

"Well, you can't go back to the Doyles' like that," said Mr. Eastwood, looking at her wrinkled jacket, stained with fluid and blood, straw clinging to her shawl and the skirt of her gown.

"No," she said, "I can't." She wasn't sure how she could go back anywhere she had been before, after the look that had passed between herself and Mr. Kensington in the lantern-light. He had been asking a question, she knew, and before she had thought about it, she had answered. Nothing would ever be the same for her again, and she needed the quiet of Yewspring, alone, to make any sense of it.

Every day that dawned brought the day that the Crestons must depart a bit closer. Mrs. Thurston had implied that her young relatives were beginning to tire of the country's winter amusements, and when the weather turned fine a few days after the Doyles' party, making travel back to town possible, Mrs. Eastwood and Rose lived in fear that they would receive a note at Yewspring bidding them farewell.

And yet when Sunday came, the Crestons were still in church but informed the Eastwoods afterward that they would be removing to town the following Thursday. Mr. Creston fixed his eyes on Rose as he said, "We hope to see you all in London quite soon." Clara's grandmother pulled away her attention just then, for Lady Eastwood felt that her eldest granddaughter's improvements were not just her daughter-in-law's duty but her own, and she proceeded to list all the masters within the radius of three villages who might be able to teach Clara something about belonging to society before she was quite shipped off to it in town.

"Oh Grandmama, it all sounds dreary," said Clara. "And what is the point of it all, anyway? Why must I be improved?"

Lady Eastwood fixed Clara with an incredulous look.

"For someone who reads so plentifully, my dear, you can be remarkably ill-informed. You must make a new match now for Rose's sake—even if you do not marry into Yewspring and she can only count on five thousand from your father, it will reflect on us all if you remain single. In other words, you must be improved so that *he*—" she had lowered her voice and now inclined her head slightly in Mr. Creston's direction, "will persevere with a hope of winning her. And need I point out that your own happiness and security can only be found in marriage? If you cannot exert yourself for your sister, pray exert yourself for your own sake. Now, who should I write to for assistance, Mr. Prescott or Mr. Horton? Mr. Prescott did do a marvelous thing for Miss Clifford down in Southam—she was quite the religious fanatic, I understand, always praying and going to chapel and refusing to go to balls and so forth. I believe they were frightened that she might be drawn to the Roman church with all her silly notions. But Mr. Prescott put her right in the end. She's married to Lord Fletcher now, in Bedfordshire, and just bore a second son. Yes, I think it had better be Mr. Prescott—"

Clara interrupted, "I cannot agree to anything of this sort unless I am satisfied that my own aims will be accomplished as well."

"Your aims? What aims? Young ladies do not have aims except for those given to them by their parents."

"Well, since I am no longer young, as you all seem fond of pointing out, I have decided to adopt some. Don't worry, I'll be as meek and docile as you like with your teachers—so long as I get one of my own choosing as well. I have my pocket money, you know, and might employ it in whatever means I like."

Lady Eastwood looked astonished. "Are you suggesting that you seek additional instruction to that selected for you? I am astounded. Your parents and I will have to discuss the matter—"

"Feel free," said Clara, seeing that the Yewspring party was heading toward the church doors. "Excuse me, Grandmama, but we seem to be leaving. I wish you a pleasant afternoon. I think mine will be, for I have plans to consider."

She left Lady Eastwood behind her as she went to join her family. She had decided she was tired of waiting for her life to begin. After all, she was closer to thirty than twenty, and life was uncertain. Since life had not yet found her, she must try and seek it instead.

But outside, underneath her umbrella as the Eastwoods and Violet walked back to Yewspring, Clara could not help thinking of her sister. Her grandmother, as much as Clara resented her imperious manner at times, was right. As long as she stayed single, Rose was held back in the search for a husband due to the uncertainty over her settlement. Violet was walking up ahead of the sisters between her aunt and uncle, and so Clara took her sister's arm as the family picked their muddy way through the churchyard.

"Shall we draw together after luncheon, Rosie? It's been so long since we did so. Or perhaps we could all read out a play—since it seems we cannot put aside our winter amusements just yet."

"All right," Rose said, her expression of solemnity brightening a little.

As they passed by a group of farmers on their way out of the yard toward the lane, Clara overheard one of them say, "...and Kensington said the yield would be increased..."

She could not help turning to try and hear a little more. After nodding to the ladies, the men paid them no heed and one of them raised his arm to Mr. Kensington's figure coming out of the church. "Kensington!" he called, and over her shoulder Clara saw that he was coming over to the men. She knew it would be unsuitable and irregular for her to stay and listen, and so she turned back to her sister, trying to hide her regret.

Rose looked at her. "Are you all right?" she said.

"Yes," Clara replied.

Rose let herself be led along as they continued through the churchyard and to the lane, nodding to those of their family's acquaintance. Clara reflected that her sister must be regretting the Crestons' departure. And yet, when she examined her sister's face, she could see, rather than longing, the faint suggestion of a smile.

Seeing Clara's look, Rose glanced away and looked down the lane. Their parents had pulled ahead of them, Mrs. Eastwood being particularly annoyed by walking in inclement weather, and Violet coming down with a cold that caused her to hasten back to the shelter of indoors. They watched the three umbrellas bob up and down ahead of them.

"What a dreary service," said Rose. "As if the rain wasn't bad enough! You would have thought we could spare a little cheeriness—after all, Lent isn't for weeks yet. Dr. Flemington looked like he was announcing the death of his mother, not proclaiming the Good News."

"He is quite mournful," said Clara. "I suppose we at least have the ham at dinner to look forward to."

"Perhaps I should change for dinner," said Rose. "What do you think of that new velvet gown Mama had made for me? Is it too hot, do you think? And what if I should spill something on it before London?"

"I think you look well as you are," said Clara. "But you know I am no judge of gowns."

They walked along for a moment wrapped up in their thoughts. Clara supposed her sister was meditating on the merits of the velvet dress or pondering whatever secret made her smile so, while she herself was listening to the birds in the trees on the lane leading back to Yewspring, some still singing despite the drizzle. She longed for the day when she would hear the swallows arrived back from their winter travels, but could not hear one amidst the other songs. It was too early, she knew, but she kept listening nonetheless.

"Clara?" said her sister.

Clara was peering up into a large chestnut as they passed it. She craned her neck for a moment more, then said, "Yes?"

"Mr. Creston asked if he could call on me when we go to London."

Clara turned to stare at her sister. Rose was trying not to appear too joyful, and much like trying to suppress a sneeze or a hiccup, was largely unsuccessful.

"Already?" Clara exclaimed. "And he hasn't even left yet!"

Rose looked annoyed. "Are you surprised that he could like me so well?"

"No, no. You have been the picture of charm, and you know it. And I am surprised not that you have many fine qualities—I am your sister and I have known this since you were born!—but that he should be attuned to them at such an early stage! From what I hear of men, they can be quite obtuse at times. Or most of the time."

"Do you think he always calls on young ladies?" Rose fretted. "I have not heard Violet mention that he asked her. And well, Clara, surely he did not ask you such a thing, since you were to be wed—"

"I cannot imagine it is a general honor he pays them, no. I

believe you have been singled out. Have your favorable impressions of him continued on this second visit?"

"Yes," said her sister. "I find him most agreeable. We talked of horses, and the races, and the merits of a chaise rather than a curricle."

Clara was glad she did not have to try and carry on a conversation on these topics, but she said "How—splendid", really trying to muster up some enthusiasm. "Oh Rosie, I am so glad you like him. And he seems to have made his pleasure in *your* company clear."

"Oh, I hope he does find me agreeable—it would be the highest compliment! And he also expressed the wish that we might have ridden together while he is here, but of course they did not bring their horses, and our weather has been horrid anyway."

"Perhaps you may meet him on Rotten Row then, and have the advantage of being seen with him by Society. But...I know little of such things, but is it quite proper for him to ask to call upon you?"

"Nothing has transpired between us to cause alarm. He has been a perfect gentleman. I believe it *is* quite forward of him to single me out, but I know little of it either." Rose looked as though she would not have insisted on an adherence to propriety if Mr. Creston's behavior had been found straying slightly from it.

"Well, I am sure he will do nothing improper," said Clara, who of course knew nothing of the sort. She was just glad that her own lessened prospects had not affected Mr. Creston's regard for her sister. She could not help gloating a little that she had not hampered it so badly as her grandmother had felt she would. They were nearly at Yewspring.

"But, please, Clara—let us keep this between us? I—I feel

odd, somehow, telling the others. It may hurt them to know that I have been singled out so, and I am sure I have done nothing to deserve it. Why, Isabella looked simply splendid on the day of our walk, especially in Caroline's pelisse, and I cannot fathom why he should prefer me to her, or anyone else. And perhaps it will come to nothing. Perhaps he will not call on us after all, and he really does just wish to be polite. I would feel so foolish!"

"Don't worry," said Clara. "You won't be made to feel foolish. I am glad for you, Rose." She wondered what it would be like to be so visibly pursued, so clearly preferred. George had rarely been in town at the same time she had, and of course in Exton every-one knew they were meant for each other. His regard for her had been matter-of-fact, calm, and as familiar as her own face in the looking-glass. She had never been wooed, never been courted. She hadn't realized she wanted to be.

"We mustn't count our chickens," said Rose. "Either of us. After all, we are both single again, and perhaps Mr. Cres-ton might simply have a high regard for our family as a whole, or perhaps Miss Creston wishes to be able to visit us and her brother must accompany her in London. Oh, but wouldn't it be wonderful if—well, we'd best not speak any more of it!"

CHAPTER NINE

Mr. Kensington left for a fortnight to fetch his family from Southam, where they were staying with friends, and the Crestons swept off to London in their *barouche*. Rose and Violet eagerly adopted Clara's suggestion of acting out plays at Yewspring while late winter snow turned straight to early spring rain outside the windows, and the three ladies occupied themselves with elaborate rehearsals, performances for Mr. and Mrs. Eastwood and their uncle Morton, who could be so little spared from his work in the country that he rarely went to town. Clara envied this excuse to stay at home, but she was not a gentleman of means who had only to consult his own pleasure in deciding whether to go or to stay. She dreaded the day that would take her to London, its presence looming ever nearer. Her father and Mr. Graham were working out the plans for the spring sowing, and Yewspring's first lambs had begun to be born as well. These were traditionally the signs that the family would go to London soon, and Clara was not sure she could persuade her mother to wait to go until after Easter. She was amazed that anyone could leave the country in spring, but her mother did not seem to see the bright green of newly-leafed-out trees or the swallows swooping over the fields, or feel compelled to seek the dappled shade of the woodlands, the forest floor crowded with delicate wildflowers that would be gone by summer. It was all parties and shops and concerts for Mrs. Eastwood, a walk through Hyde Park all she seemed to long for. Clara could not understand it.

All three of Lady Eastwood's granddaughters were surprised to see her carriage come up the drive one day when Rose and Violet were putting on their wraps for an excursion to the Reeds' store to look at cloth for new gowns. Clara was just coming down the stairs with a letter to be posted and a copy of *Hamlet* to prepare for a reading that evening when Rose opened the door for their grandmother.

"Girls," said Lady Eastwood, coming in to the hall and seeing their ragged assembly, "I came to say that we must not despair of making good use of this time in the country. I would like to hold one last party before we all depart for London. Shall we say Shrove Tuesday, so we do not violate any proper observance of Lent? I must work on the invitations. Tell your brothers to bring their friends, tell your friends to bring their brothers. Consider this my permission to invite whoever you would like. Not one of you shall sit down from dancing the entire evening if I have anything to say about it. You must all begin to set yourself at good advantage for London, and this will be an excellent chance to practice."

"Oh, how lovely!" cried Rose.

"And," continued her grandmother, "if Mr. Creston should happen to hear from your cousins in town that you enjoyed the company of several young squires here, well, so much the better. I won't have it said that we do not know anything of society here."

Clara smiled to herself amidst the squeals and joyous talk that erupted at this announcement. She had not anticipated her own pleasure in this prospect, but it was a pleasure she must not indulge just now—her letter needed to be posted. This time it was not going so far as London—indeed it was not going out of the village.

February 19

Miss Holt,

I wonder if I might seek your assistance. It has been many years since you taught Rose and I, but I still regard you as a well-connected and learned teacher. Do you know of anyone who could examine some of my drawings, and perhaps be willing to engage me in lessons again? (And pray, not Mr. Farling, if he is even still about, for he and I did not get on at all. He told me my studies of the chickens were too plain and that their plumage needed brightening up.) I know I am of an advanced age, but—you see, I have been grieving the loss of my intended in these past months, the man who was to be my future but taken from me before he even became my present. I must do something now to occupy myself.

I will call on you in a week and perhaps we can discuss the matter. There is no need to write, for my mother has too much on her mind now to be bothered with this silly fancy of mine.

And tell whoever you find that I can pay. Not much, but a bit.

I would be so grateful for your help.

Fondly,

Clara Eastwood

A week later, a parcel arrived at Yewspring as the house did its best to contain the young ladies' high spirits over the dance within its walls—this behavior was typical for Rose and Violet, and less so for Clara, but no one seemed to notice that she was unusually amenable to the prospect. For she knew that Butler Cottage would be receiving an invitation to Beechview.

When the parcel arrived, Clara had been out walking in the chilly garden, trying to collect her thoughts in readiness to convince her mother to allow her to take drawing lessons despite what Mrs. Eastwood called her "shockingly" advanced age. Miss Holt had sent an answer back immediately to Clara and offered her own services, which Clara considered better than nothing—she knew little of Miss Holt's own skill, her parents and aunts and uncles electing to hire an outside drawing master for their girls. But it would be extraordinarily convenient to study with someone in Exton, even if Clara had been hoping for someone a bit more accomplished, and so she was willing to give the other woman a chance, at least.

Violet and Rose had been upstairs going through the latter's gowns to try and find something that would suit her for the dance. Clara could hear their excited voices drifting down from Rose's chamber window, propped a bit ajar to freshen the room with the brisk February wind, as she entered the house again.

She passed the large wrapped parcel leaning against the hall table as she shed her jacket and bonnet, presuming that it had arrived for her father, walked into the sitting room, and sat down with her sketchbook. Her mother was with the cook in the kitchen, her father was out, and the only sound was the distant chatter upstairs that now became clearer and more distinct as Rose and Violet came down the staircase.

Clara heard, "Oh! Look!" and then, "Clara! Clara!" as the other two girls rushed in, Rose carrying the package awkwardly, for it was rather large and rigid.

"What is it?" she asked, not knowing whether to be alarmed or pleased to be so eagerly sought after.

"Look what has come for us!" cried Rose, thrusting the package onto her lap and upsetting her sketchbook.

Clara looked down and saw *The Misses Eastwood* written in the hand that she had last seen written on a bill of sale.

"Good heavens!" she said, her fingers suddenly trembling as she started to untie the string that bound it.

"Who is it from?" asked Violet.

"An acquaintance from the village," said Clara, afraid to

mention Mr. Kensington's name should she be mistaken in his writing.

She was not mistaken. She unwrapped the first layer of paper from the parcel and found the following note:

February 23

Southam

To the Misses Eastwood,

I hope you will not find me too forward in this gift, and beg that you make good use of it. From what I have observed of your work, I suspect that you possess extraordinarily capable artistic skills, particularly in your botanical subjects. Unless I am mistaken, I do not believe you yet possess a worthy surface for your sketching, and hope you will accept this one from an admirer who is very interested in your development as artists and naturalists. When I saw it at a shop here in Southam, I could not help but think of you. I hope it brings you pleasure and assists you in your pursuits.

Our manservant is here to help us move our furniture and brought down a very kind invitation from your grandmother inviting myself and my family to Beechview for a dance. I have already written to tell her that we will be in attendance, and do hope that I may have the pleasure of dancing with you both, though I warn you that my expertise is limited to livestock and crops, and may not extend to reels and hornpipes. I also hope to introduce you to my family, and that we may also discuss your work over the course of the evening.

Until then, please know of my warmest wishes for your health and happiness.

Yours,

Henry Kensington

Smiling, she tucked the note into her sketchbook, while telling her eager onlookers, "Yes, it is from Mr. Kensington. How kind of him!"

Rose had already peeled back the outer layer of paper, and Clara saw a small traveling easel nestled in a velvet-lined packing case. She gasped.

"Oh," she said, the word coming out in a reverent sigh. "How beautiful!"

She reached over to where the package lay in Rose's lap and lifted the easel out. Its wood was polished and silky, and its brass fittings gleamed. She assembled it by extending its telescoping legs down to the floor. It had clamps to hold a paper to the surface, a hinged compartment for storing paints and brushes, and a candle holder for painting in low light.

"How curious!" said Violet, taking up the gown she had brought downstairs with her and examining it closely in the light of the window. "Well, I think we know which Eastwood sister that was intended for. He must know that Rose is more of a musician than an artist. How thoughtful of the man!"

"Yes, how splendid, Clara!" Rose looked at her meaningfully.

Clara blushed and turned back to the easel, peering rather more intently into the hinged compartment than she needed to. She knew so little about a gentleman signaling his intent, nothing beyond what had passed for courtship between herself and George. Her education in these matters had been slight. But even she knew that such a pointed gift signaled more than casual interest on Mr. Kensington's part. And she agreed with Violet. Even though Rose's name was on the parcel, her sister had barely spoken to him—this gift must be directed at her, the communal name a way of draping a cloak of propriety around his gesture. She knew not where to look in the gaze of the others in the room, and her mother's surprised exclamations of surprise and delight when Mrs. Eastwood came in and heard the story did not contribute to her composure.

As soon as she could, she fled upstairs to her chamber with

the easel tucked under her arm, asking Rose if she might try out their present, and shut the door, still hearing the chatter of the others from below. She put the easel on the bed and sat at the window with her back to the glass, gazing at the most fitting token of esteem he could have chosen for her—the gift that out of all others, she would have liked most, had she thought to wish for it. She was giddy, or as close to giddiness as she had ever been.

After several minutes of her happy contemplation, she went to her writing table and composed a return note:

February 26

Yewspring

Mr. Kensington,

Your parcel this morning was the most pleasant surprise. Thank you for such a thoughtful gift, and one that I am sure will be extensively used, and that Rose and I vow to take the upmost care with. I am flattered that you view our drawing abilities in such a favorable light, and only hope that they can meet the high praise you have been so gracious as to bestow upon them. I have just recently taken steps to improve my skill, and your thoughtfulness could not have come at a better time.

I am pleased to hear that you will attend the dance at my grandparents', and hope to talk with you there. You will find that my skills extend only to the sketchbook (if they are even found there) and are also sadly lacking in the reels and hornpipes, so perhaps it will not be as uneven a match as you imagine, should we dance together. I would be honored to meet your mother and hope to introduce you to mine.

Until then, sir, know that your gift and your kindness have touched us immensely, and be assured of our profound gratitude.

Yours,

Clara Eastwood

She sent the note to Butler Cottage with Fiona for Mr. Kensington to read upon his return, and spent the rest of the morning sketching the geraniums in the hothouse, too content to stir.

Clara asked her mother for a private talk as they all were going upstairs to bed and followed Mrs. Eastwood into her dressing room, always a bit uneasy to enter this private part of the house. It was a place that had so clearly been her mother's and therefore set aside as a quiet retreat from the rest of the household when Clara was growing up. She suppressed the urge to tiptoe in as her mother sat at her dressing table and gestured to a chair. Rose had often come in to watch her mother dress as a child, curled up with her legs tucked under her and a cup of milk held in her lap. As she sat in her sister's old spot Clara thought of her sister's bright earnest little face as their mother chatted away to her daughter, holding out perfume bottles for her to smell, dabbing cream on Rose's tiny porcelain hands. The images came to Clara in snatches, since she had only ever glimpsed the scene through the dressing room doorway as she went down the passage. She remembered pausing at the top of the stairway and hearing Mrs. Eastwood and Rose's voices as a muffled murmur before she descended.

Mrs. Eastwood slid the rings off her fingers and looked at her daughter in the mirror. "What it is you wished to speak about, dear?" The rings landed in a dish on the table with a series of tiny *clinks*.

Clara watched her mother pluck the earrings from her ears before standing and going to the basin. As Mrs. Eastwood swabbed at her face with a cloth, her features become ones Clara rarely saw, the spots of color coming away from her cheeks in rosy smudges on the cloth, her eyelashes losing their inky prominence. Clara's own face was rarely adorned so, any color coming from emotion or a brisk breeze on her face and her eyelashes staying a mousy brown that was too pale to be called noticeable on its own.

"I was wondering if we might remain in Exton after mourning has passed, rather than going straight to town," said Clara after a moment.

Her mother paused, then continued swabbing. "Whatever for? It is bad enough that your cousins are already there without us."

"Well—" Clara knew not how to speak of her observations in Mr. Kensington without sounding conceited. "I have been thinking about the easel that Mr. Kensington sent."

"Oh yes, that was most thoughtful of him. I assume he wants to be on good terms with your father."

"Well—we have spoken several times, and—I think perhaps he wishes to be on good terms with me, as well." She felt herself blush a deep crimson.

Her mother turned and looked at her. "What makes you think so?"

Clara told her about Mr. Kensington's comment when he had come to inquire about the yearling, about their conversations during their meetings, and his interest in her drawing.

"And that's the other thing, Mama. I've asked Miss Holt to give me some drawing lessons while we remain here this spring. I should like to have more sessions with her, if you will consent to it."

"Drawing lessons? Whatever for? You're long out of the schoolroom, my dear. What we really need is for you to improve your embroidery and to work on your conversation. Perhaps Miss Holt could instruct you in these instead, though it would be *so* humiliating if it got about that you still sought a governess at your age! You'd best go to her house rather than have her come here. That way people might assume you're paying a charity call."

"Mama! One's mind does not disappear once you step over the threshold of the schoolroom. I desire to make the most of my intellectual capacities. What could be more natural?"

Her mother, now sitting at her dressing table again, swiveled to face her. "Natural? Natural is a pull toward motherhood, wifehood, toward charity to the parish. What you are describing strikes me as selfishness disguised as self-improvement. Why will your mind not turn toward finding a husband? There lies its strongest chance of fulfillment, not in books and sketching and walking about the countryside."

"Why must a husband and learning exclude one another? What if—what if Mr. Kensington does wish to pay me his addresses? How can he if I go to town?"

There was a tap at the door, and Mr. Eastwood opened it to stick his head into the room. His nightcap tassel swung as he looked from his wife to his daughter.

"Oh, Clara, you've not gone to bed? Well, I just came to say good night, Hazel."

Clara rose and went to the door, saying, "Papa, I wish to take drawing lessons from Miss Holt and for us to remain in the country for a while yet this spring. Mama insists that I can't do either."

"Well, your mother knows best about young ladies." He cast his eyes beyond her to his wife.

"I am only questioning—" began Mrs. Eastwood, but Clara cut her off.

"Papa, drawing will help me find my feet again after losing George. And—there are good reasons for us to remain in the country rather than rushing to town, I think."

"If there are, your mother and I will discuss them together," said Mr. Eastwood. "What are your objections to this drawing scheme, Hazel?"

"I do not object to it on its own merit, but I feel there are other things she should be focused on," said Mrs. Eastwood. "Deportment, for example."

"And Miss Holt could assist her in this as well, could she not?"

"I suppose so," said Mrs. Eastwood doubtfully. "Though her instruction failed to produce the results I'd hoped for the first time."

"Well then, Clara shall go and learn both drawing and how to fetch a husband," said Mr. Eastwood decisively. "As long as we are in Exton at any rate, and we shall discuss how long we intend to stay. But for now, let us say good night."

Clara did, and left her mother and father. She was not quite sure whether she had been entirely successful in her mission, now having to endure embroidery and conversation tutorials as well as drawing. But if that was the price she must pay to be taught, well—there was nothing else for it.

The weather began to make a decided turn toward spring as February turned to March, and news swept in like the breeze ruffling curtains. Clara heard Mrs. Huttleston telling Fiona about the great cart of trunks and boxes that had been seen outside the Kensingtons' cottage, for its repairs and alterations were close to being finished, and its inhabitants were not far behind their possessions. Three days before the dance, Rose and Violet had seen Haythorne's carriage in the square picking up two unfamiliar women and a little boy from the coach, Mr. Kensington there to meet them. Since her sister described the elder woman only as "very elegant" and the younger as "quite pretty, and so neat even after her journey", Clara was glad that the upcoming dance would give her the opportunity to see them for herself.

Clara went to Miss Holt's for her first lesson on the Friday before the dance at Beechview. She had nervously selected several examples of her work, and tucked *An Introduction to Botany* into her bag as a talisman, perhaps, to give her good luck. Miss Holt received her with more gratitude and solicitude than Clara had been expecting, clearly delighted to have been chosen for the appointment. Clara had promised her mother to work on conversation and needlework as well, but these must wait until the next day. Today was all about Clara's artwork, and her stomach was in knots as Miss Holt sat her at a small table near a window in her parlor, blank piece of paper and pencil in front of her.

Despite Clara's nerves, once the paper was before her she felt the familiar sensation of the rest of the world disappearing. The twittering of Miss Holt's canary in its cage by the window fell away to a vague high-pitched murmur. She had clipped a yew branch to sketch on the way from Yewspring, and held it flat against the table to study it, beginning with her pencil to make its outline. Once she was satisfied, which took some time and rubbing out with the eraser, she went over it in ink, Miss Holt murmuring to the canary all the while, holding a book open in her lap without turning a single page.

Presently, Clara heard Miss Holt come over and stand behind her to look over Clara's shoulder, then a sharp intake of breath that she was not sure signaled distress or amazement at Clara's genius. She soon found that it was the former.

"Why, Miss Eastwood, I thought you'd like to copy *that*!" Miss Holt pointed at a print of Venice on the wall opposite.

"Oh," said Clara. "Well, it *is* lovely, but I have a different purpose in mind, you see—"

"What about this one?" Miss Holt went to the wall behind Clara and came back with a painting of the countryside, one of her own, Clara assumed. She knew from her survey of the parlor that it was the only other picture hanging. "It's of Lutterworth."

"It's lovely too," said Clara, although she could not reconcile its ruined castle walls with anywhere in the neighborhood, and thought the knight riding past on his white horse unnecessary. Wherever the scene was, it was not here. And here was exactly what she wished to draw.

"I fear there's been a misunderstanding. You might remember that I have been interested in science for some time now? And what I am hoping to do is to have your opinion of my skills when it comes to things like this." She reached into her bag and pulled out the *Introduction to Botany*, opening it and flipping through until she found a page with a plate.

Miss Holt's face was becoming increasingly dismayed as she scanned the page. "Well, yes…this is nice in its way, I suppose. We must be grateful for the means of improving ourselves that we have at our disposal." She began turning over the pages of the book, squinting at the text. "You are so good to remind me. Oh heavens, some of these flower parts are most unseemly when seen up close, aren't they?"

She closed the book and but did not give it back to Clara. "Well, I shall endeavor to help you as best I can. After all, drawing is drawing, isn't it? I suppose the techniques must all be the same. And I am so eager that this arrangement between us should succeed—if I might borrow this book I will try and make out what its purpose is, so I might help you better."

Clara wanted nothing more than to take the precious book back and tuck it safely into her portfolio. She did not like imagining it in this bare room rather than nestled among her papers at home with its pages open to the plates, the corners of some pages dog-eared to mark the most important passages. Watching Miss Holt's eyes run over it like it was a fine cut of meat made her feel as if she had handed a finely crafted wooden chair to someone who so clearly needed firewood.

Clara knew as she stepped out of Miss Holt's doorway, her portfolio unsettlingly light without the weight of her book inside, that these lessons would not be what she had anticipated.

CHAPTER TEN

At last, the day of the dance arrived. To Clara, it seemed a year since her grandmother had announced the event, and her unsuccessful drawing lesson had not helped lessen her anticipation to be at Beechview. Gowns were pressed, hair was crimped, and pairs of gloves carefully selected, ironed, and borrowed and exchanged between the cousins. Clara, for once, had asked Rose's advice about which of her own top two choices of gown would be most suitable.

"Heavens, Clara!" her sister had exclaimed, seeing the two she had laid out upon the bed. "These are your working-day dresses, you silly goose! One does not wear a pattern to a ball."

She went to Clara's armoire and pulled out an olive-green silk gown with embroidery on the bodice. "This is much more suitable, and looks lovely on you. I cannot think why you do not wear it more."

She had tried to convince Clara to wear a feather in her hair, as was fashionable, but Clara loved birds too well to wish their plumage away from them and refused, so Rose had done up her thick, straight, untidy hair with plaits and ribbon instead.

And so Clara was feeling quite pretty as their carriage pulled up at the entrance. Rose, wearing an ivory muslin, caught her eye and smiled encouragingly. Clara pulled her white gloves up a bit more, still anxious that Mr. Kensington may not come after all, or would ignore her, or that she herself would trip and fall during a dance. Their father handed them down from the carriage, they ascended the front steps, and then they were inside the hall. Cries of welcome and greeting erupted as they did, for the villagers did not stand on ceremony for such an informal occasion. Had Lord and Lady Chesterson thrown a similar soiree at their grand home, all would have been meek and waited for their hosts to greet fellow guests first, but here they nearly drowned out Clara's grandparents who stood at the door to greet their son and his family.

"Clara dear, you look lovely," said her grandmother approvingly as she kissed Clara's cheek.

Clara looked about her happily as she and Rose traversed the wide and crowded hall. At every other dance she had attended, she had found the candlelight dim rather than enchanting, longing instead for clear sunlight over a meadow or the orange fire of sunset over the downs. She had shrunk from the people around her, expecting to find inane trivial food for conversation, as dainty as the dishes that would be served at supper. She expected to suffer through dances with either a pup of a lad too young to grow a mustache, or an elderly gentleman pressed into service by her mother to avoid leaving her sitting in a corner. Rose or one of her cousins would generally send their partners her way with a pleading glance in Clara's direction, a plea that the young man was only too happy to oblige, even if the price was an awkward set of dances with an ungainly cousin who wished very much not to be there.

Now—she understood the happy anticipation her sister and cousins had felt at each ball. The candles provided a depth and beauty she had never known before. She greeted her neighbors with a courteous smile, and even thought Mr. Jenkins, her uncle's decrepit assistant at the surgery, a fine dignified gentleman rather than the intolerable bore she usually did.

Every moment that lay before her that evening held the potential of meeting with Mr. Kensington, of speaking with him, dancing with him, meeting his mother and sister, and then hopefully conversing with him some more. Possibility sparkled and gleamed all about her as clearly as the golden threads woven of the ladies' gowns. She wondered that she had never been sensible of it before.

Violet had been pulled away by her good friend Miss Younge in the vestibule, so the Eastwood sisters went on ahead into the drawing room, which had been prepared for the dancing: the floor was clear, the instruments in the corner waited expectantly for their players, and chairs sat lined along the walls for those who would sit and watch the dancing. Clusters of people stood scattered throughout the room conversing, and Clara scanned them earnestly. There! Next to the windows at the far side of the room stood Mr. Kensington in a fine blue waistcoat and snowy cravat and a middle-aged woman dressed in lilac, speaking with Mrs. Thurston.

"Rose," Clara grabbed her sister's arm, "will you come with me to Mrs. Thurston and Mr. Kensington? Perhaps you might ask about Mr. Creston."

"Of course," said Rose, with a knowing look, and they walked up to the group. Mr. Kensington had watched them approach with a smile. He stepped forward and bowed.

"Good evening, Miss Eastwood, Miss Rose," Mrs. Thurston said, and they curtseyed in response.

"Good evening, Mr. Kensington," said Clara, turning to him and feeling her heart pound.

He bowed to her and Rose. "Good evening, Miss Eastwood, Miss Rose. May I present my mother, Mrs. Kensington?"

Clara knew her permission was, nominally, required for the introduction to occur, and so nodded to him and said, "We would be delighted."

Mrs. Kensington nodded to them in return. "How do you do?" she said. She was a handsome but not especially beautiful woman with fierce dark brows that showed a tendency to draw themselves together in consternation, graying hair elegantly arranged, and a turban to match her gown. Clara noted the showy plume that adorned the turban as she and Rose returned the greeting.

"You both look exceedingly well tonight," Mrs. Thurston said to them. "I was just speaking with Mrs. Kensington about what good fortune we have had to experience such an influx of young people in the village over the last few months! First your cousin's friends, then my niece and nephew, and of course you and your sister, Mr. Kensington. It is most agreeable, even for those of us who are more advanced in age, to be amongst the youthful energy you all exude."

"We are very fortunate that we have made such good friends with all the newcomers," said Rose. "Tell me, Mrs. Thurston, how do your niece and nephew get on in town?"

These two ladies, by virtue of being the two most interested in this topic, turned a bit aside from the rest and allowed the other three to begin a conversation of their own. Clara blessed her sister silently and turned to Mr. Kensington.

"I am so grateful for your kindness in sending us the easel, Mr. Kensington. Please let me thank you again for such a thoughtful gesture. I can assure you it will be put to very good use this summer."

He smiled. "You are most welcome," he said. "It pleases me immensely that you take enjoyment in it. I hope I was not too forward in bestowing it upon you, I hoped it might help express my gratitude at your help with the lambing that night."

"Oh, how does the little survivor get on?" She felt a special fondness for the lamb and wished for the liberty to go to the

Haythorne barns and see it again.

"Famously—he has gained weight nicely with his adoptive mother, even though she feeds her own lamb as well. At any rate, I am no artist myself, but I have heard that having a proper easel makes all the difference when composing out-of-doors. From what I can tell, you have done exceedingly well with the supplies at hand, but I look forward to seeing the results that you can achieve with a serviceable easel at your command."

He stopped and seemed a bit flustered. "That is, if I am lucky enough to have the opportunity to admire your work."

His mother cut in, "Do forgive my son's gesture, Miss Eastwood, which some might call impudent. He has always been prone to being overly generous, just like his father before him. I hope your family did not take offense by such a gesture, our family being so little known here. I do believe it was that generosity that drove my husband to an early grave, working himself to all hours for the people who served under him, out in all weathers and seasons. I cannot help wishing that he had not been quite so generous with strangers and perhaps he would not have left me such a young widow, with two children to provide for! And what little money was left him was given away to every Tom, Dick, and Harry who asked for help! Better to have a selfish father who lives than a foolish one who dies from being too good of heart, I say."

Clara was taken aback and did not know how to respond to this speech. Because of her distaste for them, she knew little of drawing room niceties amongst ladies, but felt sure they involved not criticizing one's late husband so blatantly in front of one's son, and a near stranger.

Mr. Kensington seemed used to bridging awkward gaps in the conversation and said to her, "My father was also a steward, Miss Eastwood, and died of fever after working alongside his men in a rainstorm."

"Ah," she said. "I am sorry for your loss—it must have been a sorrowful one for your family."

"And what of yourself, Miss Eastwood?" asked Mrs. Kensington. "Are you and your sister so fortunate as to have your father with you?"

"Yes," said Clara. "He is in good health, as far as we know. He is next to the door there with the red waistcoat, speaking with my uncle Morton."

"And the lady next to him your mother?" asked Mrs. Kensington.

"No, that is my uncle's sister Mrs. Williams," said Clara. "My mother stands next to the fireplace with my cousin Violet. She is wearing the yellow gown."

"And your uncle Morton the apothecary has three daughters?" said Mrs. Kensington.

"Yes, Caroline, Isabella, and Phoebe."

"Indeed. Are any of them marriageable? I have urged Henry to get to know the ladies in Exton if we are to stay here. An apothecary's daughter—well, I would imagine they can settle a substantial dowry. No house, of course, but we are well set up for now in that regard, thanks to his Lordship."

"Mother, I have told you again and again, I insist on choosing my own wife, and have no intention of selecting one based on her father's pocketbook. And this topic is hardly suitable for a drawing room," said Mr. Kensington firmly.

Mrs. Kensington's brows drew themselves together, looking like a streak of charcoal on a page, and her lips pursed haughtily. "So high-minded, just like your father. You forget, my son, that your salary must support four and not just one. Your wife's dowry could add to the comfort of all of us, not just yourself."

Clara was alarmed. Seeing that Rose and Mrs. Thurston had joined her mother and Violet at the fireplace, she offered to introduce Mr. and Mrs. Kensington to her relations.

"Yes, please do, since I seem forced to arrange the affairs of this family," said Mrs. Kensington. "Do not worry, Henry, we mothers will have your wife arranged by the end of the month."

Clara glanced at Mr. Kensington as they walked across the room. His mouth was set in a grim line as if he were steeling himself for a blow. He caught her eye and the line softened. He gave her a small smile.

"Mama, may I present Mrs. Kensington? Mrs. Kensington, my mother, Mrs. Eastwood, my sister Rose Eastwood, and my cousin Violet Tapley," Clara said, gesturing to each in turn."

Mrs. Eastwood said, "How lovely to make your acquaintance, Mrs. Kensington. We are so pleased you could join us so soon after arriving in the neighborhood. But—is not your daughter here as well?"

"Susanna felt unwell this evening and was forced to stay home," said Mrs. Kensington. "Heaven knows what those countryside inns are harboring, and we had such rain coming from Stony Stratford I'd be surprised if we didn't all get colds."

"Well, we hope to make her acquaintance as soon as may be," said Mrs. Eastwood. "I understand you are renovating Butler Cottage—we shall have to call on you there before we go to town."

"Someday, perhaps, we shall have a larger house," said Mrs. Kensington, eyeing the group shrewdly, "but for the present, it will do for us."

Mrs. Eastwood looked abashed, but persevered in making the newcomers welcome. In her mother-in-law's house, with Lady Eastwood's own daughters away in town, she was nearly

the hostess, and took the duty seriously no matter how unpleasant the guests may be.

Clara, for her part, was aghast at Mrs. Kensington's lack
of tact—even she, who disliked subterfuge, could be pleasant
enough to avoid offending her companions in the course of a
conversation. She could not help staring at the older woman,
trying to reconcile the polished exterior with such lack of consideration and feeling. Did she exist in a world of her own, with
the sentiments of others totally absent from her sight? Were they
simply little gnats that she might wave away? It was amazing to
her, too, that such a pleasant son could have descended from such
a mother. Would she discover someday that coldness lay dormant
in him, just waiting for the right time to emerge?

"How are you finding the countryside, Mr. Kensington?"
asked Mrs. Eastwood. "Is it similar to the last posting you held?"

Mrs. Kensington cut in over the sounds of the music beginning for the first dance. "We were lately in Somersetshire at
a very grand estate indeed. My son has been fortunate in his
employment."

Mr. Kensington bowed. "And fortunate in dance partners, I
hope. Miss Eastwood, would you do me the honor of the first?"

She smiled at him, trying to recover herself after the alarmed
speculations had run through her head like galloping horses
through a meadow, leaving muddy divots in the turf behind
them. "Of course."

He gave her his arm and they took to the floor. Clara found
him a perfectly adequate and agreeable partner, but the dance
kept them moving apart too much to speak beyond a few perfunctory comments about the weather. Clara could not be happy
with this meager opportunity for conversing, and had no wish
to rejoin the group they had lately left and so asked in the break
between sets, "Would you be very disappointed if we sat this next

out, Mr. Kensington?"

"Are you well? Have I tired you?" he asked with concern.

"No, I am quite well, thank you. I could dance the other without feeling fatigue. But I believe it would be in my best interests to leave the room so that my evening does not become monopolized." She looked meaningfully in Violet's direction, who was saying loudly to her cousin Harry Morton, who had stayed in Exton with his father, "Go dance with Clara, so Lieutenant Greene might ask me for this next!"

"Ah," Mr. Kensington said. "Might I monopolize your evening instead?"

"Yes," she answered. "You may."

They left the drawing room and walked out to the hall. A few party-goers still lingered there in little groups. It was quieter there, away from the music and larger group in the next room. They sat in a pair of chairs near the drawing-room door.

"Thank you for understanding," she said in apology. "I have found myself to be rather more disposable than I should wish at these dances. I fear I could not avoid such demands should I remain in the drawing room." She was, in truth, irritated at being unable to sit and speak with whom she liked instead of being used as a pawn in a game of chess in Rose and Violet's scheme to be partnered with particular gentlemen.

"Not at all," Mr. Kensington said in response to her explanation. "I was hoping to speak with you in a quieter manner than a ballroom can provide."

"And I you," she said, smiling.

"I am sorry about my mother," he said, as if he had been privy to her thoughts earlier. "She is not one to mince words, even when it is in her best interest to be agreeable. I had hoped she would exert herself in that regard tonight so her introduction to Exton might be a pleasant one for all involved. As it is, I suppose others will gain an accurate impression right away. I cannot accuse her of deception."

"I suppose it is better in most cases to know who someone is as soon as possible," said Clara, although she had been hoping for more agreeableness from someone who she might be spending much time with in the future. "I hope to continue my acquaintance with her, at any rate. And I hope to meet your sister as well."

"You are most kind. I am anxious that those here who—wish most to deepen their acquaintance with me, if there are any such persons in Exton, perceive and understand the natures of my relations, for we Kensingtons seem likely to remain under one roof for quite some time. And as for Susanna, she will be delighted to meet you, I am sure. The stress of moving, no doubt, made her unwell. She has a strong constitution, and I think she will be herself again in a few days."

"I hope so," she said. "We all fall prey to those treacherous damps every now and then."

He laughed. "Do you know, I do not think you especially prone to being overcome by them," he said. "I imagine you have exposed yourself to them enough that they are second nature to you."

She smiled. "I cannot say it is an affliction I often suffer from, no. But you know, most other ladies are built of delicate china held together only with cobwebs. One raindrop could be enough to shatter them completely. I am an oddity, I think."

"A very agreeable oddity, then," he said, and she turned her gaze to adjusting her gloves in order to hide her blush.

They sat and looked at each other for a long moment.

"I was wondering if you knew anything about fossils," she said finally, though the silence had not been uncomfortable. It had been the silence of two people who are not in a rush to spend all their conversational topics at once, knowing that enough time lay before them to say all that they needed.

He smiled. "Fossils? What a question! One not heard enough at balls, I think. Is there a reason behind it?"

"Only that the *Lady* had an article on them, and it was quite fascinating."

"Well then, it sounds as though I am the one who should be asking *you* about them, for I know very little," he said. "They are the impressions of bone and plant material in rock, am I correct?"

"Yes," she said. "The article said that certain areas of the country are more prone to have them than others. Limestone is often an indicator that they are present."

"Why would that be?" he said. "How did they come to be in the first place?"

With that they were off, in a comfortable but eager discourse. He had a curious mind and seemed delighted that he was ignorant where she was knowledgeable, and even more delighted that they should both desire to close the gap. If she had been asked, Clara supposed she would have remembered that Mrs. Kensington was just in the next room, but she might have been hard-pressed to recall her face. She was consumed totally with their discussion, and with Mrs. Kensington's son. She trembled a bit at his nearness. After imagining him while he was away based only on their brief encounters, and seeing him from a distance or in a group, it was as if her prior impressions had been the barest pencil outline on a page: a suggestion of the subject, nothing more. She wanted to see if what she had felt in lantern-light in the Haythorne barn returned in the brightness of a ballroom. Now he sat next to her, vividly real, and she took in all the details she had never had a chance to see—the piercing gray of his eyes, the way he rested his chin on his hand while listening to her, the wrinkles that broke out around his eyes when he smiled, which was often.

"...and Dorset is said to have the highest number of them," Clara finished. "I should love to go!"

"You shall," he said.

Another silence fell, but again it was a peaceful pause in a long interlude without a tinge of awkwardness.

"I suppose your sister is well provided for at Haythorne, but I would be happy to send her the elderberry tonic we make at Yewspring," Clara said presently. "It always helps our colds."

"You are very kind. I think she would be gratified to receive it, though the Haythorne servants have been quite attentive. As I said, moving house, perhaps, was more exertion than was wise for her. She was sorry to leave Southam, although I hope she will make friends here. But I feel I should mention, as well, that she is of a retiring nature and large gatherings are generally not to her liking. It is unlikely I shall convince her to attend many parties. But, as I said, I am sure she should be very glad to meet you, and your sister, when she is well again."

"Please do call upon us when she is," said Clara. "I am of a rather retiring nature myself and can understand her unease with parties."

He surveyed her carefully. "Really?" he said. "Do you know, Miss Eastwood, I believe you are wrong there. When I look at you, I do not see a shy woman. I see one who wants badly to enjoy society with others, but has found too few occasions to do so. I see someone who has been disappointed in what others have offered, and carries that disappointment about with her as a burden."

She was startled by his forthrightness, and looked at him thoughtfully. "That is how it feels sometimes," she said. "A burden."

"I hope the world can convince you to put it down some day," he said. "I hope I might play a role in that conviction."

She did not know what to say. He seemed to see inside of her. "Thank you," she said at last.

The dinner bell rang at that moment, and Clara saw her grandmother standing at the doorway to the dining room, watching them. Mr. Kensington saw her watching them too, as the two of them rose and he offered her his arm to walk in together.

"Your grandmother seems rather formidable," he said.

"Yes," Clara answered. "As a girl I was afraid of her, but I think I have come to appreciate her insight. Thankfully she goes to town ahead of my family and I shall have a little reprieve from her scrutiny."

He paused, turning to look at her intently. "The Yewspring party are not to go to town?"

"No," she said, looking up at him. "Not right away. I asked—if we might remain in the countryside for a while this spring, and my suggestion was agreeable to my parents. We are here at least until after Easter, although I doubt I can keep Rose here for much longer."

She could not categorize his face at that moment—it seemed like pleasure mixed with surprise, with perhaps some consternation included in the mix.

"I will tell you why I asked to stay, when next we speak again," she promised as they joined the stream of people leaving the drawing room and found their places at the long polished table. By some rapid rearranging of the cards by Lady Eastwood, no doubt, Clara was gratified to see that Mr. Kensington had somehow been seated next to her. She was gratified, too, to see that he looked as pleased as she felt. They dutifully conversed with those seated on their other sides before they were allowed to turn. Until that time, Clara had had the more taxing task of the two, for she had the hard-of-hearing Mr. Jenkins on her other side and was forced to nearly shout. In addition, her conversational common ground with him was slim indeed, and she was forced to make do with his loud stories of recent amputations at the surgery, which carried on uninterrupted save for his pauses to gulp some wine.

"Well," said Mr. Kensington when the fish had arrived and they were permitted to speak to each other, "I believe my appetite has abandoned me after hearing about that poor man's crushed foot."

She laughed. "I try not to begin my fish course with such images in my mind, either."

"To dispel them, might you enlighten me on the reason you decided to stay in the country? I thought—forgive me, but I thought it was the custom for England's finest eligible young women to go to London for the season."

She could not tell him every reason, of course, but she told him of her desire for drawing lessons.

"But the masters in London are so much more accomplished and capable of instructing you than anyone in this neighborhood, surely," he said. "I have the name of half a dozen of my tutors running through my head right now, for instance."

"Well—" she had honestly not thought of this objection, but remembered the third reason she wished to stay, "I hope to stay and sketch the countryside. It is much harder to do so in the city."

"What? You have never been to the botanical gardens? To the physick garden? To Hampstead Heath?"

"Oh," she said, startled. "No—my family attends Ascot, and the regatta, but that is the extent of the nature I have seen."

"Well, Miss Eastwood, then you have not really seen London. But I am pleased, for my family's sake, that you will remain for a while."

They spoke then only of a few common topics—he told her of his life before Exton, of stern tutors at Oxford and the release of being out-of-doors working at a lord's estate as under-steward nearby. When his father died the Kensingtons had gone to live with Mrs. Kensington's brother in Bedfordshire.

"At that time, I had two sisters," said Mr. Kensington, speaking rather quietly into his herring. "We all stayed with my uncle until I came of age to attend Oxford. My eldest sister, Elizabeth, married a naval lieutenant who was assigned to the East Indies. My nephew, Oliver, is their son. Sadly, his parents both died of the fever when he was an infant, and he was sent home for us to raise."

"Oh," said Clara in surprise. "I suppose I should have realized, when I heard of your nephew, that you would have had another sibling, since your living sister is unmarried. What a tragedy that your sister and her husband should not know their son. I am sure you provide your nephew with a good home, and how fortunate that he can grow up with his family rather than in an orphanage! What age is he?"

"He is four," said Mr. Kensington. "And I am thankful to say that he is a happy, healthy child in spite of his tragic beginning in life and the long journey he made back to us. We will raise him as well as we can, in memory of his mother, and thankfully my sister Susanna has taken on much of his care and education."

"We are very happy to have you all settled here," said Clara. "I hope Exton is your home for some time to come."

"I hope so too," he said, and he looked at her, and smiled.

Then he asked her about her own upbringing, and she told him about Yewspring until dinner ended and the crowd began making again for the drawing room. Amid the roar of voices and flood of bodies, Harry appeared at Clara's elbow.

"*There* you are, Clara! You must dance with me or I shall be forced to go with Violet, who does not wish to go with me because then Miss Younge will go with Lieutenant Greene instead of her, and she shall steal my snuff-box again. Violet, not Miss Younge."

"I *am* sorry, Harry, but I was feeling rather warm and Mr. Kensington kindly helped me find a cooler place to sit," said Clara. "Do you know, Mr. Kensington, I feel rather faint again. Might we return to our previous seats? The hall seems to have better circulation than that stuffy drawing-room."

"Indeed," he said, offering his arm.

"Harry, it's quite simple—you dance with Miss Younge instead, and then Violet will be free to dance with Lieutenant Green," said Clara before they walked off, thinking it right to put him out of the misery of trying to untangle his predicament. Harry's face lit up with relief, and Clara and Mr. Kensington saw him hurry back into the drawing-room. Their prior seats had been taken by Mr. Eastwood who had danced a set with his wife and one with Mrs. Williams and therefore felt entitled to a rest, and Mr. Dillingham's son Samuel, who had a map of the Mediterranean spread across his knees with the locations of His Majesty's ships marked in pencil. The two men's heads, one with gray at the temples and one with youthful curls, bent over the paper, their voices echoing off the tiles. Clara and Mr. Kensington seated themselves across the hall near the fire instead.

"I am sorry that Miss Younge will have lost out on perhaps a more agreeable partner," said Mr. Kensington as they sat, "but for my part, I am exceedingly satisfied with this arrangement."

"As am I," said Clara. "I feel rather unsuited to dances, much of the time. It is a pleasant change to be enjoying this one so much."

"Do you? As your partner, I found nothing wanting, and stand by my verdict now," he said with a smile. "I feel at this moment that dances are very agreeable indeed."

She laughed. "Yes, I feel the same. Though I have found the conversation at this one to be far superior than those at the others I have attended. Do you think I can count on this consistently?"

He sent her another long look. "If I am in attendance, you may be assured I will endeavor to make them as agreeable as this one for you. But tell me, Miss Eastwood, if you are unsuited to dances, what *do* you find yourself suited for? Except for first-rate botanical sketching, that is?"

"You are very kind, but are you sure that you are correct in your assessment of my skills? My drawing masters never seemed to note any special ability in my work. I fear sometimes that I am on a fool's errand."

"I suppose your tutors wanted you to paint indifferent land-scapes, and badly rendered portraits of your family members," said Mr. Kensington. "But I doubt they spent several terms using botanical texts, as I did at Oxford. The work I have seen from you, as undeveloped as it may be, is equal to what I saw in the volumes we used in our studies. I am astonished to have found such a level of accomplishment, and one that seems to have gone uncultivated by anyone who might have furthered your ability. How did you begin to draw so well?"

In truth, the origins of Clara's love for sketching held as much pain as pleasure, though these days it was a dimly remembered pain, more of an infrequent ache than a sting. She supposed it was because she tried not to think of her school days now, and rarely had a need to.

But after glancing up at him from where she was studying her lap and seeing his expression of gentle curiosity, she decided she must think of that time again, for she must tell him. She did not like the idea that he would not know this about her.

And so she told him of lessons at the Bingham Seminary for Young Ladies, lessons that—except for arithmetic and geography, subjects that she savored like sweets and were doled out with as much restraint and infrequency—both bored and frustrated her. She told him of not being able to stand the other girls' chatter over needlework, of wishing that the pupils' riding excursions were every day instead of twice a week, of learning quickly that she would often be sitting in the corner at dances. She told him of wanting to be back at Yewspring so badly that she almost wept with recognition when they attended church and heard sermons on the Israelites' exile in Babylon. She told him of looking up instead at the stained glass windows, to prevent tears from falling, and Miss Axton reprimanding her for not paying attention to the vicar.

"So you could not find a friend there?" he asked her solemnly. "And you turned to study instead?"

"The others tried to be kind," she said. "But I could hear their sighs of relief when I left the room."

She told him of Monsieur Verne, the drawing master, who let her page through his copy of *The Flora of France* and find plates to copy while the others drew teapots and fruit. When they went out-of-doors to sketch the landscapes and she preferred to pick sprigs from the garden or some quiet woodland swale to paint, he let her. And she told Mr. Kensington how, when she had been sent home to avoid the measles that had sprung up at the school one spring, Madame Verne had sent her the flora with a note saying that her husband, God rest him, would have wanted Clara to have it.

"And you never went back? To school?"

"No," she said. "The younger girls were being taught at home by that time, so they did their best with me. And in just a few more years I was out, though the balls and gentlemen meant little to me since there was an agreement between George—Mr. Eastwood—and my family. And so I just kept on studying, as best I could. One thing I will say about London, it is easier to obtain a microscope there than at the Reeds' store."

After one morning of peering through the microscope, after Clara had saved her pocket money for a year to buy it, the other girls were bored and wished only to scamper about Yewspring's lawns, shrieking and chasing one another and throwing rocks into the pond.

She sat and thought for a moment more. "I suppose perhaps I have found it difficult to explain to my teachers what exactly I was after. I find it less difficult to capture a flower than to create perspective in a landscape. My hills were always woefully steep when I attempted them. It is very frustrating, for I feel that my eye understands the dimensions that it sees, but when I try and produce them on the canvas, it does not look the same."

"But close-range subjects? Studied in detail?"

"There is still perspective there, to be sure. I try to capture that as best I can. After all, live flowers are not pressed flat against a page—they have texture and dimension. And as for the other details, to paint just the barest outline of a tulip seems wasteful to me. There is such beauty and such complexity there— in the structure of its anthers, in the sheen or dullness of its petals, in its overall arrangement. Some types seem to be different from others in the very slightest of details—but my eye can see it, and it is such a thrill! Like being able to see a pattern where others see only chaos, or like being able to recognize your friends even in pitch darkness. But if I cannot capture that beauty, that—fascinating little world, on the page, I feel as though it may go unnoticed. I suppose I feel that I must pay attention to the details that others may overlook, to bear witness to the beauty I see. It is both a challenge and a privilege, one I feel ill-equipped for at times. Much of the time, in fact."

"Yet you persist."

"Yes, it brings me more satisfaction than sorrow, and so I muddle along with it as best I can. My uncle has a set of flora in the surgery, mostly medicinal plants, of course, but Mr. Jenkins would let me look at them and sit with my sketchbook, trying to recreate the pictures. Since I do not enjoy making over bonnets, or playing whist, or learning duets, my winters have been spent thus. There are many rainy afternoons to fill here." She told him, too, about Miss Holt and the disappointing first lesson.

He regarded her, yet again, with a long intent look, one that was laced with gentleness. She felt as though he was drinking her in, and she thrilled in it

"Miss Eastwood, you are a marvel," he said. "Would you think it very forward of me if I attempted to get you some better study guides than whatever outdated dusty medicinal books you have been using? A flora of the Midlands, perhaps, with some proper illustrations?"

She blushed and smiled. "Mr. Kensington, you are too kind. The easel was more than enough—"

He leaned forward toward her, and reached his hand out to barely touch the fabric of her glove. "You have had so little aid in your endeavors," he said quietly. "I would like to do this for you, if you will permit me."

"All right," she said, color rushing into her face at his touch. Out of the corner of her eye she could see her father's head, still bent over the map. The music in the drawing room drifted in, and there in the doorway appeared a figure in lilac, its snowy plume fluttering as Mrs. Kensington searched the hall for her son. She strode over when she saw him, and said, "There you are! Henry dear, you must come in and dance with Miss Younge. She is quite forlorn without a partner, and that Morton boy stranded her in a corner for some other young lady. And how are you to make yourself known here if you do not circulate? There are not enough gentlemen, and you will make many ladies grateful to you if you ask them to dance. I have laid good groundwork with Mr. Morton, but we must keep our options open."

Clara stood. "I've kept you from the others," she said. "I am sorry. We should go in."

He stood as well, with a rueful smile, and gave her his arm again as they went in. As his mother pulled ahead of them, no doubt to make sure Miss Younge did not accept another gentleman in her absence, Mr. Kensington leaned toward her and said in a low tone, "If I was consulting only myself, I would remain in my prior seat, in the company I was in. But my mother is right— for her and Susanna's sake I must attempt to be sociable with the rest of the neighborhood. And my work as the agent will be better if I am friendly with all of the families here."

"I understand," she said. "His Lordship's agent has always been well-respected here—you must wish to do the same, and to represent him well."

He left her with her mother and rotated among the ladies of the room for the rest of the night while she danced one with Harry, another with Lieutenant Greene who stepped on her foot twice because he was watching Violet, and one with her father, who said, "You and Kensington were quite engrossed out in the hall. Did you tell him about the bull calf Bessie just had? Perhaps Haythorne would take that one as well. It seems a shame to alter him just because we can't have bulls."

"No, I didn't speak to him of it," she said. "We hadn't time." Somehow, it was true. They hadn't had time for all she had wished to say.

Clara sat out at the end of the evening, wandering back to the supper table for the second meal and then slipping off to the conservatory to survey the plants and sit for a few moments in the blessed quiet. She heard the faint sounds of the *boulanger* sounding, too soon, to end the evening. She emerged from the back of the house as the party-goers were beginning to come back into the hall, in search of either their wraps and carriages home, or more port from Clara's grandfather's cellar. She had never known a party to fly by in this way. Though her cousins and Rose might have thought her lot a very dull one indeed, having danced only four sets, she would not have traded places with them for the world.

She felt a touch at her elbow and turned to find Mr. Kensington. "Might I call on you and your sister on Sunday next and take the two of you walking after church?" he asked. "I shall see if Susanna would like to come with us. I should like to learn the plants here better, for my work, and perhaps you can help me. I trust a few things will be sprouting at least, even if they are not yet blooming."

"Yes, I believe so. I would like that very much," she said. "I will accept tentatively for Rose, if you are willing to include my cousin Violet as well, who stays with us at Yewspring."

"Yes, that would be very agreeable."

Clara's father appeared in front of them. "Clara, we're leaving," he said. "How do you do, Mr. Kensington? Thank you for being so attentive to my daughter tonight. You are very good, sir."

"It was my pleasure, Mr. Eastwood," said Mr. Kensington. "Might I help the Yewspring ladies to your carriage?"

"Of course," said her father distractedly. "Where is Harry? He owes me a pound from billiards." He craned his neck for his nephew and turned away from them.

They found Rose and Violet, and Mr. Kensington handed the ladies up to the carriage. Mr. Eastwood cornered his nephew and claimed his winnings, and Mrs. Eastwood sighed contentedly as they pulled out of the drive.

"Well, what a lovely evening," she said to her family. "Mrs. Doyle was also wearing this yellow from the Reeds' store, but I thought my gown looked better than hers. She had hers made up in such an unflattering cut for her stature! Rose, dear, you were hardly sitting down all evening! You must write Miss Creston and tell her so. But subtly, of course! And Violet, Lieutenant Green was most attentive! What a shame that his leave will end so soon."

Clara stared dreamily out the carriage window at the clear sky overhead, studded with stars, and reveled in the evening that had passed.

"Clara, you must not leave the ballroom so quickly," said her mother. "You quite disappeared for half the evening! Were you in the library with your nose in a book? I cannot always be coming away to look for you, as I did in Daventry. Really, you must exert yourself a little. It would not do for word to get out that you are an unsociable creature. You must rebuild your future now, you know."

"Mother, Clara had a lovely evening as well," said Rose. "Just look at her, she's glowing! I think it is quite in her best inter-est—and therefore the best interests of us all—to remain in the country for a while yet."

"Hmmm, perhaps you are right," said Mrs. Eastwood. "Perhaps Mrs. Clive will come to stay if I invite her—although our rooms are full—"

"I could move to Rose's room," offered Violet.

"Oh, that is most kind of you, Violet dear. And that does have the best light in the house, I think, so it will not really be an inconvenience. Yes, I will write to Mrs. Clive tomorrow and invite her."

"Do you know, I am beginning to understand why you enjoy these occasions so, Rose," Clara said with a smile. Unpleasant mother or no, her time with Mr. Kensington had confirmed every hope, answered her lingering question about what she had felt looking at his intent face in a circle of lantern-light while she clutched a newborn lamb to her. She liked him. And she felt that he liked her too. A commonplace circumstance, perhaps, but she had not had to hide parts of herself away like shabby clothes in a closet. "Mama, perhaps I might have some fabric for a new gown? Rosie, will you help me choose it?"

"Well!" exclaimed her mother, "Will wonders never cease!"

CHAPTER ELEVEN

In the week following the dance, Clara's days filled to the capacity they had before George's death had plunged her into mourning. She sketched, taking the traveling easel out on its first expeditions into the countryside, while Rose and Violet sat beside her and sewed. Even Mrs. Eastwood, who generally restricted her exercise to a turn about the garden or walking to Exton for errands or to pay calls, joined them one fine day—until a rain shower sent them all scrambling for the shelter of a tree, Clara's paints running down the page and the dye from the embroidery threads of the others staining their white cloths.

On the other days, Clara went out alone.

On Friday she went again to Miss Holt's, not optimistic about the chances of having a more enlightening lesson. And in fact, Miss Holt spent only a quarter of an hour reviewing Clara's drawings, murmuring, "Yes, this seems to be satisfactory" and "My, this little thing isn't much to look at, is it?" since Clara had only the sprouts of early spring growth to work with.

"Well," Miss Holt said, laying the drawings aside, "perhaps we shall resume the drawing next week. Let us turn to Fordyce now, for your mother has asked me to work on your deportment. Perhaps next week you could bring your sister and cousin Miss Tapley, for they could help us practice the conversation."

Clara sighed and tried to smile. "You know best, Miss Holt," she said, and fervently hoped that she was not mistaken in Mr. Kensington's regard for her—if he liked her as she was, these infernal lessons could be called to a close.

At the end of the day, as she was leaving, Clara asked Miss Holt if she might have *An Introduction to Botany* back. "Of course," said Miss Holt, "I'm just not sure where it's gotten to—" Clara found this unlikely, since the parlor was sparsely furnished and decorated. "Your bedchamber, perhaps, or the dining room?" she suggested, since these were the only other rooms besides the kitchen.

"Matilda? Matilda!" Clara could hear Miss Holt to the maid as she went down the passage. She waited a few minutes, hearing the murmur of the two women's voices from the kitchen. Miss Holt returned looking apologetic.

"We've been doing the spring cleaning and aren't sure where the book might have gotten to. It'll turn up, though, don't you fret, Miss Clara."

But Clara, did, of course. Even if the book had not cost a pound, she had missed the opportunity to study in the week between her lessons. She had already written her name on the frontispiece, to avoid such mistakes as this—and yet it had happened anyway.

Sunday brought the ladies' walk with the Kensingtons. The family attended church, and Clara saw Mr. Kensington across the aisle with his mother, a young woman quite like him in countenance, and a little boy. The group came up to the Eastwood ladies after the service as they stood in the churchyard.

"Mrs. Eastwood, may I present my sister, Miss Kensington, and my nephew Oliver?" said Mr. Kensington. "Susanna, this is Miss Clara Eastwood and her sister, Miss Rose Eastwood."

The ladies all greeted one another, and Clara struggled in the next few moments to find the shy, retiring sister Mr. Kensington had described. Miss Kensington chatted easily with the others, admired Rose's gown and Mrs. Eastwood's bonnet, and discussed the sermon with Mr. Eastwood. She seemed friendly, open, and anything but timid. She grasped her nephew's hand as he stood meekly at her side.

"I look forward to our walk after luncheon," said Miss Kensington, finally turning to Clara. "Henry tells me you are quite fond of walking, and of the flora nearby. I hope you can assist him in learning the names of the plants, for it is rather important to his job, you know. Livestock must be kept out of the poisonous patches, weeds in the crops must be dealt with, and his Lordship must capitalize on anything growing on his land that might be gathered for the good of the estate."

"I am happy to share what I know," said Clara. "But I fear I am perhaps not the best authority—we have woefully few flora guides for this county, and the ones I have seen seem to be erroneous in some instances, so my own knowledge may well be lacking or misguided." What else might Mr. Kensington have told his sister about her? She certainly was agreeable to Clara, but no more so than to any of the others. Nothing in the sister's behavior betrayed the intentions of the brother.

"I look forward to our outing, however," Clara added.

The two groups parted to take luncheon at their own houses, then Mr. and Miss Kensington were to ride their horses to Yewspring and leave them in the stable. As the Eastwoods were finishing their meal, they heard the crunch of gravel through the open window that signaled that their callers had arrived.

Mrs. Eastwood sent the young people off with a cheery wave from the door, then sat down to continue writing her inquiries to London dressmakers. Mrs. Clive's arrival to stay at Yewspring, even if it should happen, would only delay Mrs. Eastwood traveling to town for a few weeks. She had tired of the amusements and the society afforded by a country neighborhood for some time now, and really it was to her girls' advantage to be in London. Mr. Creston was there, after all. And Clara must find someone. She was writing on Clara's behalf, in fact. It would not do for her daughter to appear shabby. If one or even two engagements resulted from these exertions, they would be well worth it.

But then, Mrs. Eastwood thought, laying down her pen, there had been the surprising appearance of the land steward by her daughter's side at the dance. He had had quite the gentlemanly appearance. Mrs. Eastwood privately thought that perhaps Clara might be setting up house as a newlywed that fall as well as her cousin Caroline, returning to Exton from town to be wed. Mr. Kensington had certainly behaved in a singular fashion, whisking Clara away at the dance for such private conversation. It was enough to put notions into a mother's head, and they were generally satisfactory ones. His income would certainly be very suitable for her daughter, even with the three others in Mr. Kensington's household, and Clara would remain in Exton, which seemed to be her daughter's sole criterium for a husband. Mrs. Eastwood herself thought mucking about in the fields and conversing with the coarse cottagers who worked in them an undignified profession and one that hardly made him her daughter's equal, but there Society differed from her, and—ever its obedient daughter—she bowed to it. Her distaste for the profession was compounded by it being a reminder of her own past, for her own brother John was a steward, in fact, at an estate in Cheshire, and she did not like to think of the fact that his was the most elevated position in her natal family.

But, pushing these thoughts of her past poverty and want away, as she had learned to do many a time, she reflected that Clara's face, as Rose had pointed out, *had* been glowing on the carriage ride home, and Mrs. Eastwood did not suppose it was because of the exertion of dancing. For her part, she was not particular about how Clara was to secure her future so long as she found a way to cease obstructing Rose's chances. If this Kensington was waiting in the wings for her odd Clara, well then—so much the better. Her daughter could unite economy and happiness in one man, an enviable position for any woman of twenty-six who seemed determined to shun society.

Outside, the five walkers quickly divided into two groups, as if by design, though it seemed the most natural outcome based on their temperaments. Rose, Violet, and Miss Kensington talked away easily and pulled ahead of the other two, who kept stopping and lingering by the path to examine one flower or another that Clara spotted. The last of the snowdrops clung to the most sheltered swales, and the daffodils' yellow blooms bobbed in the breeze.

"These are all quite common," she said by way of apology. "You must have seen them before."

"Yes," he said, "but they bring me pleasure nonetheless."

They were not long into the walk, the other ladies' pelisses three colorful columns of cloth ahead of them, when he stopped suddenly and looked at her. "Miss Eastwood," he said, "I do not wish you to think me improper, but…I must ask how the death of your cousin has affected you. I—er, happened to hear that an engagement between the two of you was considered a certainty. Forgive my directness, I—am anxious to know whether you are devastated by his loss."

"Oh," she said, and felt herself blush deeply. "Well, as I said, I was quite fond of George, along with the rest of my family, and did so wish to remain at Yewspring—" The arrangement, coming from her lips, suddenly sounded mercenary and heartless. She tried again. "We did believe that we would be suitable together and that such a union would be to the benefit of both our families. But since that is not to be, I—find my future quite undecided."

"And is that circumstance a sorrow or an unexpected—opportunity?"

She thought of the letter she had written to Mr. Sowerby. She thought of one day packing her things and leaving Yewspring forever, leaving Exton and the Midlands for some other place, some other home. And she remembered the strange and thrilling feeling of her heart leaping within her when she had caught Mr. Kensington's gaze in their previous encounters, when he had looked at her with what she was coming to realize was wonder, and a tenderness that threatened to burn her with intensity.

She took a deep breath. "Some of both, naturally. Of course I grieve such a senseless loss. I grieve the future that I would have had, secure in staying here. But—as you say, it seems that the future may hold—new possibilities that I did not anticipate. As time goes on, I expect that I shall be better able to look about me to try and find them."

"Then may I confess that the news of your engagement was quite disappointing to me?"

She was gratified by his forthrightness, and her blush refused to leave her face, accompanied by a smile she felt herself unable to suppress. "You may."

He smiled too. and was likewise unsuccessful at hiding it. "Then—might I have reason to believe that perhaps, when your natural feelings of grief have abated, you may find yourself at liberty to welcome other—attachments? Not, of course, until the proper time—"

"Yes." Her answer was out before she realized it, and she

marveled that she had thought such a small short word harmless. It was like seeing lightning glancing onto a far-off peak before the wind had even picked up enough to stir a single leaf.

They went on then in happy silence, though sometimes they discussed a plant for ten minutes while the others waited, just in sight, on the path. At other times she forgot to point out any plants at all, so busy were they conversing about some other topic entirely. The walking party covered four miles, and she and he argued gently over whether or not the Kensingtons should bring home one of Lady Chesterson's new puppies (Clara was in favor—Mr. Kensington worried for the chickens in the new coop he had just built), discussed Henry's progress in Lamarck, and Clara asked him for his advice about Yewspring's hayfields, which were not as productive as others in the neighborhood. She could not bear for Yewspring to be thought inferior in any way, and he teased her gently, saying, "Are you in want of employment? Haythorne could use you." This led to talk of her drawing lessons and her hopes of, one day, earning some money of her own. He was not shocked. He did not recoil from this hint of ambition, and Clara was gratified, again, more than she could say. She had learned, too, that he was very fond of billiards and chess but never played either for money and was a passionate fencer when he had the opportunity to compete. Having never seen him at leisure, only at work or in company, she was glad to know that his pursuits were highly unobjectionable to her—and she longed to learn chess, for no one had ever taught her.

Of his family Mr. Kensington had not been as forthcoming. She inferred from a few of his comments that Mrs. Kensington was as unpleasant to live with as she had guessed. Of his sister, he only said how glad he was that Susanna and Rose seemed to be making such quick friends, and of his nephew just that he had recently taken ill after eating too many gooseberries.

***

Now the five of them stood at the gate to Yewspring with the afternoon light bathing the greening country in golden glory around them. Mr. and Miss Kensington held their horses' reins in readiness to depart.

"Thank you for the lovely walk," said Miss Kensington. "And Miss Eastwood, thank you for keeping my brother such good company. It is not often he finds a companion who can relate to so many of his interests and provide him with such contemplative conversation—I fear his household is lacking in that regard!"

"I am happy to perform that service anytime," said Clara, "and rest assured I consider it a pleasure for myself, so it is no burden."

"I am sorry to report that I must go to Birmingham for a few days, or I would beg for this pleasure again," said Mr. Kensington. "Perhaps when I am back we can walk again, or all take our horses out. We have time for several excursions before you all go to town, I hope."

"Shall not you go to London, Miss Kensington?" asked Rose. Clara had wondered this as well. Why did Miss Kensington not participate in the Season? Surely it would help her chances of meeting a husband.

"Oh no," said Miss Kensington quickly, nearly before Rose was done speaking, then paused. "I—find country life much more wholesome and agreeable to me."

"I am of your mind, and envious that your mother supports such an inclination," said Clara, although she wondered at Mrs. Kensington's forbearance when she must wish for her daughter to be married as badly as any other mother with unmarried daughters. She imagined that Miss Kensington's age must be somewhere between hers and Rose's—perhaps she was already three-and-twenty or four-and-twenty. Why then would she sequester herself in Exton, with such manners that would find her a friend in every ballroom and a suitor before the year was out?

"Ah yes, none of we Kensingtons can stand London," said Mr. Kensington, after glancing at his sister. "Alas, for there would be many familiar faces for us in the streets, no doubt. We just prefer to meet them in the country."

Miss Kensington turned to Clara, rather abruptly. "Would you mind very much if I wrote to you and your sister when you go, Miss Eastwood? I know you may be wishing for news from home, which I would be happy to provide as best as I am able. And—though I do not wish to go there myself, of course, it is always pleasant to hear news of town, if you find yourself with time enough to respond."

"Certainly," said Clara, pleased at this gesture of friendship and knowing that Mr. Kensington could never make such a gesture himself. The correspondence from London could very well be shared communally in the house, and the words she wrote to the sister reach the eyes and ears of the brother. A thrill passed through her at the thought of remaining connected to him even from across the country. "We will be in Southampton Street, number nine." Her mother had procured the lodging only a few days before, beginning the week after Easter.

"Excellent," said Miss Kensington. "A delightful part of town. I am told so, at any rate."

The Kensingtons mounted their horses and Mr. Kensington bent down from the saddle to Clara. Quietly, beneath the parting words spoken by the others, he said, "I have not forgotten about the flora. I know a bookstore in Birmingham that I can visit tomorrow evening, so I think you might expect a parcel in the post on Wednesday—I shall send it on at once since I must stay in the city for a few days more. I hope it proves a pleasant diversion until we meet again."

"Thank you," she said, looking up at him, feeling that the words were inadequate for her gratitude. She trusted that he might understand what lay beneath their surface. She hardly dared look there, afraid not of what she might find but what the world might say about it if it knew.

He gave her another long, lingering gaze, one that she was becoming used to, and yet this one made her stomach drop and her heart beat faster.

"I hope this was the first of many walks we will take together, Miss Eastwood," he said, still bent over and with the other three—joined by Mrs. Eastwood, who had stepped out to speak with the visitors—speaking too loudly to overhear.

"Thank you," she said again, "I hope so as well."

She smiled at him one last time, the horses trotted off, and Mr. Kensington turned back to wave at Clara and Rose.

Perhaps it was hindsight that colored her judgment of that moment, but it seemed to Clara that the image of him with the sunlight glowing over his shoulder, a smile on his face, the glory of the day, and the delight she had taken in it were all imprinted on her mind, so that she remembered it always. Perhaps it would have been so, even if what had transpired next had never happened.

CHAPTER TWELVE

The next morning, Mrs. Doyle called upon the Eastwood ladies. This was not an unusual occurrence, so Clara thought nothing of it save that she was annoyed that the visit interrupted her sketching of the hyacinths she had potted up and put on her windowsill.

The ladies sat in the sitting room, Fiona brought them tea, and when the door had shut behind her, Mrs. Doyle set down her cup with a *clink*. She reached for her reticule and pulled out a letter.

"My dear Mrs. Eastwood, I hate to be the bearer of unfortunate news, but I felt that you should read this."

"Heavens," said Mrs. Eastwood, reaching out and taking the letter. "I cannot imagine what can be so unfortunate."

She unfolded the letter, which was lengthy, and sat there reading it, expressionless. Violet and Rose chatted with Mrs. Doyle about the Reeds' new selection of Indian teas, and Clara asked her about the progress of a hothouse she was having built.

Mrs. Eastwood got up from her seat, brought the letter to Clara, and gave it to her.

"I am surprised indeed," she said to Mrs. Doyle, going back to her chair. "But the facts align with what Mrs. Kensington told me at the dance. I am grateful that you would share the information with us. You are very kind."

Baffled, Clara looked down at the letter.

9 March

Old Rectory, Albrighton

My dear Penelope,

Thank you for the letter—the boys are quite over their fevers, thank heaven, and we are all settling back down after all that excitement.

I especially wanted to write you quickly, dear, because the name of the new steward in Exton seemed familiar when you mentioned it. I could not think why, until I saw my next-door neighbor Mrs. Yale. I told her I had had a letter from you and that a man named Kensington had just moved to your village. This stuck in my mind because <u>we</u> have just gotten a new steward here and it made me wonder if there was some kind of epidemic going about.

"Kensington?" she said. "Kensington was the name of <u>our</u> last steward!"

You see, we feel we must warn you because this man and his family had to leave here last autumn when their secret was discovered, which it was bound to be no matter how hard they tried to hide it.

You will, perhaps, have heard that the Kensingtons have a young boy living with them, whom they claim is the son of a deceased former Miss Kensington, who married a naval man and birthed the child overseas, where both parents died and he was consequently sent back to live with his aunt, uncle, and grandmother.

It is all a falsehood. Every last word of it. The child in question is Miss Susanna Kensington's own son, born in disgrace, for there was never a marriage between his father and mother, and by all accounts was never intended to be. I do not even know who the father is, save that I believe he was indeed a naval officer who abandoned the child and his mother and slipped away overseas. However, you may be sure that there never was a second Kensington daughter, and the entire story is a ruse to keep them from being found out.

When we heard of this here, we of course believed there might have been some explanation, some mistake made. Perhaps there was a second daughter after all. I found out the parish where they had been living when the first Mr. Kensington was a steward, and had our cousin Timothy, who happens to be the curate there, look through the baptismal records. If there was a second daughter, and she was christened there as the other children were, there would have been a record. Timothy could find records for Henry, the son, and Susanna, the daughter who you have most likely met by now, but no third child of either sex, and certainly not one that could have been old enough to birth a child.

I am sorry to cause anyone trouble, but feel that you must know what kind of people have descended on your village, misrepresenting themselves as honest people. If they were that, they would have turned the girl out and never had anything more to do with her. Instead, they harbor her and tell you lies.

Lord Dayton here was so furious, he of course released Mr. Kensington immediately from his service, and I imagine the next thing they did was look about for vacancies. Did he arrive in late autumn, October or November perhaps? I believe the ladies and child went to live with some friends, and we have not seen them since. I thought to never hear their name again. Of course, we had no idea where they were to live next, and had I caught the name of Exton earlier, I might have warned you. Perhaps you could have warned his Lordship or the household of this family's deceit.

And to think I had the mother and daughter here in my drawing-room!

At any rate, my dear, I felt it my duty to share this with you so that Exton may be informed of the nature of all its inhabitants. I urge you to share this letter with any villagers who might have been especially taken in by the Kensingtons, and to consider whether it might not benefit the Lord Chesterton to know this for the benefit of himself and his household. The daughter has clearly exhibited an appalling lack of virtue and propriety—who knows what the son may be capable of as well?

Do keep me informed. I send my love to the children and Richard.

Your loving sister,

Annabelle Clarkston

Shock and disappointment overtook Clara as she finished the letter, an unlooked-for wave that loomed up suddenly and then crushed her beneath it. She felt a distinct knot in her chest, but merely handed the pages back to Mrs. Doyle and said, "Thank you for informing us. It was kind of you to wish us to be aware of our new acquaintances' history. I do hope no one in the village is too disappointed by the news. Do you know, Mother, I do not feel quite well—my headache from last night seems to have returned. Might I be excused to lie down?"

"Of course," said Mrs. Eastwood, looking relieved. Clara supposed that for all her calm words, she had most likely paled or colored beyond what an indifferent person might have upon receiving this information. She felt flushes of both heat and cold alternating with one another, and in a daze realized that her hands were tingling.

"Good heavens, what is it?" asked Rose, breaking off from her conversation with Mrs. Doyle when she saw her sister's face. "What does the letter say? Clara is never ill!"

The last thing Clara saw as she left the sitting room was Mrs. Doyle handing the letter to Rose. She knew her sister would be sympathetic once she learned the truth, the briefest flicker of comfort that flared quickly and then was driven out by the grief and disappointment again.

Once in her chamber, too shocked yet for tears, she lay

numbly upon the bed, contemplating the startling contents of the letter.

The Kensingtons had deceived them all, beginning with Lord Chesterson who hired Mr. Kensington and proceeding all the way to herself and her family. Miss Kensington a shy and retiring wallflower indeed! Clearly she was in fact fond of company, having enjoyed the company of a naval officer far beyond what propriety would dictate and been left to pay the price for what surely had been a want of restraint and decorum. It was a breach of propriety that any mother must have felt most keenly, as she could only imagine Mrs. Eastwood's reaction to Clara or Rose falling under similar circumstances. It perhaps explained Mrs. Kensington's inclination toward disagreeableness, for surely she had been blamed for her daughter's conduct. And all three seemed yoked together in a single household indefinitely—how could Mr. Kensington ever be freed from his responsibility to them? And how could she ever reconcile this news with the man she had come to know over the past few months?

And yet, even as she had these painful thoughts, Clara could not find anything in Mr. Kensington's behavior to rebuke, nor any that suggested him to be a scoundrel himself, no matter how much of one his nephew's father might have been. She would not have liked him as well as she did if he had been able to turn his sister out of his house, with child, and left her to the poorhouse or worse. Though she knew that a further acquaintance with him was out of the question, and that her parents would forbid any kind of alliance with so sullied a family, she at least could have some measure of peace in knowing that his only failing was in attempting to shield his sister from further shame, further scandal.

And at the early stage in the acquaintance between himself and Clara, how could he have been open with her about this? Though the idea that he had ever wished to deceive her caused her great pain, she knew there was no place in drawing-room talk to divulge family secrets, nor would she have wished him to embarrass his sister just so that he might clear his conscience and not be forced to lie to her. Clara's pain would have been greater if she and he had begun openly courting—here a torrent of tears began, as she realized that now there would never be a possibility of such events. And yet her pain was already strong enough that she knew their lack of engagement would not dull it, nor lessen her disappointment in Mr. Kensington's deceit.

She chose to believe that he would have told her. It was the only mark of esteem she could show him now.

After a few strangled sobs, Clara sat stricken until she heard a knock at the door. Without waiting for a response, her mother swept in. It was as if Clara mourned George still—the two of them were back in the same situation.

"Well," Mrs. Eastwood said briskly, hands behind her back and striding to the window, choosing to ignore the emotions her daughter was currently displaying, "it's all for the best, Clara. Think how humiliating it would have been if things had advanced between you and Mr. Kensington! We would have been forced to break off the engagement, had there been one, had we by chance learned of it in time! That would have been two attachments that failed to come to fruition—first George, then the one to Mr. Kensington. It would not have aided your reputation. No one receives a third proposal, my dear. We must be very grateful to Mrs. Doyle. A pity there is no time before we leave to have them for supper to thank her. I think we must go to town at once. We can stay at a hotel until the Southampton Street house is ready."

Rose had come in on the heels of her mother and gone to her sister, patting her back. "Mama!" she said now, "this is most upsetting news for Clara, as you see. I think Mrs. Doyle hardly deserves our thanks, much less a dinner. Though you must see, Clara, that she didn't mean any harm. She thought she was doing the right thing."

"And what of my feelings?" choked out Clara bitterly. "This does not change anything about who Mr. Kensington is!" She glared at her mother.

"He has participated in this ruse and taken us all in," said Mrs. Eastwood. "When do you imagine he might have told you about all this? After ten years of marriage, had it come to that, when it was too late? That is assuming, of course, that their unsavory truth had not been discovered before then. His employers are bound to find out eventually, even if he should obtain a favorable reference from prior ones. Thank heaven Mrs. Doyle has the means to enlighten Lord Chesterson quickly, before someone else falls prey to the family."

Clara shot up off the bed. "You can't mean that Mrs. Doyle intends to tell Lord Chesterson?"

"Certainly she does! For goodness sake Clara, she would be foolish not to. If the family found out the Kensingtons' character and it was revealed that Mrs. Doyle had this information and did not divulge it—well, Mr. Doyle's position in the village could be affected, not to mention their whole family's favor at the great house. I advised her to go to Haythorne straight away and ask to see his Lordship about it."

"She is going there now?" cried Clara, even more distraught.

"She has no other choice, as Mama said—" Rose said. "Mr. Doyle cannot risk having his fellow magistrate against him."

"I believe she is indeed on her way to the Hall, and I encouraged her to make her way there straightaway," said their mother. "Best strike while the iron is hot, I think. Now, you just lie down for a bit. I have some news that may cheer you. The younger Mr. Eastwood, your cousin Charles, will be arriving home from overseas while we are in London. It may be the perfect balm for this disappointment, and perhaps you might yet throw yourself into your *trousseau* shopping." Mrs. Eastwood was sadly mistaken in her belief that this would console her daughter.

"No," said Clara, getting up. "I feel in need of a walk. Just up the lane and back—I won't be long. It's just the thing I need for my headache. There's no need to come with me, Rose."

She left the room, passing a solemn Violet in the upstairs passage, trying not to betray her urgency. She grabbed only her bonnet as she went through the hall. She knew what was at stake for Mr. Kensington should the letter arrive at Haythorne. Lord Chesterson was unlikely to be lenient in this matter, just as Mr. Kensington's last employer had not been, and dismissal from the house and his position as steward was the most realistic outcome. She was the only one who could help avoid this, though she did not know how she might convince Mrs. Doyle to remain silent.

With these thoughts racing through her mind, once she was through Yewspring's gate and out of sight of the house, she picked up her skirts and ran.

Fortunately, the hours Clara had spent walking through the countryside had made her familiar with shortcuts through fields and pastures, and she clambered over stiles, rushed past bemused cattle and sheep (hoping that his Lordship's ill-tempered bull was not in her path), and cut through woodland to the main road leading to Haythorne Hall, anticipating that Mrs. Doyle had taken the long way around through the village.

Climbing over one last stile, she looked down the road toward the village but did not see any sign of anyone walking, just a cart going back toward Exton and a lone phaeton traveling north toward Leeds. She paused, wondering what to do. If Mrs. Doyle was behind her, it would be better to intercept her before she got within the gates of the estate. Perhaps she could offer to tutor the Doyle children in exchange for Mrs. Doyle agreeing to keep the letter secret. Surely saving the cost of a governess's salary would be worth her discretion. And should the truth come out, Mrs. Doyle could always claim to be ignorant. The only record that she had ever known about this lay in Mrs. Doyle's own hand—the chances of her sister Mrs. Clarkston coming forth herself with the revelation, from sixty miles away, seemed slim indeed.

All Clara knew was that she had to avert this disaster for the time being, come what may in the future. She could not stand to have her time with Mr. Kensington cut short so suddenly. After George, she was sure that it would break her.

She waited a moment more, shading her eyes against the sun to see if Mrs. Doyle would appear around the bend. There were plowboys in the fields and she nodded to them as she passed, trying not to appear too urgent. She saw nothing on the road, so crossed it and went through the gates to Haythorne's ground. As she made her way up the drive, she passed the lane that led to rows of estate cottages. One was isolated from the others and set back from the road by a high hedge bordering its garden, and bore the name "Butler Cottage" on a plaque at the gate. She could see a cart with trunks, carpets, and furniture outside, and a few men came back and forth from the house, hauling crates, chairs, and trunks inside. Knowing this was the Kensingtons' new home, and thinking of what a short-lived residence it would be for them if she did not catch Mrs. Doyle, she merely spared it a glance and rushed on.

As she came within sight of the grand house, she stopped and tried to compose herself. From that distance, she could see the Doyles' phaeton in the drive and Mrs. Doyle's back as the latter ascended the front steps and rang the bell.

"No!" she said to herself, breaking again into a run. But the door was already swinging open, the butler stood there a moment, Mrs. Doyle was walking in, the door was shut, and Mr. Kensington's chances disappeared with her.

Tears welled in her eyes yet again, blurring the beautiful garden beds and lime trees lining the drive that she might otherwise have admired. She was too late, and now her chances of happiness, so lately offered again, seemed dismal indeed. She stood there holding back sobs, trying to catch her breath, and thinking about what might come next.

"Miss Eastwood?" said a voice behind her, and Clara swiped at her eyes before turning around, for she had felt a few tears fall regardless of her efforts.

Miss Kensington stood in the drive with Oliver at her side. They seemed to have been walking in the gardens to Clara's left and come back out through a gap in the trees.

"Miss Kensington," said Clara. She knew she could not conceal her distress. She tried feebly to think of a reason why she would be at Haythorne.

"Forgive me, but are you quite well?" asked Miss Kensington. "Can I assist you in any way?"

Clara felt tears begin again. "I—I am sorry, but I have just received some distressing news," she said. Should she tell the other the truth, and be the bearer of news that would be the Kensingtons' downfall? Should she trust Miss Kensington with the knowledge that her family's deceit would soon be known?

Her decision lay in determining whether the Kensingtons had concealed Oliver's parentage out of a desire to further their own interests, or out of compassion for the difficulties that would arise should the truth be known, for both Miss Kensington and

Oliver along with Mrs. Kensington and her son. Were they enemies to be shunned, or simply making the best of their situation and therefore to be pitied, though it was now impossible to befriend them?

Clara, having no reliable guide on this matter but her own impressions of Miss Kensington, chose in a moment to trust the openness and concern for others that she had observed in the other young lady so far. If the family should really be nefarious and draw her into their web of lies, so be it. She knew where her own allegiance lay, no matter how great her disappointment about Mr. Kensington's altered status in the village. No matter how soon the whole family would depart, leaving her behind forever.

"Are you going to the Hall? Would you like to come down to the cottage for a cup of tea first?" asked Miss Kensington. "Perhaps that would help calm you. It is all a bit chaotic down there, but I think we can manage tea."

Clara said, "Thank you, yes. That would be very agreeable. In fact, this distressing news concerns your own family"—she dared not say more in Oliver's presence, having no idea what his family had already told him about his parentage—"and I would like to discuss it with you first."

Miss Kensington's face changed, becoming infused with grim resignation. "I see," she said, as the ladies turned away from Haythorne and began walking back down the drive. "Was this news related to my family's history?"

"Yes," said Clara. "And the reason for which your brother was released from his previous employment. I am afraid Mrs. Doyle has a sister living in Albrighton."

Miss Kensington sighed. "How unlucky," was all she said until they reached the cottage.

The stone house, small but well-built, had just four rooms below-stairs, the sitting-room nearly furnished but the kitchen and study still in a confusion of packing crates, trunks, and stray dining chairs that had not yet found their way to the kitchen. A maid and cook stood in the kitchen trying to order the cooking supplies as the ladies walked in.

"Molly," said Miss Kensington to the maid, "will you take Oliver up to his room and begin organizing his clothes? I fear it is still a terrible jumble up there, but the sooner we all begin staying here, the better."

When the two had left, Miss Kensington turned to the cook. "Mrs. Gregory, might we have a little tea in the sitting-room?"

The two ladies went through the passage and to the sitting room at the back of the cottage. Despite her distress and her confusion about the next proper action to take, Clara could not help observing the room with a good deal more curiosity than she might have been otherwise inclined to feel, if it had not been connected to Mr. Kensington. The parlor was of a good size and situation, positioned to capture the southern sunshine, and the windows looked out over a little swale that fell away from the house and then rose up again into a little hillside with hawthorn and sloe trees growing here and there upon it. She knew that just on the other side of that hill was her grandparents' estate.

The room itself was very comfortably appointed, with a small pianoforte in the corner near a window, large shelves for the family's books (which were not yet unpacked—crates of them still lay on the floor nearby), an ample hearth and chairs grouped around it. An elegant green paper enveloped the walls where the polished wood paneling ended, and a roomy writing desk was tucked into another corner near a window. A table currently pushed against the wall could be drawn out for card playing, Clara guessed.

In short, it was a room in which the members of the family could find occupation for themselves with enough comfort and space to do so. The miserable thought that ran through her mind now upon seeing it was that of this, perhaps, she might have been mistress.

"What a lovely room," she said as the tea things arrived. "Did your brother arrange it so?"

"Yes," said Miss Kensington. "My mother selected the paper for the walls, and the furniture of course is all her own, but Henry had new glass fitted in the windows, restored the paneling which was in very bad condition, and asked that everything be arranged as you see."

"I see," said Clara.

They were silent a moment.

"Miss Eastwood, it would be dishonest of me to pretend that I do not know what this news from Albrighton contains. I thank you for your discretion in front of my son" she said the words as naturally as if she had always referred to Oliver as such, "but since you clearly already are aware of this information yourself, you may be open with me. I hope you will allow me some openness in return."

"All right," said Clara, glad to be allowed to voice some of her feelings. "I confess that I feel betrayed by the way your family has presented itself to the village. The acquaintance I have begun with your brother, one that I very much hoped to have honesty and truth at its core, has been sullied forever by this matter."

"I do not blame you for your feelings," said Miss Kensington without a hint of distress. "I ask you only to consider what our own have been—I refer to myself and Henry, for as you may have gathered, our mother is seldom prone to the delicate feelings others experience. Henry, of course, was ashamed of my conduct when he learned of my secret, and rightfully so. But you may imagine what fate would have awaited me had he turned me out of the house. At this moment I imagine I would be working long, wearying hours as a seamstress or a laundress or worse. Should my child take ill, who would care for him? How would I pay for an apothecary to see him?

"My father, as my mother may have alluded, was so uncommonly generous that his fortune was nearly exhausted by his various good works. We always had faith in Henry to support us, and my mother maintained our household purse growing up, so we never worried about being penniless. I also expected to be married one day, of course, to someone who need not marry an heiress but would be content with my family's good name and reputation. You may have surmised, however, that that was never an option for Oliver's father and me. Though there may have been ways to force him to marry me, I found myself unwilling to unite myself to him when he was coerced so. I wished for my hand to be sought after, not a burden reluctantly taken on—a pride that time has eroded away, and I confess that there have been times that I have regretted it.

"Our residence with Mother and Henry has been our only option. As you might imagine, living with such a mother has not always been pleasant. But what mean and pitiful lodgings would I have found for us as an unmarried woman with a child? What future could my son have had, without income, education, or security? Miss Eastwood, I beg you to think of your own feelings if such a thing had happened to you, or to your own sister. One mistake does not erase the affection between siblings that builds up over a lifetime. We saw no way for our family to remain respectable without falsehoods."

Although these were the thoughts that had run through Clara's mind, and she saw the truth in them, she was still sorely disappointed that when the time had come for Mr. Kensington might have chosen to tell her the truth, he had instead chosen to deceive her as well as everyone else. And she could not help feeling that Miss Kensington must have behaved very badly to have ended up in this situation, though she would never have told the other so.

"I am sorry I could not prevent the letter from arriving at Haythorne," said Clara. "That is why I came—to try and dissuade Mrs. Doyle from revealing it somehow."

"Thank you for trying," said Miss Kensington. "Especially when you were in such distress—that was very quick thinking on your part."

They sat a moment more. Clara examined the pattern on the china cup in her lap. It was some fanciful willow that had somehow managed to sprout traditional petaled flowers, clearly violating reality. She looked up again. "What do you suppose will happen now?"

Miss Kensington sighed. "I would imagine Lord Chesterson will summon Henry as soon as he is back from Birmingham. Then we will decide what is to be done. Oh, Mama will probably be turned out from the big house—I must hurry Molly along in preparing her bedroom here. And I would imagine we will be forced to repeat the departure that we took from Albrighton. Eventually I expect we will run out of country shires to flee to. What a shame that the carpets had just been laid." She looked around the room matter-of-factly.

At hearing her worst fear of the Kensingtons' departure uttered, Clara felt tears threatening to spill over again. Her happiness, so painless to acquire, requiring only that she look over a hedge one fine autumn day—an act exactly in keeping with her wishes—now was dreadfully difficult to let go of.

"I am so sorry to hear that," she choked out, "and I am very sorry to have been the bearer of this news to you." She stood now, feeling despair beginning to set in and wishing to take her leave to grapple with it privately.

"You are blameless," said Miss Kensington, rising also. "I will tell Henry how much you tried to do in our aid. He will be very grateful."

Clara numbly took her leave and walked out of the house, dodging a pair of workmen hauling a wardrobe up the steps. She wondered if they would soon be asked to bring it out again. As she was walking away down the drive, she could see Mrs. Kensington behind her, going toward the cottage. The news must have reached Lord Chesterton. She felt ill and hurried home.

At Yewspring she found a letter waiting for her in her bedroom—Fiona must have brought it upstairs for her. As soon as she picked it up, she felt her stomach sink, for the writing on the front was her own.

Mr. Sowerby's letter had been returned to her, unopened and unread. On the front next to the address was written, *Refused by recipient.*

It fell from Clara's hand to the floor as she took to her bed.

CHAPTER THIRTEEN

Three days later, the Eastwood women sat at breakfast with Violet. Mr. Eastwood was already out of the house, have ridden over to Beechview early that morning. He had knocked on Clara's bedroom door the night before and asked if she wanted to come see the fine set of twins that one of the ewes had had, but Clara had not felt equal to meeting with anyone yet, and she knew her father would want to go to the house. She could only imagine what her grandmother would have to say about the Kensingtons' disgrace. News of it had spread across the neighborhood like water spilled onto a carpet, slowly seeping outward as it became known from household to household, no doubt aided by the circulation of servants. It was never the reason someone called, never the express purpose of stopping a neighbor in the lane, but the casualness with which it was worked into the conversation did not hamper the speed of its journey. Clara felt sure that everyone knew by now, down to the last shepherd and milkmaid.

"Clara, Clara, you must rally," said her mother with an impatient glance at her, shuffling through the morning's letters. "You look quite done in—your complexion is not aided by pining, you look quite peaked. Rose, dear, let your sister borrow some of the Virgin's Milk you just bought. All of you must appear to your best advantage when we go to town. Oh, but Violet, you needn't fret about *your* skin, dear. Your freckles are hardly noticeable, and anyway some gentlemen prefer them."

Clara could not stay to hear any more—her nerves had been rubbed raw, heightened by the knowledge that she was about to be whisked off to town entirely against her wishes. The outdoors were her only refuge, since there was no ceaseless talk of London or brisk urging her to regain her spirits, and so she fled there now, saying over her shoulder, "Please excuse me, Mama." She was down the passage and out the door without even taking her bonnet from the hall.

She could not bear to be seen, nor look on fields or cows or crops without thinking of Mr. Kensington, and so she went down the sloping lawns, across the footbridge, and up into the woods. The patter of rain picked up around her as she went, coming down through the bare branches of beech and elm until she had reached the yews, their needled canopies sheltering her. She walked uphill until she reached the top of a ridge, then walked along it trying to notice only the scuffing of her feet, the little splashes of raindrops falling around her, and the woodland plants beginning to form drifts of green in the understory. But her thoughts would wander and trace the paths they had already traveled incessantly over the past days. *How will I recover from this?* she wondered. *How can I ever be happy, when I know he will be gone in a fortnight and I shall never see him again? What fate will they have? And what fate will I have, when I had thought he might have been my future?*

And then, behind her, she heard a voice calling, "Miss Eastwood! Miss Eastwood!"

She turned and saw him, astride a fine chestnut gelding, coming along the ridge toward her. When he reached her, he swung down from the saddle and was already saying, "Miss Eastwood, I will go away at once if you wish it. I should not even presume to speak to you, but I wished to fulfill my promise to you."

She was so flustered she hardly knew how to answer him. "I—am glad to meet with you, Mr. Kensington—how fortunate! What promise do you speak of?"

He reached up into his saddlebag and took out a paper-wrapped parcel. "I had the opportunity of obtaining the flora we spoke of. The events of the past few days have taken nearly everything from me—my occupation, my family's respectability, our security. But my word I still have, and though no one in Exton believes me a gentleman, I hope to be one until my last breath. And so—I wish to give this to you." He held it out to her, grief and hope mingled in his face.

She stepped closer, took the parcel from his hand, and said, with a voice nearly broken with emotion, "Thank you. I accept it wholeheartedly, and gratefully."

He turned to mount his horse again, but she reached out a hand, suddenly aware that she was ungloved, without a bonnet, and wore only her gown without even a shawl. Her hand was red with cold, but she had not noticed until she stopped walking. "Please," she said to him, "if you have a moment to spare, I would welcome the chance to speak with you, since we—perhaps may not have that opportunity often."

He turned and stood, looking at her intently. "You may rebuke and chastise me all you like, if that is what you wish to say. I have deceived you and your family most abominably."

"No, far from it. I wish to say that my only regret on hearing of your family's past is that its knowledge in the village must take you all away from Exton. And I regret that I now have little reason to remain in the country, or any reason that my family will allow. Your sister's shame—well, I do not implicate you in it. And," she added, "I believe—at least, I have read that in such cases of illegitimacy, the father must be to blame as much as the mother. He has left her to bear this burden alone." She did not say that the only cases she had heard of had been in newspaper reports and novels. She also did not say that she felt, more than she would admit, that Miss Kensington must have been at fault in some way. This was England, not the pages of a sordid story. Men did not simply violate respectable girls against their wishes. She barely registered these doubts before brushing them away like dust off a box tucked away in some forgotten shelf, eager to get at what was inside. The brother stood before her now, and she could spare only a passing thought for the sister.

Mr. Kensington said, his eyebrows raising in surprise, "But— we are not to leave Exton."

She was astonished. "Oh? But I thought that you must wish to find work elsewhere."

"I have been offered work here," he said. "Lord Chesterton released me as his agent, it is true. But he offered to let me stay on and work at Haythorne as a laborer for as long as I wish. And he has allowed us to retain the cottage, though heaven knows how long we'll be able to afford the rent."

Clara could not help looking at him with an expression that must have verged on a very unladylike gawking. "You will degrade yourself so by accepting—such a lowly position? Forgive me, but your talents must be wasted in such a role. What a loss to someone who could have employed you, and benefited from your service! It would have been more just for Lord Chesterton to release you entirely."

"You are kind," he said, "and I will acknowledge that my dignity has been grievously injured by such an arrangement. I did not realize how much pride I had before I was faced with the prospect of relinquishing everything I had worked and hoped for. I did not realize how much I thought of myself as being above those I worked for, how much I valued my education, my knowledge! And comfort, of course, is a gift I am sure I will look back on longingly. There are many trials ahead, I think, and I am sure there will be times when I feel unequal to meeting them."

"Perhaps it is not too late to ask Lord Chesterton to change his mind—" Perhaps Clara could convince her father to let Mr. Graham go and hire Mr. Kensington instead. If he was released from Haythorne, he could go where he liked. But she knew at once that her father—anxious to preserve the reputation of both the Eastwood estates—would not place someone with an outwardly tainted reputation in such a place of prominence.

"Miss Eastwood, it was *my* request to stay on at Haythorne. Lord Chesterton would have released me."

Now Clara could not imagine what else he could say to astound her. Who would volunteer for such a degrading condition? "Whyever for?"

He met her eye. He took a step forward, and suddenly she felt how close he was, his broad shoulders less than an outstretched arms-length away.

"Because *you* are here," he said. "And therefore I have no wish to leave."

She drew in a sharp, sudden breath. "Mr. Kensington, I—"

He held up a hand. "We do not need to speak of it. I ask nothing from you. I understand, I believe, the circumstances under which you are placed. I understand that you must act, when the time comes to choose a husband, in your sister's interests as well as your own. I do not ask for any promise from you. I am only sorry to not be able to address you as I would have liked. But if I might be permitted to be in your presence, as long as you grace Exton with it, if I might just but see you now and again, to speak with you, it would be enough for me."

She was forced to look away for a moment to compose herself, and then looked back at him. "I am pleased that our feelings are so aligned," she said, "though I do not know whether that admission will give you pleasure or pain, since we are powerless to change our circumstances."

"Oh," he said, and she saw him draw in an intake of breath, then let it out again, "it brings pleasure, I assure you. It brings comfort. Your feelings honor me more than I can express."

She was aware of how long they had been standing here, aware of how it would look if they were discovered, and aware that Mr. Kensington stood on Yewspring land when Mr. Graham or her father could forbid his presence there. Every feeling in her longed to stay, to speak, to touch, but she knew she could not regard her feelings now.

"I wish I could stay longer," she said, "but I do not think it would be wise for us to be found here. I hope you will trust that my feelings are as constant and as fervent as yours, that our wishes are the same—come what may. I regret to say that I must go to town in just over a fortnight and will be away perhaps for the whole summer."

"You will come back if you are engaged?"

"Oh, yes. The only point of town is to make a match. And the only point of making a match is for Rose."

"Then I will pray both for and against your engagement," he said. "I am not sure which sentiment will triumph."

"I wish I could write to you," she said.

"As do I. But we had better not—if your family should find out, and I do not see how it could be kept from them indefinitely, no matter how trustworthy your servants might be, there would no doubt be painful consequences for you. I cannot wish that."

And now, too soon, he was up on the horse and tipped his hat to her. "I wish you a good day, Miss Eastwood. Know that our meeting has strengthened me more than I could have hoped.

And know that I wish for your happiness, most fervently."

He nudged the horse, and took off at a trot, and Clara went back toward Yewspring. She had taken only a few steps before she could not resist unwrapping the book from its paper, and ran her hands over the forest-green cover and golden titling of *Harrington's Flora of South-west England*. When she opened the front cover, there was a sealed note tucked inside, and she could not help gasping a little at her name written in his writing. She knew it was the last time she would ever see it.

She turned the note over and broke the seal (a very handsome HK in deep red).

March 15

Butler Cottage

Miss Eastwood,

You have in your hands the closest flora to this area that I could find, as promised. I hope it proves useful in your study of botanical illustration, and I hope to see your name on a volume of your own someday. It may interest you to know that I could not find a flora of the Midlands at Gardiner's Bookshop in Birmingham, and the proprietor told me he did not believe any such book existed.

Though I know we can never meet again, please know of my prayers and fervent hopes for your happiness and health.

Most sincerely,

Henry Kensington

***

If Clara had not been in love with Mr. Kensington before she left the house—which she had been, of course—that letter would have decided the matter and she would have returned to Yewspring with a heart entirely his. His unselfish concern for his sister, the unselfish concern for her he had expressed on the page, and in their conversation would have compelled her had she needed compelling. Now that the possibility of being courted by him had been taken away, she regretted it all the more.

The Eastwood households at both Yewspring and Beechview now turned their energies toward journeying to town. Clara's grandmother had long been uneasy with the idea that her children and grandchildren ran amok in London without her supervision, afraid that they were attending the wrong churches, wasting their allowances on the races and piquet, and engaging their daughters off to blacksmiths and fishmongers. And so she and Sir Eastwood were to remove to town with Clara's family and take their usual lodging just around the corner from their son's long-standing lodging in Southampton Street.

Before they all left, Clara had to try again to retrieve her copy of Priscilla Wakefield's book from Miss Holt, having heard nothing from the other about it. After yet another lesson in which Clara had sat drawing a bouquet of hothouse roses that she herself had brought from Yewspring, Miss Holt had said she and the maid were still looking for the book. Clara had been especially relieved to tell the other that she would be removing to town soon and they would have to discontinue their lessons, feeling a stab of guilt at the pinched, worried look that came over Miss Holt's face. The other had only been able to serve her pupil tea and a meagre cake split in two, and Clara knew the income, small as it was, would be missed. But there was nothing for it. She would have stayed if she could, although the lessons would have had to improve drastically for her to continue paying the other.

Clara went and called one day close to the family's departure, and Matilda admitted her after saying in a whisper, "You've come about the book, haven't you, Miss Eastwood? No matter what mistress says, I haven't seen it. Never did see it. You must believe me, for remember I served your grandmama for many years until my eyes started to go—" She resumed her normal voice and led Clara down the hall, saying, "I'll just see if she's in" and leaving Clara at the parlor door while she went on ahead.

Presently Clara was let in, and as soon as Matilda had left, Miss Holt said peevishly, "I've told Matilda time and time again that she must have mislaid your book, for I put it down one day and haven't seen it since. Right there, it was." She pointed to a small table next to the settee on which she sat. "Servants are so underhand sometimes. Matilda is better than the last maid I had, but her eyes are going and I think she must pocket things sometimes. But as you know, your grandmother recommended her and I was grateful for her assistance, and so here we are. I shall endeavor to keep looking, Miss Eastwood, but I am afraid that it may be gone for good. I *am* sorry. But perhaps you can find another copy."

Clara frowned and had to grit her teeth for a moment until she could be polite. "But I'd taken notes in that copy—what a shame." She reached into her reticule and pulled out a few shillings. "Perhaps, if you find it, you would be so good as to send it to me. Our number in town is 9 Southampton Street." She put the coins on the table next to her chair, and rose to go. She could not stand one more minute with this woman, who was clearly lying. But Clara could not accuse her without proof, and there was none.

"When do you all go to town?" asked Miss Holt as she led Clara out to the passage and then the hall door that let her out to the staircase.

"On Monday," said Clara. "My grandparents go as well."

"Oh, how lovely! When you are back please do call and tell me all about it. Is it much like Coventry, but on a vaster plane? Do you really hear French in the streets, and Latin? Do the Catholics' churches really smell like incense from the street? They say there are spices for sale in every corner market and a yard of silk goes for a shilling if you can find the right vendor. Is it true? Oh—but I hear the church bell now. I must not keep you, but do call when you return, Miss Eastwood."

Clara was glad not to have to make up praises of town that she did not really feel, and gladder still to escape from Miss Holt's company. She went out the street door and stood for a moment in front of the Reeds' shop. She needed more candles, of course. She was down to her last stub, and it would not last until they left for town. She went in to the shop.

Mr. Reed hailed her from the back room as she was paying for the candles. "Do you have a moment, Miss Eastwood?" he asked.

"Of course," she said, and Mrs. Reed unlatched the half-door to let her through to the back.

Mr. Reed went to his desk and pulled out a book. Even from several paces away, Clara knew at once that it was hers. And she knew what must have happened.

"Miss Holt came in one day and said she wished to sell this," he said, holding it out to her. "But I think it belongs to you."

She took it, feeling as though she was being reunited with a dear friend, and said, "Yes, it does."

"I agreed to buy it without looking at it closely. In fact, I even thought of you, Miss Eastwood, as someone who might like to see it. I know you always enjoy the flower pressings we get in. But after a few days I noticed that a piece of paper had been glued over someone's name on the cover and started to unpeel, and what do I find but your own name written on the inside."

Clara gasped and opened the book. There was indeed a torn spot near her name where the paper must have been.

"Well, I thought there'd been some kind of

misunderstanding, so I went up to Miss Holt's to ask her if she was sure she wanted to sell it, not knowing if you'd given her the book or not. She told me again that she did mean to sell it to the shop, seemed quite put out by my asking, in fact. I'd already paid her what she was asking, so there was nothing I could do, but it made me mighty uneasy. Forgive me, but I know she lives on but a pittance, so I didn't press the matter with her. I just wanted to restore the book to you if you wished, and to urge you to be discrete about this—mishap. We must pity her, you know, and treat her kindly if we can."

Clara was not as inclined to pity and kindness as the shop-keeper, but bit her tongue and said, "Thank you for telling me. And thank you for returning the book—I have missed it."

"Quite advanced, that botany business, isn't it?" asked Mr. Reed as he led Clara back to the front of the store. "I paged through it a bit and could hardly attend to what the author, whoever he is, meant by it all. But then I suppose I'd have to start from the beginning to understand it. Who knew flowers were so complicated?"

The London-bound party stayed at Dunstable overnight, descending from the carriages at the Sugar Loaf Inn in a bustle of bags, trunks, hat-boxes, and reticules, the ladies smoothing the wrinkles from their skirts and the maids already passing to and fro to prepare the rooms. Clara looked up at the brick building with its rows of windows facing the busy street and already felt a sense of oppressive public-ness that she felt sure would continue in London. How could she bear this shock and sorrow amid the crowds passing on the pavements, the rattle of carriages in the streets just outside the Southampton house, and the conversations, music, and callers that would fill the rooms within? How could she sit in a theater and watch a play, surrounded by ease and finery, when she knew Mr. Kensington was living a life of toil, of degradation, of want? And when his decision to lower himself had been so connected to herself? She felt she could not be easy until the disparity between them was lessened. She longed for the quiet country, though she knew it would not have been a joyful place to be.

Supper at the inn was the typical on-the-road-to-London affair: the food forgettable, the private dining room engaged for the party as claustrophobic as the carriages had been, and the fire too warm in spite of the windows being thrown open, making the back of Clara's gown stick to her shoulders. The party ate quickly and made for their rooms, the other young ladies eager to make an early start the next morning. Clara went to bed as well but saw much of the night sky passing slowly overhead that night through the inn's window, thinking of all that she had learned. Now that the Kensingtons would remain in Exton, going to town felt especially bleak. Unless she could use the time to try and be more profitable to them, for she was determined now to help not just her sister but any of the Kensingtons that she could, for any aid to them was an aid to him. To ensure that her endlessly spinning thoughts ceased their motion for the night, she reached for a candle, lit it, and took her journal from the pile of books by the bed.

April 2 (or rather, early on April 3, but I have not slept yet)

I am determined to pursue any course that will let me aid or comfort him—and I cannot do so here, as I am. As a wife, though not his, perhaps I can. I will have connections, income, and leisure to use them. I will do everything in my power to obtain what is for his good, whether it is a position, a new coat, or money to pay a doctor when he needs one, or Oliver's school fees.

Or, if no man will have me, surely drawings such as mine are needed, by someone. Surely they are worth something. And London must be the place where I find out if they are, where I find out if I must sell my heart if my skills are worth nothing.

But no matter how it is accomplished, through marriage or through my pencils, as long as I draw breath and have any of my faculties, he shall not want for anything.

CHAPTER FOURTEEN

Clara walked down Fitzroy Street while the London carriages went back and forth to her right, her cousin Harry trailing behind her on the pavement. She turned and waited for him to catch up as they approached the great house standing and staring down at its little park.

"Clara, must we go to the psychic garden again?" Harry grumbled as they stopped at the corner to wait for a coach to pass. "I was hoping to stop in at the club. I haven't had a proper game of billiards in days."

Harry had been appropriated by the young ladies as an escort and guide when their mothers could not oblige them. Indeed, the family matrons were enjoying London so much that they found themselves unable to chaperone their daughters as much as they anticipated. However, the cousins quickly divvied up Harry's time to each claim a half day of his week for him to escort them on their walks and shopping. If he had noticed that he seemed to be claimed by Violet every Wednesday afternoon and Rose on Thursdays, he had not indicated so. The girls gave him Sunday off, in respect for the day of rest.

"We're *not* going to the physic garden again," said Clara.

"Well, wherever we're going, it's too far from the house for us to be walking there endlessly," Harry continued. "It's positively ungentlemanly for me to be walking about the streets for miles on end rather than taking a carriage. Someone might see me!"

"It's just two miles," said Clara, gritting her teeth. She herself could walk there and back again without fatigue. It was not her fault Harry insisted on lounging about the club rather than keeping himself in some kind of physical condition by fencing at Angelo's or boxing at Gentleman Jackson's. The horses had even been brought down from the country so that the family could ride in Hyde Park, so as far as she was concerned Harry had no one but himself to blame for his fatigue. Still, she had to keep him in high spirits. She could not walk so far alone, nor spare the money for a carriage, and knew better than to ask that the family's curricle be loaned to her for such a purpose.

"You seek *employment?*" she could almost hear her mother say. "Why not just burn Yewspring down since you are determined to soil our family's name?"

She said cheerily to Harry, "I've brought you a bag of toffees from Gunter's and the latest *Morning Post* from Grandmother's library. You can sit outside in this lovely sunshine while I'm at my appointment." Her cousin brightened at this prospect.

Strictly speaking, she did not have an appointment with Mr. Sowerby, a conversation with whom was the object of her errand. She had written again when she got to town six weeks ago, but had not heard a reply, although this time her letter had not been returned. Though she had known that it was unlikely that the esteemed botanist would interview her regarding her work, she had at least hoped for the courtesy of a polite refusal by letter.

After getting to London, she had circled on her map places in the city where a botanist might frequent, whether as an instructor to the pupils in the city's botanical gardens or colleges, or for their own study. She had already taken Harry to Chelsea to walk about the garden there, peering anxiously at each gentle-man—most of those who seriously studied the plants there were male—in hopes that he might be Sowerby, or another botanist who might know where she could find him. The ladies at the gardens seemed more intent on conversing with one another beneath their parasols than on taking note of the plants, though she supposed that no one had ever suggested that they do more than vaguely admire the flowers in between rounds of gossip. So far she had not been successful in finding anyone who knew about Sowerby, and decided to try the London Botanic Garden in Belgravia, their destination today.

After entering it through the brick archway off Sloane Street, Clara left Harry on a bench at one end of the garden's long avenue where he could see her, then walked off in her quest. An hour passed while she anxiously peered out from the brim of her bonnet at the gentlemen who passed by. None carried notebooks or sketching easels, none consulted a flora while they looked at the flowers, and the only person who carried anything more substantial than a walking stick was the stout gardener who carted wheelbarrow-loads of manure to and fro. Finally, seeing that the afternoon was growing late, Clara approached this man, knowing that she would likely not be able to return to the garden if he thought her approach unladylike, but having no other choice.

Indeed, the man looked at her askance when she came up.

"Might I inquire whether Mr. Sowerby frequents this garden?" she asked timidly. "I—I would like to ask him about something."

He kept looking at her up and down. She was glad she had dressed with a bit more care and attempted to stuff her wayward wisps of hair tidily under her bonnet—now she would surely not look like someone of *terribly* ill repute, though she had breached etiquette entirely by approaching the gardener.

"Who wants to know?" he asked finally, wiping his hands on his jerkin.

"I do," said Clara.

He raised his eyebrows. "And why, if I might ask, miss, would you want to know Mr. Sowerby's whereabouts?"

"I wish—I wish to ask him about a letter I wrote him," she said, after a moment of hesitation.

"Well, I can't quite recall whether or not I've seen him here," the gardener said, leaning on the shovel he had been carrying with him. "I might have time to stop and think if I weren't so worried about my little son—poor chap, he's just three and terrible ill with the croup just now. I've had to take on extra work here to pay for the medicine—"

Now Clara understood where he had been going with this interlude. Clenching her jaw and ruefully tallying up the cost of this hitherto unsuccessful mission, she reached into her reticule and pulled out a sixpence. She tried to be charitable and assume the man's story was true. She made herself think of Oliver and how Mr. Kensington might one day be obliged to take on such worries about his health as she handed the coin over. It was the only means by which she could breathe onto her lately dormant sense of generosity to cause it to burst into flame.

The man bowed to her and pocketed the sixpence, saying, "Now Mr. Sowerby doesn't come here often, miss. In fact, I believe he's out of the city for the summer, staying in Dover to study fossils. But if you want to find his friend Mr. Wick— who's an accomplished botanist himself, if you'd like to speak to him—you're likely to have better luck trying the Duke of Marlborough's house, near the Palace. Wick and the Duke are good friends, so my friend Bert tells me—for he's the gardener there at Marlborough. You're welcome to try there at the west service entrance, miss, and tell old Bertie hello from his pal Nick."

"Thank you, sir," she said, and nearly ran back up the path to the bench where Harry was waiting. She tugged his arm and continued her rapid pace toward the gate out of the garden. Luckily his mouth was too full of his last piece of toffee to protest.

Soon they were traversing The Mall with the grandeur of the Palace behind them—Clara could not help but be awed by its splendor even amidst her preoccupation, but she longed for Yewspring's familiar, comforting quiet and for the time in which she had thought she might one day become Mrs. Kensington. She knew now that the path ahead of her, though flocked with smartly dressed Londoners, did not lead her back there. The only way was forward.

"One more stop," she told Harry, and they turned up Marlborough Road to the west service gate, set deep in an archway of red brick. She reached up and rang the bell, nervously twisting her reticule in her hands.

The gate swung open, and an undergardener stood there, a scrawny lad of about fourteen. When she saw him, Clara felt less out of place, less timid than she had. After all, she knew boys like him in Exton, their brows reddened with sun and their thin backs bent over the fields.

"I'm looking for Bert," she said.

About a week later, Clara feigned a cough at breakfast to be excused from accompanying the others on their walk in Hyde Park. Her mother scarcely spared her an absentminded "All right, dear," at this announcement, for Mr. Creston was certain to be in the Park and Rose had selected what Mrs. Eastwood considered a most unbecoming gown. The family had seen the Crestons often since coming to town, but Mr. Creston had not paid any attentions toward Rose that had caused Mrs. Eastwood's hopes to soar as she had hoped. In fact, Miss Creston had mentioned the day before that a young Miss Ridley had been spending time with their family, and Mrs. Eastwood had discovered that this unwelcome intruder to Rose's territory was in possession of three thousand a year. She therefore went out of the breakfast room with her youngest daughter, pleading, "Why not the pink silk we bought last week—"

The words faded as Clara was left in the breakfast room alone. There was no longer any reason to conceal a smile at the thought of what her morning would hold. She crept up to her room amidst the clatter and laughter coming from the other chambers, waited until the others left and all was still, then crept back down the staircase, bonnet in hand, and snuck out of the house, carefully shutting the front door silently behind her. She had dodged any servants that could have attested to her departure from the house, and now stood on the curb, hand raised for a hackney cab. Money was scarce, yes, but she had to get to Marlborough House alone. She carried her best gown with her, carefully wrapped in brown paper.

A quarter of an hour later, she got out at Marlborough House, asked the driver to return in ten minutes—watching the sixpence necessary to obtain such a service pass from her hand to the cabbie's with resignation and regret—and again rang the bell on the gate at the service entrance. She asked the undergardener, a different one who was doing his best to grow his first beard (with varying degrees of success depending on which region of his face one chose to focus attention), for Bert. This time she was admitted at once, and led to the hothouse. As before, her mission in coming reigned first in her mind, and she spared hardly a glance for the gardens around her, though she knew they were lovely and their beds bursting with specimens of every kind.

In the shed, Bert—a man with a thick Northern accent and as tall and lean as "his pal Nick" was stout and wide—took the bundle from her and showed her where she would find it con-cealed three days later, tucked behind a tall stack of terra cotta pots.

"'S'pose it isn't very ladylike, but you'll have to change your frock here on the day, Miss Eastwood," he said. "You can have one of the maids stand guard outside while you do."

Clara felt a thrill of daring run through her as she thought of what her mother would say if she knew her daughter would defrock in a garden shed—regardless of whether it was occupied.

Bert handed her another parcel wrapped in brown paper. "Hester seemed about your size, near as I could reckon, so you've got one of her gowns here. Cap and apron too, I believe."

"Thank you," she said.

"Oh, it's no trouble, miss," he said. "Just pleased to encounter a lady who knows a fine garden when she sees it, and if I could I would throw the gates open for erry'one to come in and enjoy. Although—" he coughed a bit into his hand, "—it is a bit incon-venient for Hester to give up her spare gown for a spell—"

She took the hint and gave him four shillings for Hester and two for himself. This was turning out to be quite an expensive enterprise, and she could only hope the end result would recom-pensate her and then some.

The butler informed Clara that her mother was waiting for her in the morning room of the Southampton Street house when she returned, and Clara came in wondering what could have torn Mrs. Eastwood's attention from the Creston saga so agonizingly unfolding.

"Where were you, dear?" asked Mrs. Eastwood. "Is your cough much better?"

"I just went down to the apothecary's," Clara lied. "For some drops to help with the cough, which already seems to be better. But I must keep up my strength, of course, so I thought it prudent to take precautions."

"I do not understand these strange illnesses that you get in town when you are so invariably well in the country," said her mother, "and in this fine weather, too! But why did you not send a servant? We cannot have it said that you were out in the streets alone."

"I—did take a servant," said Clara, hoping her mother would not seek one out to verify this story. "But I thought the fresh air would help, and it did."

"Well, that's all right then. I do agree that you must maintain your health. Especially because of what I am about to tell you."

"Oh?"

"I am most disappointed in your conduct while we have been in town. Your father and I make sacrifices to bring you and Rose to London, you know, and I would appreciate a bit more of an effort on your part in attending events and calls and otherwise expressing an interest in engaging another man. Your father and I have discussed it and we are quite in agreement about this matter. You must attend to it, Clara."

Clara thought her mother was bearing the sacrifice of being in town quite well, but said only, "I am sorry to hear that you are displeased, Mama."

"What explanation can you give me?"

She thought for a moment, knowing she could not give her the full explanation. "Well, I suppose I have not yet felt adequate to participating in the Season after my two disappointments this year."

"Two? I can recall only one," said her mother.

"George's death, of course, and my hopes regarding Mr.

Kensington," she said.

"Hopes that are to have died a swift death. Do they linger still?"

Clara told the second falsehood in the course of the interview. "No. But I do not know that I am quite ready to entertain new ones."

Her mother shifted impatiently in her seat. "I came to tell you that we saw your aunt Harriet on Rotten Row this morning, with Gertrude."

"Oh? I am sorry to have missed them."

"Your aunt said Charles is expected in town any day. His ship landed at Exeter on Tuesday, and he comes by coach to spend the summer here."

Now Clara *was* interested. Should the exhibition scheme not yield the results she hoped for, it would be prudent to have another avenue of security available. Now she supposed there was a reason to appear agreeable, as attractive as she could manage, and most of all to erase any mark of what Mr. Kensington had called "remarkable" from her persona. She could not count on this cousin viewing her unusual traits in such a positive manner.

"Oh, what wonderful news!" she said, deciding to begin at once to cultivate the personality that would be most likely to win her cousin over. "I shall write to aunt Harriet and ask her to call with him when he arrives. I desire to meet our dear cousin most ardently."

Her mother looked slightly panicked. "Pray do not appear *too* ardent, dear. We must remember that he may not share George's inclinations—"

"Yes, of course, but I am still eager to make his acquaintance," said Clara, wishing as she said the words that she were in circumstances that would have permitted her to be indifferent to her cousin. "I hope to see him soon. Was there anything else, Mama?"

Her mother still looked troubled at Clara's sudden interest, and she felt she had perhaps been a bit too heavy-handed in displaying her design.

"No," Mrs. Eastwood said, rising. "But you know, as with George we mustn't put our eggs into a single basket. Can you not try to be agreeable to Mr. Sharpe, that friend of Mr. Reynolds? He will be at the opera tonight. Four children is not so very many, you know. And he has ample funds to hire the governess and nursemaids. You would hardly know they are there."

"I shall try to ascertain if we would be compatible," said Clara, opening the morning room door. She knew already that they would not be, for Mr. Sharpe lived in Cornwall and not at Yewspring—a fact that was enough to disqualify him from her consideration. As long as Butler Cottage in Exton retained its current inhabitants, she had resolved to limit her search for a husband to Exton alone, a most inconvenient fact given that she was forced now to endure in town. But in the meanwhile, this pursuit of Charles's good opinion may secure what she needed, and she was determined to try.

As the household was preparing to go to bed one night, Clara heard a tap at her door and was surprised to see Rose open it at her "come in". Her sister had been ecstatic to be back in town, flitting from shops to the park to the theater, and had hardly stopped for an afternoon at home in Southampton Street. The only times Clara even knew that Rose was in the house was when she could hear her sister filling the spacious drawing-room with music from the pianoforte. Almost invariably, there would be the sound of other female voices from the room as well, and so Clara could not bring herself to go in. Now she was not just avoiding the chatter of young women because she found it silly and tiresome—she could not abide the sound of hope, of possibility, of their silent but nevertheless apparent belief that everything would work out delightfully for them in the end. She had put away such notions herself the moment she had finished reading the letter from Mrs. Doyle's sister. She was not sure whether she marveled at or envied the others' blithe optimism.

"What is it, Rose?" Clara asked from where she sat in bed, setting her Latin primer down in her lap. Her study had slowed frustratingly since coming to town, but despite her fatigue from walking all over town, she was now spending an hour every night on the task, and felt that she was finally improving.

Rose was in her dressing gown and carried her hairbrush with her. She came to the edge of the bed and gestured to her hair. "Will you help me? Lottie has the night off."

"Of course," said Clara, for it had been her task to unplait Rose's hair when they were young. Rose turned and sat on the bed with her back to Clara, and she reached over to begin pulling out the pins and combs that held Rose's red-gold hair in its fashionable chignon.

"Clara, I—received an offer today," Rose said softly, holding out her hand for the pins that Clara placed into her palm.

Clara's hand froze over a pearl comb and she could not help gasping. She had had no idea. "From Mr. Creston?" she asked.

Rose turned and looked at her. "No," she said. "From Mr. Sharpe."

"Mr. Sharpe! I—I cannot believe it! He has certainly spent some time with our family, but I had no idea that he esteemed you so."

"Nor did I," admitted Rose. "He seemed—well, so *old* that I supposed that if he liked anyone it would be—"

"I know," said Clara, finishing her sister's sentence. "Me."

"Because of the years only, not because of your temperaments. He is pleasant enough, to be sure, and the children are darling, but I could not envision you with him. He seems—well, a bit harried about his family at times, and I cannot help thinking that he seeks a mother for them more than a wife for himself. I am not sure it would be an especially *warm* marriage."

"Oh, Rosie, how do you feel about it? What did you answer him?"

"I told him I was honored by his notice and that I wished to consider the offer. I told him I would write tomorrow. He has obviously already talked to Papa and asked his permission. I feel—oh, Clara, I am of so many minds! I do not know which one to attend to. One part of me says that he is a kind man, devoted to his children. He has a lovely house here, and I should dearly love to be its mistress. His age is no very great obstacle, for he is only six-and-thirty—"

"To your twenty!"

"Yes, but it is no great disparity. And that must mean he is wise, and moderate, and can provide me with every comfort. Papa said the dowry agreement between them would leave more for you. Mr. Sharpe would have me for only three thousand instead of five, for he has fifteen thousand himself."

"Rose! You cannot be thinking about my interests in this! I would give you all ten thousand if it were only up to me—"

"Yes, but it's not, is it?" Rose said sadly. "And Papa is trying to be wise, ensuring that we both have money to bring to a match. And in truth, Clara, I am just happy Mr. Sharpe will take me at all." She choked back a sob.

"What is it?" asked Clara, and Rose buried her face in her hands.

"I—I so hoped that Mr. Creston would ask me," she said, in a muffled voice, sniffling. "Even for five thousand instead of ten. I hoped—that *I* would be enough to compensate for the deficit to him. But it seems—" She wiped away tears, sobbing.

Clara reached out and patted her sister's back. "Perhaps Mr. Creston is not free to do as he would wish," she said. "We know so little of the family—Rutland is not a large county, they cannot have much land. Perhaps he must boost their income through marriage."

"Yes, he has made allusions to the necessity that he marry wisely, and Tabitha says they are all quite dependent on him, but they never say what their exact circumstances are, and I cannot very well ask. But—to me, it seems as if he was serious enough about me to propose. We were hardly separated during the Tapleys' picnic, and he has undertaken a study of music so that he might understand it and we can discuss it. I believe he even asked his sisters' music master to give him piano lessons. He said the bench is too low and his knees stick up to his shoulders." Rose laughed and then began to cry again.

The image of tall, stately Mr. Creston laboriously plunking out nursery songs for Rose's sake made Clara smile even as it broke her heart a little more. She reached over and kept working on Rose's hair, which eventually tumbled down the back of her dressing gown in a gleaming coppery sheet.

"Thank you for confiding in me," Clara said. The gesture made her think of their time together at Yewspring, when she was everything to Rose. "But what shall you do?" She was thinking, uncomfortably, about the difference that seven thousand instead of five would make for her and the Kensingtons.

"Oh, I don't know," sniffled Rose, sitting up. "That's why I came. To ask you what you think I should do. What would *you* do?"

Clara would not have had Mr. Sharpe and his four children, the youngest of whom still needed a wet nurse, for all the gold in the world. And she would not have had Rose married to someone she could barely esteem for all those riches either. Mr. Creston could not be deceiving them all when there were so many other ladies in London to whom he could have paid his addresses. Clara believed he was sincerely attached to her sister, and so there was only one answer, the answer Clara wished someone could have given her. She stopped working out the calculations on the return of two thousand pounds prudently invested, and said, "It doesn't matter what I would do, Rose. But it's quite clear to me what *you* should do. Do not settle for Mr. Sharpe, and do not despair that Mr. Creston will not ask you. I feel sure that he wants to, and means to if he can. Keep yourself free for him, Rosie. Keep yourself free."

Rose turned around, smiled through her tears, and hugged her sister. "Thank you, Clara, thank you. I cannot tell you—oh, I am at so much more ease already!"

"Of course," said Clara. "Now turn around so I can brush your hair. And let us think of who might wish to be the next Mrs. Sharpe, so we can introduce her to him and clear our consciences."

Rose giggled, and Clara began to brush out the tangles in her sister's hair.

Hurry up, Charles, she thought, *get yourself to town.*

CHAPTER FIFTEEN

The day of the exhibition dawned cool and cloudy with a brisk wind, but the clouds were high and seemed liable to burn off by noon, when the exhibition was scheduled to begin. At breakfast Clara again feigned a headache, ensuring she would not be missed until at least tea time, and once again snuck out of the house, this time slipping down an alley before hailing a cab, since she was dressed in a maid's uniform and did not wish to be seen by the servants. She wondered why three empty cabs passed her by before realizing that most maids were unlikely to be able to pay the fare, and set off toward Marlborough House with what she hoped was a confident briskness, not the fidgety nerves she actually felt at walking alone through the London streets. A pair of coal porters whistled suggestively at her as they passed with their heavy cart, and one called over his shoulder, "Let's see that pretty smile then, love!"

She lowered her head and walked on, damp palms nervously twisting her skirt.

She reached the service gate, as welcoming and familiar now as Yewspring's front door, and rang, knowing that Edward or Thomas, the other undergardener, would answer. The plan was for Clara to mingle with the other servants at first, then to change into her own gown and slip out to mingle instead with the exhibition guests. She knew without disguising herself she could never have gotten through the front gates, with footmen checking names against a guest list.

She had never felt more like a fish out of water than now,

trying to appear as one who knew which trays on the luncheon tables should be placed where. One of the actual maids, Rebecca, had hissed at her, "For goodness' sake, don't let Mrs. Brown see you put the cucumbers there or she'll realize you're not on staff! One must never end the buffet with a vegetable."

Then Edward was grabbing her arm. "Look," he said, pointing subtly to a pair of gentlemen at the head of a little group of ladies and gentlemen coming up one of the paths, "that's Mr. Wick on the right, and the Marquess himself on the left."

How could this be? She knew the gates had not yet opened, and she had not yet changed into her real frock, nor retrieved the little packet of drawings she had planned to give Mr. Wick. But the chance was too good, the moment too advantageous, for her not to act now.

She had just a hasty moment to size up the men approaching them, a moment that was luckily not long enough for her to lose her willpower—she knew that if she stopped to think, it would be gone as quickly as it had appeared. The men were now close enough that she could hear their feet crunching on the gravel and see the faces of the entourage that followed them—ladies in their finest dresses, young gentlemen vying for the privilege of taking them by the arm, and several distinguished military men with their scarlet coats and clinking chestfuls of medals. The Marquess was a man of about seventy, walking in a stiff, bent-over fashion but still conversing earnestly with his guest.

She stepped forward, knowing that if she waited until a break in the conversation, the men would be far past her on the path.

"Excuse me, Mr. Wick," she said, "might I have a moment of your time?"

The trim middle-aged man beside the Marquess examined her head to toe silently in an agonizingly long moment. It thankfully gave her time to remember why she was breaking every etiquette known to man, as Mr. Kensington's face flashed into her mind, followed by Rose's.

"Who are you, young lady?" Mr. Wick asked. "Has there been some kind of misunderstanding?" He was a man of about fifty whose forehead bore a white band above his deeply tanned face where he must wear a wide-brimmed hat on his expeditions. His fashionable hat, gleaming in the sunlight, could not quite cover it. She wondered if he journeyed around the world on expeditions, if he had crossed the Atlantic in search of exotic specimens. She would have been satisfied with sketching the plants in Yewspring's garden, so long as someone paid her for it.

The Marquess now turned peevishly to a woman who Clara assumed was Mrs. Brown. "What is the meaning of this?" he demanded. "The staff are not to engage the guests!"

Clara gathered her courage, tried to take a deep breath and said in a disappointedly trembling voice, "I—I wondered if you might be so kind as to evaluate my botanical drawings, Mr. Wock. Or if that is not amenable to you, perhaps you might be so kind as to put me in touch with your friend Mr. Soweby—"

Mr. Wick looked at the Marquess in confusion. The Marquess burst out laughing. He chortled for a moment and then said to Mrs. Brown, "Hardly the tone I was expecting for my exhibition, my dear woman, but quite a delightful joke indeed! Your maid has played her part quite admirably! But," he said, sobering, "we must have no more of these hijinks once the guests arrive. We are to present Marlborough and these lovely gardens to their best effect, not that of a circus. A maid making botanical drawings!" he began to chuckle again.

Mrs. Brown, for her part, had been scowling furiously at

Clara, and now said shrilly to the Marquess, "It's no joke of mine, your Lordship, I'm not that daft to be putting impudent maids in your path! I've never seen the girl before this moment—she's not one of my staff!"

The group's heads swiveled toward Clara. She felt herself blush a deep crimson.

Mr. Wick's face was shifting from bemusement to annoyance. "I don't understand what the meaning of this is, young lady," he said. "Perhaps you are thinking of attending the Ladies' Exhibition? Although your station may still preclude you from attending—"

"The Ladies' Exhibition?" she echoed faintly. Oh Lord, had she gone through this misery unnecessarily?

The Marquess was still demanding of Mrs. Brown in a querulous manner who the woman was and how it was that she dared to speak to Mr. Wick. Clara knew from the housekeeper's baffled replies that she didn't have much time.

"The Ladies' Exhibition," Mr. Wick was saying patiently and slowly, as if to a child, "is for those of the feminine sex who find themselves drawn to botanical study. It is an ornament of the highest degree and a pride to their fathers and husbands that they produce such finely delicate drawings. Our exhibitions offer not just scientific improvement for our gentleman scholars but also result in beautiful drawings that grace many a happy home on the mantel-shelf or the wall. My own daughter has produced several fine examples."

Ah, so it was little sketches for the hallway and the margins of letters to one's aunts. At one point that might have done for Clara, but not now.

"Oh, I hope to partake in the exhibition that discusses botanical science, taxonomy, and drawings that are suitable for field guides," she said firmly, finding her courage in repulsion for anything that was merely meant for appearance and nothing more. She wanted the *more* and was ashamed that it had taken her so long to realize it.

The Marquess and Mr. Wick gaped at her, and the faces of the guests behind them bore expressions of puzzlement or disinterest, several of the young gentlemen shifting impatiently from foot to foot as they listened to this exchange, eager to get back to the pavilions where the ale was to be found.

Mr. Wick said, "But you are a servant, and a woman besides. I fear the world of taxonomy—a word that I must confess I am surprised you understand at all—is not one you can occupy. God has ordained that each sex has its sphere, you know, and science is for men. I have never understood why Sowerby encourages his oddities—that Bennet woman, for instance." He turned to the Marquess at this last. The Marquess only shrugged and shook his head.

It was as if someone had strapped an anvil to Clara's back and pushed her forward to watch her stumble, a weight she felt would be hers to bear for the rest of her life.

As if he had not wounded her enough, Mr. Wick continued, "I suggest you examine your behavior at once if you are to retain your position here."

"But—" Clara began.

The Marquess cut her off. "She most certainly *will not* retain her position here! Get yourself gone, woman, before I have the footmen throw you out!"

Clara did not have time to appreciate the irony of losing a position she had never held, as she was taken firmly by the elbow by Mrs. Brown and steered away from the group, back toward the imposing red brick walls of the house. Clara cast a hopeless glance over her shoulder as they went, her eyes filling with tears so she could hardly see the blurred figures behind her.

"I don't know who you are or how you got in here, but you'd best leave and not let us see you again," Mrs. Brown said as they marched toward the service entrance to the house. "The nerve of it! Putting yourself forward in such a way! Your mother—whoever she is—would be ashamed of you, I'm sure of it. And impersonating a maid of this house, too! That's Hester's dress, I'd know it anywhere. I insist that you take it off immediately."

Clara, still weeping and mortified both at such a display of emotion and at the humiliation she had just undergone, was allowed to change into her own gown she had brought. As she emerged from the kitchen, Mrs. Brown snatched the maid's gown from her, no doubt intending to boil the impudence out of it later. She again took Clara's elbow and steered her toward the service gate, still fuming. "After all the trouble I've put into finding good girls! What've I done to deserve this?"

They arrived at the gate, Mrs. Brown thrust her through it, and Clara heard the firm *click* of the latch after the wooden panels swung closed. The sound marked the end of her hopes, the end of her plans. She could not help standing there with her head in her hands and crying a bit more, too much in grief to care that the street sweeper boys were watching her curiously, or to realize that the packet of drawings so carefully selected were still inside Marlborough House's garden shed.

Sunday May 27

9 Southampton Street

~~Henry~~ Mr. Kensington,

I was so embarrassed by what I wrote on the preceding page— and indeed, what transpired in the events I related—that I almost tore it up to preserve my dignity and your good opinion of me.

However, I have decided in the calmer light of this morning that I knew better in my shame and embarrassment yesterday than I might have were my mind calmer and feelings cooler. My account of yesterday—written just after I returned from Marlborough House—is the more honest one, and I cannot withhold any part of myself from you, even the parts of which I am heartily ashamed. Therefore I will let it remain as it is and post it before I lose my courage.

Now that there is no possibility of a further relationship between us, you may rejoice that you need not be attached to a woman capable of such impropriety, such breach of manners. Please forgive my rashness in writing to you—I could not help myself, for I must tell someone of it, and no one here is a fit confidant. And—though you must have thought my behavior most improper and a reflection upon yourself if we had been engaged, I trust that the reproach extended to a friend is less than that of a fiancée, and less upsetting to the recipient of such news.

I understand if you think it best not to reply. The communication of my sorry errand was my only intent with this missive, save for the desire that you know how earnestly I hope, work, and pray for your happiness.

Yours sincerely,

Clara Eastwood

"Miss Eastwood, you have visitors in the drawing room," the butler said when she went down to the hall to deliver her letter. He took the carefully folded and sealed letter from her hand and placed it on the hall table. "A Mrs. Harriet Eastwood, and a Mr. Charles Eastwood."

How keenly she regretted the timing of this crucial visit! She could not help fretting over whether someone would come through the front door as the rest of the family came back from church and happen to see the direction on her letter. Her feelings of embarrassment and longing for Mr. Kensington were heightened at this moment. But there was nothing to be done. She could not keep them waiting.

Pausing before the door to press her cold hands to her flushed cheeks, Clara then went in to the drawing room and was met with a pleasant-looking woman with streaks of gray mingling against the golden hair peeking out beneath her muslin cap, sitting on a settee. She rose as Clara went to her to take her hand in greeting, saying, "Hello, Aunt Harriet."

"Good morning, dear Clara!" the other cried, grasping her hand warmly. "I hope you will forgive the early hour. We went to the early service at St. Paul's and though I knew you might all be at St. Clement's still, I could not resist looking in to see if anyone was home. I simply could not wait to make you acquainted with my Charlie. He's arrived in town only two days ago."

A male voice said, "Cousin Clara," and she turned to find a young man of perhaps one-and-twenty, dressed in the uniform of his regiment, standing near the fire. He was taller than his brother but bore a resemblance to George in his sturdiness, fair coloring with hair that occupied the middle ground between golden and red, and green eyes that stood out from the tan he had acquired from his time overseas. As he came to her, she could see that the sun had brought out freckles across his cheekbones and nose.

"I am so pleased to meet you," he said to her formally, giving her a courtesy.

She returned the gesture. "And I to meet you at last, although of course I wish the circumstances were different—"

"Yes," he said. "I expected to meet you when you came to Reedbridge Hall as its new mistress, not as a result of such sorrowful events."

Glancing at her aunt, she said, "Well, I would never aspire to be Reedbridge's mistress while my aunt was living, but yes—I had hoped to meet you in Kent as your sister-in-law. Please, sit down, and forgive me for forgetting to ask the butler for tea at once. I am a very novice hostess."

"Oh, do not trouble yourself about us, my dear!" said Harriet. "We have achieved our first object in coming already, which was to make your acquaintance. I know London is so full of things to do and places to be—I was not sure at all that you would be here after church, but decided that we had best just stop by and leave our cards, at least, if you were not in. But, here you are!"

"Yes," said Clara, trying without success not to worry about the damning letter in the hall that she had intended to drop safely into the post-box herself. And yet she must focus on the man before her, the one who could unknot all the tangles she had found herself in, if only she could convince him to do so.

"And I asked the butler whether your mama was at home, for I long for her to meet Charlie as well, and your sister! And who knows when we shall have the chance to meet again—it is so very providential that you should be here while I am in town and can introduce you to one another! Charlie must leave again in a month or two, you know. The army has consented to release him from his position, but they wish him to lead the training camps for his regiment this year. He goes to—where, darling, Sandgate? That Shorncliffe encampment? And then they say he may go all about the country—even up to York, I believe. Who knows when we all should have met again once I go back to Kent? Indeed, except for the wedding that we all so happily looked forward to, perhaps another year would have gone by before the two families met again at all! But the butler tells me that everyone else is away at church."

"Yes. But I hope they will return soon, so perhaps you might meet them yet."

"That would be lovely," said Harriet as the butler came in with the tea tray.

"Yes," said Clara. She was listening with only half an ear, watching instead her cousin Charles to see if this errand were his idea or whether it was being forced on him by his parents. He was seated opposite her and studied the teacup in his hand rather than look at her, giving away none of his intentions. Meanwhile, his mother chattered away.

"I must thank your grandmama, dear Clara, for her kind sympathy during George's passing. We certainly never expected a full six weeks from your family! It was most affecting. And I know his death must have affected you in a special way—" she took out a handkerchief and dabbed at her eyes. "But we must all trust in Providence now, and trust as well that our George rests now in peace. The Lord always provides, and always according to our merit!"

"Well, there can be no fearing for George on that score," said Clara, feeling a surge of sympathy for the grieving mother forced to make such cheerful speeches. "He lived a blameless life. We were all determined to mourn him as the close friend and relation that he was, regardless of what the family tree might say. Tell me, aunt, how long will you be in town?"

"Oh, Gertrude and I will stay on until August now," said Mrs. Eastwood. "Of course, it will be quiet until the end of Gertrude's mourning in just a few weeks. Until then, we have just a few little errands to do and several friends to pay calls on, but really we will not begin in earnest until the beginning of July, and then there is only a month before everyone goes to the country. That is why we decided that Gertrude will not come out this year after all—which is a pity, as she's already nineteen, but what could be done? She could not attend so much as a luncheon while in mourning. But we could not resist the chance to meet you."

"Well, it was very kind of you to come all this way for me," said Clara. "Do stay until the others come home. I know they would be sorry to miss you."

Mrs. Eastwood looked as if Clara had offered her a tour of Buckingham Palace. "Of course, my dear! I would be delighted. And in the meantime we can have a nice cozy chat."

Clara was not sure she knew how to have one of those, particularly with a newly-found cousin who seemed determined to stare a pensive hole into the floorboards, but smiled and said, "Indeed. I am sorry that I have not had the opportunity to know your youngest children—but Rose and I have enjoyed Charlotte's company these past seasons."

This last was a bit of a falsehood, for Charlotte had married herself off to a wealthy but insufferably arrogant baron without a thought for whether she cared for or respected him. Rose had luckily not been taken in by this mindset, resolving to find both in her own marriage, and thinking of her sister made Clara especially wish to be agreeable.

"How does she find Hertfordshire?" Clara asked.

"She gets on exceedingly well there, especially with her friends from town coming to visit," said Mrs. Eastwood, "and Mr. T's family is the leading in the county, making her quite content. She is sorry to miss this season, but her mother-in-law insisted on using the family physician when her time comes, and he cannot leave his other patients. I think Charlotte, in turn, will ask to plan on having the next babies in town as we all would have wished, but—it is best to begin one's marriage with deference to one's mother-in-law, I suppose."

Harriet looked stricken at finding herself having uttered the words, and then said hastily, "Of course, there is a great deal of affection between them, which most desirable above all."

Clara knew this was a reference to the fact that Harriet would have been her own mother-in-law if George had lived (and perhaps, still might be, if cousin Charles was at all tolerable), and said, "We all wish Charlotte and Mr. Turner every happiness and are glad they get on so well."

There was a moment of silence. Charles still seemed determined to examine the drawing room's clock, its ceilings, and its fireplace rather than its other occupants.

Annoyed, Clara felt Harriet's eyes on her and said to him, "And how was your journey from abroad, cousin Charles?"

His eyes met hers, finally, and she saw a mask of politeness slide across his face, hiding—what? She would almost say boredom. It was the luxury of a gentleman to be able to express such distaste for pleasantries openly, and she envied him for it as well as resented the effort she must now make to draw him out.

"We hit rough seas coming in to the Channel," he said, with a tone that was almost sullen, "but it was otherwise an uneventful voyage."

"I would imagine your family is glad to have you back," she said, glancing again at Harriet, who beamed at her.

"Yes," Charles said, "I think they are relieved that I am home safely. I know my mother was terrified of losing two heirs in one year." This last was said softly, and at the mention of his mother, his eyes went to Harriet. Clara saw a tenderness there she had not before.

"Yes," said Harriet simply, her eyes shining again. "I prayed you over the seas. I think Vicar Radbourne was quite weary to see me every day in the chapel, for excessive devotion must interfere with the choir rehearsals and church tidying, but I had two tasks of prayer—for George's soul, and for your safety. I could not as a mother have done anything else but haunt the pews."

"Well," Charles said, his eyes still on his mother and not on Clara, "your petitions on my account were successful, at any rate."

Mrs. Eastwood had just opened her mouth again to say something when the butler re-entered with Rose and her parents. The bustle of introductions, the smoothly executed topics of conversation that the other women carried off flawlessly—a trait Clara had never envied until now—prevented the continuation of this rather melancholy conversation. She wondered, as many do who do not possess it, how such loss as Harriet had endured could be masked with such unflagging cheerfulness, thinking of her own reaction in such a situation. And at the same time she wished with all her being to know whether her letter was still sitting out in the hall. To sit and chat now, with Charles so clearly lighting up at the sight of Rose entering the room, was maddening.

Her sister, too, seemed out of sorts but endeavored to hide it by asking Harriet, again, about her daughters, and then by seating herself next to Charles and asking him all about town. The taciturn young man shed his quietness, then, responding to all of Rose's queries with alacrity and charm. He even leaned toward his cousin in his chair, and from the circle where she sat with her parents and Harriet, Clara saw his mother's eyes fall upon the two with a wrinkle of concern between her brows. But amid all the inquiries about the other members of the family, Harriet's design to call upon Lady Eastwood as soon as could be arranged, and discussions of what the week's engagements held for all of them, Charles and Rose's *tête-à-tête* gradually collapsed itself back into the larger group.

The luncheon hour drew near, and as it did so Clara walked Harriet and Charles to the door. Harriet squeezed Clara's hand on the way out, and Clara received a more cordial bow from her cousin than she had expected based on his demeanor when it was just the three of them. Harriet invited Clara to call at any time, and the Eastwood ladies had already invited Harriet and her children to join them at Southampton Street after they went to the theater that Saturday, a prospect Clara could not help but look forward to for her aunt's sake, at least.

Clara was surprised to be summoned back into the drawing room by Rose, who stood in its doorway as Clara came back from the door. Her letter was gone—but when had it been taken away? She could only guess.

Clara was hardly through the doorway, Rose having preceded her back to her seat, when Mr. Eastwood said to his eldest daughter, "Shut the door, Clara."

When they were all seated, Mrs. Eastwood said in a high voice full of emotion, "Clara, Clara, you *thoughtless*, thoughtless creature, I do not know where to begin—"

Her husband cut in. "Clara, is it true you were seen at Marlborough House yesterday, in a deceitful position posing as a servant, accosting a gentleman and a friend of the Duke's?"

Heat crept into Clara's face, and her shame was replaced with a desire to hide her embarrassment. "A servant? What a strange notion—"

Now Rose, who had been glaring at a corner of the room's ceiling, turned to her sister, and Clara was startled by the expression on her face. Rose had often been mystified by Clara yet looked up to her and let herself be guided by her sister. Indeed, Clara had come to rely on bemusement, on affection, on gratitude from Rose. But now her sister's glare had moved from the plasterwork to herself, and Clara realized she had rarely seen her sister angry at her before.

"There's no need to try and deceive *us*, Clara," her sister said coldly. "I had it from Miss Northcott, whose brother Lieutenant Northcott was there with his officers at Marlborough. She described you perfectly, and said you addressed some important scientist about your work—and got thrown out in front of everyone! I've never been more ashamed of you!"

"And if it has gotten this far, it will be all around town by tomorrow," said Mrs. Eastwood. "What *were* you thinking? Do you realize what this could do to Rose's chances? And do you really think Charles would entertain the idea of marrying a woman who had so shamed herself and her family?"

"I was thinking of my own happiness, I suppose," said Clara into her lap. She could not, would not bring the Kensingtons into this. She knew how successful that appeal would be.

"Your own happiness?" cried her mother. "How do such dealings accomplish that? Are you happy being talked of, being ridiculed, being shamed by the entire respectable population of London? What kind of strange, malformed conception of happiness do you hold?"

Clara opened her mouth to speak, but her mother held up a hand. "I do not want to hear it," Mrs. Eastwood said. "I do not want to know why you have made us the object of scandal and disgrace. As far as I am concerned, there is no reason good enough to justify such an approach. You speak of happiness—let me tell you plainly what will bring that to you. A husband. Children. A home. That home may be in the country, should you so choose, since you seem to have such an aversion to town. But you cannot return there on your own. Marry wisely, and you will have everything you desire, even leisure to pursue this silly scribbling that you seem determined to ruin yourself with."

Clara again tried to speak, but now her father stopped her, saying, "Your mother is right, Clara. George's death cast a pall on us all, it is true. But now you must apply yourself to securing your future. The time for mourning is over. For now we have determined to portray the incident at Marlborough as the result of coercion by a shameless friend—whose name we will withhold for delicacy's sake—who wished to play a practical joke on the Duke. It is a hard story to be believed, it is true, but we can think of no other that would satisfy."

"And there are other measures we have decided must be taken," said Mrs. Eastwood grimly. "During this delicate time with Mr. Creston, we cannot risk further scandal. From now on, you will not set foot outside this house without one of us, one of your aunts, or your grandmother accompanying you. Harry has proven to be a most unwise choice as chaperone. Your pocket money relies on this, of course, not to mention your father's pleasure at bestowing any kind of dowry upon you."

"What?" Clara was shocked at this demand, her liberty for coming and going being the only thing that made London at all tolerable. "Am I your daughter, or a prisoner?"

"You have certainly not behaved as I would wish any daughter of mine to do, so it seems you yourself have chosen the latter."

Mr. Eastwood said, "I myself feel that this matter all comes down to inadequate chaperoning in the first place—"

This drew his wife's gaze and her ire. "Well, Robert, since you are so concerned, you can cancel your engagements at the club so that you can accompany Clara or be with her here at the house."

He frowned, and Clara could tell she and Rose were

witnessing the continuation of an argument long concealed behind shut doors. "It is a *mother's* duty to chaperone and guide her daughter. Not her father's. Need I remind you again where your duty lies, what is asked of you by this family that lifted you from poverty? Not in your own amusement. Not solely in Rose's conquest of Mr. Creston. You have rightly pointed out that Clara needs guidance, as she seems to be floundering on her own. So please, attend to the task of guiding her and we will all thank you for it!"

"My duty?" Mrs. Eastwood stood now and was almost shouting at her husband. Clara cast an alarmed glance at Rose, hoping to find some mutual concern, at least, for the harmony between their parents, but her sister was gazing determinedly out the street window. "Do you think I have ever, for one moment of my marriage to you, been unaware of my duties? Do you think I would not have fulfilled each and every expectation that was placed upon me? Do you think I would not prefer to have a son who would support us all, and not be so worried about the girls' matches? Some things are outside of our power, Robert. Do not blame me for them."

Her father continued to glower, and left the room, only saying on his way out, "Clara, whatever your mother decides about your comportment while we remain in town is the final word so far as I am concerned. Do not appeal to me if you find it disagreeable. I must own that I am deeply disappointed in you. I thought you cared more for the reputation of this family than you seem to—at least, in Exton you always behaved as if you did. Protect the name of Eastwood in town as well as you did at Yewspring, my dear. Such motives will not steer you wrong."

The door shut behind him and Clara was left with her mother.

"Rose, you may go as well," said Mrs. Eastwood. "Go and

compose yourself as best you can before we go to the Tapleys' tonight for cards. It will not do for you to be discomfited, my dear."

Rose stood and obeyed her mother, and once the door had closed again, Mrs. Eastwood said, "Since your silly drawing seems to be the root of all this evil, let me declare once and for all that I absolutely forbid any more investment in it. What you do with your leisure time is your own affair, but rest assured you will have very little of it, if I have anything to say. Your calendar is about to be filled, for your own good. We shall be having parties here more often, to welcome Charles and his sister to town, and you will be attending the theater, going to balls, and going out to the races. If you consider this a punishment, though most young ladies would disagree with you, be comforted by the knowledge that you hold the power to end the sentence with your own action—the sooner you secure an offer, the sooner you are married, the sooner you will have the luxury of being able to do as you wish. Husbands are not tyrants, and domestic life allows for a great deal of freedom, you will find. Have you ever seen me at Yewspring for more than three months at a time? Do you not realize that I can come and go as I wish because I am married? If you wish to enjoy these pleasures, I suggest you go upstairs and ready yourself for the Tapleys' card party as well. And wear your new gown."

Mrs. Eastwood rose and left the drawing room, leaving Clara, still reeling, amid the cups and saucers still left from Harriet and Charles's visit. It already seemed a month ago to Clara.

CHAPTER SIXTEEN

The next morning, Clara was determined to regain some semblance of normalcy after the last chaotic few days, and eager for a distraction from worrying whether she should have written to Mr. Kensington. She knew she would wonder, too, whether he would somehow be able to write back, and that the worry would gnaw away at her unless she tried to fill her mind with something else. Her parents' edict of supervising her more carefully, and bringing her out into society more often, served as an effective though unpleasant way of doing so.

And so she rode in Hyde Park with Rose and her cousins after breakfast. Rose of course had encountered Mr. Creston, who seemed very near proposing—or would have been if Clara were safely married and Mr. Eastwood's fortune had been preserved for his younger daughter. And yet Mr. Creston had still scarcely left Rose's side during the ride, and Clara tried to will away the twinges of resentment she felt over her sister being the recipient of such welcome attentions. She distracted herself by seeing how many times Phoebe mentioned Beau Brummell over the course of the morning, apparently holding this gentleman in high esteem. She had gotten to the count of thirteen by the time the young ladies returned to the house. There they were to remain only a few hours before dining with acquaintances and attending a concert that was important especially for Caroline, for Mr. Reynolds had continued in his attentions and was known to have asked her Tapley cousins many of the circumstances of her father's situation. Mr. Morton had come down to town for a fortnight, and everyone anticipated that Mr. Reynolds would use it to his advantage.

Rose dropped the veneer of politeness toward Clara she had assumed while around the others, and upon arriving home went upstairs directly without a word to her. Clara was about to follow when she was called back down the steps by the butler, who gave her a letter that had arrived while she was out.

Her first thought, heart leaping into her mouth, was that Mr. Kensington had replied, but she realized that he could not have even received her letter yet. It might not have even left London. She took the thick packet from the butler and found her name and address written in an unfamiliar hand.

Once in her room, she opened the letter and read:

May 27

Tottenham

Miss Eastwood,

I hope my interference in this matter does not give offense or further add to what I am sure was an embarrassing episode at Marlborough House, but I thought you may like to have your drawings back (you will find them enclosed). However, I do not think the fault of this incident lies with you, as you may be supposing. Rather, I blame the gentlemen involved for being so callous, so unkind, that they could not listen to the pleas of a young girl, servant or not.

But I am getting ahead of myself. My name is Priscilla Wakefield. Unlike the gentlemen who shamed you, I am interested in hearing your story because I myself am a published botanical author (a role I have assumed with no small amount of trouble and resistance from others, let me assure you). Though it is not by any means well-known outside of the schoolroom, you may have encountered my volume entitled An Introduction to Botany. *Remembering my own difficulties in securing a publisher for my work, I consider it my responsibility to further the cause of other women who wish to submit their talents to science, for the world will usually dissuade them from doing so.*

I attended the exhibition yesterday at Marlborough House and found that the staff there were buzzing with the news of your presence there the day before. I always make a point to compliment Bert on the state of the gardens—for really, they are more to his credit than the Marquess's—and, upon inquiry, he revealed everything he knew about you. He also gave me the drawings you had left behind, perhaps to clear his conscience since your errand had not fulfilled its purpose. These slim bits of information were of course not completely sufficient to determine your identity, but luckily you have signed most of your drawings (most intelligent!) and I at least had the surname "Eastwood" to work with. I took the opportunity of asking my sister Mrs. Tate, who has just had a daughter out, and she had heard of Eastwoods who came from the Midlands and reside in Southampton Street. So, here we are.

May I persuade you to call on me in Tottenham? I would very much like to discuss your work and your hopes for it. By all means, please bring your mother or your aunt or whoever your chaperone happens to be—though it occurs to me that said chaperone would not be very diligent in her duties if she allowed an escapade like the Marlborough one to transpire, so perhaps you are not encumbered by such difficulties. Please accept, at any rate, the enclosed fare for a cab to bring you here (seven miles is rather an expensive journey). We are at home any morning this week, and there is no need to write to determine which one would suit me—I am most anxious to make your acquaintance. If I should happen to be out when you arrive, please tell our housekeeper Mrs. Riley your name, and she will have me fetched from wherever I may be in the village.

I look forward to making your acquaintance, Miss Eastwood. You seem quite extraordinary.

Yours cordially,

Priscilla Wakefield

Clara had glanced at the signature at the bottom of the page before reading the rest of the letter and therefore read the text of it in a state of dazed shock. Priscilla Wakefield had written to her? It was as if the Prince Regent had called at Southampton Street or the prime minister had sent his card inviting her to come to tea. She folded the letter up and sat at the desk, turning it over and over in her hands while she thought about how to get herself out of the house.

This task was not easily accomplished, for Mrs. Eastwood had made good on her promise to fill Clara's schedule. Every morning her mother rapped at her door to inform Clara that they were leaving in ten minutes for a morning of shopping or riding, followed by calls and a dinner engagement, then the theater or any ball Mrs. Eastwood could get her family invited to. Clara told her mother she would be out of suitable gowns within a week, and Mrs. Eastwood said unconcernedly, "Oh, just put on a different sash or fix your hair differently—no one will notice."

Clara being dragged out into society had one advantage, however—she overheard Mrs. Clive tell Mrs. Eastwood at a ball one evening that her son and his wife had just taken a house in Tottenham.

"A bit out of the way—who would want to drive seven miles every time they wanted to go into town?—but such a lovely area," said Mrs. Clive.

Clara knew the son slightly, and more importantly knew that the Clives were entertaining the new Mrs. Clive's single brother, a vicar. And so the next morning she proposed to Mrs. Eastwood that the three ladies write and ask if they might visit dear Percy—whom Clara had met exactly two times—and perhaps make the acquaintance of dear Mr. Wallace—who was but a name on paper to her and whose name she had only found out through the inquiries of one of the maids. Mrs. Eastwood said, "I am glad you are applying yourself to this new task, dear. I shall call at Mrs. Clive's directly and see if she thinks such a plan would be agreeable."

And within a few days, the trip was planned. Clara, Rose, Mrs. Eastwood, and Mrs. Clive would go to Tottenham on the Monday following. But in the meantime, eleven o'clock on a Saturday evening found 9 Southampton Street's windows blazing with light as the Eastwood family returned after a concert at the Theatre Royal. As promised, Clara's aunt Harriet and her cousins Charles and Gertrude met them there for the intimate supper that had been planned earlier in the week. Also attending were Mr. Reynolds, the Crestons, and a family of long-standing acquaintance to Clara's grandparents by the name of Seymour.

As Lady Eastwood surveyed the drawing room, watching Violet flirt with the middle Seymour son, Rose deep in conversation with Mr. and Miss Creston, and Harriet speaking contentedly to Clara with Charles by her side, she could not help but rejoice in the perfect arrangement of suitors, young ladies, and parents that appeared before her. All was well.

Oh—but Miss Creston kept glancing at Charles with a fluttering of her eyelashes that Mrs. Eastwood did not quite like, and so she swept over to that young lady, taking the youngest Mr. Seymour by the elbow and propelling him along with her as she did. Charles and Clara must have every opportunity to find each other agreeable, and she did not wish to place such vivacious youth alongside her granddaughter's solemn, intent countenance. Such a juxtaposition could not serve anyone's interest except the Crestons, and Mrs. Eastwood thought one match between the two families quite enough.

For her part, Clara was not having an unpleasant evening. Her musical taste was somewhat refined, though lacking the sophistication of Rose's, and she had thoroughly enjoyed the program they had heard at the concert. Her aunt Harriet was such pleasant company that she could not but enjoy the chance to speak with her and learn of all the latest doings of the Kent Eastwoods, and she sipped away at a very fine merlot all the while. Her ride this morning had been woefully interrupted by various acquaintances, but she and the others had attended a fascinating exhibition at the National Gallery that afternoon as well. She had even squeezed in a bit of sketching in brief time she had had between returning home and dressing again to go out. After such a day of interesting diversions, all that was needed to make her blissful was Mr. Kensington at her side.

The thought of him made her look into her lap, watching the dim firelight wash across her white muslin in flickers of orange. What would he think of her, trying to capture another man's affections? And did her joy in this London day mean that she would not have been compatible with him after all? He was a country gentleman through and through. But then she remembered her delight in his company at the Beechview dance that winter, how the hours sped past. She was all too aware of her grandmother's scrutiny as Charles lingered with Mr. Eastwood rather than joining the ladies. She grimly put her wineglass down on the tray as the bell rang for supper, and she found herself going in with Charles.

"I hope you were not troubling yourself with some grim reflection just now," he said to her. "You looked terribly solemn. Might I beg the pleasure of your company at table to try and liven your mood? I trust our hostess will not object to our choosing our own seats?"

"I would be happy to sit with you," she said, reminding herself that success with Charles meant the only success she could hope for with Mr. Kensington. "And yes, it is so very informal that we may sit where we like."

And so they sat near Phoebe, Caroline, and Mr. Reynolds, and conversed together not unpleasantly. Charles seemed to be determined to make more of an effort to engage Clara, an effort she found touching and was intent on reciprocating. She was anxious to hear about his time overseas, never having met anyone as well-traveled as he, and he readily provided stories of his time abroad, though she sensed some reticence about them, generally wrapping them up with "A close scrape, but we managed it in the end" and "A nice lot, the Spanish—it's a rum thing they're papists."

"My father loves to hear your stories, I know," said Clara. "He longs for combat and conquest, I think. He can never read enough military accounts."

"I am flattered that my uncle finds such pleasure in my recollections," said Charles. "I know he must feel George's loss as much as we all do in Kent, and if I can bring him any solace with my company I am happy to do so."

"Tell me, did you enjoy your time abroad?" asked Clara. "It is so very foreign to me, this idea of sailing about and being in a different country each week. Indeed, I cannot say I have ever met anyone of a different nationality—except our Irish housemaid."

"Enjoy?" he seemed to be at a loss. "I cannot say that enjoyment was ever a consideration for me. One enjoys a thrilling horse race or a fine day out sailing during a regatta.

"I enlisted because I felt I could not ignore the atrocities committed by Napoleon, and knew my family would be proud to send one of its sons to fight such a cause. It has been an interesting career, if a frightening one at times, and I was glad to serve Crown and country."

"And—perhaps because George was the heir, it could not have been him who did so?" suggested Clara gently.

His face softened somewhat. "Yes," he said. "Poor fellow. You know, I always warned him about his recklessness with horses. I never thought I would be right about that."

"I warned him too," she said, "and never imagined it would come to pass either."

They were quiet a moment, a little island of silence amid the talk around them.

"I suppose we both needed him to live in order to gain the futures we imagined," said Charles, looking down at his plate.

"Yes. What did you imagine for yourself?"

He looked up and over at her with such sorrow in his eyes that she could not look at him for long. "It doesn't matter now," he said. "I have laid aside one mantle, but I take up another— and I willingly put it on my shoulders in George's memory. My service has taught me that happiness lies in doing one's duty, in working for the good of others."

"How selfless," she said. "But you know, someone who cares for another is not happy until that person is too. Your loved ones do not want to see you miserable."

"Oh, I shan't be," he said quickly, flushing a bit. "Believe me, cousin Clara, except for my brother's death and departing from my fellow soldiers and friends, there was nothing about com- ing home that I regret, and there is no role of George's I'm not willing to take on. Overseas was a proving ground to be sure, but ultimately, there was nothing for me there."

"Any role of George's?" she repeated. Was that a reference to the presumed engagement between herself and his brother?

He looked directly at her. "Yes," he said, "I will assume any of his roles that I am deemed fit to fill and any that will bring pleasure to the ones I care for. That has been my philosophy since I was a young boy, and I know it was George's too. Though the demands placed upon me may have changed, my resolve has not."

The group rose now to go their separate ways, and Clara's head reeled with the merlot and the implication of such words.

"Good night, cousin Clara," he said to her as his party made ready to step outside. "I wonder if I might call again sometime this week."

"Of course," said Clara, and reflected gratefully that it did not seem that Charles required as much convincing about finding her agreeable as she had anticipated. If he had truly hinted at an engagement between them, she questioned his judgment about making such a momentous decision based only on two conversations. She still distrusted, too, his comportment at their first meeting, but remembered that Yewspring was at stake and was wholly prepared to find him agreeable. After all, he had been raised by Harriet, and the ties Clara had formed with George's family need not be severed. How terrible could it be to spend her life with Charles? It was certainly preferable to marrying a stranger.

Though the clock was now striking one, the Crestons lingered on, Miss Creston playing a ditty on the pianoforte while her parents were deep in conversation with Mr. Tapley and Clara's grandfather. Mr. Creston sat on the settee with Rose, while Clara's mother looked on from where she sat playing a last hand of whist, stifling a yawn as she watched the presumed lovers.

When Clara entered the room again, Rose said, "Clara, do join us!"

Clara obediently went over to their settee, finding a nearby chair and sitting. She longed for her bed and the chance to think over Charles's words but wondered if Rose had softened towards her. However, her sister's attention was decidedly fixed elsewhere.

"Mr. Creston has something particular to ask you," said Rose, looking at her suitor with shining eyes.

"Would you and your sister favor me with the pleasure of your company on Rotten Row tomorrow afternoon?" asked Mr. Creston.

"Of course," said Clara, surprised at being so solicited. "Shall we say two o'clock?"

"Certainly," he answered, turning and looking at Rose. "I shall be here on the dot to fetch you."

Was this merely an excuse for him to sequester Rose away from the others in a manner that did not offend propriety? If not, whatever could he want with her?

All was soon revealed as the trio entered the stream of riders making its way along Rotten Row. Mr. Creston turned to her after nodding to a carriage of young ladies he knew—Clara suspected one of them might be Miss Ridley but tried to banish the thought.

"Miss Eastwood," the gentleman began, "I wonder if I might inquire as to a rather delicate matter. I know it may seem as though I make this inquiry as a stranger, for you and I have not had the opportunity to speak as often as I would like. I hope I might assure you, however, that I ask as a friend to your family and in particular to your sister."

Clara looked at Rose, who was watching her anxiously and trying not to. Clara did think of Mr. Creston as a near stranger, having spoken with him directly only a few times and having avoided many of the occasions at which he was present. But

Rose's face looking at her from the other side of Mr. Creston's bay was not a stranger's, and if Clara was not very much mistaken, her sister was once again anxious for her good opinion. And that made her answer, "Mr. Creston, you need not fear displeasing me with any inquiry that might concern Rose, or any others of my family. I believe your intentions can only be honorable."

"Thank you. I regret having to bring this matter forward, but I trust you will remember after your—attachment to your late cousin that the burdens of eldest sons are often heavy indeed, and such a burden alone compels me to speak."

"All right," said Clara, nodding in greeting as the Seymours passed them going the other way. "What is this—inquiry?" She suspected it had something to do with the dowry, for what else could bind three such dissimilar persons together?

Mr. Creston cleared his throat and looked over at Rose as if to gather his courage. Clara turned from watching them and fixed her eyes on Diamond's head bobbing in front of her.

"Well, I feel it prudent to ask if you—would be so inclined to give up your single state, if a gentleman were to address himself to you."

Clara kept watching the glossy, pinpricked gray ears standing out against the green of the track before her. "I suppose it would depend on which gentleman was performing the addressing."

She looked over to see that he was blushing at the indelicacy of his question, and felt a bit of pity well in her. "What has this to do with your burden as the eldest son?" she asked him, trying to move the conversation along without forcing him to speak again. "You are right—I do know that it can be a profound one."

"Well, as much as I wish I could report that Vineland Hall's estates have been kept with as much care and attention as I have observed in Exton, I regret very much that both the agent employed by my father and my father himself have been gravely remiss in their management of the properties, which have always been on the cusp of barely profitable. Now we have received word that the flooding damage of this spring—the river Gwath runs through our estates—has been repaired, but at a high cost. Without casting my father in a wholly uncomplimentary light, all I can say is that the Creston fortune has very nearly been extinguished. We live now on my mother's inheritance."

Clara did not need him to elaborate further to understand that he was inquiring now whether Rose's dowry would be enough to bolster the family coffers, or whether he should begin to search elsewhere. If he had not needed to marry well before these events, he did now.

"I see," she said slowly, trying to collect her thoughts. "Well—as I said before, my future and the answer to any proposal I might be so fortunate to receive would depend entirely on the gentleman who was making the offer."

"And—" Mr. Creston was truly hesitant now. She saw him look at Rose. Her sister gave him an eloquent look that spoke for her. The gentleman turned back to Clara, his resolve apparently fortified. "And what if that gentleman should be the younger Mr. Eastwood?"

So the prospect had been discussed between he and Rose, not just amongst the Eastwood family. "Can you assure me that my cousin will make me such an offer? Because I certainly do not have any knowledge that he will do so."

"As a matter of fact," he said, "he and I belong to the same club and were introduced by your cousin Harry when Mr. Eastwood first arrived back in town. I saw Mr. Eastwood there on another occasion and he approached me particularly to ask about you, having learned about my acquaintance with your family of the last several months."

"Were you able to give him a favorable report?" Her head was spinning with the implication of such a conversation.

"Indeed. I told him Miss Eastwood is a sensible, dutiful woman whose devotion to her home and family is apparent even upon a short acquaintance with her."

She was not sure what to make of this assessment, nor how Charles might feel about what he had learned, but understood that Mr. Creston meant to pay her a compliment in his appraisal of her.

"I am encouraged by my cousin's interest in me, and think well of him on my part. But you know as well as I that a lady does not think so highly of herself as to assume that a gentleman will make her an offer. Until and unless my cousin chooses to address himself to me, I will say only that I would be very happy to consider a proposal from him while thinking of his well-being and my own."

Mr. Creston smiled. Her statement seemed to be good enough for him to now engage Rose in the conversation more, and the party conversed easily enough on the rest of their ride, the relief on the two other's faces palpable.

Clara could not help but feel envious of the ease and cheerfulness they exhibited toward one another and of the prospects that awaited them if Charles should make her an offer. None of them had chosen the circumstances they were in—Mr. Creston had not asked to be born an eldest son with all the responsibilities that role entailed, Rose had not requested that her settlement depend on her sister's actions, and Clara had certainly not ever wished to be forced to choose between her own happiness and Rose's. And yet, here they were, and she could not help feeling that she paid the highest price out of them all. It was a feeling that made her a poor companion on the way back to

Southampton Street, and she sought her room as soon as they reached the house. She did not want to give Rose the chance to offer thanks, if she had been inclined to do so, or face the prospect that her sister was still angry at her. Clara could not take back what had happened at the exhibition, and in spite of the trouble it had landed her in, Mrs. Wakefield would not have written her if she had not been there. And so the trip to Tottenham the next day loomed in her mind. She wondered if she could enact the plan she had formed, for she could not be seven miles from the one woman in the kingdom who might be able to help her—and *not* try and meet with her. She hoped that even if Rose was angry about the spectacle Clara had made, her sister might have understood that.

The clock on Percy Clive's mantel sounded three, and Clara knew the party would be adjourning from the drawing-room for luncheon soon. They had walked the large garden of Mrs. Clive's son and her daughter-in-law's house, which no one had much attended to. Even Clara, who would have been envious of them on any other day, was too preoccupied with how she would get out of the house to notice much. She had pulled Rose aside before they left the house and asked her if she would go with her on an errand in Tottenham.

"What errand?" asked her sister, her tone not revealing how likely she was to comply with Clara's request.

"Just—a social visit to a friend," said Clara. "Oh Rose, have I not shown you that I am serious about Charles? I am even prepared to think favorably of Mr. Wallace. Was not this Tottenham excursion my own idea? What more can you wish from me?"

Rose sighed. "All right," she said.

And so Mr. Wallace had offered his arm to each of the Misses Eastwoods as they walked across Tottenham after luncheon to the Wakefields'. He would then walk back to the Clives' house and Mrs. Clive and Mrs. Eastwood would call for Rose and Clara in three-quarters of an hour to take them back to town. Clara willed Mr. Wallace and Rose to walk more quickly as they ambled along the lane, for every moment was precious to her. Mr. Wallace stopping and speaking with an acquaintance in the village center and insisting on introducing the Eastwoods to the other gentleman when Clara knew they would never see him again tested every inch of her politeness, already in short supply. She could hear the village clock chiming half after three as they finally wound their way to a white-washed little house set back from the lane by a rambling, lush garden.

"Oh," Mr. Wallace said, breaking off from the conversation they had all been having about the upcoming races. He stopped suddenly and looked at Clara with a furrowed brow. "The Wakefields?"

"Yes," she said. "Is there something wrong?"

"Er, no, it's just—they're Quakers," he said. "Not that I resent any attention to the movements of one's conscience, it's just that, well, they sometimes do behave most strangely—but very good folk, I am sure. Her works in the village are spoken well of, I believe."

Rose shot Clara a furious glance, but Clara could not allay any of her sister's fears as they walked up the drive. Her eye was caught by the tantalizing tangle of vines and leaves as they walked up the drive, and the flowers in the beds were beautiful, but her nervousness over meeting Mrs. Wakefield prevented her from giving it the close study she would have wished. Once Mr. Wallace had seen them safely delivered into the house, the housekeeper returning from Clara's inquiry to say that Mrs. Wakefield was much occupied at the moment but wished to meet with them, Mr. Wallace left again.

The housekeeper led Clara and Rose through a wide chilly entrance hall with a floor of stone flags into a shabby but tidy sitting room with a crackling fire in the grate. Clara was grateful that she had not had a moment alone with Rose to be chastised for keeping such unconventional company as a Quaker. And once her sister deduced that this errand had to do with drawing, Clara knew Rose would be doubly angry.

Seated on a settee of worn green velvet was a middle-aged woman whose fine chestnut curls were streaked with gray and tucked neatly under her muslin cap. She was dressed in a simple gray gown and wore spectacles pushed down to the end of her nose, to peer intently at the papers spread before her on a side table.

"Ah, the Misses Eastwood, I presume," she said with a smile. "I am Mrs. Wakefield—please do sit down. And tell me—which one of you is Clara, and which is Rose?"

Clara enlightened her as they sat, saying, "I am Miss East-wood, the one responsible for this whole fiasco. Rose," she gestured at her sister, "has no idea why I came here but kindly agreed to accompany me."

"Whatever is the meaning of this, Clara?" asked Rose, frowning. "Do you mean to say you have never even *met* Mrs. Wakefield?"

Mrs. Wakefield surveyed the sisters and said briskly after a moment, "Ah, I see the subterfuge continues. Yes, Miss Rose, this is the first time your sister and I have met, but I wrote to her and asked her to visit me. It is terribly difficult for me to get away from my work here, though I should not have been so incon-siderate as to force you to get here under false pretenses, Miss Eastwood, as it seems you must have. Now, my schedule today does not allow for much more time at home, so you must excuse my bluntness, and I suspect that our conversation will last beyond my time today. I hope you will let me call on you at your lodgings in London when I am next in town."

"Of course," Clara said.

"Now, Miss Rose, there seems to be some reluctance on your family's part to allow your sister to pursue her botanical drawing. Am I correct?"

"Oh yes, very much so," said Rose. "And I must say I share my parents' distaste for Clara's interest in it, for it has made her behave in *such* an unladylike manner! And it has brought shame upon not just herself but her whole family—we have only just convinced our acquaintance that they were mistaken in her motives—"

Mrs. Wakefield held up a hand and broke in gently. "And you find it necessary to preserve your own respectability in the eyes of a young gentleman, no doubt?"

Rose looked down at her lap and then up again with eyes glinting with tears. "Yes. And it is most distressing that Clara should deceive me now, again, after I have tried to understand why she would do such a thing—"

"No doubt," said Mrs. Wakefield, looking at Clara. "Well, Miss Rose, I beg that you accept my word as a respectable matron that your sister's reputation will not come into further harm under my watch, and by extension you need not worry about your own. I understand your concern, believe me. I know that a young lady must do all in her power to make herself acceptable to a future husband, and I remember well the days of chaperoning my own daughter. She lives in Woodbridge now, near Ipswich, and just bore her eleventh child. Does that reassure you?"

Rose looked doubtful but Clara supposed there was nothing about Mrs. Wakefield nor the sitting room's appearance to cause undue alarm. "Certainly, Mrs. Wakefield."

"Excellent." She turned to Clara. "Now, I would like to know a bit about you, Miss Eastwood, if I may ask you a few questions. You are from the Midlands?"

"Yes, a small village in Warwickshire called Exton," said Clara.

Just then a girl of about fourteen came in and curtseyed to the visitors before standing and looking at Mrs. Wakefield expectantly.

"I see," said Mrs. Wakefield in response to Clara, then gestured to the girl. "Miss Clara and Miss Rose Eastwood, my granddaughter Catherine. Kitty dear, here are your Latin papers back. I have marked the mistakes in your declinations and circled the ones you need to study further. You may work on them this evening when we are back from the maternal hospital. I would like you and Sarah to go there now to begin the rounds with Dr. Gilbert, and remind him to keep a special eye on Mrs. Thompson. She should have delivered on Friday last and that baby seems determined to keep us all waiting."

"Yes, Grandmama," said Isabella, who took the papers obediently and curtseyed again to the guests on her way out of the room. Clara was battling a surge of envy that swelled in her like an unexpected wave—what would her life have been like if she too, had grown up in a household where the girls could learn Latin as well as the boys? She thought of the dog-eared Latin primer, her struggles to understand it without someone to guide her, and the strange and wonderful sounds she made when she tried to say the words out loud. How much more knowledgeable she might be now, how much more understandable the reasons for the scientific names she dwelt on and repeated like spells to herself when she walked over the hills!

"I do beg your pardon for the interruption," said Mrs.

Wakefield. "We are quite a busy household, I fear, with scarcely a moment to spare. I established a maternal hospital here in Tottenham—the first of its kind in the London area, though the Scots have had them for ages and the Germans soon followed suit. It is appalling to me that poor women are forced to labor and bear their children in conditions unfit for the task."

"How admirable," said Clara. "I had no idea you had so many interests, in addition to your botanical book, which I think is simply wonderful."

"Oh goodness, yes, I lean toward sampling a great too many subjects, I think. Like a bird flitting from branch to branch instead of settling on one as I should have. However, science has proven to be such a delightfully prodigious undertaking, full of insights for the health of our bodies as well as the improvement of our minds through observation of the world around us, that I cannot resist all these interesting endeavors that crop up. Do you know, the chances of a woman dying in childbirth in a hospital like ours are one-third less than if she labored at home with only her servants to attend her?"

"No, I did not realize that," said Clara. Rose had blanched beneath her bonnet.

"It is quite astonishing. We are very pleased with the results and will be soliciting Parliament to approve the building of one in every village over three thousand people. I do hope that when the time comes for the two of you to bear children, you will have access to one. And speaking of children, Miss Eastwood, I deduct from your title that you are unmarried?"

"Yes. I—was to be engaged to a cousin, but he most unfortunately passed away this spring."

"And did this cousin know of your wish to contribute illustrations to a work?"

She hesitated and glanced at Rose, knowing that every word she spoke could make its way back to her mother like a fox finding a henhouse. But what choice did she have? This conversation might be the only one she would have the opportunity for. "No. I—I am not entirely sure he would have approved, if he had known, and I never found the chance to bring it up with him."

Mrs. Wakefield rolled her eyes. "Men! They are perfectly pleased when their ladies can sketch silly little cartoonish portraits or horridly out-of-proportion landscapes, but as soon as her skills turn to a really useful and beneficial turn—*that* is not to be borne! If my husband had been able to support his family as he should have, you may be sure he would not be as reconciled to my various undertakings as he is, no matter how profitable they might be. I suppose that is one of the blessings of financial need. But I do apologize, I keep interrupting you. What of your parents? Do they know of your desire, and have they any concept of your skill?"

"I think not, Mrs. Wakefield. I received so little encouragement from them in my interest that I very early refrained from showing them my work." Rose cleared her throat and shifted in her chair uncomfortably.

"So who recommended that you solicit an opinion of your work?"

Clara felt a blush spread over her face despite herself. All morning she had had Mr. Kensington's face in her mind, heard the words of encouragement he had spoken to her, and had tucked his letters in her reticule for good luck.

"A friend who was educated at Oxford," she replied. "He—was kind enough to take an interest in my work and encouraged me to take steps to educate myself." Now she saw Rose's head swivel toward her and felt the force of her sister's gaze upon her like a stone skipping off water. Just because the blow was brief did not mean that it held no force.

"And how long have you been interested in botany?"

Clara told her about her life, about her morning sketching and clandestine walks, and of her encounter at Marlborough House. Upstairs she could hear the scuffles of little feet from a nursery or school-room, and the banging of pots from a kitchen somewhere in the back of the house.

"...and I discovered your own flora just last year, but I think it is marvelous," finished Clara. "The method of instruction is so gentle and accessible, yet the plates are splendidly drawn and every detail is so correct!"

"Thank you," said Mrs. Wakefield. "I will own that I did not expect it to be as popular as it has. But, we must think of you now. I took the liberty of looking at your portfolio. If you are agreeable, shall we look it over?"

Rose said irritably, "This all sounds suspiciously like the kind of thing that so displeased Mama and Papa, Clara."

"Oh, have no fear, Miss Rose, I shall call on your mother in Southampton Street and explain everything to her, you may be sure," said Mrs. Wakefield. "I suspect she might see things differently."

Mrs. Wakefield rose and went over to a long table under a window, which let in a heavenly golden light that draped itself over the room like butter over a pastry, and picked up Clara's carefully assembled packet of drawings from the thick pile of bills, children's slates, and letters that lay across it. Heartened by the promise of the implied visit, Clara followed her, wiping her clammy palms on her skirt as she did.

Mrs. Wakefield peered through her spectacles at the drawings and began searching for something amid the pile. Despite the older woman's encouraging manner, Clara held her breath in suspense. What if all this had been for naught? What if she was to be shipped home to Exton to languish, like a broken toy no one cared for, destined to be put away onto a dusty shelf before going to the burn pile? What if this, her only method of helping Mr. Kensington, should fail? She thought of the distraught letter she would have to write him that evening should Mrs. Wakefield look kindly at her, gather up the drawings and say, "Perhaps not."

Instead, the older woman finally retrieved her paper, written closely with notes, and turned to her with a smile.

"As a whole, your work shows promise, Miss Eastwood. Well done. Especially with the lack of support and formal training that you have had, I am impressed with your technique. I applaud your friend for encouraging you to seek out a higher plane for your work than doodling on the sides of letters."

Clara felt a beaming smile spread across her face and tried, unsuccessfully, to subdue it. "Thank you," she said, feeling the commonplace phrase inadequate for her feelings. "I am indebted to you for your kindness, especially because I think so highly of your work. As a little girl, I did not know that women such as yourself existed, or I surely would have aspired to be like you and to achieve even a small measure of your work."

"Oh heavens, you flatter me!" laughed Mrs. Wakefield. "I think you do not realize how much of my work was borne out of the need to support my family and with how much desperation some of it was composed. But thank you. It is a blessing to know that one's work has had an effect in the world. Now, as I said, I do not have much time, but I wanted to give you these notes that I wrote on the plates you've included here. I do have some concerns with your use of light—some of these are terribly shadowed. And though you have done well with what I gather was a slight education, continuing to deepen your understanding of botany will improve your drawing. Don't fear, I have a proposal for your mother that I think will help you, if she agrees to it."

"Thank you," said Clara, again overcome with emotion and unable to say much else.

Mrs. Wakefield consulted her watch. "Drat! I am nearly late, which will put my schedule for the rest of the day entirely off," she said. "As I mentioned, I will call upon you in London sometime next week. Do you have transport arranged?"

At that moment, as Clara heard the distant church clock pealing a quarter to four, the housekeeper came in to say that a carriage was waiting for Rose and Clara. Mrs. Wakefield promised again to call, gave Clara back her drawings, and the housekeeper led them out to the front door. Clara wondered if she would look different to her mother when she got into Mrs. Clive's carriage, if any sign of the kindled hope in her would show upon her face. She felt as if she must have been transformed outwardly somehow by the interview, and so stole a glance in the hall looking glass as she went by to see if she looked the same. It was somewhat reassuring to see her own familiar face looking back, just as she remembered.

CHAPTER SEVENTEEN

Clara knew she had tested Rose's good nature by conceal-ing from her the true purpose of their call to Mrs. Wakefield's, though she was somewhat encouraged by her sister's reticence in the carriage on the way back to London. Mrs. Clive had spent most of the trip praising her son, his house, his wife, her own good nature in agreeing to the excursion (and in her own carriage too!), and on the good deed she may have performed by intro-ducing Clara to Mr. Wallace.

"He is so very agreeable, and not at all overly disposed to ser-monizing, as one had such reason to fear!" Mrs. Clive exclaimed as they reached the West End.

"And such a gentleman to walk with the two of you!" agreed Mrs. Eastwood, addressing her daughters. "But Rose dear, you've hardly said a word—surely you aren't worried about what Mr. Creston will think if he hears of it? I expressly told his mother that we were going up for Clara's sake, so you needn't fret. Your forehead will wrinkle most unattractively if you do."

Clara saw the opportunity to defend her sister and try and get into her good graces again, and so said to their mother, "Mama, Rose is only worried about how much longer we will stay in town. We've been here two months now, but we all know how delicate the situation with Mr. Creston is. It would be such a shame to leave before we are confident enough of my future that he feels confident in paying—any addresses to Rose that he may wish."

Mrs. Eastwood waved her hand dismissively. "Oh, we won't

go until August, Rose dear, don't worry. We've another two months left. And unless Mr. Creston takes some hare-brained scheme of going away himself to Bath or Brighton—which would be going completely against his mother's wishes, I know— he shall remain here too. Just because Clara's match must be our concern now does not mean you shall go home single, dear. Not if I have anything to say about it."

Rose brightened visibly at the prospect of staying in town, and Clara was encouraged enough to ask her sister to speak alone with her when they all got back to Southampton Street.

"Thank you, Rose," she said when her bedroom door was shut and the two sat in chairs placed in the bay window that looked out over Exeter Street. "I know you could have told Mama my real reason for visiting Mrs. Wakefield. Thank you for your discretion. I hope I may rely on it in the weeks to come?"

Rose sighed. "What is the point of this—willful rebellion against Mama and Papa? Do you not think they have your best interests in mind? And such secrecy as you seem to wish to con- tinue led to your embarrassing us all."

"I embarrassed myself, too, if that is any consolation."

"Where can all this lead but to more trouble for us all? Why should I help you?"

Clara had prepared her argument in the carriage ride home, and now told Rose a version of the truth that revealed some of her motivations for continuing to study botany—her enjoyment of the practice, her desire to improve, and the positive effect it would have on her experience in town—while obscuring, natu- rally, several others. She could not tell Rose that she wished to earn money for the Kensingtons, of course, for other questions about her relationship to them would arise. And no one must know about her feelings for Mr. Kensington, for there was no promise of secrecy Clara trusted enough to risk the possibility of

Charles somehow finding out. After the speed with which her presence at the Marlborough exhibition had become known, she was wary of revealing anything that she would not wish to hear proclaimed as fact among the family's most casual acquaintance within a week. She imagined what would happen if her parents found out—she would be married off to whoever would take her, cut off from Yewspring and Mr. Kensington, dependent on her husband for pin-money and a home. Her means of aiding the Kensingtons would be utterly curtailed, for who would teach her drawing if not Mrs. Wakefield? And where did she have to remain to be taught but in London? Whatever it took to stay there for a while yet, Clara was prepared to do.

"That's all very well for your happiness," said Rose somewhat bitterly when Clara had finished, "but what of my own prospects?"

"Well," said Clara, "I imagine it will be easier for me to be agreeable to Charles if my spirits are uplifted. Is that not reason enough to continue? And, you know, I thought Mr. Wallace amiable enough when we saw him today. If I am often in Tottenham with Mrs. Wakefield, well—perhaps we will continue to see each other. Two prospects for a husband must be better than one, surely? If I am not mistaken, such considerations are exactly in keeping with Mama's wishes."

"Oh Clara," said Rose in exasperated, resigned amusement, "do you know yourself so little? The only husband you want is the one who will take you back to Yewspring. Use Mr. Wallace as an excuse to get to Tottenham if you wish, but we both know that Charles is the man for you now. You have my cooperation, though I wish I were not asked to give it in such an underhanded way, and I hope we are both happier in the end for it. But for heaven's sake, don't repay me by making me ashamed of your conduct again!"

A week later, Mrs. Wakefield called upon the family in Southampton Street. Clara had arranged for Rose and her mother to be present, knowing that Mrs. Eastwood's approval of Clara's newfound acquaintance would rely on her firsthand judgment of Mrs. Wakefield's character, and her mother must trust Rose's judgment more than Clara's. Now, in the drawing room, with the summer sun sending golden rays through the windowpane, Mrs. Wakefield looked expectantly at Clara once the perfunctory introductions were over.

"Mama," said Clara, knowing that she was being cued, "I have become quite fond of botanical drawing, and Mrs. Wakefield has kindly looked over some of the work I have done so far."

Mrs. Eastwood looked dumbstruck. "What utter nonsense," she said, after a moment of shock. "Botanical illustrating? What could you possibly know about such a thing? And who would read such a dull book, except for dusty old men in colleges? What could have put such an idea into your head, Clara?"

"I know you may view this request of your daughter's as an unusual one," said Mrs. Wakefield, "but let me assure you that in all respectable quarters of London it will be regarded without the slightest disapproval, and that such a pursuit will not harm Miss Eastwood's reputation in the least. In fact, I believe you know one of my former pupils—Elizabeth Wallace, who is now Elizabeth Clive. Botany is a highly suitable occupation for young women, and I am sorry that my own daughter showed very little inclination toward it."

"I am not convinced," said Mrs. Eastwood. "None of my nieces, nor indeed Rose, have shown such an interest—all that tramping around out of doors, trudging through heaven knows how much mud and dust, exposed to all kinds of weather and sun that will tan one most dreadfully, even with a bonnet, and for what? To have one's name on a little sketch in an obscure book sitting on a professor's shelf somewhere? Mrs. Wakefield, I cannot see how this prepares my daughter for marriage, nor makes her a more suitable wife. She has already tried my patience and risked our family's reputation in a most appalling fashion by indulging in such eccentric schemes."

"You see, Mama," said Clara, "I believe this will assist me in creating a splendid garden wherever I am to live as a married woman. You know how important gardens are, and how much we always admire the ladies who keep the nicest ones in our neighborhood. Would not this be a good way of familiarizing myself with flowers?"

Rose spoke up for the first time. "I think it is an excellent scheme, Mama," she said. "You know how Clara is always happiest when she has long walks about the countryside. Should not we send her to the altar—whenever that should happen—with a cheerful countenance and help ensure her marriage begins on a happy note?"

Mrs. Wakefield studied Rose as she said, "Indeed, Mrs. Eastwood. A happy maiden makes a pleasant wife, I always say, which must be attractive to any gentleman. I am proposing to have your daughter stay with me, if it is agreeable to her, for some portion of each week while she is in town. I would like to help her in her drawing, and she would have the benefit of Tottenham's society as well as that in town. You have seen for yourself how genteel the area is, and how many respectable families have taken houses there. Perhaps you would be so good as to consider this idea— here is my address." She rose and gave Mrs. Eastwood a piece of paper, then returned to her chair to pull on her gloves in readiness to depart. "Please do write with any questions you might have. But since we are already more than halfway through the Season, if she could come next week so we may begin our studies, that would be very agreeable to me."

"Come and stay with you?" echoed Mrs. Eastwood, staring at the other woman with Mrs. Wakefield's card in her lap. "And have her miss all the balls and concerts with her cousin Charles in town? This is highly irregular! However, it seems that Mr. Wallace was pleased enough with you to request to visit us when he comes into town next, and so your presence in Tottenham may lead to some good after all. Clara, your father and I will confer and let you know our decision though I'm sure I still do not see the point of all this sketching nonsense when you are so very near a spinster. If we do let you go, I hope you will remember our kindness to you in our old age and be generous to us."

Any triumph Clara may have felt at the successful introduction of Mrs. Wakefield to her mother, or any happy anticipation she may have felt at the possibility of going to stay in Tottenham—actually stay with a writer and botanist!—was quelled the following morning when she and Rose returned from a walk with Charles in Lincoln's Inn Fields. The butler told Clara that her mother was waiting for her in the drawing-room, and when Clara came through the doorway, she found Miss Holt, smiling serenely with a teacup in her lap, sitting with her mother.

"Look who we have brought to be your companion, Clara!" said Mrs. Eastwood. "What lucky timing that we had already engaged Miss Holt to come down from Exton. Now you may go to Tottenham without inconveniencing any of us!"

CHAPTER EIGHTEEN

The Eastwoods' carriage clattered out of London and Clara again eyed Miss Holt warily. "Now, you are quite sure you have enough spending money?" Clara asked, again opening her purse and rummaging through for a coin. "Do take another shilling."

She handed it to Miss Holt, who beamed as she took it and said, "You are *so* kind, Miss Eastwood."

"Well, as I said, I do think you should take every advantage of enjoying yourself while we are in Tottenham," said Clara, feeling as though she had to force the words out. Her face ached from trying to maintain a pleasant smile throughout the journey. "Do not think that just because you are my companion you must remain fixed at my side—how dull for you! Think of yourself on holiday, and you may come and go from the Wakefields' as you please."

"Oh, but you mustn't come to any trouble," said Miss Holt. "I've promised your parents—and your grandmother too—that I shall do everything in my power to ensure that their good name is upheld. I am not sure, but it *sounds* as though there may have been a bit of worry on that score."

She smiled knowingly at Clara, who wished to scowl back but instead said, "Oh, you know how things get distorted when they are repeated too often. I am as committed as my family to the Eastwood's good name, and to my own future. I am quite sure I will be in good hands with you. It is only that, well, there will be quite a lot of unconventional talk at the Wakefields, for they are Quakers, you know, and hold some ideas that the rest of us may not agree with. But they are respectable nonetheless, and you must put all such talk out of your mind—even if it seems that I am participating in it."

"Participating? I am not sure what you mean."

"We mustn't be rude to our hostess," said Clara, "so it may seem to you as though I am agreeing with her in order to be polite. No matter how radical it may seem, you must trust that I am just being an agreeable guest. And—I am happy to continue providing you with the, ah, extra remuneration we discussed earlier, for as long as I am satisfied as to your discretion, why should I want for money?"

In fact, Clara did want for money because Mrs. Wakefield had instructed her to buy some good-quality vellum before she left town, but she gritted her teeth and told the falsehood. This distasteful underhanded bribery was the only way she felt assured of Miss Holt's secrecy, and secrecy was what she must have, no matter how tattered her gowns became or how badly she longed for a new book.

The two travelers found that Mrs. Wakefield was out when they arrived, and Mr. Wakefield was upstairs in his rooms with strict instructions not to be disturbed. After getting settled in their own rooms Clara and Miss Holt descended to find that instructions had been left for Clara to begin preparing a new sketch for Mrs. Wakefield to review with her upon her return. "She said to make use of the garden if you like, miss," said the housekeeper, and Clara needed no further encouragement to open the French windows and step out into the sunshine with her sketchbook. Miss Holt followed her and quickly found a comfortable seat on a bench, leaving Clara to roam about, delighting in the plants surrounding the paths. Some were familiar to her, and having been away from any kind of vegetation beyond the carefully groomed parks and the hothouse bouquets she passed in the halls of the London houses, she could not help reaching out to touch a leaf or cradle a bloom. Soon she heard the village clock chiming half-past eleven, however, and she set to work sketching an *Anthemis*, outlining the daisy's white ray flowers and the golden disc flowers in its center, bristling with pollen like a pincushion stuffed with pins.

When Mrs. Wakefield and Catherine returned home at four, Clara was just putting her little pots of paint away into their proper compartments of her easel. "What a fine one!" said Mrs. Wakefield admiringly, reaching out and touching the gleaming corner of the easel.

"Yes," said Clara. Mr. Kensington had been in her thoughts all day—at least, the thoughts she could spare from her work. "A friend gave it to me."

"Well, you shall certainly put it to good use," said Mrs. Wakefield. "Now, we shall dine and then I will look over your drawing and Catherine's sketches of the tibia."

The meal brought almost the entire household together for the first time. Mr. Wakefield, when he was at home, generally did not leave his rooms until the evening meal, and Clara had seen a maid taking a tray up to him. Despite having heard the noises of children being taught coming from the third story of the house she was surprised to find not just Catherine seated at table with them but three of her younger brothers and a sister, just seven years old, who were also staying there with their nursemaid.

"They'll be out in the garden after dinner," said Mrs. Wakefield with a smile, "and you'll know they're there soon enough. They are often with us, since their father—my son Edward—is, well, generally pursuing some scheme or another. He is often in Ireland, too, and so a bit of stability helps the poor dears."

"When shall Mama come?" asked one of the boys with his

mouth full of potatoes.

"Don't speak with your mouth full, dear. She shall come in a few weeks, perhaps, when Miss Eastwood and Miss Holt have gone away." Mrs. Wakefield turned to the guests. "My daughter-in-law, Susan is often with us as well. I wish the house were big enough to accommodate all our guests, but we have only the two spare rooms."

Clara felt terrible that she was displacing a family member and said, somewhat doubtfully, "Oh, perhaps we could get some rooms at the inn, then, or take a servants' room…" She was calculating the cost of lodging elsewhere in her head, and already finding the figure alarmingly high.

"Oh, no, no," said Mrs. Wakefield. "We must take advantage of you being here. Don't fret, Susan is just as comfortable at her own house as she is here—she just likes to be near her children since Edward is away so much."

After they dined, the younger children and Catherine went outside to the garden, still bathed in warm golden light during the warm summer evening. Mrs. Wakefield left the floor-to-ceiling windows of the sitting room open, and the breeze coming into the room made the curtains sway and ruffled the stacks of paper on the desk.

"Now," said Mrs. Wakefield, resuming her spot on the settee where Clara had first seen her, "let us review your day's work."

Clara handed the other her sketch, and Mrs. Wakefield sat with it for several minutes, occasionally making marks with her pencil. Clara winced a bit, for no one had reviewed her work with such scrutiny. Even Monsieur Verne had done no more than a brief survey of her drawings—she supposed he was not knowledgeable enough about the subject to offer her any critique.

Finally, after what seemed like a lifetime, Mrs. Wakefield

held the paper out to Clara, who sat on the opposite end of the settee, and said, "I have some changes to recommend for tomorrow. First, this was a garden specimen, yes?"

"Yes," said Clara, gesturing out the window toward the *Anthemis*, white heads bobbing in the breeze. "They looked so charming against the red brick of the wall."

"Tomorrow you must go out and find some wild specimens," said Mrs. Wakefield. "I'll draw you a map of where you might go."

"Oh," said Clara. "It's just that the garden flowers offer so much more variety."

"Yes, an artificial variety. And garden flowers can be so different from the wild forms that identifying field specimens from a garden illustration is quite hopeless. I know it is quite conceited to quote oneself, but this topic is covered in Letter Six of my book—perhaps it would be profitable to review it. Surely you've noticed this in the Midlands? Your drawings seemed to indicate that you sketched wild specimens?"

Clara flushed a little. "Yes, both," she said. "Sometimes I would begin a sketch with a wild specimen and then finish it from a garden plant, if I ran out of time to finish it in the field."

"Oh no, no, that will never do," said Mrs. Wakefield. "Always work with the same specimen, so that you do not append or remove any feature that God has put there. We must be accurate in our illustrating. We must be observant."

"All right," said Clara, stung a little by the criticism. She did try to be observant. And surely one must be the most inclusive that one could when portraying a specimen? Surely if a feature was found once, it should be considered essential to identification?

"Now, where is the proper, that is, Latin name of the

specimen?"

"Here," said Clara, reaching out and pointing to where she had carefully lettered the word *Anthemis* in the lower left-hand corner of the drawing.

"Yes, this is the genus but not the species. There are at present, I believe, five *Anthemis* species. How is the viewer to know which one this is?"

Clara frowned at the drawing.

"Do *you* know which one this is?" asked Mrs. Wakefield.

Clara's flush deepened. "Well, no. I have seen it often in our gardens, and I assumed they were all the same—"

"Never assume, Miss Eastwood. That is the first rule of a scientist."

Despite her embarrassment, Clara felt a thrill at the word.

"That shall be your evening's task," said Mrs. Wakefield, going to a bookshelf and taking down a flora. "See if you can identify the *Anthemis* to species, and add it to the drawing."

Clara went back out to the garden as Mrs. Wakefield called Catherine in to review her own work. The two pupils exchanged a wry smile as they passed each other, and Clara could not help comparing this style of learning with the others she had known. Though she knew this one was superior to learning by rote, she was also, suddenly, unsure if she could meet the challenges presented by it. Being a true scholar seemed to be more difficult than she had believed.

Mrs. Wakefield quickly assigned Clara a rigorous routine during the three days a week Clara spent with her. Every morning, while Mrs. Wakefield was often out in the village, at the maternal hospital, or teaching her grandchildren, Clara and Miss

Holt would go out for a walk so Clara could begin a sketch. She would then harvest the specimen and rush it back to the house to continue working on it after dinner, before it wilted. Mrs. Wakefield would provide feedback on the day's work and assign Clara some reading on the topic of botany. Most of it was centered around learning the science better, but Mrs. Wakefield also gave Clara the names of female botanists to research. On her first day back in London Clara snuck in a visit to the booksellers' to try and find information on Maria Merian and Elizabeth Blackwell. "We are not the first to walk this path, though it may feel like it at times," said Mrs. Wakefield. "Perhaps they will inspire and educate you." But Clara could not find any books about them.

She had other assignments during her time in town that consumed her mornings, however, the only time of day Mrs. Eastwood would allow Clara to be gone from the house. She went to the Natural History Museum once she received her pocket money, staring in awe at Sowerby's illustrations and delighting in finding some of Mrs. Merian's there as well. She went to the physick garden, the botanical garden, not to sketch but to look at the plants, the insects on them, and the birds that perched in the trees. She was overwhelmed with it all, and felt she was missing half of the things she should have been noticing.

"Expand your view beyond plants," said Mrs. Wakefield, "for they exist as a part of the great whole of nature. You will understand them better if you understand what surrounds them."

Though Clara knew this at Yewspring, she had forgotten it in London.

She was exhilarated, she was tired of being batted about town like a badminton shuttlecock, she fell asleep over her sketches in the evenings, and was discomfited when Mr. Wallace called at Southampton Street to ask after her. She fled upstairs afterward, mortified, and would have given every last coin she had to be back at Yewspring for just one day, a day when everything would be familiar to her.

She saw Charles often during her time in town. He would walk the Eastwoods to and from church every Sunday and stay to dine with them. Though Mr. Eastwood must be the fondest of them all of his nephew on account of his military background, Clara was reminded of George in Charles's demeanor, his seriousness, and his attention to them all. He listened attentively to Rose at the piano, sat and conversed with Clara's grandfather, and helped Lady Eastwood untangle the yarn for her knitting. He fenced with Harry at the club, helped Mr. Creston purchase a new horse, and asked Clara so many questions about Yewspring that she could not help growing fond of him too. It was as if he had always been among them, and yet when she saw him come around the corner of Southampton Street, she could not help feeling that George would appear as well, just a step behind him laughing and talking about the races. It was always a little jolt to her when Charles remained alone. It reminded her that things could not go back to how they had been.

One day in Tottenham, a thought struck her like a boulder tumbling from a hillside, and she asked Mrs. Wakefield, "Might I send a letter from here?"

"Of course, my dear—you are our guest, not our prisoner!" said Mrs. Wakefield, perhaps surprised by such an obvious question. "The writing paper is there."

June 25

Tottenham

Mr. Kensington,

Oh, I have so much to tell you!

The Wakefield household was not entirely solitary. In the evenings, Mr. and Mrs. Wakefield would go out to visit neighbors, many of whom were fellow Quakers. Clara and Miss Holt were generally invited as well, though Mrs. Wakefield said that they could sample Tottenham society as much or as little as they pleased. After listening to several fascinating conversations by guests of the Wakefields one night, however, in which the topics ranged from abolition to geology to the progress of the new wing of the maternal hospital, Clara quickly learned to accept any invitation that was extended to her. *Here* were topics that provided fodder for lively debate and for her own reflection afterward. She was ashamed to know so little of them, that she had been blind to the plights faced by so many other of her fellow human creatures. Looking back, she realized now that she had had blinders of bitterness and ignorance on; her time at the Wakefields' had caused them to fall from her eyes, and she marveled at the world she could see. Its beauty and complexity made her fall in love with it, even as its cruelty and senseless injustices broke her heart.

"You looked like a schoolboy with a platter of chocolates in front of him," laughed Mrs. Wakefield after one party at the house adjourned and they were all going upstairs to bed.

Miss Holt's mouth, meanwhile, was drawn more and more often into a thin line that Clara knew could only be displeasure. She worried that the pound a week she had at her disposal would not be enough to quell the reports that Miss Holt must be giving to her mother and grandmother. But she could think of nothing else, and tried only to make Miss Holt's time in Tottenham as pleasant as possible so that the other might not wish to give it up. Luckily, a spindly friendship had formed between Miss Holt and the Wakefields' housekeeper Mrs. Jones, and Clara hoped that between this association and Miss Holt's sympathy toward Mr. Wakefield (an excitable, somewhat foolish man Clara could not help disliking even before she knew that his hare-brained business schemes had driven his wife to her own projects of employment), her companion would leave well enough alone. And anyway, there were only a few more weeks left in the season, and all the families would be returning to the country to shoot. How much harm could another fortnight do?

The end of the town season brought with it some anxiety to Clara. Charles had been most attentive, but he was going off with his regiment in August to begin his assignment of helping supervise his regiment's recruits. Would he speak to her father? Had he any intention of addressing her at all? His silence and her inability to distinguish whether he thought highly enough of her to propose both vexed and relieved her. As long as she was single, she could cling to whatever barest thread of hope she could find that she might be Mrs. Kensington yet. As soon as Charles spoke, as soon as he offered her this one chance to regain Yewspring—that thread would be whisked away like a leaf in the breeze, spinning out of sight.

Her cousin gratified her by asking whether they might explore the outer edge of Hyde Park while the two families walked together the next Sunday. "We can meet the rest of you at the fountain in half an hour," proposed Charles to Mrs. East-wood, an arrangement she readily agreed to. Even Clara could not come to trouble in thirty minutes while half of London strolled the paths.

Clara asked Charles the details of his military engagement, wondering how much longer he would be in town. He replied that he was leaving for Sandgate the following Saturday.

"Oh! This is your last week, then. I am sorry we are to part so soon."

"As am I." He nodded to another young man passing them who also wore scarlet, medals gleaming in the sunlight. "I have missed England. I have missed my family. And it was delightful to make the acquaintance of all your own relations, the 'Midlands Eastwoods' I always heard so much about from George."

"Your mother will be sorry you go away again, I think."

"Yes, but even the most nervous mother cannot imagine anything very terrible befalling one in Sandgate, I think. Beyond barracks food, at any rate. But—before I go, Miss Eastwood, I have been sorry that you are so often away from Southampton Street. I find our conversations—"

She drew in a breath. What would he say? What did he think of her, truly?

"—restorative. I feel closer to George when I am with you, who knew him so well."

She could not help feeling, again, that this loss would echo in his life far longer than in hers. Mr. Kensington now had whatever claim George had had before—but a brother was not to be replaced, no matter how many years might go by. The hole left in his life could not be stitched, but she was glad he thought her capable of taking up the needle.

"I knew a part of him," she said, "the part he brought to Exton every year, and the part he displayed in town. You knew the Kent George—so between us, I suppose we have the whole man among our various pieces. I am glad that I have been of solace to you, Charles. Truly. And I am sorry if my absence meant that you were denied any comfort I could give."

He looked over at her. "If I may ask, cousin, what takes you away? Your mama said only that you were visiting friends in Tottenham. I am surprised that you wish to be so long away from town."

Oh dear, she thought, *what to say? What to conceal?*

They walked on a few more steps that felt like miles in the

silence, their feet crunching on the gravel walk. Clara fixed her eye on a bright parasol up ahead and absentmindedly watched it bob about with the lady's white gown underneath, like the stem of an elegant mushroom.

Among the various versions of the truth Clara saw that there was a common core, and one that she was sure would be acceptable. "I am fond of drawing," she said, "and I go to stay in Tottenham with a friend who is helping me improve my skills." There was so much left out of this statement—Mrs. Wakefield's faith and ideas, her publication, Clara's own objectives, the subject being studied—that she felt as though she were lying, no matter how much she told herself that there was no falsehood to be found.

"How pleasant," Charles said. "My sisters love to sketch. Gertrude has done some very pretty watercolors of the seaside— they are hanging in the breakfast room at Reedbridge, I believe."

"Ah," said Clara. She could not imagine that her acquaintance with Charles would be so brief that he would never ask to see her work. Best have it—or as much of *it* as she could—out in the open. "I am interested in floral subjects myself. Quite detailed versions of plants, their parts, and so on."

"Oh, so landscapes, then? Or more like a still life of a bouquet?"

"Er—" How to describe her work without explaining that she had longed to be a botanist since she had returned from school? How to draw a curtain over her ambitions and aims like a tapestry meant to conceal the door to a room that she did not want him to see? "More like a still life. I shall show you sometime, if you like. I warn you it's rather academic, however. Just something I like to do to amuse myself in the country."

"Well, drawing is so very suitable for a woman—so easy to put down and pick up as needed. One can fit it into the spare hours between the house and the children." He glanced at her.

"Yes," she said. This ship must tack to another wind now. "I certainly hope to continue after I am married—if I am blessed enough to enter that happy state, at any rate."

Charles looked rather flustered. "Oh, yes, I did hear— that is, my aunt Hazel did mention that—that, well, a Mr. Wallace has been at Southampton Street."

Clara was not at all surprised that Mr. Wallace's two visits had been conflated by Mrs. Eastwood into regular occasions.

"Am I to prepare to—congratulate you?" Charles had stopped and looked at her intently. Clara was pleased to see that his expression held more concern than she might have thought it wise to plan on. She could smooth the wrinkle that had appeared between his brows, and they would all be the better for it. Yewspring would be the better for it.

"Oh," she said, affecting a laugh. "Certainly not! Mr. Wallace is agreeable enough, I daresay, but I would be obliged to turn him down if he were to make me an offer. I could not be a curate's wife, always moving about. I need a home. I need to put down roots."

He smiled, unmistakably relieved, and she knew all was well. "Are you a woman or a tree?" he teased, and they continued on together.

When they reached the others, they found that the others had met with the Crestons along the way, and Mr. Creston came forward especially to greet Charles and Clara, saying with a meaningful glance at her, "What a fine pair you two make!"

CHAPTER NINETEEN

Clara was not surprised, the following morning, to find that Charles had written a note to Mr. Eastwood asking if he might have a private audience with his cousin Clara over the course of the morning, if she was willing to delay her departure to Tottenham for just an hour or two. Mrs. Eastwood had appropriated the note and thrust it excitedly to her daughter over the coffeepot.

"Oh, Clara! What else could this mean but—"

Staring at the note, Clara heard Rose say, "So soon after his return! Clara, you must have found great favor with him indeed. Oh sister, I congratulate you."

"You assume that she would accept Charles if he were to offer," said Mr. Eastwood, fixing Clara in his gaze. "What do you think of this request, Clara?"

Clara, unexpectedly, found herself in turmoil. For the opportunity to live forever in Exton, she would have done a great deal. But could she commit herself to a man whose sole feeling for her seemed to be a devotion to George? And their conversation, though pleasant enough, was certainly nothing to Mr. Kensington's. When she thought of her first meeting with Mr. Kensington, the easy, natural manner in which he had engaged her in conversation, the interest he had shown in her and her life—the disparity between him and her cousin made him appear to even greater advantage. But the very thought of him made her remember, again, that marrying well, particularly should she remain at Yewspring with the means to hire an estate agent, was the most effective means of aiding him. The person who rendered Charles Eastwood so wholly lacking as a fiancé was also the only person who could induce her to accept that gentleman's hand, and so she said, forcing a pleasant expression onto her face, "I would be happy to accept Charles's kind offer, if he does have intentions to make one."

As Clara heard the peal of a distant clock chiming eleven, Charles was shown into the drawing room. She had been sitting reading the same sentence over and over in a book while she waited, and closed the volume, clutching it in her lap while the butler brought Charles in. Her mouth was so dry she could hardly respond to his greeting—and her suitor nervously went to the window to gather his courage.

After a moment standing and smiling at her nervously, Charles came and sat in the chair nearest Clara's. She had purposely not seated herself on a settee, not yet feeling equal to inviting her future husband to sit in such close proximity to her.

"Miss Eastwood," Mr. Eastwood began, "I trust it will not come as a surprise to you when I reveal to you that I have attempted to pay you special attention almost since my arrival in London."

"It is not a surprise, Charles," said Clara, her voice startling her with its composure. "You have paid your attentions very thoroughly, and I am flattered by your notice of me."

"I am relieved to hear it," he said. "I am inexperienced in my relations with your fair sex, as you may imagine, but I was not always sure by your demeanor, which I believe to be a sign of your calm and utterly ladylike temperament, if my advances were welcome or not. And of course, I would not assume that your feelings for me are the same as they were for my brother—"

Clara felt a quick surge of guilt rush through her, which she tried to shrug off. "I am happy that the good will between our families continues in spite of George's passing."

He shifted in his chair. "Yes, as am I. My intent when I returned to England was to take up George's role as much as I am able, even to the point of offering you my hand if you were agreeable to that proposition. And after meeting with you, I felt so reassured by your sensible and calm demeanor that I determined almost immediately that our union might be agreeable to all parties."

"You will find no objection from me," said Clara, trying not to think about all the reasons running through her head informing her that she *should* object.

"That being the case," he continued, "I feel that the time has come to make my intentions known. Miss Eastwood, would you do me the very great honor of accepting my hand in marriage?"

It was like plunging into cold water—one could not think about it, one just had to act. "Yes," said Clara, almost before he had finished his sentence.

He looked pleased. "Very good," he said. "I am delighted that you are amenable to my offer."

"I am glad you think so highly of me. Believe me, I know there are many young ladies who would have been delighted to become Mrs. Eastwood."

"Well, you have qualities that they do not. You have thoroughly impressed me with the capacity for attention which you have shown these last few weeks in our conversations—I have found that to be quite rare in the women of my acquaintance. I was beginning to fear that I was very dull indeed, but the attention you have been so kind as to bestow—which, I believe, is genuine—has been very gratifying. But I fear it shall be an awfully long engagement because of my engagement with the army. I believe it will be a year before I am released."

"Good," said Clara. "That is, you must fulfill your appointment. And you are sure it will delay our wedding?"

"I believe it would be best to wait until I am fully made a civilian again, yes. Army camps can be rough and wild places under the best of circumstances, and my position is such that I will be travelling about quite often. No life for a lady, that. And then after I am done I must work with my father to obtain a house for us in Kent."

Alarm rose in Clara. "But—we shall live at Yewspring, of course."

"Oh yes, when the time comes! But your grandparents, of course, must not be displaced from their home, nor your parents. And of course, I am only your father's heir presumptive—your mother could perhaps bear an heir that would inherit all the estates."

Clara sincerely doubted it, thinking of all her mother's disappointments in past years, of bed sheets stained with blood that the maids had brought out of Mrs. Eastwood's bedroom. "That is quite prudent. Well, so long as you have no objection to living in Exton—"

"None at all, and you of course are welcome to live at Yewspring year-round should you wish it, even if I must go down to Kent to tend to the other estates. So then, my dear cousin, we shall be wed—I would imagine no later than mid-summer next. Do you think you can be patient that long?"

"Yes," said Clara. "There will be plenty of time to discuss the details. You are *quite* sure your appointment will not be shortened?"

"I think not," he said. "Unless Napoleon is so obliging as to end this conflict abroad, troops will be needed for the foreseeable future. I suppose I could press my superiors on the matter of being released early—"

"Oh, no," she said. "You must stay in their good graces. It would not do to have even a hint of scandal about your removal from the army. We must content ourselves with being grateful that you are brought back to England safely."

"You are very considerate, my dear." The phrase was woven in seamlessly, but she still felt like it was a loose thread that would one day begin to unravel the cloth. "I have been thinking of some of the details. I leave town on Friday, and you do not come back from Tottenham until—Wednesday, is it? So this is almost the last chance to see one another until I leave. We shall write to each other, of course, but I believe I should plan to come back to Exton in the autumn recess, and again for Christmas, if my aunt Eastwood is willing to have me at Yewspring. That way we may discuss the details of the settlement, and of course see each other after so many months of separation. I should like to see the estates, as well."

"Yes, that sounds agreeable," she said, forcing the words out of her mouth.

The details being decided, there seemed to be nothing more for them to say to one another. "Shall we go tell them?" Charles said after an embarrassed silence had arisen.

"Yes," said Clara.

She went and summoned the family, champagne was brought up from the cellar, and even Miss Holt, when she came into the drawing-room to tell Clara that the carriage was waiting, had a hasty glass to celebrate the occasion. The other Eastwoods came out to the pavement to bid the Tottenham passengers farewell, Rose kissed her sister with what felt like the first enthusiasm Clara had sensed from her in ages, and handkerchiefs were pulled out to be held aloft and fluttered. It was as if they were seeing off a regiment bound for war or a ship leaving the docks rather than two ladies going seven miles' distance, but Clara felt she had earned it. She had already told Rose and her mother to spread the news of her engagement about the family, and indeed she knew it would be all over town at large by the afternoon. She wanted all to know her triumph—her grandmother, Mrs. Doyle and Annie Clemons and Mr. Dillingham in Exton. Let no one say that she did not deserve Yewspring. Let no one say that there was anything she would not do for it. Her hand belonged to Charles—her life and her future bound to a man six years her junior who thought she drew pictures of bouquets in her spare time. Nothing was out of the question when it came to getting Yewspring back, to restoring Mr. Kensington to his rightful place. All that had been asked of her was her freedom. She left it behind her in Southampton Street as the carriage turned the corner.

"But why are you so anxious to get back to Exton?" asked Mrs. Wakefield, brows drawn in consternation. "I would have had you with us for the whole autumn, if your mother could spare you that long. Your work is progressing, yes, and I cannot deny you have a natural aptitude for the work, but you still have much to learn. And Belle's house would have accommodated you and Miss Holt if you were to travel with us to Woodbridge in a few weeks—the children are hardy enough now to take rooms in the attics, which would not be so very hot or cold during the autumn."

"I am grateful more than I can begin to express to you for your help," said Clara. "But I've been away from Yewspring too long. I miss it, and—I am just not meant for town. Being here has been the best thing about it."

Mrs. Wakefield raised her eyebrows. "Even above this offer from your cousin?"

"Oh, well…I suppose that has not quite sunk in yet."

Mrs. Wakefield sighed. "I cannot presume to know you well enough, Miss Eastwood, to advise you as to which way you are meant to live in the world. But I must admit that except for your family connection, this seems a strange match indeed. I sense neither affection nor friendship in your feelings toward him, though those may grow in time. Is there some reason you find yourself compelled to marry? If my question seems impertinent, know that I ask it in your own interest. Marital relations can be strained enough by circumstances even with esteem, affection, or understanding, and it is best to begin on as solid a foundation as you can. The winds of life will buffet you enough, believe me. I am trying only to save you from unhappiness, if I can."

"I must marry because I must be at Yewspring," said Clara, feeling that the other woman, attached as she was to her neighborhood and the work it brought her, would understand this motive.

"Indeed? Does your father stipulate so?"

"Oh, no. I just wish to be there. I cannot spend my life anywhere else. I have it in mind to convince Charles to take a house in Exton for us, rather than living in Kent."

"You have some objection to Kent?"

"As I said, I wish to remain at Yewspring. I have no reason to object to Kent, so far as I know—although George did get so ill from living there."

"Yes, but they have those marvelous canals now that help clear the air. I think you would not fear for your health if you were to settle there." Mrs. Wakefield seemed to be probing, and Clara could not help shrinking from the scrutiny.

"I thought—you are attached to Tottenham, are you not? And to London, where you were raised? Surely you cannot think that one place is just like another, that landscapes can be exchanged seamlessly?"

"Yes, but if circumstances had arisen to take me elsewhere—to the Continent, to Edinburgh—such a scientific city! What a joy it would have been to live there!—I would have attended to those circumstances. No landscape will ever bring you happiness if you do not bring it with you, you know. Nor can any landscape be enchanting enough to lift one out of sadness or regret—not in the long-term, at any rate. And for myself, the happiness I have found, what drips and drabs of it life has seen fit to give, has come when I am active, when I am useful, when I am wrestling with some great idea. Those circumstances have arisen here, but I do not suppose they would not have arisen anywhere else, and I simply would have learned another place's flora in my walks. But this is beside the point. I suspect that your eagerness to marry has something to do with money, as it so often does for us women. Am I correct?"

Clara told her about the arrangement of her and Rose's dowries. "And now that I am engaged," she finished, "I cannot believe that Mr. Creston will be long in making his addresses to Rose."

"So you have thrown yourself on the sword for your sister?"

"I hardly think marrying Charles and living at Yewspring qualify as throwing myself on the sword," said Clara with a smile. She hoped it hid the uneasiness churning in her like waves smashing into cliffs.

"Leaving you two thousand."

"Yes. Charles will be happy with it, I think. My expenses hardly signify."

"I am so displeased with this system of only giving money

to women when they marry. How, as a culture, are we ever to advance the cause of women and ensure happy marriages when we restrict a women's ability to capital to the married state? Would your father give you the money outright? Then you might marry or stay single as you liked."

Clara had never thought of this potential solution to her difficulties, considering herself bound first to George, then to Mr. Kensington and Yewspring—both schemes had required marriage, and so married she must be. "Well, not now that I've accepted Charles," she said after a moment's thought. "I don't think he would risk displeasing Aunt Harriet and all the others. I think I must go through with the match now—a prospect I am not displeased with."

"What a pity," sighed Mrs. Wakefield. "I still think you should appeal to your father and ask for the money. Why should men always have it all?" She looked out the window and said softly, as if to herself, "They can be so foolish with it."

Clara could not answer these questions, and Mrs. Wakefield's dissatisfaction with her engagement could not lessen her determination to marry Charles, nor was her mentor's persuasion to stay longer successful in convincing her. She must get home again, as soon as she could.

The next evening brought several visitors to dine at the Wakefields'. Two couples that were frequently at the Wakefields came, and a houseguest staying with one of the families—Dr. Roger Stanley, a surgeon from Somersetshire. He was a tall, robust man of about fifty with graying hair combed neatly over his balding pate, and Mrs. Wakefield and Clara quickly discovered that he was an amateur botanist.

"Lovely, these," he said, gesturing to some of Mrs. Wakefield's illustrations that were framed in the drawing-room. "As good as Sowerby's, Mrs. Wakefield."

"Thank you," said Mrs. Wakefield. Behind them they could hear a lively discussion of Mrs. Edgeworth's latest novel beginning, with interjections of "*Most* horrid!" and "But was Lady Glenthorn really so bad?" already flying about the room. Clara could even hear Kitty's voice amid the chatter. From over Dr. Stanley's shoulder she could see Miss Holt's frown deepen into a scowl. Clara knew from flipping through the pages of the novel in town that her companion would not approve of the material, and so called her over.

"Miss Holt has been kind enough to accompany me here so I might study with Mrs. Wakefield," said Clara. "My family are all otherwise occupied in town."

"How good of you," Dr. Stanley said with a bow to Miss Holt. "You must have a great deal of respect for the study yourself, ma'am, to be so accommodating with your time."

"Yes," said Clara, casting a glance at Miss Holt, who had turned a bit pink. "Miss Holt was my governess."

"Ah, you must be responsible for Miss Eastwood's interest, then."

"Oh, not at all," said Miss Holt.

"Oh, you ladies, always so modest!" He beamed at Miss Holt. "I have an instinct for these things—here stands before me a woman of not only genteel meekness but true accomplishment."

Miss Holt—and Clara, grateful for this diversion to keep the other's attention—thought it wisest not to contradict Dr. Stanley. Mrs. Wakefield stepped away from the group with a polite smile, saying, "I must see to the tea-things."

"Do you have any botanical projects afoot, Dr. Stanley?" asked Clara.

"Oh, yes," he said casually. "I'm thinking of writing a flora for

Somersetshire. It's so terribly difficult to find experts who know the plants—not that I believe I deserve *that* accolade—and our residents are quite ignorant of the species found in the county. But my old schoolmate Becker—Johnathan Becker, do you know him, Miss Eastwood? His daughters are about your age, I should think—no? A pity, they were lovely girls, though girls they are no longer. I believe old Becker has something like ten grandchildren now—at any rate, Becker is a publisher and has agreed to put out whatever I can assemble in the next year or so. I treated a very bad case of his gout about three years back and the dear fellow has always wished to repay me, I think."

"Oh!" Clara was flooded with excitement and with envy for this opportunity, which seemed to have presented itself to Dr. Stanley as easily as Rose received invitations to balls. "I have often wished for such a flora for the Midlands. When will you do your collecting?"

"Collecting? Oh, I suppose I could make a few jaunts about the countryside, but I shall work mostly from books. There are descriptions of almost every plant in England these days—the ones for the proper species just haven't been compiled. It shall be a task for the long winter evenings, I think."

Clara was tempted to call Mrs. Wakefield back over and tell her about this shockingly unscientific plan. What self-respecting botanist could simply assume which plants were present without actually laying eyes on them? What if the prior descriptions were erroneous and the new guide perpetuated misunderstanding? And, to Clara, divorcing the plants of the page from the physical counterparts they represented was madness. One might as well be writing fiction. But—this poorly-laid plan could, if she were careful, present an opportunity to her as well. And who knew when another might come?

"And—" she cleared her throat, "what if your publishing

friend were to supply the costs to take collecting trips? He might do so, if he felt it would increase the quality of the book. Which, as a fellow student of the subject, I believe it would."

"Oh, cost would be no object. It is more the matter of time away from my practice."

"Ah," she said. "And what about—illustrations?"

"Oh, I'll use the ones in the books I find. What's been done once needn't be done again."

This was the door she had hoped would crack open. She edged up to it and hoped Miss Holt would not notice her intentness on reaching up to nudge it ajar.

"I have been studying illustrating with Mrs. Wakefield," she said. "Would you let me lend my services to your flora? I am not at her level yet, but I think I am passable. And I think original plates would make the flora more valuable. More respected. Even Mr. Sowerby draws all his own plates."

"Well," Dr. Stanley said, rubbing his chin, "such a scheme might be feasible."

Yes, if there is any money to be had in this, thought Clara. "Perhaps you could write to your friend—Becker, was it?" she said. "Better yet, I shall write him myself."

Triumphant, giddy, Clara floated up the stairs after the guests had left, and found a letter waiting for her in her room, brought in the last post of the day. The joy in her soared higher when she saw the handwriting on the address, then plummeted into the depths of her core. She opened the envelope with shaking hands.

July 11

My dear Miss Eastwood,

You do not know how much joy your letter has brought me. You do not know how greatly I treasure it. Forgive the long interval between posting your letter and my reply, I beg you, for we are in the midst of harvest and hardly have a moment of leisure. I regret very much that it has kept me from writing to you, but we must work while we can since winter will bring weeks of idleness. Know that I think of you every hour—nay, every quarter hour.

I wonder what you are reading. I wish I were there to speak with you about books, about plants, about our days here. About everything.

And that was when Clara finally began to weep.

CHAPTER TWENTY

Mr. Eastwood found himself at the center of a whirlwind of business arrangements with not one but two young men over the course of the week following Charles's proposal to Clara. As soon as she returned from Tottenham, Clara found that Charles and her father had worked out all the details of her marriage settlement, with her new suitor taking her on the terms that his brother had intended to. Clara had two thousand that would come with her upon her marriage, leaving eight thousand for Rose. She was not to remain single long after her sister became engaged—Mr. Creston wasted no time asking for Rose's hand just five days after Charles had spoken to Clara. His proposal, of course, was accepted with alacrity and pleasure.

To his future sister-in-law, to whom he must have felt a debt of gratitude for attaching herself in such an obliging way, Mr. Creston took pains to give a cordial notice as he took his leave after making his addresses. In his final congratulatory wishes to her and her fiancé, she felt sure there was meant to be a marked tone of friendship and geniality where before there had been watchful caution. Of her ability to esteem her brother-in-law, she was not as certain, doubting she could hold him in as high esteem as others might have. His father's poor management of the family estates might be reflected in the son and must say something in general about the family who so little understood their role as steward and provider in the county—such neglect and folly vexed her exceedingly. But she hoped nonetheless that he would make her sister a happy woman, and that all within the Crestons' sphere would prosper.

No sooner had the door closed behind Mr. Creston than the room fell into a happy clamor, for Violet, Caroline, and Mrs. Tapley were in attendance. They all fell upon Rose in joyful commotion, each grasping her hand and offering their congratulations. It had turned out to be the year of matches, after all the fruitless ones before, for Mr. Reynolds had made his offer and Caroline was blissfully picking out her *trousseau*. The mothers' past disappointments were forgotten now; indeed, the aftereffect of their trials was only to sweeten the pleasure of these triumphs now, just as a bitter medicine makes a bite of strawberries afterward twice as delightful. Three engagements in a single summer! It was good fortune of the highest magnitude, and despite the fact that all of them had come about because of a connection to Exton rather than London, Mrs. Eastwood and her sisters-in-law still thought the expense and inconvenience of coming to town worth the trouble. Rose, for one, would reside in town much of the year as Mrs. Creston, so the connections she had formed there would not be wasted. And Mrs. Creston she was to become with all speed, with an Exton wedding planned for the beginning of September.

The night after Mr. Creston's proposal, Rose came to Clara's room before bed and asked, "May I come in?" so timidly that Clara's heart, locked as it was in the dread and guilt of her own engagement, could not but feel the tenderness she used to when Rose would be afraid of the dark and come knocking at her door to climb into the bed with her sister. It was a side of her sister she had rarely seen since coming to town, especially after the exhibition.

"Of course," she told Rose, setting her book aside.

Her sister came in, shawl wrapped about her, hair in its paper curlers, with a smile so serene and content that Clara remembered that there was a second reason she had accepted her cousin Charles.

"I just wanted to say, Clara, that James and I are ever so grateful that your engagement with Mr. Eastwood has enabled our own," said Rose. "And to ask if you will be my bridesmaid on the wedding day."

The request touched Clara. She knew her sister could have chosen any of their cousins to attend her at the wedding, and that it could be argued that any of the others had been a more compatible companion than she had to Rose in the past months—and indeed the past years as Clara's unconventional interests consumed so much of her time and attention.

"Of course," she said. "I would be glad to attend you."

Rose had been hovering near the door and now went to the window to fidget with the curtain tie, avoiding her sister's eyes.

"And—Clara, you are not making yourself a sacrifice for me, are you?"

"A sacrifice?" Clara was determined not to reveal too much of her discomfort around the subject of her own engagement. Innocence was the best approach. "Whatever do you mean?"

Rose sighed, as if she were the older of the two and Clara the young, wide-eyed girl just out of the schoolroom, gaping at the world. "I could not be easy if I felt you still had thoughts of Mr. Kensington and engaged yourself to cousin Charles just to smooth the way for me. Do you?"

"Do I…?"

"Have thoughts of Mr. Kensington?"

"It would be entirely inappropriate for me to do so. Mama and Papa would never consent to a match between us. And I determined long ago that my first love—my only love, really—is Yewspring. The course that best secures my future there is marrying cousin Charles, who has given me no sign that I shall regret doing so."

"But do you care for him at all?"

Clara went to the window and pulled the curtain aside to see if it was raining, for she wished to see the moon. "I hold him in high esteem. He is doing a very honorable thing, engaging me in George's place, thinking so little of himself and what he may have wished to do had he not been made heir." Outside, only inky darkness and the pinpricks of stars met her gaze, and she settled the curtain back again.

Her sister looked a bit pacified at Clara's words. "Yes, I suppose it is a noble thing for Charles to do. But I care so much for James—I quite prefer him to every other man I have met. He is so charming, and so agreeable! And I confess his smart ways appeal to me. I am eager to become a woman of Town, vain though it may be, and he has shown so much consideration for me in that regard—before we all leave he has already arranged for us to tour three houses we might take. Do you think someday perhaps you and cousin Charles will come to care for each other so?"

Clara knew Rose's admiration of London life was a harmless vanity but one that would sunder her sister from her nonetheless. Ignoring her heart, which if she had not known was already broken seemed to be breaking anew, she said cheerfully, "Oh yes, I am sure we will. Neither of us expect romance, you know, especially at this stage of our relationship. At present we esteem and admire one another, I believe. What better way to help affection grow than by letting it do so in its own time? We shall do quite well, Rose, and I think you and Mr. Creston will too. You may go to the altar with a clean conscience. In fact, I command it, in the last act of authority of an older sister!"

And so it was that Rose and Mr. James Creston were wed, as planned, on a warm September morning, exactly to Mrs. Eastwood's specifications. Mrs. Morton had made casual mention that a double wedding that included Caroline and Mr. Reynolds might be less inconvenient for Dr. Flemington. But Rose, one of the two daughters coming from the male line of the Eastwoods, would naturally have overshadowed her cousin, thought Lady Eastwood, and so Caroline was to be married the following Monday instead. Rose wore light blue and a demure smile that Clara knew hid both ecstasy at finally becoming Mrs. Creston after nearly a year, and a modest fear of her wedding night. The groom looked both nervous and thoroughly delighted at the same time. After the breakfast at Beechview, they swept out of the gate with Rose waving cheerfully to the guests who remained on the steps to see them off. They would honeymoon in Nottingham before going to Rutland for the autumn shooting, with Violet and Mrs. Tapley going as far to Measham with the second pair of newlyweds the following week before going to Rutland as well. There Violet would stay with Rose until Christmas, when the Crestons would come back to Exton. Clara had been invited to Rutland as well, but she could not go until November, for she was engaged to spend a month during the autumn in Somersetshire with Dr. Stanley. They were to select field sites for a spring collecting trip, Clara was to make some preliminary sketches for the flora, and help Dr. Stanley inventory the existing floras he owned as well as procure any others that would be useful.

Miss Holt had already agreed to accompany Clara to Somersetshire so that Mrs. Eastwood might remain in Exton for the all-important shooting season, though Rose's parents had also scheduled a visit to Rose in Rutland during the course of the autumn. Imagining what Miss Holt had returned to upon their return from town—the dark, spare rooms over the store, weak tea and weak broth, the cheapest cakes from Tifton's bakery, the long unchanging hours sidling by, marked by the clock on the mantel—Clara was not surprised that Miss Holt had offered her services before the trip had even been brought to Mrs. Eastwood. But even the thought of spending another four weeks being watched over by Lady Eastwood's proxy could not hamper Clara's anticipation. They were to leave in a fortnight.

She woke the morning after the wedding with a spring in her step and a smile she could not contain, beaming at the early autumn sun coming through her window. Luckily, Mrs. Eastwood had gone to Coventry for the day to help Mrs. Morton get provisions for Caroline's wedding breakfast, and her father was already out with Mr. Graham, so Clara's day was entirely her own. She stopped at the kitchen and received, as she had requested the night before, a cold repast of bread and butter, cheese, and a cup of tea. She took it in the garden, delighting in the birds singing above her in the leafy canopy of the trees and wondering why in the world anyone ate indoors in fine weather. Taking her dishes back to the kitchen, she then spent the morning happily engrossed in the garden, papers spread out on the work table she had brought out, the latest edition of *Ackermann's Repository* with her journal at her side to take notes. Finally, she went back inside to find the pile of letters on the hall table, as she had been expecting. She found the one with her name on it that she had been hoping had arrived, read it quickly, and broke out into a smile.

When she could hear the Exton church bell tolling twelve, she told the servants she was walking to the north fields, and set off hoping to find Mr. Kensington. She took the lane that led past Yewspring's drive, which ran next to several of their neighbors' houses—one of whom, an elderly gentleman whose estate bordered Yewspring but one house, passed her in his pony cart, tipping his hat to her as he went by and calling, "Do give my regards to your grandfather!" for he must have assumed she was cutting across the fields to Beechview.

She continued on as the lane went from a cart-track to a narrow footpath between hedgerows, weaving back and forth at the ridge of a hill that marked the border between the steep fields above her and the ones below. Above, she could see the distant movements of the tall corn plants where the harvesters were moving through, and occasionally a figure would appear at the margin of the field.

She glimpsed Daniel Fulbright, called to him, and asked as he came over to the hedge, "Do you know where Mr. Kensington is?"

"Yes, Miss Eastwood. 'E's over near the wagons, a bit west of 'ere. Can I fetch 'im for ye, miss?"

"Would you? I will bring you a fine jar of earthworms from our garden to thank you. But, Daniel—" he had already started off, gleeful at the promise of such a precious prize for fishing, "please pull him aside to ask him to come. I must speak with him about a rather personal matter, and would prefer it if you did not announce to the group."

"All right, miss." He was off, and soon Mr. Kensington came through the rows, coming out at the hedge a bit behind her. Her heart skipped a beat again, this time for more pleasurable reasons, and she walked down to meet him, though they stood on opposite sides of the hedge, there not being a stile nearby.

He smiled and removed his hat. "Good afternoon, Miss Eastwood."

"Good afternoon," she said, returning the smile and drinking in the sight of his face, a pleasure that she seldom could anticipate or enjoy. He had tanned further from his weeks of work, and a sheen lay upon his brow from the hazy heat rising from the fields.

"Daniel told me you were by a 'great big tree, the kind with gray bark, sir.' I presume he meant this rowan, but I was sorely tempted to teach him the name, for I fear for his generation if they lose their knowledge of nature. Another time, perhaps. So the newlyweds are safely off? I heard the church bells yesterday."

"Yes, Rose has already written to my mother, I think."

"And they looked happy when they left?"

"Very," she said. "I think Rose must have been longing for that day for a long time now. She was radiant. And Mr. Creston—James, I suppose I should say now—looked so relieved it is as if he had just gotten a bill of clean health from his doctor."

"Lucky man! To unite happiness and practicality, to gain the wife of his choice and the funds so badly needed not just by him but by those who look to him—well, I cannot but envy him. But today is not the day to dwell on that. Spite is not a tonic but a poison, and I shall not sip from it. To what do I owe the agreeable surprise of your presence? And how might I persuade you to bestow it upon me more often?"

She laughed. "If it were left only to me, you would need only ask and I would be there," she said gently.

"I know," he said. "But thank you for saying it."

"I came to give you some news. Might I convince you to take your dinner break? And perhaps we can sit under that 'great tree with gray bark'?"

"All right," he said, and at the corner of the field came over the stile. They sat in the shade of the tree, and Clara rejoiced that here they could sit so near to each other, his arm less than a foot from her own. He pulled out his bundle of dinner, and she winced at the sight of the meager portion of bread and cheese, with a lone peach carefully packed in a cloth.

"Will you share this with me?" he asked, beginning to rip up the bread.

"Heavens, no," she said. "You have earned every bite of it, I am sure. And I will go to my own dinner soon."

He took a piece of bread, topped it with cheese and handed it to her. "Just a symbolic bite, then. I do not know when I shall have the pleasure of sharing a meal with you again. Indulge me, if you would."

She smiled, took it, and they ate together. After a moment, during which he too, seemed to want to drink in her face, he said, "What of your news?"

She smiled. "Would you consider perhaps taking some time off from field work?"

He smiled as well. "Nothing would please me more, or rather, I would happily trade *this* labor out-of-doors for labor out-of-doors that would engage my mind as well as my body. But the bills must be paid, and Oliver grows so quickly it is as if he is determined to ruin my pocketbook with new clothes, cheeky chap."

Her joy at the proposal she had to offer him swelled up in her. "What if you could perform such labor at a third more per week than you earned here?"

He looked astonished. "I would thank Providence for sending such labor to me and accept it gratefully, of course."

"Then you may thank me in Providence's stead," she said, "and the sweetest recompense would be to be in your arms as I wish to be, but—I am getting ahead of myself. I am commissioned to perform botanical drawing on a Somersetshire tour this fall with Dr. Roger Stanley."

"That's wonderful! What—"

"There's more," she cut in, holding up her hand. "You may congratulate me after I finish, and perhaps there will be reason for us both to be gladdened by this expedition. I know you have some knowledge of the county, and that you have drawn maps for Lord Chesterton, and so I asked Dr. Stanley if he might find your assistance useful to help select field sites, carry our equipment and drive us about, and to draw the maps for the flora he is writing. He agreed, and his letter of introduction to you should be here within the week, I wager. And—I have some idea of what you make here, and solicited Dr. Stanley to pay you that and more. Since my own pockets are not deep, I will shamelessly preposition those who have more funds than opportunity to spend them."

A smile burst out on Mr. Kensington's face as well, making him look like a thrilled boy who has just galloped on a swift horse for the first time. "Miss Eastwood—" he began, overwhelmed with emotion.

"Clara," she said firmly. "Please, Clara."

"Why have you done this? The torture of being near you without calling you mine will be overshadowed by the pleasure of this task and the knowledge of your nearness—but nothing has transpired to make your engagement to Mr. Eastwood impossible. Why have not you cast me away? It would be better for you to forget me, you know."

"Oh, I could never do that. I can more easily picture myself burning Yewspring to the ground. It is as I told you when I wrote—my primary wish, since we are not to be together, is to position myself in such a way that I might be useful to you, and this opportunity was too wonderful to resist."

His hand drifted to her face, and he looked at her like she was the princess in a tapestry, a Madonna, a Venus. Though she knew she was only a maid in the shadows of some fine portrait, not its subject with shining curls and luminous eyes and swathed in fashionable linen, she let him think her beautiful, and smiled. She had never known that such exquisite pleasure, the pleasure of loving and being loved in return, could ever be mixed with such sharp pain—the thought of wedding another almost undid her; she almost suggested they catch a carriage bound for Gretna Green. She would, thereafter, always have a fondness for rowan trees, such bliss that she stole in those few moments under one of its branches in the dappled shade of the bank, while the summer insects hummed around them. She fancied that they made sounds of approbation, that nature itself delighted in their nearness to one another, no matter that he could not touch her as she wished.

She soon realized how long she had kept him from his work. "I must take my leave, lest you are missed. But please watch for Dr. Stanley's letter, and accept his offer as soon as you can, if you are so inclined. Weeks with you would strengthen me for the winter to come, I think, and perhaps that time would be a comfort for you as well."

He looked up at the sun. "I despise the day for its speed in passing. I would have stretched this half hour into years if I could. You see, I doubt very much that your presence will be a comfort to me, knowing that you are promised to another, and while we have sat here I have almost convinced myself that you are free to be my wife. But if this collecting trip will be tortuous, it is a torture I happily accept. It is far better than waking every day and knowing that I will not see you, that we shall not speak."

He stood, held out his hand and helped her rise. His touch sent tingles up and down her spine. She smiled, pressed his hand, and they parted. All the way home, she tried to quell each dreamy smile, only for another to take its place. Despite herself, despite everything that would unfold, she was happier than she could ever remember.

The group traveling from Exton—Clara, Miss Holt, Mr. Kensington, and Fiona and Matilda to attend their mistresses—went separately from Mr. Kensington to Somersetshire. Clara, knowing that Miss Holt would know of Mr. Kensington's reputation, had not told her companion about his presence during the trip. Miss Holt frowned when Mr. Kensington was shown into Dr. Stanley's parlor, but in company she could not do more. When she pulled Clara aside that evening before they went to bed and said, "Mrs. Eastwood would not like this, Miss Clara, not one bit," Clara replied, "Oh? Whyever not? Mr. Kensington is staying at the inn, not here at the house with us, and it is not *my* fault we need a cartographer. Don't fret, Miss Holt, no harm will come to me, nor to you. I hardly think this even worth mentioning to my parents." She was straying close to a cliff, she knew, but it was always in the back of her mind that she faced a lifetime with Charles, and so chose to risk tiptoeing along the edge, watching stones skitter down into the abyss beyond.

The group was based at Dr. Stanley's house for a fortnight, where he went to his surgery during much of the day and then spent the evenings discussing the arrangements for the flora with Clara and Mr. Kensington. During the day, the other three drove or walked to find nearby field sites, and Clara worked on sketches while Mr. Kensington made notes for his maps. While they were out, working in some woodland hollow or beside some stream swollen with autumn rain, Clara would sometimes walk off a short distance with Mr. Kensington, leaving Miss Holt perched on her canvas stool with a book, glaring at them disapprovingly. In this way, they snatched conversation together like birds after crumbs, always agreeing with a rueful, regretful smile when it was time to return to their chaperone.

He had slipped Clara the first volume of a book one evening while they were sorting through Dr. Stanley's collection, showing her the identical one that he kept. "I hoped we could read it together," he had murmured to her, and her guilt at the expense he had taken on to buy two copies was paired with pleasure at the prospect of reading with him. By alternating stints with books in Dr. Stanley's library, as well, they got through several volumes during their time staying at the house. The books Mr. Kensington chose were exactly the kind of books she had longed to read but no one would ever have given to her or even imagined her capable of understanding—interesting, elegant treaties of natural history and land management, explorer's diaries from the jungles of the Amazon and the heart of the African continent, essays linking the religion of church to the rapture of the soul when viewing nature. She had no idea her mind had been so closed by narrow writing on fashion, feminine meekness, and fanciful descriptions of the natural world that left out many pieces of evidence. She also had had no idea that now her mind could stretch so far, could delight in so many different topics that challenged her; her time at the Wakefields' had confirmed that there were many horizons in the world, stretching beyond the drawing room and the nursery, and she eagerly chased the subjects that most appealed to her. Of these, no unifying thread could be found except that they were complex, took in the world in all of its brutality, its apparent randomness, and all its unique features. Where these subjects could, they found order, and where they could not find it, instead responded with awe and wonder.

"My God, Clara," said Mr. Kensington one day after a stealthily executed argument, loving but fierce, over whether England should send military forces to assist in exploring its new colonies, "your mind is even more fearsome than I supposed, and at long last, it is awake."

Not all of their discourse was amiable. One rainy Sunday

afternoon while Dr. Stanley was called to the surgery and Miss Holt was in bed with a headache, Mr. Kensington laid down his book after a pleasurably comfortable silence, the fire crackling in the grate, and said, leaning toward her, "There is something that has been weighing on my mind, and I—I wonder if I might be bold enough to ask it of you."

She laid aside the sketch she had been working on, and said, "Of course. You need not fear asking me anything." In spite of herself, her heart hammered, asking, *What if he were to offer? What would I say?* He had come to sit beside her, and she arranged her hands in her lap to hide their trembling and looked at him expectantly.

"I am wondering if you would, perhaps, be better served by breaking off your engagement to Mr. Eastwood than by marrying him."

She looked away uneasily. "I cannot pretend the idea is not an appealing one, but I cannot see a way that it could be accomplished. Yewspring would be lost to Charles while I would be shunted off to Rutland with Rose someday, if she would have me. Not to mention the fact that I would be separated from you, permanently. I believe it would break my heart."

"But must your income come from your husband? Clara, you have a gift, and one that might give you some measure of independence and comfort. I beg you to consider it as a means by which you might support yourself. Perhaps your father would give you your dowry money if you asked. If you could convince him that your happiness is better secured in this way than through marriage—he is not a cruel man. He will not deny you, I think."

"I wish I shared your opinion. He is not cruel, you are right—but I have come close to sullying his name and making him the laughingstock of London, the father of eccentric Miss

Eastwood who embarrassed herself in front of the Duke of Marlborough. He wishes me married as much as my mother and my grandmother."

"It is so maddening, when you would want so very little to live on! Your wants are not excessive. You are so close to independence, dearest, and I cannot help feeling that you should grasp for it more ardently."

"I wish it were only a matter of my own comfort," she said. "For as tenuous as the spinster life is, I would accept it if it meant I could provide for all those whom I wish to protect. But with Yewspring, I can do so much more for you and your family. I think Charles would give me an allowance of ten pounds a month, and since my own wants need not come out of that, well, it is very much more that I could give you."

He sighed and rubbed his face with his hands. "Please forgive my interference in this way, but when I knew of your talents, I had hoped at least to find you with a devoted father, who had been attentive to and cultivated your gifts. Then I could have slept at night. But to find you at every juncture to have been so misunderstood, or so neglected! To have no one tell you that you might be able to provide for yourself, when you think the only choice is to attach yourself to a stranger! Mrs. Wakefield's attentions are the only consolation when I think of how you have been treated."

"I know it is painful for both of us to think of me being married to Charles," she said gently. "But I think we must resign ourselves to it being the best course of action, even if Yewspring did not hang in the balance. The fact that it does should strengthen our resolve. My influence there will benefit both of us, and the workers as well. I have not forgotten my duty to them."

Mr. Kensington let out another sigh, then after a moment said, "I trust your judgment. If you think you are able to bear what your marriage will ask of you, then I respect that decision. We shall be separated either way if we are to attend to practicalities, so I cannot consult my own happiness in this matter."

She swallowed hard. "Mr. Kensington, no matter what may happen, know that I am yours in heart and mind, no matter what."

"And I am yours," he said. "The knowledge of our love gives me great peace in spite of everything that separates us. I have lost much in my life, but so long as I have the knowledge of your regard for me, I consider myself fortunate enough for three men." He made a motion as if to take her hand, then checked himself.

She reached out hers and took what he had withheld.

"I wish I could be so selfless," she said. "I have spent so long without the hope of love, and now find it hard to let it go. I still am in happy disbelief that it has found me, when I did not even know that I wanted to be sought."

"Believe it, my Clara," he said, and, emboldened perhaps by the solitude they had stumbled into, lifted her chin, and kissed her.

In their bliss and the intensity of their attention on each other, and with their back to the entrance, neither of them saw Miss Holt slip away from the open doorway, her cheeks burning.

CHAPTER TWENTY-ONE

During the last fortnight of their autumn efforts, the group traveled about to various villages to inspect their study sites. They rose each morning at the inn, breakfasted quickly, and gathered their supplies for a morning of collecting. Fiona had accompanied the ladies from Exton and was perfecting her stitching, hoping to be asked to go to town and serve in the Crestons' new household, and brought her hoops out with her to work on, perched on a stool beneath a parasol. Clara's heart had gone out to her when she said contentedly on the second day, "It's like being a real lady, Miss Clara, and I don't know when I'll be off my feet for this long again."

Mr. Kensington had selected sites ahead of time, with the consultation of Dr. Stanley, and they spent half the day or more walking out and collecting, with Clara making quick field sketches, and then went back to the inn to examine specimens, work on the maps for the flora, and for Clara to continue her drawing. Every second or third they went on to another place, and they could hear the gunfire of gentlemen hunters echoing through the countryside even with the carriage windows up.

Dr. Stanley spent the evenings delving deeply into existing floras to best determine the identification of the plants, and Clara soon learned to finish her sketches for the day quickly in order to sit at his elbow and pester him with questions. Mr. Kensington's eyes shone proudly as he watched her in the firelight of the room they had appropriated as a study off the inn's common room. As all three of them had an interest in plants and Clara had learned enough from her studies to convince Dr. Stanley to take her seriously, the discussions were lengthy and sometimes became quite passionate. Clara had been alarmed to find that Dr. Stanley was, at best, a dedicated amateur and his knowledge often strayed into error. When she tried to suggest corrections to his classifications or descriptions, asking as gently as she knew how whether the leaves of a plant had been arranged alternate rather than opposite one another or if the bark of a particular tree had had nodules rather than rings on it, Dr. Stanley said only, "Perhaps, my dear. You draw what you see and leave the text to me, mmm?" Mr. Kensington glared at him when he heard such things, saying with a clenched jaw, "Miss Eastwood may have a point there, sir. Perhaps you could attend to her ideas."

"I think you will find that Miss Eastwood has been engaged for her sketching, not her knowledge of Latin," said Dr. Stanley, chuckling. "Medicine and botany go together hand-in-hand, you see, and Becker was delighted to have me write this because of my profession. Leave the quibbling over genera and families and traits to me and him, and all will be well."

Mr. Kensington's face echoed the outrage that Clara felt at this condensation, but she knew they both must swallow their indignation. Her name and that of Mr. Kensington were not even to appear on the flora's title page, with the plates and maps only indicating who had created which. And Clara felt sure that such attribution could easily be overlooked.

As the party went upstairs to their rooms that night, Mr. Kensington caught Clara's arm and said softly, "You must write to Becker, and to Mrs. Wakefield. You *must*."

And so Clara did, as much as she loathed being thought ungrateful or entitled. *These errors cannot continue*, she wrote to Mr. Becker. *Any self-respecting botanist will know them at once. It will undermine the credibility of the project—and of the publisher that prints it.* To Mrs. Wakefield she wrote, *How do I make him listen? How do I bear the fact that he might make these mistakes simply because he is a man? How shall I get through this next fortnight without strangling him?*

Her worries soon multiplied as she began to notice a change in Mr. Kensington during the last week of their trip. He became more silent and involved less in their lively conversations around the fire and out in the field. One morning he wore a fierce scowl and could not be coaxed into looking at Clara from over his plate of kippers. In response, she was silent and anxious, and not able to give voice to her feelings.

"My my, what has gotten into the two of you today?" asked Dr. Stanley, cheerfully ladling himself another scoop of the porridge, which was so viscous it clung to the spoon and he waved it about vigorously to free the sticky gruel. "Let us end this little collecting jaunt on a cheerful note, if we can."

Clumps of oatmeal flew out and onto Mr. Kensington's sleeve as Dr. Stanley's portion finally landed into his bowl with a defeated-sounding *schluck*.

"Oh, for God's sake," said Mr. Kensington, leaping up from his chair in irritation. "I will be glad never to see a pot of this swill again."

Clara looked up at him in surprise. It was unlike him to be so abrupt and short-tempered. His ill humors generally resulted in quiet silence, not angry outbursts.

Mr. Kensington looked embarrassed at his outburst. "I—I apologize, Dr. Stanley, ladies," he said. "I should have better manners, and really the porridge is of no consequence, Dr. Stanley."

"My dear fellow, you look quite put out, but I imagine you

are not relishing the thought of returning to Exton and continuing your labors. This must have been an excursion more suited to your talents. Most understandable. I only wish I had the means to offer you a permanent position, but even I shall not write enough floras to engage you for much longer," said Dr. Stanley.

Glancing at Clara, Mr. Kensington said, "Thank you, sir, but discontent is no excuse for me to act in such an ungentlemanly manner. I apologize. I—I think I shall see if my horse is ready." He left the room.

That evening, Clara sent Fiona up to their room early and asked Dr. Stanley for a flora she knew he had not brought down from his own room. No sooner had the door closed behind him than Clara went over to Mr. Kensington and took his hand. "My love," she said, "is something the matter? You have not been your usual self these past few days."

He looked up at her silently for a moment, pain flickering with the firelight over his face. "This is torture," he said softly, "such exquisite torture that I would not give up for the world, but torture nonetheless. To be so close to you each day and unable to touch your hand! To listen to you argue with Dr. Stanley about the correct family in which to place *Cheiranthus* and not be able to tell him how badly mistaken he is not to listen to you! And every night to sleep apart from you, divided only by a wall or two, when every fiber of my being wishes to hold you in my arms."

"That is all? You wish only to hold me? How chaste," she teased.

He lowered his head. "That is not all, of course," he said. "But a gentleman does not speak of such desires, and trying to be a gentleman is the one dignity I have left to me. Do not tempt me beyond what my imagination already torments me with, my love. And every day brings your wedding closer."

She knelt to be level with his face, so marked with pain when she wished it to be cheerful and unburdened. She knew she must return to her seat before Dr. Stanley returned.

"I am sorry," she said. "I was so caught up in the idea that we could be together that I did not consider how difficult this might be, for both of us. But I could not bear to take only stolen walks and a glance at you every Sunday at church into my marriage, whenever it comes—I was selfish and wanted more time with you than that. I apologize for my thoughtlessness."

She took his hand and squeezed it, and hurried back to her chair as Dr. Stanley came in with the volume held triumphantly. "Ah! Now we shall get to the bottom of those rascally mustards," he said.

By the time they had reached the last village, Clara was soon making mistakes on simple drawings and mislabeling the plates she had once spent hours poring over to make sure every detail was correct.

"Come come, Miss Eastwood," said Dr. Stanley as their penultimate evening of work began, "do apply yourself to these *Agrimonia* plates, and for heaven's sake refrain from portraying them in that lurid orange color as you did last week. It was most inaccurate, and far too gaudy of a shade for a self-respecting English wildflower."

"I'm sorry, Dr. Stanley," said Clara.

Mr. Kensington was reading at the grate of the inn's fireplace and looked over at her. She could feel his gaze like a flame that was far enough away to merely create a pleasant warmth. She knew that if she was face to face with him, her face would burn in his intensity.

As they all went up the stairs to their rooms an hour later, Mr. Kensington dropped his books, looking at Clara deliberately as he did so. She stooped to help him gather them, and he slipped her a note as she did so.

When her door had shut behind her, she unfolded it, heart hammering, and read,

My feelings are too hot just now to do us both justice, but look under your door in the morning for another, calmer note. Suffice to say now that I burn for you with everything in me and would happily ship Mr. Charles Eastwood off to Abyssinia to be assured of your freedom to accept my hand, if you would take it without your parents' approval, a dilemma I do not wish upon you. At least as your husband I might defend you against that buffoon! But these thoughts are useless—I only took up my pen to urge you not to let me distract you from your work, and instead passion has gotten the better of me, spilling out my pen like stray ink. Forgive me, and wait for my next note. H.K.

She tossed and turned all night, debating with herself as to what would be the best course of action. In the early morning light, as she heard the first stagecoach of the day rattle into the innyard below her window, there was a *shft* at her door and she sprang out of bed to get the sheaf of pages that was lying just over the threshold.

October 17

I am sorry for the selfishness I expressed earlier. I have paced my room for hours, thinking long and hard about the dilemma we are in. I cannot bear this torture any longer, of knowing that you do not have the respect you deserve. I have written a frank letter to Dr. Stanley and it is already with his servant, waiting for him to read it in the morning. I have written one like it to Mr. Sowerby and to one of my professors at Oxford, to see if they can assist you in any way and to warn them of Dr. Stanley's errors.

My wish to help you is matched only by my unhappiness at being

so parted from you. I fear it shall drive me mad. Never have I been more unhappy; never have I had such an exquisite reason for being so. Your parents will never consent to a match between us, especially now that my family has taken on such poverty. If I can but keep a meagre roof above my head and the heads of Oliver, Susanna, and Mother and ensure we are fed and clothed, however poorly, it will be all I can do. Your father would be a cruel man indeed to wish this fate on his daughter.

I have no doubt that Mr. Eastwood's chances of providing you with a comfortable home are altogether higher than my own—even if only because he does not bring three mouths with him that need to be fed. Four people's board does not accommodate a fifth very well, though God knows I would give you my own portion in a moment. And then, there would have been children—but that is a path we must not look down, lest it cause us both pain. Bachelorhood is surely the best way of life for me now. T

here is nothing for it, Clara. My sweet Clara. I will not ask you to bear my disgrace nor to give up your beloved Yewspring. I know how much it means to you, how much it is already a part of you. You were meant to be its mistress and work for its future. I am convinced that all of your books will be written from its hothouse (in the winter, of course, for in the summer you shall be too busy studying out-of-doors to attend to such indoor matters). This vision will give me solace whenever I think of it.

It is clear that being together is painful and distracting to both of us, and I fear this will continue to our detriment and those who depend on our work. I am gone on the first stage coach today and will stay away from Exton until you are married. Please, my love, don't try and find me. Don't try and follow me—and you may rest assured I will not go back to Butler Cottage.

I will think of you always and love you for the rest of my days,

Henry

She burst into tears and ran to the door of her room and opened it, not caring that she was dressed only in her nightgown without even a dressing gown over her. How could he leave her like this? Surely he wouldn't have gone yet. Surely this was a test to see how much he meant to her—she was now forced to admit to herself that he was everything to her, Yewspring or not—and she would knock on his door to find him smiling and waiting for her, his hand outstretched and waiting to pull her close.

She tiptoed down to the door she knew had been his, knocked, and not hearing an answer, tried the knob. The door swung open to reveal only darkness, and she chastised herself for failing to bring a candle. She shut the door, went back to her room and retrieved one, hoping she had not woken Miss Holt, and went back to Mr. Kensington's chamber.

The dim light of her taper revealed an empty, neatly made bed, his trunk by the foot of the bed—locked, without a key to be found anywhere—and three pence left for the maid and porter left on the desk. She sobbed, sunk to the floor by the desk, and cried for a quarter of an hour, not knowing anything until Miss Holt came to the doorway with her plaited hair mussed and shivering in the threadbare nightgown that gave Clara a shock of guilt even as she cried.

Miss Holt sighed, raised Clara up, and said, "Come along now, Miss Eastwood. Your mother and father won't like it a bit if you were found in this room, nor would Mr. Charles Eastwood, I imagine. Come along now."

Clara mutely followed Miss Holt back to her room, and upon reaching her bed surrendered herself wholly to her tears and a night of restless wakefulness.

In the darkness of the late autumn dawn, as rain beat down on her windowpane from clouds that had gathered during the night, Clara got up, dressed, and went back down the hall to Mr. Kensington's room, knowing that the porter would soon be up to collect his trunk so that the room could be prepared for the next guests. She sat at the desk, clutching the pages of Mr. Kensington's letter tightly while she waited. Presently the door opened and a boy of about fifteen entered. He stopped in surprise when he saw her there, and looked toward the trunk in confusion.

"I beg your pardon, miss," he said. "I thought this was Mr. Kensington's room—"

"It was," she said firmly. "I waited here to ask you where he asked you to send his trunk."

The boy shifted uneasily on his feet and looked up at the ceiling beams nervously. "He—he told me that no one was to know where he was going, miss," he said after a moment.

She had expected this reply, and rose with her purse in her hand. "Might I convince you to change your mind?" she asked. She opened the purse and rummaged through it. "I would be happy to give you a tenpence to jog your memory."

His face darkened a bit. She could see the first few traces of blue on his face where whiskers would one day grow. "I'm sorry, miss, he was very insistent in his note."

She pulled out some coins. "What about a shilling? A pound?" She hated the desperation in her voice and the agitation with which she thrust the coins out to him.

He held up his hands, and shook his head. "I'm sorry to cause you any distress, but I won't do it. Mr. Kensington seemed a gentlemanly fellow and I've got to honor his wishes, both for my own peace of mind and my position here, miss. I know Mr. Hall wouldn't like my defying the guests like that, and there's six children at home behind me and my mum needs my wages, begging your pardon."

He stepped decisively around her and picked up the trunk, hoisting it up onto his shoulder.

"Please," Clara said, as he walked out through the door, but he did not stop, did not turn back, and she watched the last hope of her happiness step over the threshold and disappear around the corner.

Two days later, Clara and Miss Holt made their way home, having parted ways with Dr. Stanley.

"You were an immense help, Miss Eastwood," he had told her. "I look forward to our work in the spring."

Clara thanked him, not sure whose presence caused her the greatest irritation, his or Miss Holt's. And yet the only way to leave Exton, since her mother was to be away so often, was to submit to be chaperoned. And as unpleasant as it may be to have Miss Holt guarding over her, Clara could not bear the thought of what waited at home. She wondered all the way back to Exton how she would ever look forward to returning there again, or return to the life she had led before. At least she had had the prospect of sometimes seeing Mr. Kensington, of building up her portfolio so she might tell him what she had been working on. And now she had nothing. It seemed impossible that the war within her would ever settle to a gentle truce, that the mountains and chasms that she felt her heart was now made of would ever smooth themselves into a level plain. The result of this emotional turmoil was a general feeling of misery. And yet when the carriage pulled up to Yewspring's door in the October dusk, its golden windows beckoning, she remembered that at least it offered her one consolation. Here, she could be left alone.

However, shortly after Clara returned, Charles requested

to trespass upon the kindness of his aunt and uncle for a week, during a brief recess in the army's training schedule. Clara was discouraged to find that her misery over Mr. Kensington was not lessened by the company of the man she had agreed to spend her life with, but rather heightened. They were, quite frankly, not often together, for Mr. Eastwood quite hoarded his nephew's company for masculine pursuits, and the two were often out shooting, closeted in the study discussing military invasions, and down at the pub most evenings.

Charles did sit dutifully next to the pianoforte while she played, learning where to turn the pages, but she was dismayed to find his eyes turning often to Phoebe and Violet when the others visited Yewspring. They were altogether nearer his own age, and such comparisons made her feel old and decrepit. Altogether she was restless and dissatisfied, and longed to be stalking through Yewspring's garden beds yanking up weeds or churning a batch of butter down in the dairy. At least these would help relieve the feelings that stalked her like demons and waited for her in the darkness of her bedchamber to keep her up at night.

On the one walk she could manage to make herself take with Charles, while Mrs. Eastwood and Mrs. Tapley trailed behind them at a distance as reluctant chaperones, he seemed uneasy, clearing his throat repeatedly before bridging the gaps in their silence with polite questions about her family, and the neighborhood. After several of these exchanges, Clara stopped to look at the last willowherb blooms of the season peeking their delicate white faces out from under a hedgerow.

"Oh!" said Clara, "these have increased since last year. I never saw them before two summers ago, and have been watching these. I wonder where they came from? I have not seen any others nearby from which they could have seeded."

Charles paused briefly. "Such a plain little flower!" he said. "I confess I far prefer the more showy garden varieties, though perhaps it would be more virtuous of me to try and find some beauty in our wildflowers. And since they give you pleasure, perhaps you might teach me their names. You said this one was birchherb?"

She corrected him gently, wondering how in the world they would get along together. Until she saw Annie Clemons coming toward them on the path, going home for the day. That made her remember why she would consent to be Charles's wife. The other dropped a curtsey when she saw Clara and Charles, though without her usual smile. She was about to hurry on her way, but as she passed Clara noted her red-rimmed eyes and furrowed brow.

"Mrs. Clemons," she said, "is everything all right?"

Mrs. Clemons turned back, and Clara saw her eyes touch on Charles.

"This is my fiancé, Mr. Charles Eastwood," Clara said, to put the other woman at ease. "You need not fear speaking before him."

"Oh! We'd heard the happy news that you're still to remain at Yewspring," said Mrs. Clemons, "and I should have recognized you, sir, given your resemblance to Mr. George. I'm not myself today, is all—it's my Sam." She broke off in a sob, her hand going to her mouth.

"Oh dear," said Clara, stepping toward Mrs. Clemons. "I hope he is well?"

"Oh, yes, he's all right. Only he's lost his job in Liverpool." Mrs. Clemons eyes shone with tears. "And my Simon's terrible poorly just now, so we've been counting on Sam's pay to help with his medicine."

"I'm so sorry," said Clara. "I know Mr. Clemon's consumption is always worse going into winter. You must feel this terribly. And Sam is a good worker—they were fools to let him go."

"Thank you, Miss Eastwood. I'm sure he'll find something. Liverpool's big enough that he'll naught have trouble finding work. But it's a blow, to be sure. Mr. Morton's always been kind enough to be lenient with our payment, but it's an ill-timed loss all the same."

Clara did a mental survey of Yewspring to see whether there was any work she might offer Sam Clemons. He was about her age, married just a year. Getting him back now might mean decades of benefit for him and the estate both. "I wonder if Mr. Graham might have something for him?" she wondered aloud. "You said Sam kept the books at the Corn Office, didn't you?"

Mrs. Clemons nodded. "And me who can hardly cipher a grocery bill! It's wonderful, to be sure."

"I'll speak to Mr. Graham," said Clara, making up her mind. She had almost forgotten Charles was standing there, listening.

"Have you always been so involved with the estate?" her fiancé asked as they continued on after saying goodbye to Mrs. Clemons. She could not tell from his tone whether he disapproved.

"For the last eight years or so," she said. "Since I came back from school. Though I've always loved it."

"I can see that," he said. "And I could see that woman thinks highly of you. I thought she'd never stop thanking us. Though I played no part in it, and I can't imagine we'll be here much after we marry. This Graham fellow seems to have things under control. We needn't interfere with it, I shouldn't think. And someday when we have Beechview, well—it's good shooting country, isn't it? A few weeks in the autumn should be enough to keep us Eastwoods in good standing here." He smiled a bit, watching her closely.

"Well, we can discuss that as we get closer to the wedding," said Clara lightly, not wanting to spoil the day. She must tread carefully until there was a ring on her finger. But she knew she would fight for longer than a few weeks' residence in the county, and she marveled that Charles knew her so little to think that she wouldn't.

The two ended their walk by taking Mrs. Eastwood to Exton to be fitted for a new gown. It was a Saturday and the town was busy as the villagers did their shopping before the coming Sabbath and harvesters brought wagons to and from the storehouses. The other two left Mrs. Eastwood at the dressmaker's, where they agreed to meet her in an hour, then strolled along the main street. They saw Ned coming out of the livery stables, and he and Charles began talking of their hunters. Clara let her gaze drift over the street scene before her, with the carts piled high with crops passing to and fro, servants calling to one another with baskets slung over their arms, and children sent out and about on various errands joining up into little groups.

Amidst the wagons and horses, she saw Mr. Fulbright astride a fine chestnut whose coat shone in the gentle afternoon light. After she had looked at it a moment, half-distracted by the men's conversation next to her, she recognized it as Mr. Kensington's horse Achilles. She felt herself flush involuntarily at the shame Mr. Kensington must have felt at having to sell such a beautiful animal, and to have the village note its change of hands. She turned away, feeling physically pained.

Clara and Charles went on, and paused for a moment at the window of Reed's store.

"Oh!" Clara said, looking at a handsome green-covered book in the window. "*The Forest of Montalbano!* I so long to finish it, but we all take turns buying books and then share them around. It is Phoebe's turn to buy it, I believe, and she is always short on her allowance, so it may be some time before I see it."

Charles looked peeved. "You cannot mean that you read those dreadful novels? I do so hate to interfere with any pleasure of yours, but it would be very unbecoming for you to indulge in that sort of reading material after we are married. From what I have heard, there is very little to be found on the pages of those popular books. Indeed, I have been thinking about your reading while I have been away. Do you know what would be a fitting tribute to George's memory? I will send you a handsome copy of the translation of *Essai sur l'architecture* by Monsieur Laugier. He is a Papist, sadly, but his work is nonetheless much more suitable and instructive than a silly novel. Perhaps you might draw up a few little sketches for my mother in honor of George—she would have such appreciation for such a gesture! I am sure such literature as that novel is already beneath you, and will be more so when you are a married woman."

Clara was horrified at this sudden and unexpected constraint upon her deportment, and only managed a faint, "Yes, I am sure that will be quite instructive."

They walked back to the dressmaker's to collect Mrs. Eastwood, and Clara saw Mrs. Kensington entering just before them, carrying a large bundle.

At the door of the shop, Charles stopped and said, "I know it is silly, but I always feel a bit awkward in such places. I always feel that I might spy something I shouldn't if someone moves a curtain at the wrong moment. Why don't you collect my aunt? I'll wait." He moved away from the door and stopped at the corner with the air of a soldier taking up his guard duty. Clara supposed he felt like he was. She assured him that she could manage without him, and went in to the shop. She stood waiting for her mother to emerge from the fitting room, while Mrs. Kensington was at the counter speaking with Louisa, the shopkeeper's daughter. Mrs. Kensington's back was to her, but Clara could overhear their exchange.

Mrs. Kensington was saying, "I've come to pick up more work for Susanna. She claims she's done with the first lot, and ready for another, though how she's managed to become such an expert seamstress, I've no idea. She was always a dawdler with her sewing as a girl."

She handed the bundle over to Louisa, who took it and went to the shop's back room, emerging a moment later with Mrs. Vincent the dressmaker, who said to Mrs. Kensington, "I'm very sorry, Mrs. Kensington, but we're out of work just now, and I don't believe we'll have a need for your daughter's services after all. We do appreciate her willingness to help us, and I have here the wages we agreed on for the first lot of work. She might try the netting collective up in Whitley, if she can net."

Mrs. Kensington took the money and said sarcastically, "What a shame. And here I've been forced to take messages and negotiate wages like a common charwoman, and for what? And I must say, the note from you that I saw promising good, steady work for the foreseeable future was quite misleading if you anticipated this outcome. I'm tempted to believe that Susanna's reputation has caused you to reconsider."

Mrs. Vincent looked offended and said, "I do have a reputation of my own to uphold, you understand. I've offered the kindness I could, and can't do any more."

"What a bunch of tripe," said Mrs. Kensington, taking the money from the counter with a vicious swipe.

Mrs. Vincent said coldly, "Good day, Mrs. Kensington. You needn't come here again unless as a paying customer. We don't object to your business in the least, if that's any consolation."

Mrs. Kensington said stiffly, "Oh, you needn't worry that we would trouble you for your services. Good day."

Clara had hoped and prayed her mother would appear before the end of the conversation, but now Mrs. Kensington turned and passed by her on the way to the door. Clara felt the other's gaze sweep across her with intense dislike, even as she curtseyed to acknowledge the older woman, aware of Louisa and Mrs. Vincent's watching her as she did. But so close to Mr. Kensington's mother, who surely knew where he was, she could not help turning to try and stop the other woman. "Mrs. Kensington, could I—"

The older woman paused in the open door of the shop for just a moment, then briefly turned her head to say firmly, "Good day, Miss Eastwood."

The shop bell sounded as Mrs. Kensington shut the door decisively, and Clara was left to ponder this exchange among the mannequins and bobbins of thread.

 CHAPTER TWENTY-TWO 

"I'm sorry, Dr. Stanley," said Clara. "Do you know, I don't feel quite well. I think I'll keep working on these plates in my room, if that is agreeable to you."

The spring sun streamed in the window, though she knew it was likely destined to be changed into one of the frequent showers that had accompanied them throughout their second collecting trip. They had gone back to several of the villages they had passed through the previous autumn, to capture the spring flora, and now near the end of their trip they had journeyed further north to new territory in the county to check their plant lists against the areas they surveyed.

"All right," Dr. Stanley said in answer to Clara's request. "Yes, you haven't been yourself these past few days. Perhaps some rest would perk you up and get you back into the fine form you exhibited early on this trip. When Mr. Thompson returns from his scouting trip, I'll have him take up the maps for tomorrow."

In the hallway, she met Fiona, who had been unpacking Clara's trunk, headed toward the common room with a letter in her hand.

"For you, Miss Eastwood," the maid said, handing it to her. Clara shifted her portfolio to her other hand and took it.

"Thank you, Fiona," she said as she turned the letter over. It was from Charles.

May 1

My dear Clara,

I am delighted to write with the news I have to share. I have been released from my position much sooner than I expected—you need not worry that it was on the grounds of any offense. Far better, I am being commended for my service and awarded the Gold Cross medal by His Majesty himself. My father, upon learning of this news and my hastened discharge from the service, has kindly agreed to install us at the old rectory of Reedbridge Parish. As you receive this letter I will likely be on my way to inspect our new home and ensure that it is fit for my fair fiancée.

Once I am satisfied, I shall return to town where I shall procure a license for us to be wed—shall we say it is to be St. Paul's, since it is so close to Southampton Street? You may join me for the wedding as soon as is convenient for you in the next month or six weeks. I would be grateful if you would send me your intended date of arrival in London by return post, so that I can make the necessary arrangements for the church.

Depending upon what my father can settle upon us, we may choose a frugal or a rather more lavish honeymoon (straight down to Kent for the former? A trip to Weymouth if the latter?). I shall bow to your wishes, but really I would rather go straight to Reedbridge so that we can get settled. You are such a sensible, agreeable person I am sure you will agree. And my mother is eager to have us close—I know it would please her to have our society as soon as possible.

I look forward to your reply and our forthcoming union, my dear. I hope the expedition is going well and that you are enjoying yourself—our gardens will surely be the finest in Kent with the knowledge you are gaining.

Yours affectionately,

Charles Eastwood

Clara slumped down on the rickety chair in her room, stunned. She had known, of course, that the wedding would one day arrive, but as long as Charles was safely away, still travelling about and present only in his letters, it had been easy to push the thought out of her mind and carry on with her work. Secretly, she had been sure that some sudden turn of events would prevent the marriage at all.

Now, with their future home all but secured and her reply to him the only thing holding back the wedding, she was flooded with dread and remorse. She would have to relocate to Kent, one hundred and fifty miles from Exton, much too far to visit more often than once a year or perhaps even every few years. This, of course, meant that her chances of seeing Mr. Kensington would be slim and infrequent indeed, whenever he did return to Exton.

Nonetheless, she did not see an alternative to it. If she had, she would have taken it long ago. Yewspring would be hers, and that must be enough. She stared out the window at the dimly lit inn courtyard, sent out a desperate plea for forgiveness to Mr. Kensington, wherever he was, and got up, wiped away the tears that had claimed her with a vengeance, and sat down at the table to write her reply.

May 6

Charles,

Thank you for your letter. Your plan is agreeable to me, but I must make the necessary preparations when I return to Yewspring in a week or so, so I must ask for the full six weeks in order to do them justice. I should hate to begin our wedded life in a state of haste or ill preparation. Shall we say that the wedding will be on the morning of Saturday June 15? I could travel with Mama and Papa to town on the Wednesday or Thursday preceding, which should give us time to make any final arrangements. I shall pack only what I need for the wedding and the journey and have the rest of my trunks sent on to

Reedbridge from Exton when I leave there.

Our work here continues as well as can be expected. I hope you are in good health and shall see you in a few weeks. We will be travelling back to Exton on the 14th or 15th of this month, so pray send your next letter to Yewspring.

Yours sincerely,

Clara Eastwood

In her garden at Tottenham, Mrs. Wakefield walked about with Kitty, who held a book in her hand and was reciting a list of chemical elements with their atomic weights. The early May morning was blustery and tossed about the boughs of the trees, laden with new leaves, that hung over the wall.

"I think you will find, my dear, that the two newest elements are potassium and barium, not sodium and boron." Mrs. Wakefield said to her pupil. She stopped and frowned. "In fact, that is an error as well, since Monsieur Courtois has just discovered iodine, I hear. I have an article about it inside—just wait a moment and I'll go fetch it."

She left her granddaughter in the garden and went in to the drawing room, where the maid had left the post. Sifting through the pile of letters with one hand while she rummaged through the drawer of her secretary, she found one that made her pause, take it up and open it, walking to the window to read it in the light. With a few *tsks* here and there as she read, she folded it up after a few minutes and stared out into the garden, where through the open window she heard Kitty's voice reciting the elements dutifully. She watched the girl circle round and round the lawn, chanting "Copper, lead, gold, silver..." as if the words were a spell or a prayer.

Her grandmother turned from the window, sat down at her

desk, and began to write. After a time Kitty came in and was ready to recite for Mrs. Wakefield again, but her grandmother only handed her the article and said absentmindedly, "Read this for now, and we'll pick up the discussion later. Something has come up that needs my attention."

Finally, Mrs. Wakefield sealed her letter, rang for the maid, and told her, "Take this down to Harley Street yourself at once, Lucy—there is no time to lose. I need this letter to be in Mrs. Creston's hand today. Ask her if she would be so good as to send her reply by you, if she does not need time to think over my proposal. And if she does ask for more time to think it over, pray stress that this is a matter of urgency!"

Clara was surprised, as she half-heartedly went through *trousseau* linens in the storeroom one afternoon several days after she had gotten back to Yewspring, to hear wheels on the gravel of the drive through the open window. She looked out to see the Crestons' carriage drive through Yewspring's gate. Rose alighted, wearing a very fine traveling ensemble, and swept into the house with her maid trailing behind her, laden with parcels from London.

Mrs. Eastwood was with her youngest daughter in the passage when Clara came downstairs.

"—such a surprise!" her mother was saying. "Why did you not write and tell us you were coming?"

Rose saw her sister come down the steps and went to her, embracing her affectionately. "I could not resist the chance to see Clara once more before the wedding," she said. "And at any rate I had already planned to go to the Lakes at this time, so I just *had* to come for a day or two on my way up and bring you the wedding presents." She gestured to the maid behind her. "Therese, please take those to my sister's room—the third door on the right, up the stairs."

The maid went, followed by Fiona who was to make Rose's room ready, then prepare a room in the attic for Therese.

"But your aunts do not know that you are here! Heavens, and Mrs. Morton was going to dine with the Doyles tonight—but I must see if she can reschedule since you are here," Mrs. Eastwood was saying as the three women went into the drawing room.

"Oh, mama, don't make anyone change their plans because of me," said Rose. "And anyway, my aunt Tapley already knows that I meant to be here, because I am taking Violet with me to the Lakes. It is such a short trip before we return to town for Clara's wedding that James did not wish to come, and I need some company."

"Oh, how lovely," sighed Mrs. Eastwood. "I would give my right arm for a holiday! It is so very dull here after London—I am almost glad to never have had the opportunity to go before we took you girls. I would not have been satisfied with anything else if I had been there, I am sure, and it is very much easier on one's pocketbook if one can be content with a country life. I know *my* pin money disappeared quite quickly in London—it was most alarming."

"Well, Mama, you may come stay with us anytime you like, and need not take a house of your own. After all, Clara will be at—Reedbridge, is it? You need not stay here if you don't wish to. And after the wedding, I've taken lodging in Yorkshire until September when we go to Scotland—come to us then. There will be plenty of room for Fiona if you choose to bring her, as well. I am sure Therese would appreciate her company."

"Oh, what luxury to travel wherever you wish! It has been one of my greatest joys as a married woman, and I see you have embraced it as well," said Mrs. Eastwood happily.

"Oh, Mama, travel *is* lovely, but London almost makes me never want to go anywhere else! And James is simply the most delightful husband—even after eight months of marriage, I still get a thrill when I remember that he is my *husband*, and me his wife! Speaking of marriage," said Rose to her sister, "I must see your *trousseau* while I am home, Clara. I hope you did not pick your silver from Herrod's, for theirs is quite inferior to Harding and Howell's. Caroline was on the verge of going to Herrod's but luckily wrote to me first. It would have been disastrous if she had chosen a service that the scullery maids scratched within a month."

Clara did not know whether her service had come from Herrod's, her grandmother having selected it, but she assumed that that was where Rose had gotten this advice, so simply said, "I think I have avoided that disaster as well."

Rose then systematically moved on to the bed sheets, night-gowns, dressing gowns, furniture, and table linens that Clara (or, more often, her grandmother) had selected, found all to her satisfaction as a married woman, and the ladies then retired to dress for dinner, Mrs. Eastwood still fretting over Mrs. Morton's dining engagement. A solution was found by instructing the diners to come to Yewspring after they were finished and receive the London news from their niece, which pleased everyone except Mr. Morton, who was forced to cut short his game of whist at the Doyles'.

The family party was broken up the next morning when Rose and Violet swept out of Yewspring's gate, merrily waving their handkerchiefs out the carriage windows while their mothers stood forlornly with Clara out on the drive.

"Ah, to be young!" said Mrs. Eastwood as the three went inside. "I am quite envious of you girls, Clara. Rose married in

London and you nearly so, both with such respectable men for husbands, Caroline with her little one on the way, and Violet off on a summer holiday! Your lives lie before you rather than seeming to be over as middle age descends. Take care you enjoy your blessings and your youth, my dear."

"Yes indeed," said Mrs. Tapley sadly. "And when one has so many sons, they hardly need a mother, so I feel quite desolate with Violet gone. At least Charlotte has daughters with which to occupy herself."

Clara thought that her own youth, at any rate, had brought more torments than delights, but said only, "Maturity, at least, brings wisdom, which cannot be said of youth. I envy those who can see the best path to pursue and follow it without doubt, without—regret."

If her mother and aunt thought this was a peculiar statement from a young lady about to be married, they did not comment on it but rather drifted into the drawing room despondently while she went upstairs to furtively work on sketching amidst the chaos of linens, boxes, and trunks in her bedroom. Among the mess of papers, books, and paints were the crumpled drafts of letters to Mr. Kensington, letters she had composed against her better judgment, that she knew she would never send, and did not even know where to direct.

With what seemed to Clara to be unprecedented alacrity, the last week of May flew by, and she met the beginning of the month of her wedding with despair. She had overheard Mrs. Huttleston telling Fiona that her husband had reported that Miss Kensington had taken a position at the inn as a serving maid, and that the family had taken to attending church in the next village over.

"A Dunchurch parish man must have caught her eye, them

all being so disgraced here," Mrs. Huttleston had said. "They must need all the workers they can get in that house. I cannot imagine the brother'll remain unmarried long, though heaven knows who will take him. It's a blessing you and Miss Holt were with Miss Eastwood on that foolhardy trip last autumn, or Lord knows what would have been said about her in the village."

These words had filled Clara with a mix of jealousy at the idea that Mr. Kensington would court another and fierce anger that his reputation was still so low, but she bit her tongue and scratched away so fiercely on the pages of her journal that the nib ripped through to the sheet beneath and left ink-spots. She took to pacing in her room until late at night, feeling her bedroom walls imprison her like a cage, angrily packing her clothes and wrinkling the expensive French sheets of her dowry as she stuffed them carelessly into trunks. Her only consolation was a letter from Dr. Stanley proposing one last collecting trip to Somerset-shire in June. Clara wrote back accepting happily and arranged to return to Yewspring just before she was to leave for London. She could not help looking forward to the chance to walk and draw and study once more, although her mind shied away from what would come after.

The night before she was to leave for the collecting trip, Clara's sense of confinement and desperation overpowered her, and she crept down the stairs as the house slept, unlatched the front door, and picking up her skirts, ran out into the fields. The waxing moon shone bright and a few stars still sparkled despite their competitor, but the night air, which she had hoped would drape itself over her body like a cooling balm, did not bring her the peace she hoped it would.

She went to the yews, feeling a thrill at being out in the darkness, when the world told her she must be asleep, or at the most should not stray from the yard. She reached the ridge and looked down at the house, its windows dark and its stone walls pale in the moonlight. It was the last time she would be at leisure to look on it before she was Mrs. Charles Eastwood. She wanted to spend a few moments to bid it farewell before she came back as a new person.

The concept startled her. Her surname would not change, but she would become someone else, it seemed.

But perhaps she already had.

She remembered the weeks of mourning George, of lying crumpled in her bed staring up at the ceiling.

She remembered wanting to tell someone, anyone, that Miss Holt had taken her book. She remembered touching the place on the front cover where her governess had tried to cover the name *Clara Eastwood*, a tear on the front page and the remnants of sticky paste covering the letters of her name like a wound.

She remembered riding beside her father, his hand outstretched to show her where he was going to have oats planted instead of wheat. She remembered the excitement and hope of seeing the plowed furrows, ready for the spring's sowing.

She remembered Annie Clemons' face when Clara told her Sam could work for Mr. Graham.

She remembered Rose's smiling words before her sister had left for the Lakes. *I still get a thrill when I remember that he is my* husband, *and me his wife!* She had not needed to ask her sister if she was happy. Even Clara could see it.

She already had become a new person, it seemed. The world had disappointed her, but it had also offered her gifts that she had almost been too bitter to accept, too blind to appreciate. Until Mr. Kensington had helped her see the resentment she carried. She realized, with a shock, that he must know its look so well because his mother bore it everywhere she went. His words made her realize that she did not wish to become a copy of Mrs. Kensington. She wanted to accept people as they were, to make peace with the fact that they would never be who she would have made them. Her sister would always prefer a street of shops to a walk in the country. Her mother would always run from the pain Yewspring had brought her and call it "going on holiday". Charles would always miss George, her father would always wish Clara had been a son. *Spite is a poison, not a tonic*, came Mr. Kensington's words, and she knew she would never forget it again. She had been sipping it for years and not realized. She felt the mantle of disappointment slipping off her shoulders, and wondered what would fill its place.

She walked the four miles over to Butler Cottage, not knowing what she hoped for, save some sign of his presence, some indication that he was alive and still in this world, though she might never lay eyes on him again.

Her heart pounding, she cut off the main road and approached the cottage from the little hillside behind. From her vantage point she could see over the garden wall to the lawns now plowed up and planted with vegetables. She could see the light of a candle sitting on a table out in the little kitchen yard, but nothing else. Clara's rebellious heart, forgetting it had no cause for joy, leapt into her mouth. In a moment, she became aware that a figure stood out in the yard, and was staring up toward her. The figure disappeared further into the yard after a moment, and she stood still, not sure whether she had been seen in the darkness.

She was about to turn away and go back to Yewspring when she heard, "Who's there?" from the gate leading out of the garden.

With horror, she saw the glint of moonlight against the

barrel of a gun, pointing her way. She gasped, and stammered, "It's—not an intruder! Please don't shoot!"

Miss Kensington lowered the gun when she heard Clara's voice, then swiftly walked through the gate and came up the hill.

"I'm sorry, Miss Kensington," said Clara as the other drew near her. "I—"

"Why have you come?" Miss Kensington cut her off.

"I—was just out for a walk, and—"

"Don't pretend this was an accident, Miss Eastwood," said Miss Kensington. "Why have you come?"

Clara sighed. "To say I'm sorry," she said.

"For what?" The gun was dangling from Miss Kensington's hand, but Clara knew it could be raised again.

"For making your brother unhappy. For keeping your family here. Since I cannot tell him so myself, please tell him—" A sob escaped her throat. "Tell him that I think he should become an agent again. He should try again elsewhere."

Miss Kensington looked at her. "That would mean leaving," she said.

"Yes. It pains me to no end. It will hurt me the rest of my days, I think. But his knowledge is too great to be left unused as a laborer. Will you tell him I said so? I leave tomorrow for Somersetshire and leave soon after I return for London, to be married."

"It cannot come too soon," said Miss Kensington. "Your household may not have been privy to the details of your entanglement with my brother, Miss Eastwood, but such reticence in our family was disposed of when I found myself with child and abandoned. My mother and I heard nothing but your name from my brother's lips this past year, and are thoroughly ready for you to be gone and married."

"I beg your pardon," said Clara, offended. "I do not believe I deserve such enmity. You, of all people, should know how limited a woman's options for respectability are and why I must follow through with my engagement. Where is your compassion for me and for your brother? We must be parted forever."

"Compassion?" repeated Miss Kensington. "It is compassion for Henry that has formed my opinion of you. One does not pity the cat that torments the mouse but instead wants to grab it by the scruff of the neck. What hope is there in his love for you? What outcome can there possibly be besides heartbreak and pain? The sooner you are gone, the sooner he can heal and move on with his life, just as I have. Just as he must."

"I hope time and a cooler head make you think better of me," said Clara. "For it was never my intent to hurt him nor to be dishonest about my feelings. But until women have some other means than marriage to make a way in the world, and until we are allowed to consult our hearts alone when we marry, I see no other course."

"And what obstacles are those, pray?" asked Miss Kensington. "The only ones I see are your refusal to accept poverty as the price if you were to marry Henry, and a reluctance to give up your father's estate for the sake of affection. No, affection is too feeble a word for what he feels for you—you have chosen property over love, and I am not sure I can ever forgive you. Instead of confronting these insignificant obstacles, you choose to bind yourself to a man you do not love. How can I respect that? And how can your daughters expect anything more for themselves than a loveless, false marriage of convenience if their mother has modeled one so well?"

"You may wish me to be a heroine and a martyr for the cause of women everywhere, to make a statement by pledging myself to the man who already has my heart, but what good would it do, in the end? Unless I can be a blessing and a help to him, and contribute to his ease and happiness, I refuse to be his wife. To add another mouth to feed to this household, and then the children's mouths that would follow from our union, to watch him work himself into an early grave and burdened by fatigue and labor would be torturous to me. He has had enough trials and enough people who depend on him as it is. "

"A fact I am conscious of daily," spat Miss Kensington, "thanks not only to my conscience but my mother. Thank you for your selflessness, which conveniently preserves your own reputation and security."

"Will you at least write and urge him to come back to Exton?" Clara asked. "I will be gone by the time the letter arrives, wherever he is, and if he is determined to come back to resume his labor for Lord Chesterson, he may do so safely. I imagine his wages have been sorely missed."

Susanna studied her again silently. "He is employed elsewhere," she said at last. "We have had wages from him every fortnight. And if he were home, I would make you rattle the shutters and wake everyone else, just to give you a taste of the humiliation you seem so loathed to experience, no matter what the rewards of love and happiness could have brought you and he both. Go now and leave our family in peace."

Clara complied with all the speed she had in her, cheeks burning with embarrassment and anger, and ran halfway back to Yewspring before she finally felt the angry flame in her subside.

CHAPTER TWENTY-THREE

Despite the late night before and the knots in her stomach over her conversation with Miss Kensington, Clara awoke the next morning and could not help feeling a spring in her step as she finished her packing, ate a hurried breakfast, and climbed into Yewspring's carriage with Fiona. They picked up Miss Holt and Matilda and were just leaving Exton when she was surprised to feel the carriage lurch to a stop. Clara looked around the carriage and saw the other three's brows wrinkle in concern as well, and lowered the window to speak to the driver. Her unspoken question as to why they had halted was answered by a messenger on horseback speaking with the driver. When he saw her put her head out the window, the messenger nodded to the driver and approached her.

"Clara Eastwood?" he asked.

"Yes," she said.

He held out a letter to her, and she reached inside to get a reticule for a coin. He waved her away. "No need, miss, it's already taken care of."

Puzzled, Clara held up the letter to the light from the window. What could have been so urgent that they had been stopped? She saw Rose's handwriting on the paper in her lap, and turned it over to break the seal.

June 1

Grasmere

Oh Clara, you must make haste at once to Gretna Green! The most dreadful thing has happened! Violet has run off with—you will never believe it—Lieutenant Green, who was stationed in Exton all that time ago! She left me a note saying not to be alarmed but that they were in love and intended to elope to Scotland! I am so distressed and alarmed, for Violet took my purse with her to pay for the journey and swore up and down in her note to pay me back when they are married. She must have known that if she had consulted me, I would have refused to help her. It is so shameful for her to have to sneak off and marry without her father's consent! What would people say?

I have already written James to tell him to come at once with some money to rescue me, and the innkeepers have graciously allowed me to stay until he arrives. But I have no way to get to her in time to convince her not to make this terrible decision.

If you leave right away, you may yet make it there in time to stop them, for I found her note but an hour ago. When you get to Gretna Green, check the Blacksmith's Inn for them. I only hope it is not too late, and that you are able to talk some sense into that silly girl before she ruins her own life!!

In haste and distress,

Rose

Clara gasped, gave the letter to Miss Holt, and leaned out the window to order the carriage to turn around and take her to Exton to get the coach to Scotland. Violet must not also be the victim of marital folly. She must save her cousin, since she could not save herself.

Two days later, as the long summer evening was drawing to a close and darkness beginning to creep over the countryside, the Kendal coach pulled into the main square of Gretna Green. Clara climbed out, rubbing her eyes as she came out of the uneasy doze that had overtaken her. She had dreamt of bandits peering their scowling faces into the coach, of the coach overturning, of the coach underwater, and this unease clung to her as she looked about the square. Fiona climbed down after her and they stretched their legs and arms after the cramped, stuffy ride. It was just the two of them—they had sent Miss Holt and Matilda on to Somersetshire so this detour to Scotland would not be discovered. Except for a few market vendors still packing up their stalls, and the sound of voices and laughter coming from the brightly lit windows of the pub, propped open to catch the evening breeze, the town was quiet and buildings were gathering their occupants in for their supper.

Clara peered into the dark, reading the signs that hung over the shops. "I don't see the Blacksmith's Inn here," she said after a moment.

The talkative farmer's wife who had befriended Fiona on the day's journey overheard them and said, "The 'Smith Inn, you say, love? It's down that road there a quarter mile." She pointed to one of the streets that led off the square. "The Dixons that run it is good folk, and it's right next to the smithy, if you're needing his services." She winked.

"His services?" Clara asked, baffled.

"Oh Lord, child, one doesn't just come to Gretna for the scenery! The smithy is where folk slip off to get married because our smith can perform the ceremony—no preacher needed here! Though there's other 'anvil priests' who can do the job just as well, if you've an objection to the heat of the smithy. I believe Mr. Dixon himself at the inn can perform a ceremony. But I can see that you've not come on that score, and beg your pardon if I've given offense."

"It's quite all right," said Clara. "As a matter of fact, we *are* here on marriage business, but we hope to prevent one rather than see it accomplished."

"Well, best of luck to you," said the woman, and she went to meet her husband who waited in a cart for her across the square. Clara watched them embrace fondly before trotting off, and felt a pang. If Violet really loved Lieutenant Green, how could she tear them apart? Why should her cousin be denied the chance to one day get off a coach and see the man she loved waiting to take her home?

She and Fiona set off with their bags down the road the woman had indicated and soon came to a brick building bearing the words "Blacksmith's Inn". Next to the inn, separated from the back alley by a little lawn, was the smithy itself, now dark and shut up for the night. Clara and Fiona walked in to the inn's dining room, which was beginning to fill for the evening meal. Clara scanned the tables for Violet and her affianced, but did not see anyone she recognized.

"'Ere for a room, ladies?" called a middle-aged man bringing out tankards of ale from the kitchen. "Or just for supper?"

"A room, if you please," said Clara. "And supper to follow."

They followed him to a desk with a large register laying atop it and a row of keys hanging behind.

"How many nights would you like, miss?" the proprietor asked Clara.

"Just one," she said firmly. "We'll be leaving in the morning, if all goes well. Might I inquire if you have a Miss Tapley staying with you? I—am hoping to surprise her at her wedding and was told she might be staying here."

He scanned the list of names on the register. "No Tapley, miss," he said. "But you're welcome to look at the guests, if you'd like. Some young folks don't feel quite comfortable puttin' their true names down, in case Father or Mother is in pursuit. We try and run a confidential business here, long as folks can pay." He turned the book around and pushed it toward her.

Clara scanned the list of names and did not see Violet's anywhere, nor any names that she suspected could have been invented by her cousin or that were written in her hand.

Another name caught her eye as she read, however, and she gasped. *Mrs. J. Creston* was written in Rose's writing near the bottom of the page.

She pulled Fiona over to the desk and said, "Rose is here!" Could Violet have assumed Rose's name? How then could the handwriting be so much like her sister's?

"Do you know, I thought I saw her maid, Therese, going upstairs just a moment ago, Miss Eastwood," Fiona said. "But then I decided I must be mistaken. Heavens above, what could Mrs. Creston be doing here? She's already married, isn't she? And she's supposed to be at the Lakes!"

"Do you know if Mrs. Creston is in?" Clara asked the proprietor.

"I believe so, miss," he replied. "Shall I go up and check? And will you still be wanting the room for yourself, then?"

"Yes," said Clara. She wasn't about to leave until her sister, or Violet, explained herself.

He tapped the blank spot at the bottom of the register. "Sign here, please, and that'll be a guinea."

She wrote *Clara Eastwood* on the ledger and reached for her reticule.

The innkeeper, however, had spun the book back around, and when he saw her name, said, "I beg your pardon, Miss Eastwood. Your lodging's been paid. We've been expecting you, and your room is already prepared. I hope you don't mind looking out toward the stables, as our garden view rooms are all occupied. Something about the summer air makes folks want to do drastic things, and brides and grooms seem to like looking at gardens rather than cobblestones."

Clara looked at him incredulously. Could he have her confused with someone else? "But I myself did not know I would be here," she said. "How could you have known I was coming?"

"I don't know, miss. Mrs. Creston reserved your room when she came. Best ask her. Shall I fetch her now?"

"Please do." She could not remember when last she had been so baffled.

Mr. Dixon went upstairs and returned a few minutes later. "You're to go up, Miss Eastwood. The room is number five."

She and Fiona went upstairs and wound their way through a little passageway to a door with a polished brass "5" on it. Clara raised her hand and knocked, not knowing what to expect on the other side.

Rose opened the door and said, "You're a bit later than we expected, but supper shan't be long now. Come in! You must be exhausted."

She led the other two into a sitting room with bedrooms opening onto either side and a table laid for supper, and seated herself on a settee near the fireplace. The door to the bedroom opposite opened, and Violet emerged.

"Hello Clara, Fiona," she said cheerfully as she made her way to the sitting area. "I do hope your trip was not too arduous. I know when we came up it was terribly bumpy and dusty, and that was in Mr. Creston's fine carriage, too—I can only imagine what the coach would have been like."

Clara looked from Violet to Rose and back again. "Do you

mean you both came here directly? Rose, you said you were stranded in Grasmere! How could you let Violet come here with this foolish scheme? And Violet, need I point out that you are about to make a terrible choice in this elopement? It will ruin you, it will break your mother's heart, and you will never be permitted in your father's house again."

"Oh Clara," said her sister. "Save your censure until you know what has really transpired. And for heaven's sake, haven't you noticed that *you're* the one engaged to the wrong man?"

"Noticed?" Now Clara was tired, confused, and filled with dread and anger at the thought of returning to Exton. "How could I not notice, when every day I am faced with the prospect of spending my days with Charles? Charles, who lectures me and thinks Yewspring is just a place for him to shoot partridges and wants me to stop reading novels? His mind is full of the army and pretty girls and carriages and pleasing his mother. Do you think these qualities have escaped me? Do you suppose I can be hopeful that time will remedy them?"

Rose took two letters from the table at her side and handed them to Clara. "You had better read these first, and we will answer all your questions after that."

Clara opened the first and read:

May 27

Exton

My dear Miss Eastwood,

~~*Miss Rose*~~ *Mrs. Creston will no doubt explain nearly everything to you, but she cannot explain my part in this scheme—at least, she will not know everything that led me to assist you.*

You remember, during our drawing lessons last spring, that you left a book with me (Mrs. Wakefield's, to be exact—who knew that I would one day meet the author, who is in spite of my misgivings quite distinguished!). I asked you to leave it with me, intending to study it and gain a better understanding of what you sought by soliciting my assistance.

It was the end of the longest, cruelest winter of my life. Matilda (I don't suppose you remember her—she is my maid and used to work at Beechview for Lady Eastwood) was having problems with her eyesight, and we had to have your uncle Morton in to look at her more than once. It cost a pretty penny, even though he does not charge full price for his tinctures since we are associated with Beechview. And then I fell ill in January, an ailment that was no doubt not helped by the fact that we had to ration our fires. Poor Matilda was sleeping in the kitchen to be near the grate, and my bedroom was the only other that we could heat. Your grandmother, as thankful as I am for her patronage, was reluctant to increase the allowance she gives to Matilda and I. It seems there was something amiss with the estate's grain that year—it did not sell as well at market as expected. Something about the market being flooded just when it was offered, or some such thing, and so she said we must make do with what we were given.

And so when your letter came, and when you left the book with me, I was so desperate that before I had time to think better of it, I sold it to Mr. Reed for his store. I thought I could use the excuse of Matilda's eyesight to say that we had misplaced it. I am ashamed of what I did, and after some self-reflection I went to the Reeds to ask for the book back so I could return it to you. (though heaven knows how I could have returned what he paid for it—it was spent on wood and a girl to help Matilda before the coins even touched my hand). Imagine my distress when Mr. Reed told me he had already given it back to you and told you where he got it. I knew you must have found me out. From that day on I waited to hear from Lady Eastwood turning me out of my lodgings. But when I never received a message from her Ladyship on the matter but rather was asked to come to town to be your companion, I concluded that you had kept my shameful act from your family. I have been in your debt ever since, and when I stumbled upon you and Mr. Kensington together one day in Somersetshire, I knew your secret might repay the debt of you keeping my own. I hope my assistance might help settle the score between us.

If you should return to Exton, you will find that Dr. Stanley has honored me with the offer of his hand, and I will be gone to my own wedding as you return from yours. He has flattered me with his attentiveness and good opinion of me during the two collecting trips. However outlandish I may find your science, and however unseemly I think it to put oneself forward as you and Mrs. Wakefield have, I cannot deny that in this case, I owe the pursuit a great debt.

Be well, Miss Clara, and do come see us if you are ever again in Somersetshire.

Sincerely yours,

Bertha Holt

"Oh, Miss Holt," sighed Clara, unsure whether her emotion was old pain re-remembered, pity, or gratitude. Perhaps it was all three.

"She's better off now," said Rose. "Think of her in Somersetshire with a legion of servants to command, rather than be commanded herself. I like to picture her eating chocolates in front of a roaring fire with her feet propped up on the grate."

"With this Dr. Stanley fawning over her!" giggled Violet.

"I do not think he is the fawning type," said Clara. "But since I knew nothing of his attachment to her all the while we were together, perhaps I should not hazard a guess. But what does she mean by all this talk of a wedding, and a debt repaid?"

"You were distracted on that trip yourself, silly goose," said Rose with a smile. "Open your next letter, and hurry!"

Clara obeyed.

May 24

Tottenham

My dear Miss Eastwood,

If you are reading these words, your sister and cousin have performed their tasks admirably and you are in Gretna Green as planned. I hope you are not too angry at them for deceiving you. You should know that I am responsible for this entire scheme and that they only aided me when I asked.

But, you must be wondering, why on earth would I concoct an elaborate plan to bring you to Gretna Green? Not so that you could prevent an imprudent marriage on the part of your cousin (how very lucky that she is unmarried and could play the role of runaway bride! I was worried that the recent outburst of weddings in your family might have spoiled things), but so that you might enter into a marriage of your own. Mr. Kensington is staying across town at the Russet Pheasant and should be with you within the hour. I urge you, before it is too late, to marry him before you throw your life away. I knew you would not come to Gretna for yourself, so your cousin agreed to concoct a story. Put any thoughts of her danger out of your head and begin thinking of the danger that you now have the chance to escape by becoming Mrs. Kensington.

You may think I am doing this out of the goodness of my heart, but while I will think of your happiness with great pleasure, the truth is that I cannot afford to lose your skills as an illustrator. Your sister tells me that Mr. Eastwood was reluctant to "allow" you (such a vile word when used about one's husband!) to go on the collecting trip last autumn and that he expected you to give up drawing upon your marriage. In contrast, Mr. Kensington's presence and aid on that same trip convinced me that he would not think so little of your abilities. With so few avenues of employment open to us, when we have the talent and the inclination to contribute to society, women would do well to find supportive husbands when we can. The thought of you throwing away your chance was repulsive to me. Do you think the kind of man who encourages his wife in her scientific interests grows on trees? I am astonished that you found one at all in such a small village as Exton. Pray, do not squander your good fortune, and remember the women who are less fortunate in their marital relations.

As for the moral cost of breaking your engagement to your cousin, let us weigh it against the moral costs of <u>not</u> doing so. Your illustrating would be nonexistent, so science would suffer as well as your own mind and soul. Your husband would be sadly mistaken in your feelings toward him, so your relationship with him and your sense of integrity must also suffer, as I imagine it already has over the course of your engagement. I firmly believe that a wife and mother must be the moral compass of her household, and deceit has no place in that calling.

Finally, it sounds as though the Kensingtons desperately need another earner in their house to prevent them from falling into perpetual poverty (your sister has related their downfall to me), and the proceeds from your illustration could contribute to their comfort and welfare. You seem to have confused your fate as Mrs. Eastwood with your fate as Mrs. Kensington. Illustrating will not be as closed off to you as the latter as it would be with the former. I understand there is Miss Kensington's child to think of, and would hate to think that you had driven him into the poorhouse because of your own stubbornness.

I suspect you have discounted the idea of your marriage to Mr. Kensington because it is the outcome that will bring you the most happiness, and, by virtue of your temperament and what our society calls "eccentricities", have never learned to trust your own joy as a guide. Let this be a lesson to you: happiness cannot be the only consideration when making a decision, but neither is it necessarily the sign of a wrong action. We must only possess a fair scale with which to measure the merits of various actions for ourselves and others, which I fear in this case you do not have. Therefore, I lend you mine and hope someday you will be able to do the same for someone else. At times it is possible for the choice we most hope for to be the right choice. In these cases, we must thank Providence and receive the resulting blessings with gratitude and humility, as the good Lord has ordained.

Trust me, there will be pain, sorrow, suffering, and grief along with the joy, for such is the nature of human life. You would not escape them by marrying Mr. Eastwood, and you will not have the respect and love between man and wife that can at least ease so many of those burdens. I also feel compelled to mention that Mr. Eastwood deserves the undivided love and care of a wife whose heart is not attached to another.

In my view, the only things you lose by marrying Mr. Kensington are the respect of those who do not understand the true Christian charity exhibited in his acceptance of his sister, and the disappointment of Mr. Eastwood (and, I hear, his mother, who it seems is quite fond of you—but the price you must pay to be her daughter-in-law is too great), which I trust cannot be long-lived. He will no doubt find a more suitable wife by and by. In the meantime, I leave it to you to decide whether those losses are too great to bear, though I question your intelligence if you come to that conclusion.

And how did this all come about? Because you did not shame Miss Holt, she wanted to help you in return. Putting kindness into the world often returns it to you. She wrote to me and told me that she stumbled upon you and Mr. Kensington in Somersetshire. When he left abruptly, she and her maid tracked him down in Derbyshire through her Exton connections, and then I had my son Edward lead him to Scotland on an imaginary endeavor. I do not think he will mind the deceit, for it will get him the wife he has longed for.

I close now in the hope of hearing from you soon as Mrs. Kensington, and in the hope that, if children bless your union, you raise them to expect the same relationship of respect, love, and deep joy in one another when they seek their own spouses that their parents model for them daily.

Send me your new address when you know it, so that we can discuss details for the next flora. Yorkshire has not yet been done and I hear the heathers are quite fascinating.

Cordially yours,

Mrs. Wakefield

Clara was not surprised to find that she was weeping as she finished the letter, though she did not know whether they were tears of relief, shame at Mrs. Wakefield's rebukes and the memory of her past conduct, or disbelief that such an unlooked-for conclusion to her engagement was possible. She could not believe that after having released her hopes, standing with empty hands, this had been given to her.

She had fled into Rose's bedroom while reading the letter, holding it before the dim light of the little fire in the grate, and now wiped away her tears and tried to compose herself.

In the outer room, she heard doors opening and closing and various voices coming in and out. At the sound of Mr. Kensington's voice among them—a sound she had thought she would never hear again—a few more tears sprang up in her eyes. This time she could identify them as being borne of unadulterated happiness, a kind she had never known. Self-doubt had always been the companion to every one of her joys, entwined with each like a vine whose delicate tendrils belie the strength with which it is wrapped around its host. Its absence was at once thrilling and profoundly disorienting.

As she sat sobbing, a knock came at the door. She wiped her eyes and went to open it. Mr. Kensington stood there in a rumpled tailcoat, dark circles around his eyes, looking anxiously at her. After a moment, however, he broke out into a smile of a strength Clara had never seen before, and she answered it with one of her own.

"May I come in?" he asked formally, and she looked around him to see Fiona, Therese, Rose, and Violet seated at the sitting area, each trying hard to look preoccupied with an important yet invisible task. Therese had picked up a piece of sewing without a needle and was gamely trying to mime the act of sewing, and Violet had grabbed a nearby book and was looking at it upside down.

Clara looked at them and laughed a little, then grabbed Mr. Kensington's jacket and pulled him inside.

CHAPTER TWENTY-FOUR

In the dim room they did not speak for a long while, but when they did, he took her face in his hands and said breathlessly, "How long I have ached to ask you this question, and with what hopelessness I contemplated my chances of ever doing so! You do not know how often I spoke these words at night to my silent room into the darkness. Clara, my love, you are the only woman I could ever give myself to. Will you marry me in the morning? I shall beat on every door in town until I find a man who can perform the ceremony, if you say you will be my wife."

"Yes," she said through her smiles and the tears that seemed to be her lot that day, "with everything I have in me. I have been your wife in heart for many months now, so we have no choice but to make it legal."

Again they chose the sweetness of not speaking, since they had an entire lifetime of conversation ahead of them, until Rose came and told them to go eat their supper.

Clara stood at the mirror in Rose's room the next morning, the window flung open to catch every bit of the summer morning, though the birdsong she would have heard at Yewspring was replaced with the rattling of carts and horseshoes upon the cobblestones of the stable-yard and the voices of those sent about their morning errands. In the room next door, the maid had flung the carpets out onto the sill, and she could hear the *thud* of the beater as the dust of another season flew from its fibers.

She had made the journey to Scotland in a plain, everyday gown in her haste to get there, which had begun its journey merely ink- and grass-stained and was now wrinkled, had gravy on the skirt where she had spilt her chop at an inn, and was draped all over with the fine dust of the stagecoach. She had been standing in her petticoat staring dismally at the wreck of a gown when Rose had pulled from behind the dressing screen a lovely one of gray silk with lace trimming with a flourish of triumph.

"Therese pulled this out of your jungle of a bedroom!" her sister had said triumphantly as she laid it across the bed.

Now, in her wedding garb, Clara felt quite pretty. Violet had gone out to get roses for the bride's bonnet, and now Clara heard her name being called from the yard below. She went to the window and there saw Violet holding an armful each of pink and yellow roses aloft for her inspection. Mr. Kensington was next to her, dressed in a freshly pressed tailcoat.

Violet called up, "Which ones, Clara?"

Rose had come to the window with her sister and looked over at Clara, laughing at the look of panic on her face. "Pink, Vi!" she called down to her cousin, who nodded approvingly and disappeared into the inn.

Mr. Kensington looked up happily at his bride-to-be, grinned, and triumphantly held up a wedding ring.

"Just a plain band, but it was all I could find on such short notice," he called. "I hope it's all right."

"Of course!" she called back down. "I won't be taking it off, so the plainer the better for sketching."

He smiled. "The minister will be at the church at nine o'clock—I asked for eight, but he said it was bad enough as it was that he would have to wake up the two witnesses."

It was only seven-thirty, so she ducked back inside and Rose put the finishing touches on her gown.

"Will you go back to town after this?" Clara asked her sister.

"No, I decided to take Violet to the Lakes after all," said Rose with a laugh. "It's the least I can do after all the trouble I've put her through, though I anticipate that this will be the last elopement of the trip. Sit now so I can fix your hair."

Clara did so and looked at her sister standing behind her in the mirror, then caught up Rose's hand and squeezed it. "Thank you for all this, Rosie," she said. "I do not know how I shall repay you for your kindness."

"The knowledge that you will be as happy with your husband as I am with mine will be reward enough," Rose said with a smile that was quickly replaced with a more solemn expression. "Though—Clara, I fear it may be very hard going for you. I would not have done this if I did not think the joys of your marriage would outweigh its sorrows, but…you will be cut off from nearly everyone you have known. Perhaps only a single servant, no holidays, no society—are you prepared for all of that?"

Images flashed through Clara's mind like the undersides of cards being shuffled: of her and Miss Kensington gamely trying to make supper, of trying to turn the worst of the grocer's wares into soup, of burning bread. She saw herself trying to mend a torn gown, of jagged stitches that pulled the fabric into an ugly pucker like a scar.

And, most painful, she saw Yewspring. She thought of Annie Clemons's sons with no one to call them home again and offer them work. She saw the house with a stranger's family in it, let to anyone who could pay the rent. She saw planting and lambing and weeding and harvesting and slaughtering, wagons piled high with hay, piglets in the sties, the woodland swales thick with flowers, their sides awash in blue and white and yellow. She saw all of it going on without her, and she almost wept to think of it, her own reflection in the mirror going blurry for just a moment. She remembered standing under the yews in the moonlight just a few nights before, accepting what had been given to her, deciding that happiness was not everything. But it was not nothing, either, she realized as she looked at her sister in the mirror.

So she said to her sister, "I am not sure anything could prepare me for what might follow. But I have lived long enough without Mr. Kensington to know that I choose difficulties with him over whatever ease I might have had without him. That I should have made that choice from the beginning. I am grateful to you for helping me make it now."

Rose smiled, a little sadly. "Then it is very fitting that your happiness should be accomplished in such a remarkable way. A commonplace engagement would never have been suitable for you. Now look straight ahead so I can fix these plaits."

Violet came in with the roses, looking for Clara's bonnet.

"If only you had brought your newer straw bonnet," she sighed to Clara. "Ah well, I shall drape the brim with roses and no one will see the weaving coming undone." She took it into the sitting room next door.

In the mirror, Clara looked at Rose who still looked sober while she pinned Clara's hair.

"Surely Rosie, you will not cut me from your acquaintance after all this? Surely you believe that this is the right choice? Perhaps we might come to Rutland—"

Her sister hesitated and fixed her gaze on the scuffed floorboards at her feet. "I would very much like to be able at least to correspond with you," she said finally. "But I do not yet know how James will feel about this matter, for he also does not know about the true purpose of my supposed holiday. He thinks I am really in the Lakes for this whole time. I will do everything in my power to convince him as firmly as I am convinced myself of the merit of this match. I hope that his good judgment will prevail in this matter, but he was raised in a very conventional household that placed strong value on their respectability, and it may be a long process to persuade him, though I swear to persevere as long as it takes."

Clara said in dismay, "I see now that severing my closest relationships will be a heavy burden indeed. Is there nothing you can do to advocate for us, Rosie? Especially to Mr. Creston, so that Mr. Kensington and I may at least have our relationship with our siblings intact?"

"Of course, I will do everything in my power to share my convictions with our family. But surely you understand that husband and wife must present a unified face to the world, and one must not undermine the other if their marriage is to flourish. Until Mr. Creston can wholeheartedly support the idea of you and I continuing to have a relationship, I must give him the respect he deserves as my husband and abide by his wishes."

"How degrading for you to have to stifle your own wishes for that of your husband!"

Rose laughed. "Oh Clara, you have much to learn. But I do not expect nothing from my husband in return. I plan to make my own wishes and desires very well known to him in this regard, and just as I will acquiesce to him, I expect him to listen carefully to my feelings and to understand how ardently I desire not only unity between him and I, but unity between you and I as sisters. That is a motive he will not be able to set aside lightly."

"Thank you," said Clara. "I am already grateful for your support."

"You are most welcome. And no matter what, you must send me your new address when you have it. I will not consent to be completely cut off from any correspondence from you—if nothing else I must at least be able to communicate between you and the rest of the family. I hope our relatives are all destined for many more years of life left, but it would not do for you not to know if one of them fell sick or departed this world."

"All right," said Clara.

"Do you know where you will go?" Rose asked, giving a final tug to Clara's crown of braids and then going to sit by the vanity.

Clara and Mr. Kensington had discussed their plans late into the evening before he went back to the Russet Pheasant to make his own preparations.

"We have enough money to get back to Exton again, for I brought enough for Violet's return fare as well as my own. And he has a bit of money from his last place in Derbyshire. We will use those funds to stay at an inn for a night or two on the way back home to have a bit of a honeymoon, since we will have to begin our new life immediately after we return to Exton."

She blushed at the implication of the word *honeymoon*, but Rose only smiled knowingly and said matter-of-factly. "Yes, you should take advantage of wedded bliss while you can, since heaven knows you may find little of it enough when you get back. I gather Miss Kensington is not terribly fond of you, and Mrs. Kensington sounds most unpleasant."

"I do not know that our relationship will be the happiest of in-laws," said Clara, smiling ruefully. "But I have been surprised over and over again these last few days. I suppose I should not speculate on what the future might bring. But Miss Kensington's dislike of me seems to be centered on the unhappiness I caused her brother by continuing in my engagement to Charles, so per-haps she will forgive me once she seems how thoroughly I have repented of my actions."

"I do hope so," said Rose. "And what about Charles?"

"I shall have to write to him today," said Clara. "Our wedding was to be only a week from tomorrow, and by the time the letter reaches him it will be very late indeed. I am sorry to cause him pain, but the sooner he knows, the better. To be truthful, I am more disappointed in losing his mother as my mother-in-law than him as a husband. I shall write her separately and say how sorry I am that we shall not meet again."

Violet knocked on the door and stuck her head in. "It's time to go!" she said cheerfully. "I've already sent Mr. Kensington on to the church since he was pacing so nervously up and down the passage outside. I think the Dixons were getting annoyed with him—he nearly upset the chambermaids going around blind corners. And anyway, he is not to see his bride until the ceremony."

The three cousins went downstairs. Fiona and Therese wanted to stay behind at the inn to arrange the wedding breakfast, but Rose said, "No, you must come along to the church."

The party of five set off, retracing the route Clara and Fiona had taken the night before to the main square, then following a side road from the square north to the church, set back a bit from the street.

Clara's heart fluttered in her chest. Was she really about to marry Mr. Kensington? Twenty-four hours ago her life had been on a path she could see no way of leaving, and now she was to have her happiest dream realized, so unexpectedly!

Therese and Fiona went in first to ensure that the groom and minister were ready, just as the bells rang the hour. They came back out to say that everything was prepared, and Violet went in with them.

Rose took Clara's arm. "I shall do what Papa should have done and walk in with you," she said. "I never expected to give away a bride!"

They went in to the quiet church, sunlight streaming through the stained glass, to the little group of figures at the altar. The minister stood there in full vestments, with Mr. Kensington at his side. Her groom looked at her, drinking her in. Rose brought her to the front of the church, declared that she gave Clara to Henry on behalf of the entire Eastwood family, and sat in the front pew with Violet, who was already weeping copiously.

The minister said, "Dearly beloved, we are gathered here in the sight of God, and in the face of this congregation, to join together this Man and this Woman in holy Matrimony; which is an honorable estate, instituted of God in the time of man's innocency, signifying unto us the mystical union that is betwixt Christ and his Church; which holy estate Christ adorned and beautified with his presence, and first miracle that he wrought, in Cana of Galilee; and is commended of Saint Paul to be honorable among all men: and therefore is not by any to be enterprised, nor taken in hand, unadvisedly, lightly, or wantonly, to satisfy men's carnal lusts and appetites, like brute beasts that have no understanding; but reverently, discreetly, advisedly, soberly, and in the fear of God; duly considering the causes for which Matrimony was ordained.

"First, it was ordained for the procreation of children, to be brought up in the fear and nurture of the Lord, and to the praise of his holy Name.

"Secondly, it was ordained for a remedy against sin, and to avoid fornication; that such persons as have not the gift of continency might marry, and keep themselves undefiled members of Christ's body.

"Thirdly, it was ordained for the mutual society, help, and comfort, that the one ought to have of the other, both in prosperity and adversity. Into which holy estate these two persons present come now to be joined. Therefore, if any man can show any just cause, why they may not lawfully be joined together, let him now speak, or else hereafter forever hold his peace."

There was a pause. No one burst in, having pursued them from Exton. No one spoke. Clara, feeling that she ought to try as a matter of form, cast about for a qualm to this marriage and found none.

"Who comes this day to be joined in holy matrimony?"

Mr. Kensington said, "I, Henry Frederick Kensington, do so come this day."

The minister asked, "Where do you reside?"

"Exton, Warwickshire."

The minister turned to Clara. "Who else comes this day to be joined in holy matrimony?"

Clara replied, "I, Clara Elizabeth Eastwood, do so come this day."

"And where do you reside?"

"Exton, Warwickshire."

"Are each of you single and unmarried as of this day?"

They answered that they were.

The minister continued, "Mr. Kensington, do you come here of your own free will and accord?"

Mr. Kensington looked at Clara. "I do," he said with a smile.

"And do you, Miss Eastwood, come here of your own free will and accord?"

Clara thought of the long carriage ride of the last two days, of the quiet, calm joy and contentment that had swept over her like a wave over the last twelve hours, a deeply grounding peacefulness that had anchored her already and let her greet this dawn with a confidence she had never felt before. She looked at the man who would shortly be her husband and said, returning his smile, "I do."

The minister turned to a table at his side and filled out a portion of the marriage certificate. Violet's sniffles were the only sound in the quiet church. Clara looked around her at the emerald and burgundy light streaming in, still unbelieving and yet feeling that this was the moment, over all others, that belonged to her and her beloved.

The minister finished writing and said, "Please face each other and join your right hands."

All else fell away for Clara but Mr. Kensington's face, his gray eyes gleaming with a joy that nearly smote her the way that his unhappiness had smoldered when she caught his gaze each night that autumn on the collecting trip.

"Mr. Kensington, do you take this woman to be your lawful wedded wife, forsaking all others, kept to her as long as you both shall live?"

"I will," said Mr. Kensington.

"Miss Eastwood, do you take this man to be your lawful wedded husband, forsaking all others, kept to him as long as you both shall live?"

"I will," said Clara.

Then Mr. Kensington said, "I Henry take thee Clara to be my wedded wife, to have and to hold from this day forward, for better for worse, for richer for poorer, in sickness and in health, to love and to cherish, till death us do part, according to God's holy ordinance; and thereto I plight thee my troth."

The cards of her future flashed again, and Clara thought of nursing him, of bearing him children, of thin soup every day and going to bed together each night. She saw chilblained hands, washing hung to dry in the parlor, and her husband's face held tenderly between her hands. She watched the life she might have had disappearing around a corner like a carriage bound for somewhere else. She watched Yewspring slip away.

Through her tears, in spite of her trembling, she said, "I Clara take thee Henry to be my wedded husband, to have and to hold from this day forward, for better for worse, for richer for poorer, in sickness and in health, to love and to cherish, till death us do part, according to God's holy ordinance; and thereto I plight thee my troth."

Mr. Kensington took her ring from his pocket and gave it to the minister, who gave it back to him and said, "Put this ring on the fourth finger of her left hand."

As he did so, Mr. Kensington said, "With this ring, I thee wed, with my body I thee worship, with all my worldly goods I thee endow in the name of the Father, Son and Holy Ghost, Amen."

She did likewise for his ring, and then the minister said, "For what God has joined together, let no man put asunder."

Clara looked down at the band, the light from the windows reflecting off its surface, and though it was still her own hand, she felt a thrill. The gold on her finger and its glint of sapphires and amethysts proclaimed to her that it was possible for anything one could imagine to shift, to grow, to change.

After thanking the minister, and Mr. Kensington heartily shaking his hand several times, they left the church with Clara on her husband's arm and with the marriage certificate in her hand. The other three went on to the inn while Clara and Mr. Kensington walked slowly around the square, then down the little lanes radiating out from it, looking at the shops and houses.

Mr. Kensington, from time to time, pulled her into an alley to kiss her out of sight, though once the butcher's boy passed by and whistled loudly in approval, making them jump apart hastily. They looked at each other and laughed, then Mr. Kensington said, "I have nothing to be ashamed of—I shall kiss my wife if I feel like it. God knows I have waited long enough for that privilege," and pulled her close again.

After three-quarters of an hour, they went back to the inn and upstairs to Rose's sitting room for the wedding breakfast, which consisted of a fine array of cake, ham rolls, chocolate, and grapes that the inn kept on hand for such occasions. Mrs. Dixon also sent up a carafe of her best wine with her compliments to the bride and groom.

Just as they had drunk to the health of their parents and grandparents, and toasted the newlyweds, a knock came at the door and a serving maid came in without waiting for an answer.

"I beg your pardon," she panted from her flight up the stairs, "but a Lady Eastwood is here-" Before she could finish, Clara's grandmother herself swept in, resplendent despite what must have been a long journey in a carriage, neatly dressed in a traveling coat and with a hat full of feathers that added to her air of height and grace.

She wordlessly took in the table and the array spread out upon it, the newly-weds and Rose and Violet, who had festooned their own bonnets with the yellow roses Violet had bought that morning.

Rose said weakly, "Hello, Grandmama."

Lady Eastwood's nostrils drew in with a quick breath of fury, then she said stiffly, "I see I am too late to prevent this highly foolish wedding. Since my efforts to stop it have been wasted, I will instead use it to inform you, Rose, Violet, Clara, that you will no longer receive a penny of your inheritance from your grandfather and I. How could I reward such disobedience and lack of regard for this family's respectability with a financial gift upon my death? I hope whatever satisfaction you derive from this perverse event will be ample compensation for this loss.

"Clara, I bid you goodbye forever. You are never to set foot on our property again, and I shall leave the premises immediately if I find myself in the same vicinity as you. I am shocked and ashamed that you have thrown the principles of your upbringing away so carelessly."

Clara opened her mouth to reply, but her grandmother waved away her objections and turned to Violet.

"Violet, let this be a lesson to you as you select a husband of your own. I must also point out that your note of amused triumph in this mad scheme to Caroline nearly prevented it from being carried out, as she divulged that information to me as soon as she received the letter. Did you forget that I was visiting her in advance of the baby's arrival? If our horse had not thrown a shoe in Leeming yesterday, your premature triumph would have led to the only proper and fitting outcome for this venture, which is for it to have failed completely and for you all to return home in shame. I insist that you come back to Exton with me immediately.

"Rose, I expect a letter of apology and explanation as to your involvement with this disastrous idea and shall write you a reply correcting whatever misconceptions led you to enter into it. Following this transaction I will consent to acknowledge you, but not before. Come now, Violet."

"Just a moment, Grandmother," said Clara, rising from her seat where she had sat with anger simmering quietly as her grandmother spoke. "I hope you reconsider your threat to disinherit Rose and Violet. How will Violet's chances for a respectable, prudent marriage be helped by lessening her inheritance?

And there is no reason that anyone need know that she and Rose were not in fact at the Lakes as they planned. Rose is already respectably married, and any suspicion would harm her reputation without cause. Leave them out of it. Mr. Kensington and I could easily have planned and executed this elopement ourselves, and until you leave this room and reveal otherwise, that is exactly what we shall say happened.

"As for my own punishment, it is severe indeed and does not befit the obedience and devotion I have shown you hereto, but I will not argue against it. I will only say that if you cannot see Mr. Kensington's goodness and his compassion toward his sister, I relinquish all claim to be known as your blood or inherit your wealth." She looked down at Mr. Kensington and took his hand. "From henceforth, my marriage shall be my wealth, and my allegiance lies with my husband first and foremost. So long as I have a roof over my head, I want nothing more."

She looked back up at her grandmother, still holding her husband's hand. "You may go now. Let us finish celebrating in peace."

Her grandmother looked at her furiously. "You silly, stupid girl," she said. "I hope you remember those words when you wonder how you will feed your children and worry whether they shall go to the poorhouse. I shall consider your plea to spare Rose and Violet. In the meantime, we shall carry on as if nothing has happened, but do not consider my mind made up. Violet, you shall carry on to the Lakes as planned. I will leave this wretched place at once and leave you all to consider your actions. I pray they do not torment you as they will torment me to the end of my days."

She turned on her heel and swept out.

The other four now looked at each other. The food had gone cold as they sat. Violet had paled at the mention of her letter to Caroline and now said, "I'm sorry about the letter, Clara. I'm sorry, Rose. I did not mean to betray us—I was simply excited about the trip and the chance to help you."

"It's all right," Clara said. "You had no ill intentions. And I hope she decides to spare you both from the disinheritance. I would feel awful if she carried through with it and you had to suffer because of me."

"I know it's no use now, but should I inquire how much you were to inherit?" asked Mr. Kensington asked Clara.

"We think it would come to a thousand pounds each," said Violet.

Mr. Kensington leaned forward and buried his face in his hands. "A thousand pounds," he groaned longingly from between his fingers.

Clara laughed and put her hand on his back. "My darling, we live by our own luck and hard work now," she said. "What an adventure! A thousand pounds would have prevented it entirely."

CHAPTER TWENTY-FIVE

Fog hung over Liverpool in the chill January air, and the sea was a sheet of iron that sent up wave after wave onto the harbor wall, leaving its stones dark and slick. The ship *Friends* sat waiting at the dock, ready for her departure the next morning, and Clara and Mr. Kensington finished loading their parcels into their cabin from the cart waiting at the bottom of the gangway. Clara looked at the little space around her, wondering how it would get them through the three months of sailing ahead of them. Mr. Kensington was already arranging their botanical books at the cabin's little table near the porthole.

She went over and said, "We can do that tomorrow, Henry. Let's go enjoy our last night on land."

In the cabin next door, they could hear Oliver's little voice piping cheerfully to his mother as she arranged their belongings. The young people had left Mrs. Kensington at the inn—she had declined to go to the docks with them, saying that the time she would be onboard would be long enough for her.

Mr. Kensington looked down at the little row of books sitting next to a pile of drawing paper and Clara's pencil box. "All right," he said.

They collected the other two, left the ship and paid the driver of the cart, then walked to the inn where they were staying, Oliver chanting a sea shanty he had learned from the captain and skipping ahead of them. After a quick supper and retiring to their rooms, Clara and Henry lay together in the narrow bed, shoulder to shoulder, looking up at the splintered ceiling beams.

"Are you apprehensive, my love?" her husband asked her.

"Yes," she admitted. "I do not relish the prospect of being sick for weeks on end, or contracting some awful disease, or getting caught in a storm."

He took her hand. "I know," he said. "I hope we arrive safely and in good health. But I stand by our decision, and I think it is for the best."

"So do I," she said. "Try and get some sleep now, darling. I must write Rose so that I can send the letter before we embark."

He held her for a moment, kissed her good-night, then rolled over, and she heard his deep heavy breathing that she knew even after a mere six months of marriage meant that he had fallen quickly into sleep.

She put her dressing gown back on in the chilly room, wrapped a thick shawl around her, and propped a thick book against her knees to use as a writing surface.

January 6

Liverpool

Dearest Rose,

I know this will come as a shock to you, but I wanted to write before we sail tomorrow so that you do not wonder if I do not write this winter. Henry and I are departing tomorrow morning on a convict ship bound for Australia, named Friends, *and will arrive sometime in March or April, God willing. Please let James know again how grateful I am that I am able to write and tell you, even if he could not be persuaded to let us meet in person.*

The last few months in Exton were harder than I imagined. It was very humiliating to have Mama and Papa cut me as they did, and to have no society beyond the laborers and tradespeople we encounter every day, who are mostly good-hearted but cannot understand why I would throw away my former privileges. It has been a strange and disorienting experience to have those who my family employs as our social equals now. Last week we had a little dinner in farewell to Exton, and Aunt Charlotte's maid attended!

Henry and I have tried to carry on educating ourselves, having intellectual discussions whenever we can, but we are often so tired in the evenings that we have very little energy for writing, reading, or my sketching.

We decided this fall that we must go away and find a place where we might earn better money, and thought of the colonies. In Australia we will also have the benefit of no one knowing of the Kensingtons' downfall. We hope there will be botanical expeditions we may join as further exploration is done, so that I can continue sketching and building my knowledge and Henry can perhaps join on as cartographer as we did in England. His family comes with us—his mother unwillingly but without any other recourse, and Oliver of course in a spirit of youthful excitement to be sailing on such a ship. My sister-in-law must leave with regrets, but I believe shares our desire for a new beginning, where her past cannot shackle her as it did in England.

Please send your next letter care of:

Mrs. Charles Harley

2 Godwin Street

Sydney, New South Wales

It may not reach me for ten months or a year, but please continue to write and I will send you a new address if I have one. We are hoping to stay at Mrs. Harley's boarding house first and perhaps look for some land after that, though we may have to work on someone else's property first while we save our money. Mrs. Wakefield has been informed of our move and promises to pass along any information she gets about Australian collecting.

And now I must say farewell, sister. Though we have encountered difficulties during our marriage, as I imagine most couples do, and though I understand more now than I did about the trials of poverty, I am so grateful for my Henry and that we face our life together. Though we may have more burdens to bear, we are stronger and more able to meet them together than we would apart. He understands me unlike anyone I have ever met, a gift I was so foolish as to almost squander, and I plan to spend the rest of my life repaying the debt I feel to him for allowing me to be exactly as I am, without reproach. This half year of our marriage has convinced me that I will not regret the choices I have made, nor the years that led to them, nor even the reckoning that we have been through. We have emerged from it ready for this voyage, ready to see what lies ahead.

I hope and pray the same for you, dear sister.

Fondly,

Clara Kensington

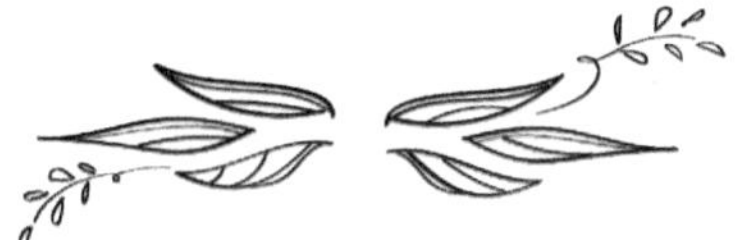

HISTORICAL NOTE 

Most of the people and places in *Yewspring* are fictional, but Priscilla Wakefield is a real historical figure. The author of seventeen books and an educator, activist, and Quaker, she lived from 1751-1832. She was clearly exposed to botany and the sciences in her youth and wrote *An Introduction to Botany*, intended to be used by students studying at home, in 1798. Wakefield also founded various charities, including a maternal "lying-in" facility, in Tottenham and is credited with starting the first savings bank in England. Her book *Reflections on the Present Condition of the Female Sex, with Suggestions for Its Improvement* was published in 1796 and critiques prevailing attitudes about women's labor in the late eighteenth century—including those inherent in the economic theories of Adam Smith. The eldest of ten children and eventually mother to three, she was active in intellectual and religious circles throughout her life. When she died at the age of eighty-one the author of her obituary wrote that "in her efforts to improve the rising generation…she was eminently successful" (*The Gentleman's Magazine*, 1832). While Clara and the assistance Wakefield gave her are works of my imagination, Wakefield's many endeavors of service and education are very real.

As of early 2023, there is a website run by Margaret Burr and Noel Treacy devoted to Priscilla Wakefield's legacy in Tottenham. The address is priscillawakefield.uk.

To those who want to learn more about botanical women in England during the eighteenth and nineteenth centuries, I recommend Ann B. Shteir's *Cultivating Women, Cultivating Science: Flora's Daughters and Botany in England, 1760 to 1860* and Anna K. Sagal's *Botanical Entanglements: Women, Natural Science, and the Arts in Eighteenth-Century England*.

ACKNOWLEDGEMENTS 

For their encouragement as I was taking my first steps as a writer, I'm grateful to Jeff Dodd and Dan Vice. Thank you to the M.A. faculty at Mercy College for supporting my work there, particularly Dr. Christopher Loots and Dr. Sean Dugan. Elise Hooper and my Historical Fiction classmates at Hugo House helped me refine my writing and research and were a great source of camaraderie. Thank you to Erika Mailman for her kindness during our Blue Pencil session and for telling me to keep chasing the dream. Nicole Dieker offered insightful editing and feedback that immensely helped the story.

For the past three years, I've been impressed over and over by the knowledge of Jane Austen and the Georgian/Regency eras so generously shared by the members of the Jane Austen Society of North America. For their support of my work and this project, I especially thank Michele Larrow and Brenda S. Cox.

Several good friends embraced *Yewspring* as soon as they heard about it: Thank you, Rob, Katie, and Annie.

Thank you, Shiela Pardee, Aditi Vyas, and Julia for walking with me on this writing journey and for the insightful feedback. Your generosity and encouragement have been priceless, and I'm humbled to receive them.

Lucia Rinolfi at the British Museum guided me through the process of gaining rights to use the cover image—the book wouldn't be the same without it.

A thousand thanks to Alaina Kowitz for working tirelessly to make the book beautiful.

One of the biggest blessings of my life has been growing up in (and marrying into) wonderful families who have always been my north star. It's been inspiring to spend my life alongside people who live their own lives so well and who have given me so much. Thank you, Kassas, Kowitzs, and Van Cleaves.

As with all my projects from stick-figure drawings to degrees, Mom, Dad, and Alaina have supported and cheered on my writing (and made me an Austen fan forever with our VHS of the 1995 *P&P*). I'm grateful to them for that, and for much more than will fit here.

Thanks to J, who teaches me all the time what it means to live and love well.

Profound, profound gratitude to Ted, for being *Yewspring*'s first and staunchest reader and giving me thoughtful feedback through all the drafts. Thank you for helping me fix "Charles's personality disorder," take risks, and grow as a writer (and a person, and a wife). Love you, like you, forever grateful for you.

ABOUT THE AUTHOR 

Cecily Van Cleave worked in the natural resources field for a decade before earning an M.A. in English Literature from Mercy College. Her thesis on Elizabeth Gaskell and George Eliot was chosen as the program's Thesis of the Year. Her writing has been published in the journal *Persuasions*, *The Copperfield Review*, *The North Columbia Monthly*, and various anthologies. *Yewspring* is her first novel. She lives in rural Washington State with her family.

Visit **cecilyvancleave.com** for more information & updates!

www.ingramcontent.com/pod-product-compliance
Lightning Source LLC
Chambersburg PA
CBHW021441310726
48971CB00005B/1450